INFINITY
ALCHEMIST

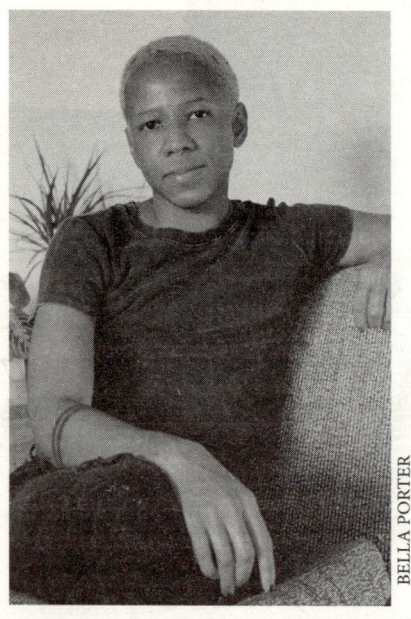

BELLA PORTER

Kaeen Callender is the bestselling and award-winning author of multiple novels for children, teens and adults, including the Stonewall Honor Book *Felix Ever After*, *Lark & Kasim Start a Revolution* and the National Book Award for Young People's Literature winner *King and the Dragonflies*. Their adult fantasy, *Queen of the Conquered*, was a World Fantasy Award 2020 winner for Best Novel, named one of the 100 Best Fantasy Novels of All Time by *Time* and one of the 50 Best Fantasy Novels of All Time by *Esquire*.

'An author with a powerful point of view.'
CASEY McQuISTON

INFINITY
ALCHEMIST

KACEN CALLENDER

faber

First published in the US by Tor Teen,
an imprint of Macmillan Publishing Group, LLC in 2024
First published in the UK in 2024
by Faber & Faber Limited
The Bindery, 51 Hatton Garden,
London, EC1N 8HN
faber.co.uk

Printed and bound by CPI Group (UK) Ltd, Croydon, CR0 4YY

A CIP record for this book is available from the British Library

ISBN 978-0-571-38383-2

Printed and bound in the UK on FSC® certified paper in line with our continuing
commitment to ethical business practices, sustainability and the environment.
For further information see faber.co.uk/environmental-policy

2 4 6 8 10 9 7 5 3 1

For the younger me
who always wanted to write a YA fantasy

THE EIGHT HOUSES
OF NEW ANGLIA

HEAD HOUSE OF ALEXANDER: Leaders

HOUSE OF KENDRICK: Redguards

HOUSE OF LUNE: Diviners

HOUSE OF ADELAIDE: Healers

HOUSE OF GALAHAD: Merchants

HOUSE OF ALDER: Keepers

HOUSE OF VAL: Scientists

HOUSE OF THORNE: Engineers

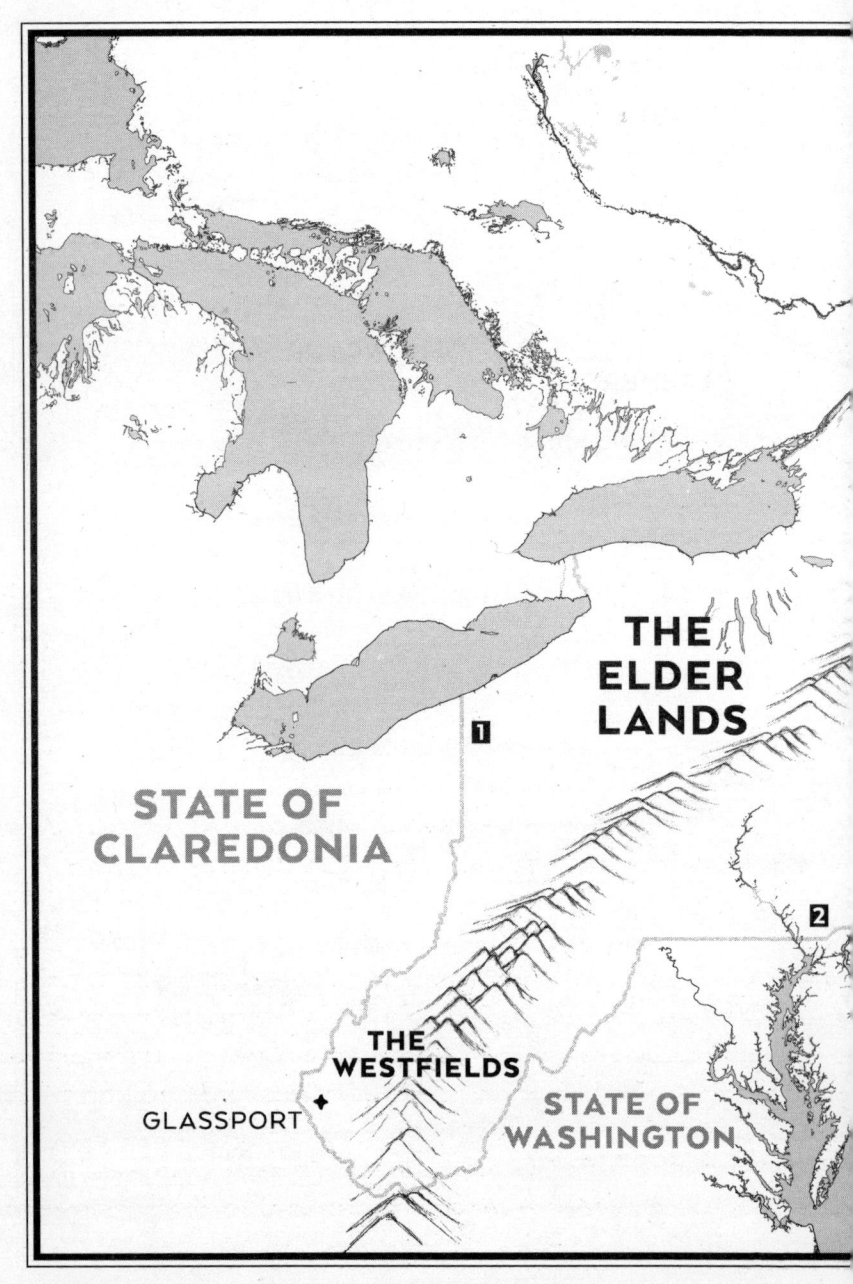

THE
ELDER
LANDS

STATE OF
CLAREDONIA

1

THE
WESTFIELDS

GLASSPORT ✦

STATE OF
WASHINGTON

2

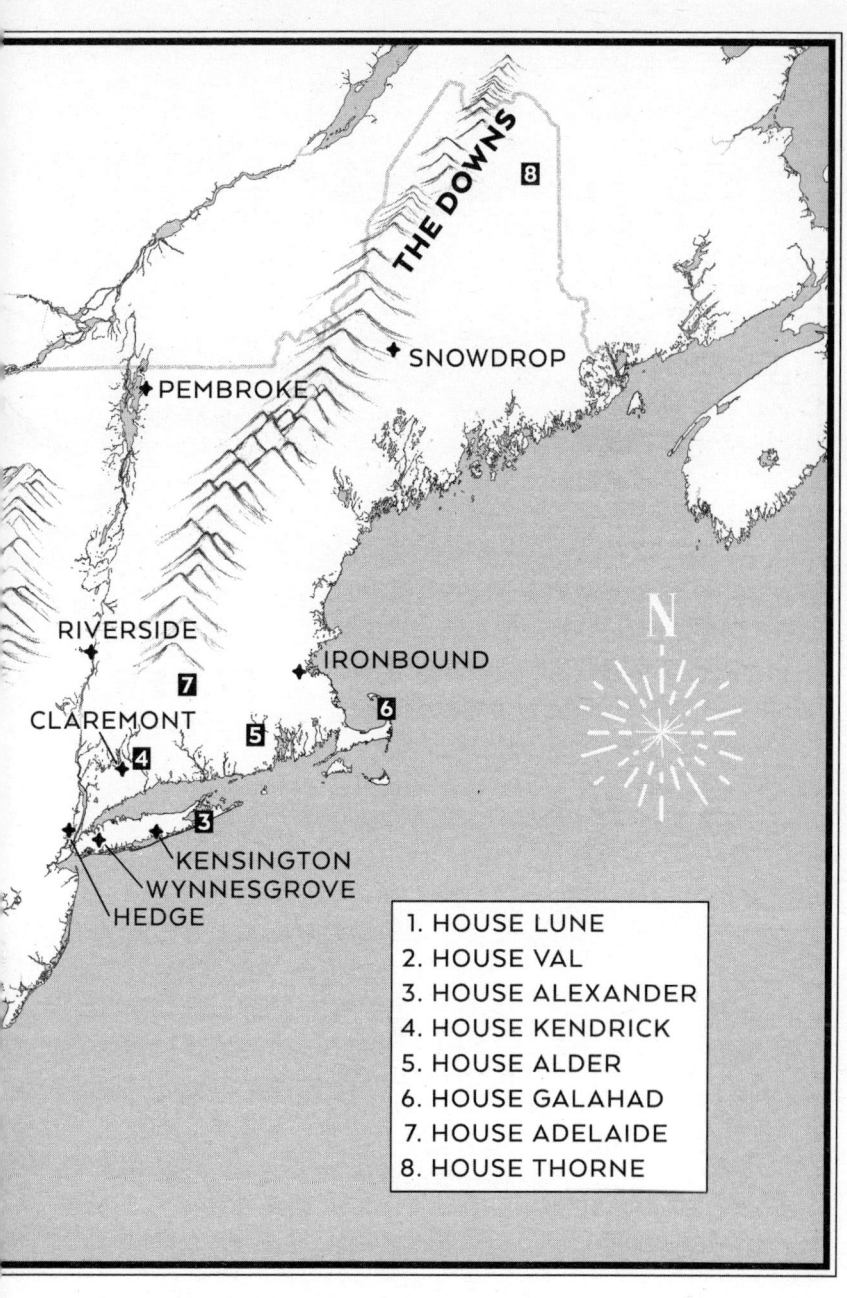

THE DOWNS

8

SNOWDROP

PEMBROKE

RIVERSIDE

7

IRONBOUND

CLAREMONT

5

6

4

3

KENSINGTON
WYNNESGROVE
HEDGE

N

1. HOUSE LUNE
2. HOUSE VAL
3. HOUSE ALEXANDER
4. HOUSE KENDRICK
5. HOUSE ALDER
6. HOUSE GALAHAD
7. HOUSE ADELAIDE
8. HOUSE THORNE

INFINITY
ALCHEMIST

1

Snow drifted from the gray sky—slowly at first, lazily, the sort that was caught on eyelashes and tongues. Ramsay gripped her mother's hand as she crunched across the frozen dirt, ice like glass shattering beneath her boots. The thin white trees were covered in knots that looked like dozens of eyes watching as they passed. Puffs of steam left her mouth as she breathed hard, trying to keep up with her mother's long strides. Ramsay's many questions had been ignored. She was only told to hurry, don't stop now, they were almost there. Ramsay complained that she was cold, but Amelia only tightened her grasp.

"Come along," she said, voice gentle. "It's almost time."

They crossed a frozen river. Her father had always told her not to walk along the river in the winter. The surface was too thin. It could crack, and she could be washed away, never to be seen again. Her mother let go of Ramsay's hand and told her to wait there, right there, right where she was. Ramsay pulled on the ends of her shirt nervously while she watched her mother walk to the other end of the riverbank, back onto the solid ground of snow. She stood in a clearing of the trees and looked over her shoulder at Ramsay with a loving smile.

The snow began to fall faster, then—hard enough that Ramsay had to shield her eyes from the ice that stung her cheeks. The world became a white blur. The snow turned red. It fell to the ground, drops spreading like blots of ink. The blood dripped from Amelia's cheeks. Her smile faded as the screams began.

2

Ash was lost in thought, as usual, when he saw the alchemist he wanted to meet. Gresham Hain strode through the beige stone corridor with purpose, surrounded by a group of chattering scribes. Ash had only ever seen Hain in grainy black-and-white photos in the texts he'd written, but it was definitely him. He was a pale-skinned man nearing his sixties, but his back was straight, frame muscular, and though his hair had turned a stark white, it was full, gray stubble on his jaw. Ash had heard that Hain sometimes visited the college. The man was an advisor to House Alexander, but he was technically still a professor, though he rarely taught classes or took on apprentices. Ash had often imagined this moment—imagined finding enough courage to march up to Gresham Hain and tell the man his name.

As Ash watched Hain striding toward him, his anger grew. The rage became a mirage of heat that glowed from his skin, a second pulse inside him. Ash's hands clenched into fists. Ash hated Hain, hated him enough to want to scream at him and hit him and—

"Excuse me," Ash said. His voice cracked. "Sir Hain, I'm—"

Hain walked past, speaking to a scribe. He hadn't heard Ash—hadn't even spared a glance. It was like Ash wasn't there. A scribe gave Ash an odd look and seemed moments from asking him why he was standing in the middle of the corridor, and didn't he have anything better to do with his time? The anger faded and died until it was replaced by numbness. Ash bit down on his teeth, ducked his head, and walked in the opposite direction.

It was a cold, nasty morning. A misty rain hung in the air. Ash knelt in the dirt beside a stone bench as he patted a new layer of soil. Each flower, every plant had its own energy. The wilting hydrangea there, for example—Ash could feel that it had a calm, slow, rhythmic vibration, perhaps an acceptance of death, transforming from one state of the physical into the next. Its petals were shriveled and brown. Ash held it in his palm as he looked over his shoulder.

The campus was shrouded in a thick yellow-gray haze, stone buildings disappearing in the fog. The students and professors were in class, no one else in sight. Ash looked back at the flower and shut his eyes. He imagined the hydrangea in full bloom— pictured in his mind every detail, from the velvety softness of the petals to the dew glistening and dripping onto his hand. Alteration was tier three, but it wouldn't require much alchemic power for something so small. Energy sparked inside of him, a flint lighting flame. He felt the heat grow under his brown skin, spreading through him—

"You don't have much love for this job, I see."

Ash stood and whirled around, heart hammering. He let go of the flower and dropped it to the dirt. It was in full bloom, just as he'd imagined, dew on his hand. Frank stood behind him in his usual workwear overalls, hands in his pockets. The man was almost seven feet tall, but he snuck around like a cat. Ash couldn't be convinced that Frank wasn't also secretly practicing alchemy and hadn't simply materialized out of thin air.

Ash gave what he hoped was a charming, sheepish grin worthy of forgiveness. That grin, plus his floppy brown curls and big brown eyes, had gotten him out of trouble before once or twice. "Saw that, did you?"

Frank was often in a foul mood, but it was made even fouler now. "You must not have any love for your freedom, either," he said.

"I didn't know anyone was here." But even Ash knew that was a sorry excuse.

"Maybe you could try explaining that to the Kendrick," Frank said, not even the hint of a smile on his face. Ash sometimes felt that Frank took it upon himself to be a fatherlike figure a little too much.

"You wouldn't call the reds on me, would you?" Ash asked. "You'd be down an assistant."

"I made do without you before," Frank said. "I'll be just fine without you again."

The two stood in silence for one long moment, staring each other down. Ash was used to being on his own, and he wasn't very fond of obeying anyone—but Ash needed this job, and besides, Ash appreciated Frank and his gruff straightforwardness. It was a breath of fresh air, in a place like this.

"Sorry," Ash said. "It won't happen again."

Frank eyed Ash as if he wanted to continue his lecture, but thankfully he only gave a nod before he carried on across the lawn, disappearing into the haze. That's often how the man operated: like an unaware energy that had forgotten it was no longer alive, walking from one dimension and into the next. Ash sighed, dusting his hands off on his cotton overalls, and pushed the wobbling barrow in the opposite direction, back toward the greenhouse.

Ash had been technically hired as a domestic of the college to fold sheets and wash dishes in the kitchen, but Frank, for some unknown reason, had taken the boy under his wing in the past few months, asking for his assistance with various groundskeeping tasks. Even if Ash was annoyed at the man, he was also grateful. He preferred to be outside, hands in the dirt, than in the shadows of the college's corridors, hiding from the gaggles of laughing students and the professors with their cold stares.

It wasn't quite that they eyed Ash like he was mud tracked onto expensive rugs, or that they insulted him in the halls, though that did happen, too, a whispered sneer about the state of his clothes and hair, and oh, yes, the one girl who had laughingly said that

Ash would be cute, if he wasn't so short and didn't smell like fertilizer. It was more that, for the most part, they didn't even look at him at all. It was as if Ash was invisible to them, or that he didn't exist; that he wasn't even worthy of enough attention to show disgust, let alone respect.

Ash had applied to Lancaster. Just a year before, he had saved enough sterling from his part-time job at the docks to send off an application and take the entrance exams. He'd worked hard for years before that—hours of studying alone at night, bent over texts, because he'd convinced himself that he could have a shot at becoming a student of the college. Any and all financial need would've been met if he'd been accepted, and he would've greatly increased his chances of passing the license examination. Ash had tried to earn an alchemist license before on his own, without studying at Lancaster, but the sheet of paper had been designed to only allow an elite few to pass with its endless, ever-changing questions about random trivia focusing on the history of alchemy and technique of various tiers. The exam didn't let Ash *show* what he could do, prove that he deserved to pass—and so he'd failed each of the three times he took the test.

With a license, Ash could find a job in alchemy, doing something he actually loved—and with the money he earned, he could've applied to any of the eight Houses. His life would've changed. But it quickly became clear that it didn't matter what Ash did, or how talented he was, or how hard he worked. He would never belong. *Thank you for applying to the Lancaster College of Alchemic Science. Unfortunately, due to the high number of applicants . . .* The thought alone filled Ash with shame, the fact that he'd believed someone like him could make it into some fancy college for magic.

It was a cruel irony that Ash ended up working at the college instead. That was something alchemists often wrote about in the texts he'd read: the infinite universe as understood through the finite human brain was a tapestry of threads that often paralleled one another, synchronicities sometimes appearing as cosmic jokes. Ash hated his job and the constant reminder that he wasn't seen as good enough, but it was the only one he'd been able to find that offered a decent enough wage. And Hain. Yes, that had been a part of Ash's decision to apply to the college and to take this job, too. But now that he had seen Gresham Hain in person, Ash realized that he was too much of a coward to meet his father. Meeting Hain had been his only accomplishable goal in life, and now even that he couldn't achieve. It was a depressing realization.

The barrow squeaked as Ash pushed it along the path lined by buildings, toward the campus gardens and the glass greenhouse. Ash's stomach grumbled as he entered. He couldn't help it—he was often hungry, especially after practicing alchemy. Ash and Frank kept their tools hung up and leaning against the far wall, and long tables held pots of seedlings that were Ash's babies, cared for until he planted them in the ground. Ash exchanged the wheelbarrow and gloves for a rusting watering can. He heaved it up into a sink, water gushing from the faucet and into the opening until it was full.

The campus buildings had ornate white stone and stained glass windows along green paths of damp grass and dirt that lined the main courtyard and its lawn. Ash had practically every room and office memorized. He knew that Vanderbilt Hall's dusty, shadowed, and mostly abandoned classrooms were where students sometimes liked to shut doors and have their fun, from the sound of giggles and groans; that it was better to avoid the Trumbull Tower late at night, when certain energies had a habit of playing the piano that was left in storage, taking pleasure in startling whoever was near, laughter echoing through the realms whenever Ash jumped at the sudden banging of keys.

Ash also knew that the Giddings Library held some of the rarest texts on energy alchemy: electrodynamics, manifestation, nonphysical explorations of the quantum, and more—all once known as *magic*. Ash had always had an unquenchable curiosity for the science of magic. He wasn't a student nor a professor and so would swiftly lose his job if he were ever caught, but sometimes he couldn't help but stay on campus late at night and steal through the stacks long after the library closed, learning what he could by moonlight.

Magic was an outdated term, used rarely, though Ash found he liked the energy of the word. Magic. The word implied universes unknown and adventures undiscovered, power unfulfilled and possibilities that were endless. Magic was once thought to only be gifted to the unique or special, the *chosen ones*. Now it was commonly known that every single person in the world had the capability to become an alchemist.

Legally, however—the House Alexander had created the law almost a century before that only licensed alchemists were allowed to practice energy of the higher tiers. The first tier was legal for all—it was the energy of existence, of breathing and blinking and feeling, not something any human could really help. The second, the tier of channeling more energy past a standard measured point, was still legal without a license, too. It was the kind of alchemic practice that was usually seen among artists and musicians and dancers and athletes—the sort of alchemy that would have an audience whispering that the performer had a certain *glow* as they performed.

Tier three and upward, however, required a license. Ash tried and failed to ignore the bitterness that spiked in his chest. Yes, emotions such as anger and resentment were energy, too, and he was embarrassed that he couldn't figure out how to transmute and release these emotions so that he wouldn't feel so trapped by them. All the texts he read gave the same instructions, but no matter how he tried, he struggled to accept where he was in life and find joy in small pleasures. There was still so much potential he had, so many impossible dreams he hadn't yet reached. Attending Lancaster, receiving his license, finally being looked at with *respect*. But that was all they were. Impossible daydreams.

As Ash arrived at Boylston Hall, he realized he'd been

distracted by his many thoughts and taken too long on the walk from the gardens. He only had a few minutes before the bell rang and the corridors filled with students, something he preferred to avoid. Ash dragged the watering can up the steps, pushing open the heavy front doors with his back.

Not all the buildings of Lancaster were extravagant—Ash had been surprised to see the faded wallpaper and scuffed floorboards of various Halls, the college at times keeping its older charm—but Boylston was the main manor of the campus. It was practically a fortress towering over the courtyard, filled with a mixture of offices and lounges and classrooms, with shining white marble floors and golden ornamental wallpaper. Ash's first destination was a sitting room for guests. He watered the large-leafed monstera in the corner before he moved on to the administrator's office where five older adults sat at their desks, barely giving Ash a glance as he watered the pothos plants, careful not to let a drop fall onto the stacks of papers. In a small private library for instructors, where Ash couldn't help but stare at the titles of each of the cracking faded covers, he watered the hanging philodendron.

Ash was just thinking to himself, rather proudly, that he'd managed to whip through this errand without the bell ringing when he entered the lounge. It was usually empty at this time of the day, but now, for some unknown reason, there were students. One sat at the chess table on the side, playing a game by herself, while two more students sat on the sofas in front of the dim fireplace, speaking lowly. They all wore the college's uniform of plaid pants and tucked-in, buttoned-up shirts and ties. Ash stopped at the door's threshold. It slammed shut behind him on its own, grabbing the students' attention. They glanced over with some surprise, then gave Ash the familiar look—the *oh, it's no one* realization, eyes sweeping from his face and down to his shoes, before they turned away again, back to their conversation and solo chess match.

Ash hesitated. He knew firsthand how cruel the students of

Lancaster could be when they were bored, and even worse was that, no matter how much he wanted to, he couldn't fight back—not if he wanted to keep his job. But Ash had already pissed Frank off enough for the day, so he took a deep breath as he walked to the spider plant on the fireplace's mantel, raising the watering can above his head with trembling arms.

"Anyone could travel to a realm of another density," one boy on the sofa said snidely. He was interchangeable with any number of students on campus. He had yellow hair and light-colored eyes and an air of wealth about him. He raised his chin as he spoke, as if he had an implicit understanding of his own worth that Ash wasn't sure he would ever find for himself. "Haven't you read the teachings of Henry Bates?"

Ash's ears perked up. He'd just finished a text by Henry Bates a few nights ago. Over a century before, the man had theorized that, because the universe was a complex woven system of infinite realms, and humans were a part of this universe, then humans could also travel to those realms, leaving their physical bodies behind—if they had enough alchemic power to do so, anyway.

"Yes, of course I have," the other brown-haired student said. "You aren't the only one attending this college."

"It sometimes feels like I am."

The stories Ash heard painted the higher realms as universes containing an endless number of worlds and dimensions, too infinite for the human mind to comprehend. Ash had tried to reach the higher realms, but this was tier-six alchemy, the most difficult form of all, and he'd only ended the night with a headache. Some famed alchemists claimed to have been successful over the past few decades, but there wasn't any way to prove that they were telling the truth. There were the darker stories, too—tales of alchemists who'd lost their minds in their attempts, caught between dimensions and unable to return to the physical realm.

"I'm not saying it's *impossible*," the student argued defensively. "Only that it would take years of training if it was. The physical body is too much of a manifestation in this reality to drop it and enter the nonphysical realms easily."

He was repeating lines from a text Ash had read a year or so ago now, by another scholar whose name Ash was forgetting. Ash slowly lowered the watering can as he listened.

"You're mistaking your definition of *you* with your *physical body*. If you have a true connection to Source, then you'll realize that you *are* Source," the other student said, "and so anything you imagine can be created and become reality."

Ash almost rolled his eyes. Yes, the boy was right, of course— but it was such an overused phrase that it felt unoriginal and pretentious to repeat now. The line was seen in nearly every single text on alchemy, this constant reminder that everything in existence was a conscious extension of Source—

"Can we help you?"

Ash looked up, startled. The two boys were watching Ash. He realized he had stopped to listen to them so intently that he'd been staring at their shoes. He hesitated, then shook his head quickly.

"No," he said. "No—I was just leaving."

He tried to do just that, making his way to the exit, but the yellow-haired boy held up his hand. "Hold on," he said, and Ash hated that he had no choice but to do as he was told. As an employee of the college, it had been made clear that he was expected to follow any orders given by the students and professors.

Ash clutched the watering can's handle so tightly that his knuckles ached. The boy stood slowly, several heads taller than Ash. "Weren't you ever taught that it's rude to eavesdrop?" he asked. "Especially as a servant."

The brown-haired boy sneered from the couch. "Listening in on conversations isn't exactly a part of your job description, is it?"

Ash tried to swallow the fire burning inside him. "I'm not a servant."

"What was that?"

"I'm the groundskeeper's assistant," he said more loudly, ignoring the small voice that whispered at him to stop. "I'm not a servant. And even if I was . . ."

"Even if you were . . . ?" the blonde boy said, smile growing even as his eyes narrowed. "Well? Go on."

It pained Ash, knowing that he could run alchemic circles around both boys if he'd been given the chance. The words were on the tip of his tongue. *I'd still deserve respect.* But fear found him first. Source, why was he such a coward?

The two students laughed at his silence. Entertainment, Ash realized—that's all he was.

"*Groundskeeper's assistant,*" the blonde repeated. "You should be out on the grounds, then. Not here, interrupting our conversation."

Ash nodded, hating himself and the words he bit out of his mouth. "Yes. You're right."

"An apology, perhaps?" the blonde suggested.

Disgust and humiliation raged through Ash. "I'm sorry," he heard himself say. "It won't happen again."

The yellow-haired boy nodded slowly, eyeing him. Ash stared back, unable to hide the anger that smoldered through him, even as he was afraid that the boy would, on a whim, decide to alert the college and have him fired. Luckily it seemed to be too much effort for the student, maybe already bored with Ash's presence. He sat back down on the couch with another lazy gesture. "You're dismissed."

Ash nodded and hurried from the room, trying not to outright run, ashamed that he'd depended so much on the boy's mercy. Ash often wondered what the true definition of power was. Some alchemists claimed that power was Source—feeling aligned to the energy within all beings, the oneness of all creation, seen and unseen, infinite and unending, and knowing without any doubt that he was as powerful as the universe itself. But if that was the case, and Ash was as powerful as these alchemists claimed, then why were there so many people who had the power to decide if Ash was worthy or not?

There were few professors' offices with plants that needed Ash's watering, but one had so many that the space felt more like a jungle. Ash's nerves spiked as he came to the door. The wooden nameplate read *Ramsay Thorne*. The Thorne name was infamous, connected to a gruesome past that Ash preferred not to think about. He couldn't help but feel vibrations of fear whenever he came to this office. Ash was lucky to have never met Ramsay Thorne, but he'd glimpsed the professor from across campus. He'd never seen Thorne without a scowl, and the professor was avoided by everyone, from what Ash could tell—workers and students and other professors alike.

He took a deep breath and pushed the door open. The heavy curtains were pulled shut, only a sliver of white light shining through, dust particles dancing past. The office's faded Damascus wallpaper still had golden tints, and the floorboards were heavily scuffed and scratched, perhaps by shoes that had a tendency for pacing. The room was cramped, made even smaller by the bookshelves that lined the walls. The single mahogany desk was piled with towers of papers that threatened to collapse and even more books, many of them open and stacked on top of one another, breaking the spines, notes scrawled across the margins. The sight offended Ash. He so rarely had the opportunity to study texts that if he ever got his hands on a book, he treated it with special care, afraid to wrinkle a single page.

And there were the plants themselves: ferns and clusters of snake plants and hanging vines from the top of the shelves. Ash knew from Frank that Thorne didn't want anyone to come into his office at all, but that the professor so often traveled away from campus impromptu that someone was needed to look after the plants while he was away.

It was as Ash was emptying the last of his watering can that something on the desk caught his eye. Ash often struggled to control his curiosity in this office. Fear was a large motivator—he couldn't imagine being caught reading a book by an angry Ramsay Thorne. But today, there was a paper on top of all the mess, and the single stream that slipped in through the curtains shined upon the yellow parchment like a spotlight. Ash saw at the top, underlined several times, *dis. book of source.*

He wasn't sure what the *dis.* meant, but Ash knew about the myth of the Book of Source just as much as anyone who studied alchemy. Legend told that the Book of Source was a sacred text and that its reader would become an all-powerful alchemist, so aligned with Source that they'd be able to create entirely new realities, to live in their body immortally, to give and take away life with a single thought alone.

It was just a legend, of course, a fairy tale. There was no proof that such a script ever existed, and even if it did, stories of the text had likely been mistranslated and exaggerated over the passing centuries. It was ridiculous to think that a single book could really offer a person so much power. Ash was surprised that someone like Thorne, a professor at a serious institution like Lancaster, would have notes about the Book of Source at all.

Curiosity piqued, Ash bent closer to the paper to attempt to discern the messy scrawl.

text = energy manifested—tethers power into this reality
symbol of manifestation:

And there was an odd shape drawn on the paper itself. It was a hexagonal pyramid, but one pyramid, pointing up, was on top of another, pointing down. The lines that defined the shape were like a cage, sketched in a bright blue pencil, unlike the messy notes taken in black ink. Ash held the paper up, inches from his face, as he inspected the shape. Ash didn't always think his decisions through, and he was prone to taking unnecessary risks, but especially now he felt a rush of energy—an inspiration to create that overwhelmed reason. Maybe it was the same sort of inspiration that had poets running to find a piece of paper and a pen or a musician longing to touch their piano's keys. Ash could see the shape even as he closed his eyes.

Creation alchemy was tier four, one of the more difficult forms of alchemy. Alteration depended on taking a physical substance and matter and altering it, shifting it, with the imagination. But rarely—oh, so very rarely—an alchemist like Ash was able to pull enough physical substance from the air and atoms alone to create something new. Ash imagined each particle connecting to another, forming the thin line, the color, the angle of the shape. He felt his body heating with energy, felt as if he was rushing forward, as if time had sped up, and there was so *much* energy that he felt like laughing, as if his body couldn't contain the heat and excitement and joy of creation, and he could feel chaos dancing at the edges of his mind also, the chaos that called to him, the chaos that he feared, because he could understand, too, how easily an alchemist's mind could break if they entered into that unknown, just as so many had before him—

Ash opened his eyes. The shape floated in the air. Ash plucked it and held it in his hand, warmth fading. The object was as small as a newly budded rose, silvery light cast on Ash's skin before the glow died down as well. Its lines were thinner than Ash had imagined, and he hadn't managed to pull enough physical matter to create the shape fully. But it was still there, this thing that he had made. He felt a soft pride as he smiled.

"What're you doing?"

Ash's smile dropped as he spun around. His heart stuttered as Ramsay Thorne stepped into the office.

3

Thorne wore a gray coat over an unwrinkled collared white shirt and black corset vest. His dark hair, tumbling to his shoulders and wet with dewdrops from the morning's misty rain, was a stark contrast against his pale skin. Ash had heard that Professor Thorne graduated from the college at the obscenely young age of eighteen before he'd returned to Lancaster one year later as the youngest professor in the college's history, despite the Thorne heir's past. How could Lancaster even trust a Thorne enough to hire him?

His brows were raised, eyes hooded with apparent boredom, as he looked Ash up and down and back up again.

Ash froze. Even if he tried to speak, he wasn't sure a sound would come out.

"I asked you a question." Thorne walked farther into his office and shrugged off his coat. "What," he said again, dropping the coat onto the back of a chair, "are you doing?"

Ash swallowed audibly. "Nothing. I wasn't doing anything." He clutched his creation in his hand, hidden behind his back. If Thorne saw it—saw with his own eyes that Ash had practiced alchemy—he would undoubtedly have Ash fired, possibly even arrested.

But he'd clearly been doing *something*. The man looked away from Ash and to his desk, with its messy stacks of papers and books. "Were you practicing alchemy?" he said, voice low, some amusement coloring his tone. It wasn't a particularly kind amusement.

Ash's breath caught in his throat. "I—no, I—"

But alchemists tended to have senses that helped them feel when magic was in the air—and the higher the tier, the sharper the sense. Ash was more visual. He would see flashes of color and light in the aftereffects of alchemy. Others who were more auditory reported hearing the tendrils of sounds like instruments, and some described different tastes and smells. Ash wasn't sure what the professor had seen or heard or smelled or tasted when he walked into his office, but it was clearly enough that he'd already known the answer to his own question.

"But you're not a student," the professor said, as if Ash was a simple but annoying problem to an equation he was trying to solve. "And I'm assuming you have no license."

Ash hated that this was a correct assumption to make. "I was only looking at your desk," he insisted, trying again, hoping that Thorne would doubt his senses. "I shouldn't have. I'm sorry. I'll leave—"

Thorne gestured lazily. A sudden gust of wind slammed the door shut behind him. "It's my responsibility, unfortunately, to alert the Kendrick."

Ash went cold. Frank had warned Ash that this would happen if he was caught, but it had never felt like a real threat until now. Ash was eighteen, so there wouldn't be the excuse that he was a child who deserved leniency. In prison, he'd be under constant scrutiny, unable to get away with even the smallest vibration of alchemy. Ash knew that this would be the most painful punishment of all.

"Please," Ash said, voice now hoarse, though he had a sinking feeling that begging for mercy wouldn't help. Thorne strode across the room to his desk, ignoring him. "Please, you have no reason to—"

"No reason?" Thorne scoffed, pausing in disbelief to turn to Ash. "Imagine me, returning to my office, exhausted and still with a night's worth of work to complete, only to find a strange boy has broken in and illegally practiced alchemy." He turned back around again, shaking his head and muttering something that sounded like *unbelievable* beneath his breath.

"I didn't break in," Ash insisted. "I'm the groundskeeper's assistant. I was watering your plants." He pointed with his free hand at the forgotten can on the floor as evidence.

"Wonderful," Thorne said, sarcasm flooding his voice as he reached for the telegraph machine, buried underneath paper on the corner of the desk. "One less crime to report."

Ash was desperate. "But if you call the Kendrick, you'll have to deal with questioning and redguards and—"

"Better to deal with all that," Thorne said, "than risk it being discovered that I knew you illegally practiced alchemy. I'd have my license revoked."

Ash reached across the desk for Thorne's hand as he picked up the receiver. Thorne made an appalled sound of the *how dare you* variety as he pulled away, but Ash continued. "Please, I'm sorry—"

"Perhaps you should've considered how sorry you'd be before you broke the tier laws."

Ash's annoyance splintered through his fear, or maybe he was angry *because* he was afraid. "But it's a fucked-up law," he argued, even as Thorne put the receiver to his ear. "Everyone should be able to practice alchemy."

The man's smirk twitched. "Is that so?"

Ash knew this wasn't helping his case, but clearly begging for mercy wouldn't help him, either. Maybe arguing for his freedom could make this professor budge. "We're all made of energy," Ash said quickly. "We all practice alchemy naturally, with every breath and every thought and emotion. To say that only a conveniently wealthy few can legally become alchemists is bullshit."

Ramsay watched Ash for one long moment, as if the equation had become more interesting. He put the receiver down with a click. Ash's heart slammed against his chest as he tightened his fist behind his back. The professor leaned against the edge of his desk, arms and legs crossed as if this was nothing more than a casual classroom debate. "Don't you think there are some who would be too dangerous to become alchemists?" he asked. "It wouldn't be fair, would it? To put the general public at risk."

Ash thought it was ironic that a Thorne of all people was suggesting this, but then again, maybe it was because Ramsay *was* a Thorne that he was especially qualified to speak on the dangers of alchemy. "And none of the licensed alchemists of Kensington or Lancaster are dangerous?" Ash said with a small laugh. He sounded breathless. "They're probably more so than anyone else."

"Do you honestly believe that?"

"*Yes*," Ash said. "The wealthy and powerful are willing to step on the backs of others to get where they are."

Thorne considered this, but only for a moment before he pushed off from the desk. "Maybe you're right, but it doesn't matter in the end," he said, tossing up a hand that seemed to say, *Oh, well, what can you do?* "The law is still the law, and I won't risk my position protecting a boy I don't even—"

He paused. Something had caught his eye. Ash looked behind him and saw that he stood in front of the sliver of the window not covered by the curtains, and that his hand was reflected.

"What is that?" Ramsay asked quietly. "Behind your back."

Ash shook his head. "Nothing."

"Show it to me."

Ash was expected to do as ordered, but this he would not do.

"I already know you've practiced alchemy. There's no point in trying to hide the evidence," Ramsay whispered. He spoke gently now, but his eyes were hungry and intense with energy. Ash swallowed and pulled out his hand. The blue hexagon glimmered. Ramsay stared at the object in Ash's palm for a long moment, long enough that Ash couldn't tell what Ramsay was thinking or feeling. The professor's expression was carefully blank as he took a step closer and picked up the object with long fingers, then reached out for the paper on his desk, still staring at what Ash had created.

"I—I don't know, it was an interesting shape, and I felt inspired—"

The look Ramsay gave him made Ash's mouth snap shut. Ash began to fear he'd done something truly egregious besides breaking the law. Though he was afraid to ask, he pushed the words from his mouth. "What does it mean?"

An annoyed twitch in the corner of Ramsay's mouth was his only sign of emotion. "You created this," he said.

"Yes," Ash agreed.

"Creation is one of the most difficult forms of alchemy. Only licensed alchemists who've been studying for decades are at all successful."

Ash wasn't sure what to say. Clearly, he wasn't a licensed alchemist. It felt as if Ramsay was arguing against his very existence. "Well, I'm not one of them."

Ramsay clenched his jaw. "Who taught you alchemy?"

"No one. I learned on my own."

Thorne seemed on the edge of a laugh, though the humor didn't reach his eyes. "That's completely unheard of. No one *teaches themselves* alchemy."

Ash's annoyance was starting to catch up with him now, too. Thorne might've scared Ash, but it turned out the professor was just like anyone else at Lancaster: an arrogant dick. "Maybe it seems impossible to someone like you."

"Someone like me?"

"Someone who doesn't think anyone is talented or intelligent unless they've paid for it."

Ramsay's eyebrows rose in surprise. Ash knew he'd said too much, especially if he hoped to get out of this unscathed.

"You seem to have made a number of assumptions about me," Thorne said, voice low.

"And you haven't made any assumptions about me?"

Thorne gripped Ash's creation in his hand, staring at him as if at a loss for words. Ash had a feeling that this was a rare occurrence.

"Why?" Thorne finally asked.

"Why what?"

"Why have you taught yourself alchemy?"

Exasperation ran through Ash. He raised his hands at nothing, unsure of how to answer that question. "Why do people teach themselves how to sing or dance or paint? I don't know. I wanted to learn, so I did."

Thorne's eyes had become hooded again, jaw clenched as he watched Ash, nodding slowly.

Ash swallowed. Maybe there was still a chance he could get out of this. "Listen, I'm really sorry," he said. "You can have that, if you want," he offered, gesturing at Ramsay's hand. Even if losing his creation pained him, it was nothing in comparison to losing his freedom. "And I promise I'll never set foot in your office again."

The professor paused, still refusing to look away from Ash. It was unnerving. He seemed to be consumed by some internal conflict in the taut silence, so thick that Ash could practically feel the thoughts that swirled through the professor's mind brushing against him.

Finally, Ramsay spoke. "The universe is a woven tapestry, made of threads of energy streams that we think of as *life*," he said, "with Source aware of each and every single string."

Ash squinted in confusion. "Okay," he said, unsure of why Ramsay was telling him this.

"There are often synchronicities in our organized universe," the professor continued, maybe not realizing or caring how odd he seemed. "Moments when we might think that something is a coincidence but is actually Source delivering what was asked, because we are, after all, Source as well, creating our own reality with our thoughts and desires."

Ash gave up on understanding where this was headed altogether and simply watched the professor as he began to pace back and forth. The man was unpredictable, swinging from one end of the emotional spectrum to the next without any warning or explanation. Ash wasn't sure if this would prove to be a good or bad thing. Energy began to grow in the room as Thorne paced. It felt like a storm, a blast of wind, might rip through at any moment, creating a vortex of loose papers and throwing books to the floor. Ramsay spun to Ash suddenly, and Ash took one decidedly long step back.

"A man complaining that he doesn't have the house he wants may be dismayed to find the home he currently owns has burned down, but was that not Source delivering what he requested? Now he's on the path to the house of his dreams."

Ash dared to ask a question. "Am—am I the house?"

"In a sense," Thorne said, eyes narrowing into a slightly more condescending gaze. Ash suspected that Ramsay was impressed he'd kept up, though Ash wasn't sure if this was a compliment or an insult.

"I have needed . . . *assistance*," Ramsay said, "for some time."

"Assistance?" Ash repeated.

Thorne held up the hexagon. "In my meditations I saw that, when this object entered physical reality, it would be a sign that Source has woven one important, life-changing thread with mine. I'm assuming that you—you, what is your name, anyhow?"

Ash considered lying, but he knew that Ramsay would figure out the truth once he asked enough questions around campus. "Ashen Woods, but I go by Ash—"

"I believe that you, Mr. Woods," Ramsay continued, "are the help I've needed."

Ash's head was spinning with the overload of information. He frowned as he watched Ramsay walk back to his desk and return the paper to its proper place on top of the mess. "Why would *I* be that thread?"

"This is an independent project," Ramsay said, ignoring Ash's question. "It's unfunded by the college, and it's not something I can give you the details on, for the simple reason that I don't know or trust you."

"But you want my help?"

"Yes," Ramsay said.

"You want my help with a project that I'm not allowed to know anything about?"

"Yes," Ramsay said again, as if this was perfectly reasonable.

Ash glanced at the paper on Ramsay's desk. "Does it have something to do with the Book of Source?"

Ramsay's gaze cut into him. He was quiet for a long while, silent and cold enough that Ash began to regret his question. "What do you know about the Book of Source?"

"Nothing, except for what the legend says." Ash watched Ramsay's blank expression carefully. "But that's all it is, right? A legend."

"That depends on who you ask, I suppose."

It was clear to Ash that, if he were to ask Ramsay, he would say that the Book of Source was very real.

Ash wasn't sure what to believe. It was like hearing that dragons existed after all, a childhood tale come to life. If the Book really did exist, and it was able to make its reader an all-powerful being, more powerful than any human to have ever lived, then it was also incredibly dangerous and would be better off burned, ashes scattered to the wind. Still, at just the thought of seeing the Book, having all his questions answered and being handed a path to such power, Ash's heart began to beat just a little harder.

"But what do you want with the Book of Source?" Ash asked.

Ramsay only eyed Ash for a moment before he said, "Enough questions for the day, I think." He closed his hand around the object and sat at the chair behind his desk, throwing his feet up onto its corner. "I need your answer. You'll either assist me with my plan or not. I'm keeping this, by the way."

Ash crossed his arms. "I think I deserve to know a few more details before I agree to do anything with you."

Ramsay cocked a single brow and met his eye, and Ash began to put two and two together, perhaps more slowly than he should have.

"Are you going to blackmail me?" Ash said, voice lower with anger now.

"Blackmail? No, no," Ramsay said. "I'm merely going to suggest that you agree to work with me, and in exchange, I will not let your employer or House Kendrick know that you've illegally practiced alchemy."

"So, blackmail."

"If that's what you would prefer to call it."

Ash's anger was sometimes difficult to control. It could be as sudden as a lightning strike and could similarly leave behind a trail of destruction in its path. He hated being taken advantage of, hated being used—and especially by a conceited House heir like Ramsay Thorne.

Ramsay's smile dropped. Maybe he sensed the impending danger. "Another deal could be made," he added.

Ash frowned. "What sort of deal?"

Ramsay lifted his chin. "Clearly you are—talented," he landed on. "Not many would be able to pull off what you did today, especially for someone who has never received proper schooling."

"It depends on what you mean by *proper*," Ash said.

"I didn't mean to suggest—" Ramsay paused, then started again. "You never attended a private institution."

"That's right," Ash said. He didn't like Thorne's arrogant gaze.

"You've gone without any formal training in a college, and yet . . ." Ramsay glanced at the object in his hand again. "I've never seen so much raw power before in all my years at Lancaster."

Warmth filled Ash. He'd spent many lonely nights reading texts he'd stolen from bookstores or taken from the college's library without ever once hearing an ounce of praise. He was ashamed that some part of him was pleased hearing validation from a conceited House heir. "What's your point?"

He didn't expect Ramsay's next words. "I can teach you," he said.

Ash didn't think he'd heard Ramsay correctly. "What?"

"I could teach you in exchange," Ramsay told him. "If you assist me in my project—"

"Which I still haven't been told anything about—"

"Yes, precisely—then I'll teach you what I can. I'll help you learn alchemy. I can even prepare you for the license exam, too, if you'd like."

Ash felt a jolt of excitement at the thought. A professor at Lancaster would know what he'd need to memorize to pass the written exam, and Thorne was even offering to teach him alchemy on top of it all. But . . . "Just a few minutes ago, you were going to send me off with the reds," Ash said. "Now you want to illegally teach me alchemy so that I'll help you?"

"Yes, yes," Ramsay said dismissively, waving a hand back and forth. "I'm a self-seeking, egotistical narcissist who doesn't actually care about the law, especially when it comes to my selfish ambitions. What's your answer?"

Ash felt his own desire bubbling up and threatening to boil over, but he was still uncertain. He shook his head. "It's too risky. What if we're caught?"

"It seems like you're looking for a reason to refuse my offer," Ramsay said, and sounded disappointed for it. "I was under the impression that you *want* to learn."

"I did—I do—"

"We would take certain measures," he interrupted. "I would ensure your safety. As long as we're in agreement, you will be under my protection. Now, what will be your next excuse?" Ramsay asked. "How will you try to convince me and yourself that this is the path you're not meant to take because you're too much of a coward?"

Ash watched, slack-mouthed, as Ramsay stood, taking his time as he crossed the office and stopped in front of Ash, staring down at him. "Well?" Thorne asked, voice quieter now, desperation in his eyes. "Do you agree?"

Ash wanted to say no—wanted to watch Thorne's smug face fall. But his body had betrayed him. At the suggestion that Ramsay might teach Ash alchemy—that he could potentially receive a license of his own, even if it was a far-fetched plan—it felt as if Ash had been delivered exactly what he'd wanted most in life, too. Maybe Ramsay was on to something, and Source really had orchestrated this scene just so that their lives would collide.

"Yes," he said, feeling as if the word had pushed itself out of his mouth. "I agree."

4

The sitting room was damp, its walls slick with mold. Dying embers in a fireplace flickered. The room smelled rotten, like blood had soaked into the carpet. Sir Pentridge Val was nervous, unwilling to meet Hain's eye, sweating and pale and already a ghost.

The two men spoke. Val wiped his brow and looked as if his heart would beat itself to death, but Gresham only stood with his back turned, hands clasped behind him.

"You don't even have information on where it's hidden."

"This is the only option."

"How do you know with any certainty this will work? So many deaths—"

"You agreed to assist me, Sir Val, did you not?"

"In funding the search, yes—but this—"

"There's too much at risk for you to back out now."

But the man shook his head. "I don't want any part. I refuse to have a hand in a massacre."

Val started to turn away, but Gresham reached out and grasped his neck. Val gagged. He couldn't breathe. Even after Hain let go, there was something lodged in his throat. Val coughed, and a flower petal fell. He looked up with wide eyes, a shadow falling across his killer's face. He gasped for air, reaching into his mouth, fingers digging. He gagged as he pulled out a peony. But still there were more, petals and unfurling flowers falling from his tongue. He sank to his knees, hands grasping his neck. Hain watched until the light left the man's eyes.

*

Lancaster College's campus stood on the outskirts of Kensington in the suburban neighborhood of Wynnesgrove, with its tree-lined cobblestoned pathways and white town houses that had windows with curtains of lace. It was an hour-long walk home. Ash could have taken the trolley, but it was three sterling each way, and he preferred to save his coin for rent instead. He ducked his head as he walked through the wealthy neighborhood, afraid to meet anyone's eye, scared that someone would stop him and demand to know what he was doing there with a threat to call the reds. It was only when the houses became a little smaller and the trees began to disappear that he breathed more easily. He reached the iron bridge that crossed the gray river, into his borough of Hedge.

Hedge was essentially its own city, even larger than Kensington, if only because there were more people with nowhere to go. Ash followed the raised railways. A train clanged by overhead with a rhythmic pounding on the tracks until it screeched away. Abandoned apartments had boarded windows. People looked over their shoulders. Factories burned smoke in the distance so that the blue skies had turned a lifeless slate gray. Ash hurried through the roads of cracked pavement, knowing which ones to avoid. Calls echoed through the streets, and Ash paused when he saw a group wearing the white robes of House Lune. Its followers marched and shouted about the Creator and his enemies, though who they were yelling to, Ash couldn't tell. "Repent!" one man leading the group shouted. "Burn away your sins! Hang the alchemists, and save them from their ills!"

A familiar anger spiked through Ash, but what good would it do for him to pick a fight with a group of Lune followers? If they found out he was a practicing alchemist, they would become a mob, and he'd end the night with a rope tied around his neck. He ducked his head as he pushed past the crowd that'd gathered to watch.

"Alchemy is a *sickness*," the man continued to the cheers of white-robed followers. "It's against nature to steal the energy of the Creator, to manipulate the gift of life for selfish human greed! Alchemists are a *danger* to this world—"

Ash burst through the crowd and turned the corner into an alley. He leaned against the wall, held up his palms, and waited for them to stop shaking. It shouldn't surprise him, how much strangers hated him for existing, but still, their hatred always managed to take his breath away. He inhaled slowly, let out a shaky exhale, and continued on.

He passed lines of row houses until he reached his own. His apartment was on the second floor of a box of faded red brick, packed into a street of abandoned storefronts and pubs. It was the same home his mother had died in. Ash had seen it coming. Didn't mean it hurt any less.

He stomped up the creaking stairs and unlocked his door. The apartment wasn't much to look at, but it was still home. It had one room, with a kitchen that had a single counter and a rusting refrigerator and stove and a table where he ate and did his studies. There was a mattress pushed into the corner beside a fraying couch. The walls were plastered with research notes that Ash's mother had once complained about.

Ash's mom hadn't been like the conservatives who wanted to outlaw alchemy altogether, but she didn't see the purpose in practicing it, either. She'd never understood why Ash loved magic so much. Ash assumed it was a similar reason to why musicians loved instruments, or why sculptors loved clay. She hadn't understood the physical pain that would grow in Ash's chest the longer he went without letting light emit from his hands.

Ash stripped off his shirt and sighed in relief as he unlaced his black binder. He had tried a thousand times to flatten his chest with alchemy, but human bodies were too complex manifestations of Source and, outside of injuries and illness, couldn't be permanently altered. His corset binder was several years too old and the lace was fraying, but it would have to do. He kicked off his shoes and dropped onto his mattress. He was surrounded by books. Books he'd found on the sidewalks, books he'd borrowed from libraries, and a few he'd stolen, too. Some were books that his father had written. Gresham Hain had popularized the connection between divinity—Source—and the science of magic.

Hain had delivered the basics of alchemy to the masses. Whereas before, the average person like Ash believed that alchemy was only for the rich and powerful, thanks to Hain, more and more began to understand that they *were* alchemy. He explained that chaos was the original spark of energy, from which Source became aware of its own consciousness and created the universe. Chaos, in a sense, *was* Source: a raw explosion of energy that then organized into the threads of existence. Two sides of the same coin. Ash sometimes felt the original spark that was at the core of life and alchemy. He wanted to reach for that spark when he practiced, to feel its unfiltered power—but chaos was also dangerous to tap into, alchemists sometimes losing themselves in the uncontained, limitless energy.

Hain wrote that because Source was created from energy, and every vibration in the universe was a part of Source, this meant that every living being was Source as well. *To understand Source, and your role in this magnificent universe, is to look at a tapestry. Each thread weaves together to create the whole; but I suppose the single thread believes it is separate as well.*

This was considered blasphemous by House Lune, who taught their followers to praise Source as the Creator, a divinity outside of themselves and not within. Many Lune followers were the most steadfast of the conservatives and claimed that the founder of their House, Sinclair Lune, would one day return to life and smite all alchemists and other forms of evil from the earth.

When you see that we are all Source, all divinity, all fragments of the Creator, then you also see how each and every one of us is fundamentally deserving and worthy. But Gresham Hain was a hypocrite. Weren't all the great men? He had impregnated a twenty-year-old servant when he was twice her age, ignored the letters she had sent begging for help, and left her to die, abandoning her and her child. Maybe this had been why Samantha Woods couldn't stand magic. It'd reminded her too much of Ash's father.

Ash sat up on the edge of his mattress, hugging his knees, hands sore from a day's work. Ash hadn't even been sure what he would do when he met his father. He imagined attacking the man, screaming at him to acknowledge Ash as his son, to apologize for abandoning him and his mother. Now he could see that wanting to meet his dad had been childish, a boy's dream. What had he thought? That the man would apologize and, overcome by love, pull Ash into his arms?

Now what? The question echoed through him. Meeting his father for the first time had been his only achievable goal for so long, for so much of his eighteen years, that Ash wasn't sure what else he had to live for.

But now a new goal was beginning to grow. His daydreams didn't seem so impossible anymore. Ramsay Thorne's offer to teach him alchemy wasn't just a coincidence. Ash hadn't been accepted to Lancaster, but he would still find a way to earn his license. He'd become one of the most powerful alchemists of the state. Ash would force his father to look at him, to see him and bow his head in respect. He would force his father to acknowledge that Ashen Woods was his son, and to realize that Ash had been worthy of so much more.

Ash sighed as he flopped back onto the mattress. The day had been more exciting than usual, and it'd taken a lot out of him. But even then, he couldn't help but reach for the nearest text, flip it open, and begin his studies for the night—and this time, he searched for any mention of the Book of Source.

※

Ash bit back a bleary-eyed yawn as he stomped out of his apartment complex's door the next morning, stuffing his hands into his green jacket. The sun hadn't even risen yet, but unloading at the docks before heading to the college was a quick part-time job that would ensure he made rent—assuming that the manager didn't cut Ash's pay, anyway. There were enough people desperate for work that he could get away with it.

Tobin was waiting outside, finishing the last of a cigarette. His usual lighthearted grin had been replaced with a clenched-jaw frown. Sure, things had been awkward between them for a few months, but this was different. Tobin was miffed. He had been ever since Ash applied to the college, and the tension only got worse when Ash started working there. Ash could've explained that his father was a professor, but the topic of Gresham Hain felt especially vulnerable and not something he could speak about, even to Tobin.

"Trying to get us fired?" Tobin said as a greeting.

"Sorry," Ash grumbled. "Overslept." He locked up, pocketed his key, and they were on their way.

Tobin was taller, bulkier, slower in his movements and his nervous glances, while Ash was shorter and leaner. Helpful, when it came to quick escapes. Ash and Tobin had spent a few months in a juvenile detention center together when they were twelve—Tobin had been thrown in for beating his stepfather to hell and back, and Ash had been caught stealing a book. They became inseparable. Fought for each other when no one else would. Tobin would watch Ash's back while he stole extra rations, and Ash would kick the shins of any kid who tried to mess with Tobin and race away before they could catch him. The pair made a good team. When they got out a few months later, they'd cut their palms open and had a bloody handshake, a promise that they were willing to die for each other, leaving identical scars behind. It was the kind of promise only kids would make, but still, it meant something to Ash. Friends were hard to find in a place like Hedge.

Tobin flicked the end of the cigarette to the ground. "Can't believe I let you convince me to take this job."

Ash couldn't meet his eye. How long had it been since that disastrous night, and he was still embarrassed? "It's good money."

"Could've made better money if we joined Baron," Tobin said.

"Baron? He'd just use you until you're knifed in the gut in some alley."

"Not if I'm smart about it."

"Right," Ash said with a grin. "That's the problem." He laughed and dodged a hand that aimed to smack the back of his head.

Tobin rolled his eyes, but at least he was smiling now, too. "Think I can't survive Baron? Can't be any harder than what we're dealing with now."

Most guys like Ash and Tobin who lived in Hedge ended up working for Baron, pledging themselves to the gang like it was a House, and in a way, maybe it was. Maybe that's what the Houses were, too: gangs, but with more money and the power to say that they weren't. Ash had managed to resist pledging to Baron so far, and he hoped he would never have to.

"Only other option is to walk south," Tobin said. "Cross into the Union." New Anglia hadn't been to war with its bordering states in almost two hundred years, but none of the neighboring nations were particularly friendly to Anglians, since land had been stolen, the territory expanding to the south and west. Colonization at its finest.

"Come on. Our lives aren't so bad, right?"

"Waking up before sunrise is pretty shitty in my book."

Ash shrugged. "Well, you don't have to come if you don't want to."

Tobin let out a weary puff of steam. "And hear tomorrow that you were found hanging from the railways for pissing off the wrong person?"

Ash smirked, relieved at the truce Tobin offered, as miniscule as it was. "I'm a fast runner. When have I ever gotten caught?"

"First time for everything," Tobin muttered.

Ash and Tobin weaved through the city streets, avoiding the groups of men crowding around corners. The narrow alleys and lanes had big round cobblestones, slippery after a late-night rain

shower. A putrid smell and the buzzing of flies gave Ash and Tobin enough warning to cross the street and cover their noses and
mouths with the ends of their shirts. On the other side, a swollen
corpse hung from his neck on the side of a crumbling wall, a sign
reading that he had offended the Creator, though it was impossible to tell the crime.

There was silence, but only for a moment. Tobin was never
comfortable with quiet, even when he was angry. "If you could
join any of the Houses, which would you pledge to?" It was an old
question he'd asked Ash a million times when they were kids, the
sort of question that was made of dreams of a better future.

"If I had the money to pledge to any of the Houses, you mean?"
Joining a House had its costs: There would be the application fee
and, if accepted, the entrance fee, along with the monthly taxes—
and the more popular the House, the more expensive. It could
be upward of a thousand sterling per month. Ash was lucky if he
made the two hundred sterling he needed for rent. Lune was the
only House that allowed followers to join for free, though they
requested tithes and donations.

Tobin grinned. "If you had the money to pledge to a House,
you wouldn't be in Hedge."

"And that's the truth," Ash mumbled.

"I'd probably go with Kendrick," Tobin said. "Become a red
who does the chasing instead of being chased for once."

Ash snorted, but he couldn't blame Tobin—that desire for
power was intoxicating sometimes. People could join any of the
eight Houses because it was what they wanted to accomplish in
life: to be a merchant in House Galahad, or to become a healer
in House Adelaide; to study history and language in House Alder, or to go through combat training and become a redguard in
House Kendrick. The Houses were an automatic *in* to the upper
classes and social circles where grifters like Ash would never be
welcome. But pledges went beyond life paths and careers. There
was an old idea that with each House, you could find your *people*:

those who had the same dreams, the same morals and values, sometimes even similar personalities. You could find your true family. But in that case, in a way, being Houseless meant that Ash had found his people, too: the ones everyone else had decided weren't worth acceptance.

"Speaking of Houses," Tobin said. "Did you hear some lord got killed by the docks? He was a cousin to one of the Heads."

Ash frowned. "What was a House lord doing down there?"

Tobin shrugged. "Who knows? But now reds are all over the place. They don't give a fuck about Hedge until one of their own is killed." He frowned, as if lost in thought for a moment. "People are saying flowers were stuck in his throat."

"Flowers?" Something clenched in Ash's chest. Sounded like alchemy.

Tobin wouldn't meet his eye. "Another reason for people to hate alchemists, I guess."

Tobin could secretly practice alchemy if he wanted to, just like Ash and any human being who breathed—but, well, sometimes Ash feared that Tobin might believe the people who said alchemy was evil, even if he never told Ash to his face.

5

Ramsay had been loved, once. The Thorne name was one of the lesser dynastic lines, yes, but it was a House family all the same. She'd been a part of the group that pranced around her boarding school campus, eating together in the dining hall and studying together in the library in full view of everyone who envied them. Ramsay had been so naïve, then.

"I need to speak with you, Ms. Thorne."

She was sixteen years old at the time. She followed the dean into the woman's office and sat in front of the desk, confused. This was the first time she understood what it meant to be looked at with disgust.

"There's been an incident."

"An incident?" Ramsay repeated.

"Your parents," the dean began. She clenched her jaw. Ramsay could feel the dean's waves of emotion. Rage twisted with grief. "Your parents have done something horrible."

Ramsay felt like she was falling. Her voice was hoarse. "What happened?"

She insisted on attending their execution. It was in Kensington Square, in the heart of a city of white brick roads and grand stone architecture. Ramsay didn't have an opportunity to say goodbye. The Kendrick redguards wouldn't let her near the prison where her parents were kept. She stood in front of the gallows and forced herself to watch as they were marched forward, hands bound. Her father—he wouldn't look up from his feet, but her mother stared back at the crowd with defiance. "What is death?"

she called, her words met with jeers as a rope was slung around her neck. "Death has no meaning. My being is immortal."

When Ramsay's father finally met her eye, it wasn't the empty gaze she was so used to seeing. He shook his head once. He pressed his left thumb into his right palm.

Ramsay squeezed her eyes shut when the doors below them clanged open and the cheers rang.

The thumb to the palm was a symbol among alchemists. The eye in the center of the palm signified clarity. Clarity was necessary, when faced with the unorganized, unanchored, infinite power of chaos. And to cover the eye in the center of the hand? Misunderstanding, uncertainty—chaos. Ramsay had often wondered, over the years, what message her father had meant to send.

※

Ramsay had directed Ash to come to the library after closing hours, with instructions to use the side entrance that Ash had already discovered was left unlocked. The Giddings Library was spectacular. It was one of the largest buildings on campus, several stories high, with a domed ceiling of blue glass that left designs of dim moonlight on the patterned tile below. The second and third stories were mezzanines that overlooked the first, and each floor sprawled into a maze of halls and rooms stocked with books by category, with some private offices for silent study.

Ash climbed the steps, hand gliding up the polished wooden railing. As much as he loved the library, it was eerie in the nighttime, as if there was an unseen energy watching him. Ash couldn't help but glance over his shoulder as he walked down a hall on the third floor. When he reached Room 308, he pushed open the door to find Ramsay already there, standing by the window in a vest and trousers, similar to what she'd worn the day before. She barely glanced up from the book she was reading as Ash stepped inside, closing the door behind him.

"You're late," she said, snapping the book shut.

Ash bit back his annoyance. He was already in a foul mood. There'd been a lacrosse match, and Ash had been asked to stay behind later than usual to clean the stands. Lancaster students treated the grounds like a trash can. "I was working."

She slid the book back onto its shelf. "You aren't the only one of us who has work. You need to be more mindful of my schedule and not waste my time."

Ash frowned. "I'm barely ten minutes—"

Ramsay glared. "I wasn't aware that the number of minutes determines whether you're formally late or not."

"It doesn't, but—"

"Whether one minute or one hour, late is late."

"Is it that big of a deal?" Ash said, exasperated.

Ramsay's eyes flashed. Ash subdued the instinct to take a step back. "I have studies and assignments to grade, Mr. Woods," she said, voice low. "And, even if I could afford to, I don't *want* to spend any time waiting around for *you*."

Source, Ash wasn't sure that he liked Ramsay Thorne very much, no matter how much he needed her. "Right. It won't happen again."

If Ramsay could tell how annoyed Ash was, she didn't care. She gestured at one of the two large chesterfield chairs, a small wooden table and golden lamp in between. Ash took his seat, glancing up at Ramsay through his lashes curiously, despite his irritation. He'd heard that Ramsay was someone who shifted genders. This was rare and often a marker of exceptional power. People like Ramsay were thought to have lived hundreds of thousands of previous lives, experiencing so many genders that their energy felt no need to settle on only one. Some people who had no gender were theorized to have reincarnated from a future when gender no longer existed—at least not as the world currently thought of it, as simplified binaries rather than infinite energy manifested into physical bodies. Those who, like Ash, felt uncomfortable with their assigned gender at birth were people who had likely lived most of their past lives with a particular identity. Ash knew this for a fact—he'd had multiple dreams as the men he'd once been, too.

Most people were taught how to sense energy, at the very least—fancy schooling and licenses unrequired—and a person could choose to share their gender with others around them. It was something Ash had learned to do at a young age. He projected the fact that he was a boy so that strangers could sense and feel who he was, a simple knowing that would appear inside a person's mind, as easily as realizing that the sky above was blue, or sensing that another person was happy or sad.

Ash tried to get comfortable in his seat. "You have to admit, though," he said, "it's not like your work is hard."

This caught Ramsay's attention. Her gaze cut to his icily. "And how would you know if my work is *hard*?"

He hesitated, sensing the danger. "It's—well, being a professor isn't as draining as being a groundskeeper, is it?"

She quirked a brow. "You think that I'm a professor?"

Ash paused with confusion. "You're not?"

"I'm nineteen, Woods."

"Yeah, but—but I heard—"

"And you believe everything that you hear, I take it? Did you also hear that the world is flat? Oh, maybe I should tell you that you owe me half a million sterling."

Ash was now certain that he didn't like Ramsay Thorne at all.

Ramsay pulled out thin twine from a pocket and wrapped her hair into a bun, strands falling into her face, which she swiped away impatiently. "I'm a graduate apprentice."

That's where the misinformation spread, then: as an apprentice, Ramsay would teach at least one class a semester as she continued her own independent studies. Ash felt tendrils of jealousy. She'd been given her own office and was even paid to learn alchemy. "I'm funded for research on Source geometry," she said, then added dismissively, "Those are the reoccurring patterns throughout the known universe that replicate—"

"I know what Source geometry is," Ash mumbled.

Ramsay eyed him. "Yes. You seem to know a lot that you technically shouldn't. Not through legal means, anyway."

Ash frowned. "You're going to judge me for that while you offer to illegally teach me more?"

Ramsay tilted her head to the side. "I wasn't judging you, Mr. Woods. Only observing."

Ash didn't enjoy being scrutinized. He felt like Ramsay's gaze had begun to analyze him, watching every flicker of emotion that ticked across Ash's face. She didn't seem to mind that he knew she was staring, eyes narrowing. He was about to ask her to stop when he felt it—the tingling that spread across his skin. Ramsay was reaching out with her own energy, feeling his vibrational patterns, and from the slight look of distaste, he knew that she didn't like what she sensed. Well, the feeling was more than mutual. As she reached out to him, Ash could detect her rigidity, her vibrations that were practically straight lines, boring in comparison to his own uninhibited dance. She seemed to be the sort of person who would rather follow rules and formulas than venture out into the unknown.

"Don't you think you should ask for permission before you start poking at my energy field?" he asked her.

"If we're going to work together, I think getting to know you is reasonable."

"Most people get to know each other by *asking questions*," he muttered. "Well?" he asked when Ramsay said nothing else. "What did you think?"

She pressed her lips into the slightest smile. "Do you really need to know my opinion of you that badly?"

"No," Ash said, only a little defensively. "I was just curious if you thought we'd work well together to find the Book of Source."

Ramsay's expression was wiped into an unreadable mask. "I'd prefer if you didn't broadcast that."

"It's not like anyone else is here."

"No one else is here in their physical form, that's true," she said. Ash knew what she implied: Some alchemists had mastered remote viewing, leaving their bodies behind to travel across the physical with their energies alone, able to watch and listen to others unseen. Yes, it was possible someone could be in the room at that very moment.

But, still. "I can't think of many alchemists who would spend their evening spying on a groundskeeper and an apprentice," Ash said.

Ramsay lifted her chin, staring down at Ash. "You underestimate the average alchemist's desire for the Book."

"The average alchemist doesn't believe the Book exists."

"Oh, we know it exists," she said. "Maybe outside academic circles, you're told that the Book is just a legend, a myth—and sure, there are notable alchemists who publicly deny its existence, too—but it is real, Mr. Woods, as real as you or me."

"If it's real, then why do so many pretend that it's not?"

"Isn't it obvious?" she said with a tone that suggested it indeed was. "The fewer people who know of the Book of Source, the fewer people there are to search and fight for it. There are many alchemists who would love nothing more than to find the Book," Ramsay told him, "and are more than willing to do anything to get it. Especially when their rivals are nothing but a groundskeeper and an apprentice, as you've so aptly put it."

Ash felt a lurch of fear. He'd agreed to assist Thorne, yes—but he wasn't willing to *die*. "And—uh—just how dangerous will this plan of yours be, exactly?"

She only gave a vague shrug, as if Ash's concern didn't matter. Something else seemed to have sparked her curiosity as she watched him. "You're not afraid of death, are you?" she asked him.

"Afraid to die?" he said, bewildered. "Yes. Yes, I am."

Her eyes softened. "But you're an alchemist. All alchemists know that death isn't the end. These lives of ours—they're only illusions. Dreams. Our energy leaves our body, and we return to

Source, or perhaps decide to take another jaunt on Earth. What's there to fear?"

Lost potential. Dying, before realizing his dreams. Ash knew that he would only get to live this particular life once, even if he lived thousands more, and he wanted to fulfill his goals. Earn a license. Be recognized as a powerful alchemist. Prove himself worthy of his father's respect.

Maybe it wasn't death that Ash feared but the idea of dying with regret, thinking in his last moments of everything he'd failed to achieve.

But he wasn't about to admit this to Ramsay Thorne of all people. Ash didn't trust her. And the more that Ash considered Ramsay's words, the more he wondered if *Ramsay* was willing to kill to get what she wanted, too. Amelia and Silas Thorne were mass murderers. What was to say that Ramsay's goal of finding the Book didn't involve killing others?

"The Book of Source . . . it can't be used to hurt people, can it?" Ash asked. He knew full well that it could be used for exactly that, but he wanted to see Ramsay's reaction.

"It depends," was Ramsay's only response, distracted. She'd opened a notebook of what looked like hastily scrawled instructions and was skimming the pages.

"Will *you* use it to harm others?" Ash said, firmly enough that Ramsay finally looked up.

She blinked at Ash, as if hurt by the suggestion. "No," she said. "Source, of course not." There was a bitterness in her expression for a moment as she looked back down at the notes again, a pinch between her brows. "Though it's a common misconception, I can promise you that I'm not my parents."

Ash flinched. It must've been difficult for Ramsay to grow up with a mother and father who were among the most-hated people in all the history of the state. "Sorry," Ash said after a quiet moment.

Ramsay gave a stiff nod. "I understand the concern, but rest assured, I would never hurt another person if I can help it."

Ash wanted to believe her, but questions kept trickling through his mind. What *did* she want the Book of Source for, then?

She tossed the notebook to the side so that it sailed through the air and landed on the ground. Ash was starting to see how her office became the disaster zone it currently was. Ramsay leaned against the chair's armrest rather than sit in it, long legs crossed, trousers rising to show black socks beneath. "Let's not waste any more time," she said. "We'll need to be fast if we're going to have any chance of finding the Book first, before anyone else."

Ash's eyes widened. "We're not going to try to find it *tonight*, are we?"

"Don't be ridiculous," Ramsay said, ignoring Ash when he bristled. "The Book itself is a physical manifestation of limitless energy, sealed away somewhere in New Anglia, if the lore is to be trusted. It could be anywhere. No one simply decides to find the Book, or existence would be undone. We would already be thrown into chaos."

"How do you know others are searching for it, then?" Ash asked.

"Because others are always searching for it," Ramsay said. "Probably not many who are on the right path, granted—but I've come far enough to know what I've needed, what has been missing, for me to find the Book." She met his eye briefly, and Ash felt a strange fluttering of embarrassment as he realized that she had needed *him*. "But every generation of alchemists comes closer to finding the Book, relying on knowledge that came before them— and just as I've found what I've needed, it's possible that other alchemists have, too. They could be further along than we are. Now," she said, and sliding into the chair, "close your eyes."

Ash hesitated but did so, feeling an uncomfortable warmth in his chest spreading up to his neck. "What're we doing?"

"An exercise. There will be some odd side effects to this, by the way."

By the way? He opened his eyes again. "Don't you think that's something you should've told me first?"

Ramsay ignored Ash's question. "Then, breathe in through your nose—"

"Wait—what about the side effects? What are they?"

"—and exhale through your mouth in rapid succession."

Ash let out a heavy sigh. It seemed he wouldn't get a clear answer from Ramsay, so he closed his eyes again and did as he was told, surprised when he heard Ramsay begin to match his breath.

"Keep your eyes closed," Ramsay said. Though her own were shut, she somehow knew when Ash peeked. Ash closed his own quickly, cheeks heating. He focused on the breath, hearing Ramsay's coincide with his, a rhythm that they eventually fell into.

They continued for seconds, minutes, what began to feel like hours. Ash's lungs felt like they would burst. He'd just started to consider outright asking Ramsay what the point of this was, when he felt it—a buzzing, a hum, a ripple in the air. The ripples came faster, the bright red of his energy mixing with the deeper purple of Ramsay's, her energy sinking beneath his skin and setting his bones on fire—

Ash saw the image of a woman, as if in a dream—standing in a forest of snow, turning to him with strands of black hair stuck to her cheeks. He heard distant screams.

When he opened his eyes again, Ash was no longer in the library.

6

Images flashed before him: a mountain bathed in the pink of a sunset, racing through a tangle of trees at night, the depths of water with light shining from above, his mother clasping his hand as she struggled to breathe—

Ash wasn't sure he was in his body, but in that moment, he could also feel that it didn't matter—his body was only the imagination of Source, the single photon of light that was existence itself, a concept usually too infinite for his brain to comprehend, but now he could see that there was no beginning or end, no creation or death. *Ash* was a character he, Source, had created, as was Ramsay, pretending that they had separated from one another when they were only fractals of the same energy. Ash could see how he was Ramsay, too.

Ashen. Ramsay's voice echoed in his mind, but there *was* no mind, no body for Ash to cling to—

—a boy's smile as he touched the palm of her hand and fields of green grass that were endless and the blood that had crystallized into snow—

Ashen, focus on me. Focus on my voice.

He felt like he was spinning at a million miles, no sense of *up* or *down* or *left* or *right*, visions flickering too quickly, and the *heat*— the rush of energy threatening to explode—

It was chaos, Ash realized vaguely. The original spark. Chaos had always been at the edges of his alchemy, untamed and inviting him into the unknown of unending power—and once he was there, Ash wasn't sure that he wanted to leave. Why go back to his body, to this illusion he had created, to a world where desires that would never be filled were slowly killing him, where he couldn't escape his own thoughts and wants and fears?

Control yourself. Ramsay's voice echoed. *Come back. Now!*

Ash gasped. His eyes flung open. He sat in the library. His hands trembled when he raised them. Ramsay's eyes were already open, watching him closely. Neither breathed.

"What was that?" Ash asked with a hoarse whisper. He thought he might be sick.

Ramsay opened her mouth, but even she seemed at a loss for words.

"Were those the *side effects?*" Ash demanded, voice shaking. "Losing my fucking mind?"

"No," she said quickly. "We were only supposed to sync our energy. Matching each other, like instruments starting to harmonize." She broke her stare, blinking rapidly as she stood and began to pace, shaking the tension out of her hands. At least she'd been affected, too, her polished veneer shattered. "There are theories that all beings harmonize in our purest forms of Source—"

"Thorne," Ash said, barely able to keep his voice stable. "Tell me what the hell happened."

Ramsay's expression was carefully hidden, but maybe it was because of the aftereffects that Ash could feel her waves of discomfort and even shame. "I didn't think this would work so quickly," she said. "I had the intention of traveling to the higher realms, but—"

"The *higher realms?*"

"I figured it would take several synchronization sessions, at least a month, before we could even consider successfully reaching them."

"We can't have gone to the higher realms," Ash said, even as he could feel the truth settling. "It's impossible."

"Alone, maybe," Ramsay said, eyebrows furrowed. Ash had the distinct feeling that she was rambling out loud to herself now, rather than speaking to him. "Our frequencies wouldn't be nearly high enough, but with synchronization—I hypothesized that, if I found the right person, together we could act like a springboard of sorts, propelling our energies even higher than if we'd been alone. We harmonized much more quickly than I expected," she said again, as if this was a problem scrawled across a chalkboard and she wouldn't be able to focus on anything else until she'd solved it.

"What does that mean?" Ash asked, impatience growing.

Ramsay paused, maybe hesitant to admit the possibility. "It likely means that we're a high vibrational match." She swallowed, then added quickly, "Not completely surprising, I suppose. If this is one large orchestration of Source, then of course the person delivered to me would be—"

"Excuse me," Ash said, "but my purpose in life isn't to be *delivered* to you." He felt like he'd been dragged into a game he hadn't been given rules or instructions for, and he was officially tired of playing it.

But Ramsay only ignored him, rambling on. "It's probably because we're on opposite ends of the vibrational spectrum that we balance each other well. Your energy is so uncontained. Chaotic. It's no wonder that you began to lose yourself so easily." Was it Ash's imagination, or was this said with scorn?

"And your energy is, what?" Ash asked. "Tidy? Neat?"

"Exactly that," Ramsay said, as if this was obvious. "I am controlled, measured, and disciplined. It's why I was able to anchor myself. These are key personality traits to becoming an expert alchemist."

"But you're the one who admitted I'm powerful."

"I said that your *energy* is powerful," Ramsay said, this time with definite scorn. "You, as an untrained alchemist, are not." Ash tried to interrupt, but she spoke over him. "You have a lot to learn, beginning with the need to control yourself. Your energy is overpowering and exhausting," Ramsay said with some complaint. Ash found that he wasn't sorry at all.

"But the realms have been described as different worlds," he said.

"We didn't *reach* the higher realms yet," Ramsay said, "though we were on our way. With practice, and you grounding yourself so that you don't get lost in the chaos again, we could very well reach the higher realms within a week."

A week? Excitement mixed with dread at the thought. Ash didn't fear the chaos so much as he feared himself—feared that he might decide to stay and never return to the physical world again.

Ramsay began to speak rapidly, muttering to herself as she paced. "A better setting would be conducive—one with energetic barriers, perhaps—"

"What were those visions?" Ash asked.

Ramsay's eye twitched at the interruption. "Our minds adjusting to the frequency of the higher realms," she said impatiently, as if this was something Ash should've known.

Ash thought of the alchemists who sometimes lost their minds attempting to reach the higher realms. Maybe it was because they hadn't adjusted to the frequency quickly enough, their thoughts reduced to a slideshow of images. That, plus the chaos that had beckoned him in—the heat, the waves of energy rushing over him, with no sense of time or physical reality . . . Ash couldn't think of a worse hell, being trapped in his body, his brain loose with chaos, and seeing the endless images of the higher realms flash through his mind, unable to make it stop—

The visions were like a dream, difficult to remember the details as they melted away, but one image came back to him then.

"The woman standing in the snow."

Ramsay stopped pacing.

Ash watched her. "Did you see her, too?"

Ramsay wouldn't look at him. "Yes. I saw her."

"Who was she?"

Ramsay returned to her seat, sitting stiffly. "My mother."

Ash's shock silenced him, but only for a moment. "Is that what always happens?" he asked, anger growing. "When we go to the higher realms, we'll see visions of each other's—what, lives?"

"Memories, in a sense," Ramsay said. "Yes. As we synchronize, we'll begin to see visions of each other's pasts, our consciousness filtering out of our physical forms."

"Don't you think that's something I should've known first?" Ash demanded. He felt exposed. If he had seen and heard Ramsay's memories so clearly, like they had become his own, then surely she'd seen Ash's, too. He tried to remember if there'd been a particularly private vision of him, his mother, his life in Hedge—working by candlelight as he tried not to let his fear and loneliness find him, thinking only about what his life could be instead. Ash didn't have anyone he felt safe enough to share so much of himself with, not even Tobin, and certainly not a conceited House heir like Ramsay Thorne.

"Couldn't you have warned me?"

"I suppose I could have," Ramsay said, surprised by the suggestion. When she saw or maybe even felt a flash of Ash's anger, she added, "Maybe I should have. I'm sorry," she told him. "I don't always have the—ah—*social skills* to know how other human beings operate with one another."

Ash heard what was unsaid: She didn't remember how to act because she'd been so ostracized for the past few years of her life. Another consequence of her parents. Ash's anger dimmed, but only slightly. "Fine. But I think I deserve to know more about your plan if I'm going to risk my mind and my life."

Ramsay crossed her arms uncomfortably, glaring at the floor, not meeting Ash's eye—but she couldn't disagree.

"Why do you want to go to the higher realms?" he asked her. "How will this help you find the Book of Source?"

Ramsay's grip tightened on her arms. "First, we need instructions on finding the Book."

"Like a treasure map?"

Ramsay stared at him. Ash shifted in his seat uncomfortably and decided it was best not to interrupt again.

"No, not like a treasure map," Ramsay said slowly, small condescending smile growing. "We're not in a children's fairy tale about pirates and lost gold. I'm not sure what form the instructions would take, and they won't be easy to acquire, either. I only know that the answer is in the higher realms."

Ash blinked at her in confusion, already going against his decision. "But the higher realms are infinite, from what I've read. Where would you even know to look?"

Ramsay hesitated. There was more that she was keeping from him, he was sure of it—even more than what he'd originally suspected.

"Tell me," Ash said, "or I won't help you. I don't care if you call the Kendrick on me. I'm not going to risk so much without even knowing why."

She opened her mouth and inhaled sharply, then let out a breath, as if she'd wanted to continue fighting but couldn't think of a reasonable argument. Finally, she nodded. "The Book is difficult to find because, even after reaching the higher realms—if successful—alchemists don't know where to begin their search. The realms are, as you've said, infinite, and we can't simply think, *Tell me how to find the Book of Source*. There are too many energetic protections and barriers. But we alchemists are a collective, and like Source itself, we're always expanding, evolving, building what has been left to us by generations of alchemists past."

Ash wasn't following, but he was getting more used to Ramsay's rambling explanations that had no direct answer. He leaned back in his seat and waited, listening.

"I'm lucky," she said, chancing a glance at Ash, "that I'm in a generation that can depend on the research and knowledge of those who have come before me. I have a starting point that can push me in the right direction, as long as I can make it to the realms."

Ash could feel her breathlessness, her fear, in admitting the truth. "If we're going to work together," he said quietly, "you're going to have to learn to trust me eventually anyway."

Ramsay seemed to agree, though reluctantly. She nodded. "My parents," she said. "I want to meet my parents in the higher realms, and I want them to tell me where I will find the Book of Source."

7

Marlowe was sometimes called the invisible girl. She'd gotten very good at slipping in and out of rooms unnoticed in her thirteen years. It was like a game to her, to see how often she could escape unseen, sneaking through the marble and stone halls of the estate of Lune without doing her chores. *"Your work is how you show your gratitude and love for the Creator."* This was what she and the other orphans of Lune were told. They were expected to be grateful that they had a belly full of food and a place to rest their heads. Marlowe wasn't so convinced.

She hid, curled up inside the cupboard of one of the many sitting rooms. She'd run away hours ago, certain that she'd be sick if she was forced to listen to even a minute more of Lord Peterson Lune's lectures on sin. Marlowe was already often lashed for laughing too loudly at breakfast or not paying attention during afternoon prayers. She wasn't afraid to be lashed for this, too.

She'd managed to find a comfortable enough position, even hunched and twisted in the cramped space, to drift in and out of sleep. She only woke up, startled, when she heard voices.

Marlowe peeked through a crack in the cupboard. She bit back a gasp, her heart hammering. Peterson Lune himself and a man she didn't recognize stepped into the room, Mistress Davies, the old hag, bowing as she left them with trays of teas. The doors closed behind her.

The two men sat opposite each other and spoke as if continuing a previous conversation. "I'm sure we could come to an understanding," the strange man said. He was tall, with white hair and the shadow of a beard. Marlowe decided she didn't like him. She had a nose for such things.

"You're so intent on pushing your sinful agendas, Sir Hain," Peterson Lune said.

"Come now," the man replied. "Save your convincing speeches for Lord Alexander. We both know of the *sins* you and your House carry."

Marlowe didn't dare to breathe. She'd never seen anyone speak to Peterson Lune in such a way. She wondered what *sins* he referred to.

Peterson Lune, surprisingly, glared but said nothing.

"Let your current proposition to Lord Alexander rest," Sir Hain said. "In return, I think you might find we have more in common than you think."

Lune scoffed. "And how is that?"

"You raise a great deal many orphans here on the estate."

Peterson Lune paused, but only for a moment. "It's our burden to take on the charitable tasks that no other will."

"Yes, well," Sir Hain said, "it's also come to my attention that you've been making quite a profit by selling the children."

Marlowe shrank farther into the cupboard. She'd heard the rumors, too—the whispers that some children who were requested to aid Head Lune in a private task were never seen again. Was that what had been happening to the children who disappeared? Her heart hammered so loudly, she was certain she'd be heard.

Lune was tense. "I don't see how you can hold something like this over me, Sir Hain. You've benefited from this business in the past as well."

"I've adopted children from Lune for a fee, that is true," Hain replied. "But this other business of yours, I've heard, is more sordid in nature."

"Are you making an accusation?"

"Such a wide net you cast across the Houses," Hain said. "I'm not certain how the families will react to discovering you've let so many of their secrets slip. Smiles to your face, perhaps, and a dagger to the back."

Lune's hands were clenched. "Say what it is you want, Hain."

Hain smiled. "Like I said: I only hope that we can come to an understanding."

"An understanding where you attempt to control my House? This won't stand."

Sir Hain got to his feet, turning for the doors, leaving Lune behind. "*Attempt* to control?" he repeated. "I don't think this is much of a power struggle, do you? Go to Lord Alexander. Explain that you've rethought your proposal." The man reached the doors. "And I think that I'd like to adopt again, too."

He opened the doors to a flood of light and walked out of the room. Lord Lune sat still, trembling with so much anger that Marlowe was certain he'd release a bellowing scream. Finally he stood and left as well, footsteps fading away. Marlowe didn't waste any time in pushing open the cupboard doors and racing across the sitting room, out into the hall, turning the corner—

She ran right into someone. She looked up, heart falling, as Mistress Davies glared down at her. The woman immediately grabbed Marlowe's ear and twisted hard enough that tears sprung to her eyes. "And where have you been?" she demanded, hand already raised to begin walloping Marlowe right then and there.

"I was praying to the Creator in solitude—"

Mistress Davies slapped Marlowe's cheek. "Insolent girl," Davies said with gritted teeth. She wrenched Marlowe's wrist, pulling her.

"Where're you taking me?"

She was ignored. Dread trickled through Marlowe as she was dragged through the halls. The estate was built around the central courtyard and its gardens. It was where every member of the House and the attendants were expected to meet each morning, afternoon, and night. It was empty now, save for the line of children, those who shared Marlowe's room and some younger, too—the ones who hadn't vanished over the years or fallen ill and died because the Lune followers said that the Creator would save those worthy. Marlowe didn't consider any of the other children to be her friends. They all looked nervous as they whispered—why were they there, what had happened?—and Mistress Davies walked back and forth, glaring at anyone who didn't stand up straight and keep their mouth shut.

There were sudden footfalls, and Peterson Lune himself walked into the courtyard—followed by the very man Marlowe had seen in the sitting room. If she hadn't been there to witness their argument, she wouldn't have known that anything was wrong. Both men smiled at the children.

"Someone lucky will have a new home with Sir Gresham Hain," Peterson Lune said, arms wide. If he thought this would be met with celebration, he was wrong. He received skeptical stares instead.

Sir Hain started to walk the line of twenty-something children, eyeing them all. Marlowe's skin crawled as he came closer. She saw that everyone else's gazes were fastened to the floor—but she couldn't help but watch Hain as he approached and stopped in front of her, staring down at Marlowe as if he'd been idly wandering an antiques shop and something had caught his eye.

Mistress Davies hissed. "Lower your gaze."

But Sir Hain raised a hand. "That's all right." He looked at Marlowe's cheek. There was a cut from the slap. "You're bleeding."

"I was punished," Marlowe said.

"Did you deserve your punishment?"

"No," she said without pause.

Mistress Davies looked ready to beat her again. "Insolent child—"

Sir Hain crouched in front of Marlowe. "You're not afraid of much, are you?"

She gave a shrug. "Should I be?" She looked at Mistress

Davies, then looked at Lord Peterson Lune, too, who frowned. "I already know I'm going to burn. That's what I'm told each and every day. This world will be engulfed in flame, and Lord Sinclair Lune will only save the worthy. I'm not one of them. There isn't anything on Earth scarier than burning up, is there? I might as well learn to be brave."

Marlowe assumed Sir Hain would be disgusted with her, too, and turn away. She didn't expect him to stand and gesture at her.

"Are you sure?" Mistress Davies questioned. "She's a wild and rebellious creature."

Sir Hain met Marlowe's gaze again. "Then she's exactly what I'm looking for."

8

Ash couldn't think of anything but Ramsay Thorne and the Book of Source in the following days. He was distracted as he watered plants and pulled weeds, lost in thought as he pushed the wheelbarrow down the path. He remembered the last conversation he'd had with Ramsay.

"Does your gender change often?" Ash had asked. He'd been about to leave, hand on the knob of her office.

Ramsay had given him an odd look. It wasn't rude, per se, to ask about a person's shifting gender—but it wasn't a common topic of conversation, either. "Maybe about once a day or so." Maybe Ramsay was more curious than she'd wanted to let on, too. She'd crossed her arms. "Does yours?"

Ash shook his head. "No. I've always been a guy. That doesn't change. Do you care," he asked, unsure of why he was suddenly so shy, "how you're referred to?"

"Not particularly. I've figured a good rule of thumb is just to refer to me as how I identified when you last saw me, since you have no way of knowing my gender otherwise."

Ash wondered vaguely if Ramsay's gender had shifted again. Tight nerves pinched through him at the memory of their last meeting—at the thought of attempting to reach the higher realms with Ramsay again. If he failed, he could lose his mind. If he succeeded, he would, apparently, meet the state's most-hated mass murderer of all time. It didn't exactly seem like a win-win situation.

Except for the Book, he thought vaguely. There was still a

chance that he might be able to see the Book. Perhaps read for himself the secrets of the universe.

"Found yourself a lover, did you?" Frank said gruffly as he and Ash seeded new pots of lavender. It was a quieter day, which meant that Ash could enjoy the calm of the greenhouse with Frank. The older man chuckled when Ash spun to him, eyes wide. "You have that head-in-the-clouds look about you."

"That doesn't mean I have a *lover*," Ash said with a shudder—he hated that word, *lover*—and turned away from Frank, digging a finger into the fresh soil of the pot in front of him.

"But you *are* in love," Frank said with confidence.

Ash snorted at the thought of being in love with someone like Ramsay Thorne. They were barely acquaintances, much less friends, and nowhere near *in love*. Thorne was a self-centered, rude, arrogant know-it-all who looked down her nose at Ash, just like any of the other students and professors at Lancaster. No, of course Ash wasn't in love with Ramsay—but he could see why Frank would be mistaken. Ash couldn't stop thinking about her, after all.

The glass walls were fogged with condensation. Budding sage and rosemary and lavender scents mixed, making the air sweet. "What do you know about the Book of Source?" Ash asked Frank.

Frank scooped fresh soil into another pot. "Nothing. That's alchemist business."

He'd said this with a disgusted tone. Ash hesitated. He hoped Frank hadn't been someone who thought alchemy was evil all along—but if he was, he hadn't said anything when he caught Ash practicing.

"You don't have anything against alchemy, do you?" Ash asked with a forced smile.

Frank didn't speak for a moment as he kept working. "When I was your age," he finally said, "I was taught alchemy is a sin. Spitting in the eye of the Creator. If you'd asked me then, I would've said yes, I've got something against alchemy. Now?" He shrugged as if he didn't have an answer. "I'm the groundskeeper of Lancaster College, ain't I? I'm old and tired and don't want to fight young peoples' battles anymore. As long as you keep your alchemy to yourself," he said, voice growing harder, "I don't much care. Just do your job and do it well."

Ash felt the heat of disappointment and growing shame. Frank had always been good to him. The man had mentioned, once, that he'd also grown up across the bridge in Hedge. Maybe that's why he'd gravitated to Ash, wanting to guide him. But now there was a coldness between them, and Ash could see it, too—the slight stiffness in Frank, the way he couldn't quite meet Ash's eye. They fell back to their work in silence.

*

Without even knowing that he'd been tested, Ramsay let Ash know that he'd passed her initial interview and that she would meet him in a location that they would use for future sessions from that day forward. The instructions passed on by an impatient messenger, messily scrawled across the sheet of protected paper with ink that revealed itself only for Ashen Woods, asked Ash to go to Ramsay's office—but when he arrived, she wasn't there. The room was in shadow, red light of the setting sun filtering in through the closed drapes. He squinted at the instructions, confused.

Close the door behind you and speak the password Snowdrop.

Snowdrop. He shuddered. The choice of word seemed macabre. Still, he did as he was told, frowning all the while, afraid that this was some sort of joke, though he didn't think Ramsay had enough of a sense of humor. He snapped shut the door, sighed, and said, "Snowdrop."

Nothing happened. He twisted to look over his shoulder, thinking that maybe Ramsay had been hiding in the corner so that she could laugh at him, then faced forward again. "Snowdrop!"

Still nothing. Ash's frustration grew. He stepped forward, grabbed and twisted the knob, and threw the door open with the full intention of storming out of Ramsay's office, upset that he had trusted Thorne at all—

He was no longer in Boylston Hall. Ash had heard of portal doors, but he'd never experienced one for himself. He stepped through the threshold with awe, closing the door behind him with a click. The other side of the door was painted a chipped purple, different from the plain oak on the side of Ramsay's office. It was dark, wherever he was. The windows showed a night sky that was either heavy with rain clouds or fog, Ash couldn't tell which. The room didn't look like any of the seminar classrooms or offices of Lancaster. It looked like the sitting room of an abandoned manor. The wallpaper was a deep emerald green, some spots torn and stained yellow. The hardwood floor was scuffed and scratched. A fireplace had glowing orange embers.

There were two large plush chairs beside the fire. Ramsay waited in his seat, one ankle over a knee. A book was in Ramsay's hands, as usual, but his eyes were narrowed on Ash. His icy glare gave Ash the distinct feeling that Ramsay was planning how, exactly, he would kill the boy and get away with it. It was only terrifying because Ash knew that Ramsay could succeed, if he really wanted to.

"You're over ten minutes late, Mr. Woods," Ramsay said.

Ash clenched his jaw. "I had to finish up some tasks."

Ramsay's cheek muscle twitched. "You always have tasks. Maybe you should—I don't know—consider finishing them ten minutes earlier."

Ash glared. "You're acting like my job is easy. I promise you, it's not."

"You always seem to have an excuse," Ramsay said, gaze even colder.

"It's not an excuse. It's an explanation. And you could have some empathy," Ash said. "I don't get to waltz away from my responsibilities whenever I want to." Ramsay rolled his eyes, but Ash continued. "I have an actual job and bills I have to pay and—"

"Do you ever stop complaining?"

"Do you even know what bills are? Do you have to worry about paying rent?"

"Endless whining. You ask for my sympathy," Ramsay said, condescending smile planted on his face. "Why should I give it to you? So that you'll feel justified in how miserable you are?"

"I'm not *miserable*—"

But Source, that couldn't have been further from the truth. Ramsay seemed to pick up on that little vibration. "You act like your life is out of your control. As if you can't change—"

Ash would've liked to throttle Ramsay. "Change—what, my life? How?"

"—couldn't help that you arrived late—"

"*Your* fucking Houses make it impossible to change anything!"

"—instead of *taking accountability*." Ramsay paused, a shudder in the air. "Maybe then you'll learn that your whiny excuses are the real blocks and that you're getting in your own way."

Ash felt an infuriating flash, the buildup of frustration exploding with a wave of heat. "That's what privileged assholes like you always say."

"Asshole?"

"*Get out of your own way, oh, yes, I have a million sterling given to me by my daddy, stolen from other people mind you, but your mindset is the real reason I'm better than you!*"

Silence filled the room as Ash realized he'd just insulted the one person who had the power to turn him over to the reds. Ash hadn't given much thought before he'd spoken, but what else was new?

Ramsay's mouth quirked. The fact that he was clearly unamused made his expression that much more worrying. "You're making quite a few assumptions without any evidence," he said, "including that I think I'm better than you."

Ash tried to interrupt, but Ramsay continued with a steady gaze. "I've never once said such a thing, so is it possible that this is what *you* think—no, what you fear? That everyone around you is somehow better, for whatever reason that you tell yourself—our wealth, our looks, perhaps our charm. Maybe that's your real issue, more than anything else: that you're losing a war that doesn't even exist, a competition you conjured in your own mind. Losing a fight against yourself is, in my opinion, pathetic, but it really doesn't matter to me, either way. That seems like a problem for you to handle without letting it bleed into our agreement. So, please—*pull yourself together and arrive on time.*"

The discussion was over. Thorne made that clear by snapping his book shut. Ash's rage deflated into smoldering defeat. Source, Ramsay was vicious. Ash had to remember himself. He'd decided to put up with Ramsay so that he could learn alchemy. He needed Thorne if he was going to have any chance of passing the license exam. "I'm sorry," he said after a moment. "For calling you an asshole."

Ramsay gave a *hm* of acknowledgment, eyebrows raised as he stared at Ash with his arms crossed, but said nothing more.

Ash surrendered by breaking the tense silence. "Where are we?"

"My family home in the Downs," Ramsay said, uncrossing his leg and standing to make his way across the room to a shelf. "We'll be more secure here, with the energetic protections I've put in place."

Ash twitched. It was like he'd suddenly walked in on Ramsay naked. In Ash's experience, homes were only shared with friends and loved ones, and Ash was neither. He curiously glanced around the room, surprised that Ramsay would live in a place that seemed to be falling apart at the seams. The Thorne dynastic line was hated, sure, but it was still a House.

"I didn't realize you were allowed to create portal doors at Lancaster," Ash said, talking mostly to cover his discomfort.

"I'm not," Ramsay replied. "I'd be reprimanded if any of my

superiors found out, maybe fined or put on academic suspension. But, well, I'm assuming you're not going to tell on me," he added with a sardonic smile.

It was ironic: Ramsay's energy had felt so orderly and disciplined, but maybe he only followed the rules closely when it came to his own alchemy since, as long as it benefited him in some way, he certainly seemed willing to break every other rule in existence.

"Why risk it?" Ash asked.

"I was given the option to live on campus," Ramsay said slowly, as if carefully choosing his words, "but I've found over the years that it's better to . . . avoid my peers."

It was unexpected, that Ash felt a little sorry for Thorne.

Ramsay didn't meet Ash's eye as he sucked in a quick breath. "Enough small talk. We have a lot to do tonight—starting with your lesson." Ash's brows raised in surprise, earning a brief smile from Ramsay. "You held up your end of the bargain and followed my instructions, so I'll hold up mine."

Even while he was still angry at Ramsay, Ash felt like an excited little boy, unable to help the eagerness that fluttered through him. Wasn't this something he'd wanted for nearly all his life now? An official lesson in alchemy, even if it was from a graduate apprentice and not a professor, and even if it was given by an arrogant, infuriating person like Ramsay Thorne, was something he'd written off as impossible, once. Ash wanted to hold on to his annoyance with Ramsay, but he could feel it fading, replaced by excitement.

Ramsay turned his back to Ash and went to a cupboard in the corner of the room, opening the drawers and rummaging through until he returned with an unlit candle that was long, thin, and white. "Now," he said, "I need a clear understanding of your technique level."

Technique? Ash's face fell. It was his least favorite subject. Authors of his texts would go on about when to take a specific breath and how to direct energy and—well—Ash preferred to just *do* it, imagine what he wanted and watch his creation come to life. Technique was too organized and limiting for his tastes.

Ramsay stared blankly at the candle, and a flame blinked into existence. Ramsay closed his eyes, and with a whoosh, the flame died back down again. Ash could see purple light dancing around Ramsay's skin, but only for a moment. Ramsay gestured at Ash.

Bringing a flame to life was tier-four creation alchemy, though fire was considered relatively simple to create. It only took an awareness of energy already in the air—imagining the gathering of that energy, fire flickering to life . . . This should be easy for Ash.

He took a breath, shook out his arms, and raised his hand to the candle. He closed his eyes as he imagined the flame—the spark, the heat, the fire—

"Shit! Ashen—"

Ash opened his eyes. The flame had enveloped the entire candle and nearly burned Ramsay's hand. Ramsay dropped it, and the fire took to the wooden floor. Ash gasped and raised both hands, gripping them into fists. The fire sizzled out of existence, scorch marks left behind.

"I'm sorry," Ash said immediately as he looked up, expecting to find an enraged Thorne, seeing that Ash almost burned down his house—but he was surprised to see Ramsay's bemused brow raised instead.

"Are you trying to kill me?" Ramsay asked. "Has that been your plan all along, to get out of our agreement?"

Ash didn't think Ramsay even knew *how* to make a joke and was baffled that Thorne chose this moment to have a sense of humor. It seemed impossible to get a read on Thorne's eccentric unpredictability. "No," Ash said, "though now that you mention it, not a bad idea."

Ramsay bent over to pick up the half-melted candle, examining it. "Remarkable," Ramsay said. "You failed one of the easiest tests given at the college."

"Feel free to hold off on the verbal lashing," Ash muttered. "I've had enough for the night."

"You would've been kicked out of Lancaster for this."

"Are you serious? Because I can't light a fucking candle?"

Ramsay shrugged. "My year-one students are able to control a flame by the end of their first semester. Failing a test like this would show that the student is—well—hopeless."

"Why do I have the feeling that you're enjoying this?"

"Why in the name of Source would I be enjoying this? You're my partner," he said, then quickly amended, "my *alchemic* partner. Your weakness will only drag me down, too."

Ash's embarrassment—and anger—grew. "I'm not *weak* just because—"

Ramsay ignored him, tossing the mess of a candle over his shoulder. "How is it that you can practice complex tier-four creation alchemy—bring an entirely new object into existence—but you can't light a candle and control its flame?"

Ash's shame burned just as hot as his fire had, but Ramsay didn't seem to notice. His confusion seemed to mix with genuine curiosity as he faced the puzzle that was Ash Woods. It was only a few moments before the answer dawned on him. "Ah," he said. "In your independent studies, you didn't happen to skip the fundamentals, did you?"

Ash's expression said it all.

Ramsay released a frustrated sigh, pinching the bridge of his nose. "You decided to attempt the more complicated forms of alchemy first, rather than the basics? Learn how to create objects, before you even learned how to control candlelight?"

Ash couldn't see what was so astonishing about that. "There isn't any point in starting at the beginning when my goal is to get to the end."

Ramsay raised two frustrated hands and clenched them into

fists. "*What?* Mr. Woods, the *beginning* is what gives you the foundation, the building blocks—"

"I have enough of a foundation to create complex objects, right?"

"—to become even clearer and more concise in your technique," Ramsay told him. "It's incredible, truly, that you've managed to grow to where you are now without a foundation in place."

Ash blinked with surprise at the unexpected compliment, cheeks warm.

"Think of how much more powerful you'll be when you know the fundamentals," Ramsay said. He added dismissively, "You need to learn control."

"I disagree," Ash said without missing a beat.

Ramsay gave Ash a bewildered look. "Your energy is an explosion waiting to happen. You have no discipline."

"Is that what you write on your students' reports? *Not enough discipline.*"

"Discipline is necessary if you're going to have any chance of earning a license."

That hit a nerve. "*Controlling* yourself is just *limiting* yourself," Ash said, voice raised. "You're cutting yourself off from your own power."

"What's the point in having power if you can't control it enough to funnel it into purpose?" Ramsay asked, voice also rising and sense of humor now gone.

Ash looked away with annoyance. "I've funneled it into enough purpose to create, haven't I?"

"There isn't enough consistency. You never know when one error will result in harming yourself or others. If you were to learn technique," Ramsay said, "you could pass the alchemist-license exam." And Ash could see the hunger in Ramsay's eyes, too— could hear what was left unsaid: They could also make it to the higher realms.

"In any case, I'll begin our lesson, now that I know your

technique level—which is to say, nonexistent." Ramsay gestured at Ash to sit in one of the chairs beside the fireplace. He cleared his throat, grasped his hands behind his back, and seemed to Ash to be a touch nervous, as if he was about to begin a presentation in front of an actual class of dozens of students.

Ramsay began. "You could think of this physical world, this dimension, and the infinite number of dimensions we can't yet see, as a song played by an orchestra. And if you're made of energy, then you can, of course, orchestrate energy as well. You only need to learn how to pluck the strings."

Ash raised a brow. "I already know that, Ramsay."

"Yes, well, this is the opening lesson I give my first-years," he said, annoyed at the interruption, "so you'll just have to make do and listen, won't you?" Ramsay sighed and adjusted his glasses before continuing.

"Alchemy," Ramsay said as he paced across the room. Ash could almost picture it, the apprentice in front of his class with his stern and solemn expression. He snorted. "It's composed of three key elements. What are those three elements?"

Ash recited from a book he had once read. "Imagination, belief, and power."

"What is imagination?"

"Alchemic creativity. Focusing energy into existence."

"Belief?"

"Faith—trust in your ability as a creator."

"Good," Ramsay said. "Now, what is power?"

Ash was silent.

"It isn't a trick question. Surely you know the answer."

Ash wasn't so sure. He knew what alchemists claimed—connection to Source—but he also knew that, despite his own connection, he was often powerless. "It's when one person has the ability to beat the shit out of another," he said sarcastically.

Thorne gave a quick, unimpressed smile. "Is that truly what

power is?" he asked. "Is that how we define the powerful? Whoever can *beat the shit* out of others?"

"That's how we define power in New Anglia, isn't it?" Ash said. "The Great Houses are in control. The Alexander family leads the Houses because they won the war."

Ramsay seemed to consider this. "But how does the ability to win wars translate into the power to—say—create a flower?"

Ash hesitated, biting his lip. "Honestly? I don't think power can be defined."

Ramsay tilted his head. "And why is that?"

"Because human language can't completely describe the immensity of what *power* truly is. It's impossible. Our brains can't comprehend it."

"And yet here we are," Ramsay said, "comprehending."

"We're *attempting* to comprehend. We'll never fully understand until we die and return to Source."

"But we *are* Source," Ramsay said, gaze flicking up to meet Ash's eye. "We might not understand the logistics with our human brains, and we might not be able to put it all into words, but we can feel what Source is, what power is, because our energy is still a vibration of Source. Don't you feel it now?" he asked, gaze focused on Ash's. "I know that you can. I feel your energy growing in you as I speak."

It was what all alchemists knew, what was repeated again and again in the texts Ash read—but somehow, Ramsay spoke in a way that Ash couldn't dismiss. His pulse quickened. The growing rush of energy danced over his skin.

"Let me offer you a definition," Ramsay said. "Power isn't something that's found externally—taken from others, or created by feelings of superiority. Power comes from within because Source is found within."

Ash swallowed. Suddenly, he couldn't look away from Ramsay. Ramsay held his gaze, dark pupils widening in the silence.

Something taut was between them. It felt like gravity, trying to pull them closer. Neither moved nor spoke.

Ramsay turned away abruptly, clapping his hands together. Ash blinked, looking at the ground. "Now," Ramsay said, "we'll continue with a few exercises so that we can get your technique to where it *should* be."

Ash bit back a groan but sat straighter in his seat, ready to begin.

9

Ash hurried through the cold drizzle and found Tobin already waiting for him outside the Street Cat pub under the gabled roof. The pub was hidden away in an alley near the Mallow docks, the white lights of Kensington shining through the heavy fog in the distance. Ash and Tobin shook hands, palms with their identical scars pressed together. Ash tried not to blush when their skin touched.

They stepped inside. Wooden walls and creaky floorboards smelled like beer and piss. It was warmer, at least. Men with pale skin and pink noses sat at the counter and round tables, turning to look at the two, eyeing them before deciding they weren't worth any trouble.

Tobin chose a table and chair toward the back, sitting heavily with a sigh. He'd been offered a full-time job at the docks, and in the last few days, his face had been tight with exhaustion. After they ordered cheap whiskey and Ash asked for a couple of bowls of greasy fries, Tobin knocked his knuckles against the wooden table, not meeting Ash's gaze. "I—uh—I decided to pledge to Baron."

Ash lowered his voice, glancing around and leaning in. "Baron? Are you sure that's a good idea?"

Tobin clenched his jaw, swirling whiskey around in his glass. "Not everyone can find a fancy job at some college."

He still seemed angry that Ash had even applied at all. Ash wasn't sure if Tobin was upset that he'd tried to leave Hedge and his best friend behind, or if Tobin was angry that Ash had dared to dream that he could be good enough for a place like Lancaster.

He'd known higher society would be angry that he hadn't stayed in his place, but he hadn't expected that from a friend, too.

Ash leaned back in surprise with a pinch of hurt. "My job's not that fancy," he said. "And where I'm working doesn't stop me from seeing that you shouldn't pledge to Baron. He'll own you for the rest of your life."

Tobin's glare cut into Ash, making him flinch. "*Hedge* owns my life, Ash—and it owns yours, too. You're just so stuck in the clouds, trying to learn magic and dreaming that you can get out of here, that you refuse to see the truth that's right in front of you."

Ash's hurt was quickly turning to anger. "And what's that?"

"You want to kiss ass as if you'll get to join a House and become a licensed alchemist, but you think those rich assholes would ever let you? They *hate* people like us. They'd rather kill us themselves." Tobin drained the rest of his glass with one swallow. The silence went on long enough that Tobin sighed, crossing his arms. "Listen," he said, "I'm not trying to give you a hard time. I'm just trying to be your friend, all right? You need to wake up. Stop trying to learn that alchemy shit. Pledge to Baron and start saving so you can live a better life here, in Hedge."

Maybe it was because of Ash's pride that he said what he did. He hadn't meant to tell anyone, not even Tobin, what he'd been up to at Lancaster lately. "Actually," he said, "I have been learning alchemy."

Tobin stilled with surprise.

"With someone, I mean." Ash swallowed, and something inside whispered he'd said too much, gone too far, but Ash's impulsiveness could be difficult to control once it'd already started to surge. "I found a teacher."

"A teacher?" Tobin squinted. "You're not allowed to learn anything unless you get into the college, right? Who would teach you and risk the tier laws?"

Ash bit his lip. "It's a long story."

Tobin shrugged. "I've got all night."

Ash paused. This was *Tobin*, his best friend since they were kids. He used to tell Tobin everything, so why was he hesitating now? "It's—uh, it's actually Ramsay Thorne."

"*Thorne?*"

"Yeah. He's an apprentice at the college."

"As in Amelia and Silas Thorne's kid?" Tobin snorted as if this was a joke, his eyes bright. "You're messing with me, right?"

Ash shook his head. "No. I mean, we got caught up in something—"

"Caught up in *what?*" Tobin asked, flabbergasted, like there could be no reasonable explanation for why Ash would be working with Ramsay.

Ash hesitated. Source knew he shouldn't speak so openly about Ramsay's plans, especially in a pub in Hedge—someone could overhear, and there was no telling who was a Lune follower and who would be willing to string Ash up, a sign that he'd offended the Creator around his neck . . . But he also felt a genuine excitement that he wanted to share with Tobin. He never did think his decisions through. "Ramsay's asked for my help," he said, lowering his voice, "finding the Book of Source. He can't get it without me."

Tobin watched Ash, as if waiting for the punch line, then said, "You're serious."

Ash bit his lip and nodded.

"The Book of *Source*, Ash?" Tobin said. "Will you be hunting for goblins while you're at it?" He raised his glass to the barkeep, signaling for another.

"I didn't think it was real at first either," Ash said.

"And you do now?" Tobin asked. He didn't bother hiding his irritation.

Ash leaned away. "I—well, I don't know what to think," he said. He also wouldn't have thought it was possible to travel to the higher realms before. "What if it *is* real, and we actually manage to find it?"

"It'd probably be the end of the world," Tobin said.

Ash frowned. "Why do you think that?"

"A *Thorne* wants to become all-powerful, and you're asking me why I think the world would end?"

"Ramsay wouldn't hurt anyone. And even if he wanted to, I wouldn't let that happen," Ash said. "I'd be able to read the Book also. I could stop Ramsay."

"Oh, so you would become an all-powerful alchemist now, too?" Tobin said. Though his tone suggested he was teasing, his energy wasn't amused. No, Tobin wasn't as extreme as the mobs of Lune followers, but maybe there was still a part of him that believed alchemists were overstepping the laws of nature.

Ash didn't know what to say. He shook his head for a moment, even as he felt the truth lingering. Yes, of course he would read the Book if he had the chance. "I—well, it doesn't matter," he said quickly. "As long as I help Ramsay, he's offering to teach me alchemy."

"But a fucking *Thorne*, Ash?" Tobin said, leaning in closer now, looking at the other boy as if he'd lost his mind. "That piece of shit's family killed *hundreds* of people."

Ash clenched his jaw. He felt an inexplicable urge to defend Ramsay. "That was his parents. Ramsay—I don't know, he's different. A smug asshole, yes," he said, "but he doesn't want to hurt anyone."

"How do you know that?"

He didn't, Ash realized. He had no proof that Ramsay was someone he could trust. It didn't help that now, Tobin was looking at Ash as if his friend was just as evil for learning alchemy from a Thorne. That hurt more than Ash was willing to admit. He and Tobin had been so close, once—close enough that Ash had wondered, sometimes, if he was in love with his best friend. Almost a year ago, Ash decided to be upfront and told Tobin exactly that, and one thing led to another, and the two shared a drunken night in Ash's bed. That night was something Ash was often too embarrassed to think about, though a part of him was also grateful that his first time had been with Tobin. It was obvious from the awkwardness and their inability to even look at each other the next day and sometimes even months later that they were meant to stay platonic friends. It was a miracle that their friendship had survived a night under the sheets—and disappointing that it seemed it couldn't survive alchemy.

Their conversation ended with a tense silence. Tobin finished his drink, and they left the pub together, hands in their pockets and shoulders hunched against the biting cold. Tobin suggested they walk through the docks as a shortcut. Clouds of mist hung in the air through the Mallow. There was a scent of salt and rotting fish. Warehouses were lined by the tracks, and on the other side of a road were the docks that stretched into the horizon, disappearing into a haze of smoke and fog. Boats and ships rocked up and down and clunked against the concrete with every wave.

Ash heard the footsteps that followed. Their stalker didn't even attempt to hide. Tobin sighed, as if too tired to deal with being attacked tonight. He spun around. "Can I help you?" he shouted.

The person stepped out of the shadows, a slash of yellow light falling across them. Tobin and Ash froze. A young woman with light-brown skin and bright red hair walked across the cracked pavement in heeled brogues. Her tweed coat suggested that she belonged in Kensington, not the Mallow docks of Hedge.

"No," she said, smile gleaming. Her gaze flicked to Ash. "But you can."

He frowned, exchanging looks with Tobin. "Do I know you?" he asked as he looked at the woman again.

"Not yet," she said. She raised a hand as if she meant to greet them. It was the only warning Ash had before it began to glow gold. He shouted at Tobin to get down, throwing himself at the other boy. They landed on the ground in a heap just as a ray of searing light blasted over their heads.

Ash's heart thundered as he leaped to his feet. The woman raised both hands now, smile twisting in concentration. Ash clenched shut his eyes and imagined a shield of red light rising from the ground, impenetrable—

A second golden blast, stronger than the first, exploded against a red wall that had appeared before Ash, shattering on contact. He was thrown back from the blast, but Tobin was already on his feet, dragging Ash to his and starting to run.

"Who the hell is she?!"

"I don't know!"

"Why is she trying to kill us?!"

"I don't know, Tobin!"

Another blast of light exploded, hitting the wall of a building they raced past. Ash could only hear the smacks of footsteps, his thumping heart echoing in his ears and air wheezing in his throat. He looked over his shoulder. The woman was fast, too fast for someone running in heels on wet pavement. She stopped, hands raised.

For a split second, nothing happened—but then hot energy shot past Ash. The outline of her form appeared over and over again, surrounding him, created from nothing but light particles like images made of embers. The line of women held up their hands, palms forward, and Ash could feel a binding twist around him like the threads of spiderwebs wrapping around his arms and legs, attempting to cocoon and imprison him. He closed his eyes and imagined a jolt of electricity zapping from his core and through the threads. The wall of women vanished in a wave of sparks, and the real woman yelped in surprise and pain. Ash kept running, following after Tobin and beginning to surpass him—

"Keep going!" Ash shouted.

Tobin's face was purple and slicked with sweat, chest heaving.

They raced around a corner, feet sliding on pebbles. Tobin was a few paces behind. He wouldn't make it.

Ash slowed to run beside him. "Head to the train."

"What?" Tobin said hoarsely, wheezing. "But she'll follow you."

"That's the point."

"No—no way you can take on a fucking *alchemist*—"

The woman was only a few blocks away, quickly gaining.

Ash clenched his jaw. "She wants me, not you. I won't let you get killed."

"And I won't leave you behind!"

But Ash gave Tobin a determined look, one that meant it didn't matter what Tobin said because Ash had already made up his mind. Tobin growled in frustration and grabbed Ash by the collar of his shirt, pulling him close. "You better make it out of this," he said in Ash's ear, before they gripped each other's hands, pressing their scars together.

"I'll find you after," Ash promised.

Tobin turned on his heel and ran.

Ash sucked in a deep breath and hurled a ball of red-hot energy over his shoulder. There was an echoing boom behind him, but he sprinted without stopping to see if he'd hit the woman. He raced through the maze of warehouses with only the light of flickering streetlamps, weaving through the abandoned streets, feet splashing through mud. His legs started to shake. He grew dizzy. He turned a corner, breathing hard. The docks were eerily silent now, no sound following him. He slowed down and looked over his shoulder and saw, with relief, that he'd finally lost her. When he looked forward again, he gasped.

The woman was waiting right in front of him, as if she'd materialized out of thin air. Ash skidded to a stop, but she grabbed his neck. "I didn't realize you were an alchemist, too," she said. "I would've been more careful if I'd known."

Ash choked, hands scrambling at her fingers, trying to pry them open as the woman lifted Ash off his feet. She was only a few inches taller than him, but she managed to hold him a foot off the ground.

"How *did* you learn such high-level alchemy? I didn't see that you were a licensed alchemist or a student when I looked into you."

Ash tried to hit her hands, her wrists, lungs burning.

"Ah, well," she said, grip tightening. "I suppose it doesn't matter."

Ash threw out a hand. Sand flew into the alchemist's eyes. She clenched them shut, grimacing, but she still wouldn't let go.

"Unfortunately for you, Ashen Woods," she said, slowly opening her eyes once more, "it seems that Thorne needs you to find the Book." Her smile twisted. "And we can't have that, can we?"

Ash's vision was blurring. The woman's voice sounded faint. The adrenaline, the fear, the anger of being caught and trapped, of being treated like he was nothing, as it seemed he always was—

A burst of energy exploded. The woman flew backward until she smacked into a brick wall. Ash fell to his knees, coughing and gasping. He tried to push himself to his trembling feet—he needed to *run*—

"Well, you're a powerful little shit, aren't you?"

He looked up. The woman glared. She seemed bored as she pushed herself up, disheveled, but the energy coming off her in waves told a different story. Ash gasped and threw up a shield just as a dagger of golden light flew for his throat. Another sliced into his shoulder. He grabbed it as he scrambled backward, blood leaking between his fingers.

This was the end. He would die here, without ever having earned his license, without ever forcing his father to acknowledge him. Ash would die if he didn't fight.

He started to draw energy from the air, from the stone and water beneath him, from the particles passing by on the night breeze. Ash had read enough about materialization. It was tier-five alchemy, dangerous if attempted incorrectly. *Home. Take me home.* But he didn't have enough oxygen in his blood. He didn't have a level enough breath or mind, this was obvious for the alchemist to see.

She froze. "Stop," she said, backing away. "What're you doing? That's dangerous—you might—"

Ash didn't hear her over the crack, the series of pops as energy flooded into the unstable space he'd created. Ash's eyes widened. He raised his hands, a barricade shimmering just in time. The explosion shot him back. The railway tracks split, crumbling. A crater blasted into the ground and the nearby warehouse. Debris and embers drifted through the sky.

10

Ash heard shouts and screams vaguely, as well as the sirens in the distance. He groaned as he dragged himself to his feet. A pile of rubble stood where the alchemist had been. She was dead, there wasn't any doubt in Ash's mind—he'd killed an alchemist from Kensington, and to the Kendrick, it wouldn't matter if it'd been in self-defense, especially when he wasn't licensed. He'd be hanged before week's end.

He couldn't return to his apartment. The alchemist had said she'd looked into him, and if she had, it was possible that others knew about Ash, too. He struggled not to tear himself apart as he thought back about the reckless conversations he'd had with Frank and Tobin, not taking Ramsay seriously when he'd warned Ash that other alchemists could be paying attention, listening in on them, willing to do anything to get in their way—

He limped through the streets of Hedge until the bridge appeared. The neighborhood of Wynnesgrove was quiet and peaceful so late at night, but he still jumped at every shadow, afraid that it was another alchemist or that a Kendrick redguard had already caught up with him. Ash made it to the college campus, the stone buildings intimidating in the dark. He wasn't sure where else to go. He couldn't hide with Tobin and endanger him, and at least if an alchemist began to attack Ash at the school, he'd be surrounded by other trained alchemists who could help him. There was the other possibility, of course, that surrounding himself with alchemists right then might be even more dangerous, but that wasn't something Ash wanted to think about.

It was hours before the sun would rise. The sky was a dark

purple, a rare night that was clear of clouds. He walked through the gardens and into the greenhouse. He stood at the sink and splashed water on his face, wincing at the sting of his shoulder and the bruises around his neck. He broke off a stem of aloe and rubbed the gooey substance on his cuts, and when he was finished, he found a corner to curl up in. He couldn't sleep. Questions raced through his mind. Who had the alchemist been, and how had she known about Ash and Ramsay? How many others were there, possibly even watching Ash at that very moment?

The sun began to rise, a soft-pink light illuminating the air. Ash could barely focus on his work as he made the rounds with his watering can. He dragged the can to Ramsay's office first, knocking on the door and cracking it open, but his heart fell when he saw that the apprentice wasn't there. The office and its mess of books and papers were unchanged since the last time Ash came. They had plans to meet in Ramsay's home later that evening, but Ash wasn't sure that the news of the attack could wait.

Ash hid from Frank throughout the day—as long as Ash completed his tasks, the older man didn't always need to know about his comings and goings—but the bruises and cuts earned him alarmed looks from the students he passed on the lawn, and it was only halfway through the day that he realized there were brown spots of dried blood on his shirt. He hadn't had a shower, and he was beginning to smell. Ash decided to spend the rest of his day hiding in the greenhouse, and when it was late enough that classes were over, he snuck to Ramsay's office once again.

The apprentice had come through at some point—books were shifted, and a pair of round glasses were left on top of a pile of papers. Ash closed the door, took a breath, and said, "Snowdrop."

He opened the door to the dark sitting room. Ramsay was standing by the fire, reading as usual, and she looked up with a smirk. "*Early* today, Mr. Woods? I never thought I'd—"

She saw him—his face, the bruises, and the blood on his shirt.

"Source." She immediately clapped the book shut and tossed it to the side, hurrying over to Ash and raising a hand. He flinched. "I want to check your vitals," she said with concern, frowning and already eyeing his limbs as if she could detect internal injuries by sight alone. "Is that all right?"

He swallowed and nodded.

Ramsay was focused as she swept a hand over Ash's forehead and cheeks. Ash could feel the tingle of energy as she worked and saw glimmers of purple that faded into a light blue. "What happened?" she asked.

"I was attacked."

"I assumed you didn't trip and fall," she said with only some sarcasm. "Who attacked you?"

He took a breath. This was what he'd been dreading. "I'm not sure," he started slowly. "I only know that she was an alchemist."

Ramsay's hand froze. Her gaze snapped to Ash's, clearly knowing there was more. She waited for him to speak.

"She—ah—knew, somehow," Ash said, "that I'm working with you. That you depend on me to find the Book."

"Shit," she breathed. "I was afraid someone might've been—but I took every precaution, even when we were meeting in my office, setting energetic barriers—but maybe they'd found a way . . ."

She trailed off before she looked up at Ash, and he realized it didn't matter what he said next or how he tried to defend himself. She already knew exactly what he'd been afraid to say.

"Who did you tell?" she asked, voice low.

He hesitated. "My friend. But he was attacked, too, and there's no way he would've—"

"It *doesn't matter*, Ashen," Ramsay said, rage growing. "I've told you, haven't I? I told you to be careful. Alchemists—some could've created energetic grids so that *any* time *anyone* calls the Book of Source by name without protections, they can find the person talking about it, listen to them, discern if the information is helpful—kill them, if necessary. You must only refer to it as the Book, if you refer to it at all."

Ash thought of the conversation he'd had with Frank about the Book of Source. If what Ramsay said was true, then that might've been the moment alchemists began to listen in on him, to follow his movements—and for the woman to have heard him tell Tobin outright that he was helping Ramsay . . .

Ramsay cursed under her breath as she continued to scan Ash with her hand, down one shoulder and arm and across the collarbone to the next. "You're intolerable," she said.

Ash clenched his jaw. "I'm sorry. I wasn't thinking."

"It seems you rarely are," Ramsay snapped.

Ash glared at her, pulling away. "It was a mistake."

"A mistake that nearly cost you your life," Ramsay said. "Stay still."

"You don't care about my life," Ash said.

"Oh, is that so?"

"You only care about your *assistant* helping you get to the higher realms."

"Do you often make a habit of telling people what they think and how they feel?"

Ash wasn't sure what to say to that.

Ramsay swept a hand over his ribs. Even though she wasn't touching him, the trace of energy felt like fingers brushing against his skin, even beneath his shirt. Ash's face warmed. He glared at the floor as she fell to one knee and ran her hand down his legs, knees, and shoes.

She took an impatient breath and stood. "You have no broken bones," she murmured.

"I think I would've known if I had broken bones."

"The bruise on your neck will fade. But this gash on your shoulder could get infected," she said. She met his eye. "I'm not the strongest healer, but I know enough. May I?"

He swallowed nervously. He'd never, in all his eighteen years, had another alchemist heal him. He'd made his own attempts with smaller cuts here and there, but he just didn't have the patience that healing required. "Yes."

Ramsay shook out her hands, then closed her eyes and placed one on her chest, over her heart, and the other directly on Ash's shoulder. Her long fingers touching his skin made his pulse race. This was especially embarrassing when he realized that Ramsay would be able to feel his quickening heartbeat under her hand, too. She gave no reaction. She only breathed as a lighter purple shined from her skin. Ash remembered the texts he'd read explained that tier-four healing alchemy required compassion—an unflinching empathy, a reminder that every being in existence was worthy of unconditional love and acceptance, that they were pure Source energy beneath the layers of pain and hurt and fear.

Ash's cut began to tickle, then tingle and itch. The warmth spread across his skin, and he glanced up at Ramsay, wondering how it was possible that she, who was so sarcastic and condescending and cold, could find it within her heart to heal. The warmth ended. Ramsay's hand pulled away. She inspected her work, and Ash twisted to see a thin raised scar.

"Not perfect," she said, and seemed disappointed in herself for it, "but good enough."

Ash rolled down his torn sleeve, suddenly feeling self-conscious. "Thanks."

She didn't answer him as she sat in one of the two chairs, legs crossed. "What will you do now?" she asked.

He knew what she meant. "I don't know. It's probably not safe to go back to my apartment—"

"No, it's definitely not safe."

"I stayed in the greenhouse last night," Ash said. "I could get away with sleeping there for a while, as long as I wake up before Frank arrives."

Ramsay suddenly seemed uncomfortable as she looked away from Ash. "You could stay here," she suggested.

Ash froze. He didn't know what to say. "Here?" he repeated. "As in—here?"

She quirked an amused eyebrow. "Would you like me to define the meaning of *here* for you? Yes, Mr. Woods—*here*, in my home."

"With you?"

"Well, I'm not going to sleep outside." She shrugged, as if this was a perfectly reasonable thing to offer someone who was barely an acquaintance, though she couldn't quite meet his eyes. "It'd be safer. I have generations' worth of barriers and protections that prevent anyone from spying on my home, much less attacking it. No one would know where you are, if there are other alchemists watching you."

Ramsay's points made her invitation tempting, but Ash still couldn't move past the fact that he'd have to spend any more time with her than necessary.

She seemed to read his mind. "There're multiple wings and chambers for you to choose from. We wouldn't have to cross paths at all," she said, "except for when we're meeting for your lessons and our work."

And there it was. Ash could see Ramsay's real motivation. If Ash stayed in her home, that also meant they could get closer to finding the Book of Source. Ash frowned as he remembered the conversation he'd had with Tobin just the night before. Was there any way for Ash to know that Ramsay wasn't just as dangerous as the other alchemists who were willing to kill for the Book?

"Why do you want it?" Ash asked.

She looked up at him with a frown.

"What will you do with the Book once you have it?"

It seemed for a long moment that Ramsay didn't plan to answer him. Finally, she pushed away from the chair and stood. "Don't you trust me, Ashen?"

"Ash," he said. "I hate being called *Ashen*."

She stepped closer to him. "Ash, then," she said. "It'll be difficult for us to work together if you don't."

"How can I trust you?" he asked. "I don't know you."

"That's the purpose of our exercises. You'll get to know me."

"Getting to know you won't help if you turn out to be a psychotic murderer like your parents."

He'd gone too far. It was like he'd slapped her across the face. She jolted, taking a step back. "I'm not like my parents."

"No? You're desperate to find the Book of Source. Weren't they, too?" he asked.

"I'm not the only one—"

"Isn't that why they killed all those people? That's what everyone says," he said, before Ramsay could answer him. "Everyone says that the Thornes massacred hundreds of people in a sacrifice—"

"I *know* what everyone says," Ramsay said, voice quiet but cold enough that Ash snapped his mouth shut. "I know that the world sees my parents and now me as the villains, and it's easier, isn't it? To have an obvious villain so that you can feel like the hero instead."

Ash swallowed and watched as she paced away, turning her back to him for one long moment. She took several deep breaths, maybe to compose herself, before she spoke again.

"What my parents did was irredeemable," she said softly. "I'm not looking for forgiveness for their actions. I only want to take accountability."

"Accountability?"

She turned, but her gaze was still on the floor. "I want to atone for my parents' wrongs," she said. "It's the only goal I've had since their executions. I've wanted to find the Book, just as they were unable to. I'd dreamed, even, of reading it myself and having the power to bring back to life every person they'd killed—and to bring my parents back to life, too," Ramsay added with shame. "An immature dream. Nothing more. As the years passed, I realized there was only one course of action I could take to truly atone."

Ash feared that he already knew the words that would come from Ramsay's mouth. He had a difficult time ignoring the pit of disappointment when she inevitably said them.

"I want to find the Book and destroy it," she said, "so that it can never be used to harm again."

*

Ash was surprised that Ramsay didn't immediately demand that they begin their exercises for the night. "You wouldn't be any use in your condition anyway," she said. "Rest, and we can begin again tomorrow."

The manor's run-down state wasn't confined to only that room. The stone walls slick with water and mold made Ash feel like he was in a dungeon, and there were very few windows. The ones they passed only showed far-below trees and cliffsides and low-hanging clouds. Ramsay's tour was brief. She showed Ash the formal dining room, with its long wooden table and chandelier made of antlers, and she pointed to the kitchens, a maze of counters and an iron stove. There was a crate of fruit, but that was all. Ash got the overwhelming sense that Ramsay didn't eat well, not like she should.

"Are you hungry?" Ramsay asked. When Ash nodded, she said, "Help yourself."

Ash picked up a pear and bit into it. It was softer than he would've liked. If Ash was going to stay, he would need to figure out what to do about food. "Don't you want dinner?"

She shrugged. "Not really."

Not really? Ramsay had practiced healing, which took a significant amount of vitality, from what Ash had read. "But you need to renew your energy, right?"

"I don't cook very often, since the college's dining hall provides meals."

"But we're not in the college now."

Ramsay smirked. "Look at you, nagging me. I didn't realize you cared."

Ash rolled his eyes and took another bite. "Forget it."

Ramsay looked like she would very much regret the next words out of her mouth. "Would you *like* me to cook something?"

Ash glanced around the kitchen. "With what?"

For a moment, she seemed offended—but then she looked around the kitchen, too. "Fair point."

"Don't you ever—I don't know—fix your own meals?"

Ramsay sighed. "Sometimes, but, Source, cooking is an endless chore. I need to eat three times a day, plus preparing the meals takes time and grocery shopping is a pain, and it's so much easier to grab something with high sugar—why're you looking at me like that?"

Ash shook his head. He pictured Ramsay working through the mornings and afternoons and nights, forgetting that she should eat and grabbing an apple with impatient annoyance, as if needing food was an inconvenient interruption.

Ash's heart soared when she showed him the library. It had scuffed wooden floors and torn black-and-gray striped wallpaper. It wasn't as large as the college's, of course, but it was still two stories, and each wall had floor-to-ceiling shelves.

Ash walked with wonder to the closest shelf, running his fingers along the spines. He saw a book titled *Inquiries of the Akash*. The Akash was said to be a library that connected all universes and dimensions, holding all knowledge—where anyone could go to ask any question and have it answered. The only problem was that no one in the physical realm had access to it. Ash had thought the Akash was just a legend, too, but now he wasn't so sure.

"Are they all alchemic texts?" he asked Ramsay.

Ramsay blushed. "Not all, no."

Ash tilted his head in surprise. "What else is here?"

"Reading isn't only for work," Ramsay said stiffly. "Some people read for pleasure, too, you know."

She turned before Ash could ask more questions, and with a grin, he immediately knew that the first chance he had, he would be back in the library, scouring the shelves for the sorts of books Ramsay read *for pleasure*.

Ramsay slowed down and opened another door to a guest bedroom. It had a large four-poster bed frame with red drapes. There was a wardrobe that was far too large for Ash's few things and a stone balcony that looked out over the mountaintops. Ash walked inside and saw another open door leading to a bathroom with a rusting claw-foot tub.

Ramsay spoke behind him. "Will this be sufficient?"

He turned to her, unsure of what to say.

Ramsay seemed embarrassed as she rubbed the back of her neck. "I know that it isn't to the standard of other House manors."

"This is more than I've ever had." He tested out the bed. The sheets smelled musty, as if someone hadn't been in this room for years, and maybe they hadn't, but this didn't bother him. It was the softest mattress he'd ever touched. "Thank you," Ash told her. "For letting me stay and healing me and—just, thank you."

Her cheeks pinkened. She took a quick breath, as if impatient with her own reaction. "You're welcome. I'll see you tomorrow, Ash."

11

One night, Ramsay sat on a stone bench in the Pembroke gardens, hidden by the roses. She held her hand and cried. Blake Quintrell had shoved her in the middle of the dining hall, in front of the entire school to see, and she'd fallen and skinned her palm on the stone floor. Ramsay wasn't even sure why she was crying. Her hand didn't hurt very much, and she wasn't sad because of her parents. She hadn't been close to them. They'd sent her off to Pembroke, and when she came home to the Downs in the summer months, their heads were always bent over papers, whispering and scribbling notes, glancing up to meet her eye, only for her father to stand and walk across the room to shut the door. Ramsay knew that her parents had only been concerned with having an heir for the Thorne name. That was the only reason she'd been born. She didn't miss them now that they were dead. But, still, she'd never felt quite as alone as she did then.

Ramsay jumped to her feet when a shadow appeared, but it was only Callum. They'd been friends once, before her parents' killings. She'd been part of the small group of House heirs at Pembroke, treated like royalty. She and Callum had been especially close, even though the Thorne and Kendrick families had never been allies. Ramsay had even disliked Callum once, just because of his last name alone, before she saw that he wasn't so bad. Ramsay had even begun to like him, perhaps more than she should. She'd wondered sometimes if Callum felt the same. Those days seemed like a lifetime ago now.

Callum had always been a tall and gangly boy, limbs that

seemed too long for him to know what to do with, with dark brown skin and short curls. He froze when he saw Ramsay and swallowed nervously, like he wasn't sure what to say.

"Why're you here?" she asked, clutching her wrist. Her palm throbbed.

He gestured at her hand. "I wanted to make sure that you were okay."

"Aren't your friends wondering where you are?" she asked, bitterness settling. She could've used Callum *making sure she was okay* months ago, when her parents were first executed, but he'd been like everyone else—suddenly unable to meet her eye, hurrying away as if he hadn't heard when she called his name. Callum's betrayal had hurt more than anyone else's. Ramsay had decided, then, to steel herself against other people—to get used to the fact that she would be friendless and alone for the rest of her life.

He took a step forward. "May I?"

She clutched her hand to her chest, staring at Callum's outstretched palm—not trusting it, not after the way Blake and her other former friends had treated her. But Callum's dark brown eyes were as gentle as Ramsay remembered, warm and hesitant. This was what Ramsay had always loved most about him. Callum was different from the other House heirs. She could see that he tried to prove to the world that he was strong and brave, the Kendrick warrior he was expected to be—but his biggest secret was that he was kind.

Ramsay gave him her hand. He held it as if it was a flower, gently cupped in his palm. He swallowed and closed his eyes. She could feel warmth exuding from his body—could feel the love that he felt for her, the love that she'd started to feel for him, too. Her skin began to itch as the cut closed. Ramsay and Callum had studied alchemy before in secret, even though they could've been expelled from Pembroke if anyone saw. No one was allowed to practice alchemy unless they were accepted to a college, and if any of the faculty caught Ramsay, they would gladly take the chance to get rid of her, as many parents had already demanded. Her palm was healed, but neither seemed to want to let go.

"Thank you," Ramsay whispered. She turned to leave, but Callum reached out and touched her elbow.

"I'm sorry," he said. "I'm sorry for—Creator, I'm sorry for everything."

Ramsay narrowed her eyes. "Why're you sorry?"

"Because—well, it isn't like you did anything wrong," he said. "Your parents—they did something awful, Ramsay. They killed so many people."

She squeezed her eyes shut. It was something she tried not to think about.

"But you didn't do anything wrong," Callum whispered. "You shouldn't be punished for their mistakes."

"Everyone thinks that if my parents could do something so awful," she said, "then I might, too. And what scares me most is that I'm afraid they're right."

"No," Callum said immediately. He stepped closer, still holding her hand. "I know you. You're the person I'm closest to, closer than Blake or Gavin or anyone else, and I—I know you would never hurt anyone."

Ramsay had started to cry, the pain built in her chest overflowing now with the touch of kindness that she was shown after months of being treated like the monster she feared she was.

Callum continued. "You're a good person, Ramsay. I know that you are."

She wanted so badly to believe him.

The next time that Ramsay saw Callum in the dining hall, he glanced up at her, eyes widened—and he looked away again, as if he hadn't seen her at all. And the next evening, she hid away in the gardens, daring to hope that he would come and overjoyed when he did. This was the dance they continued, night after night.

※

Hedge and Kensington were separated by a gray river, where the Isle of Kingsland rested offshore. The shining white city centered around the House Alexander, a golden barricade and Kendrick redguards with their swords at their hips surrounding an also all-white manor of intricate architecture that had survived even the Great War. There was a rumor that Alexander's was the only manor in all the state to have portal doors that accessed every major House, giving Lord Alexander such power that he could waltz into any one of them, completely unannounced. Even the Houses that hated alchemy depended on it. Marlowe wasn't sure why she found that so amusing.

She strode down a tree-lined street where the manor of House Alexander stood over white town houses and cul-de-sacs of brick roads, streetlamps wrapped in pretty vine. She clacked down the sidewalk and up the front steps to her door, fiddling with her keys. The powdered makeup had hidden her bruises well, though there was still an angry red scab across her temple. She'd done her best to patch up the gash, but healing wasn't her specialty, and Marlowe couldn't go to House Adelaide, not without explaining why she'd nearly been killed in an explosive battle with another alchemist. Marlowe was lucky she'd managed to imagine herself wrapped by a protective shield, and even with that, she'd had several broken bones and fractured ribs.

Marlowe pushed open her door with a tired sigh, then froze, her gaze snapping up. Her entryway was in shadow. The sitting room was also dim in the late afternoon, the windows facing away from the sun. Her eyes met the energy she'd sensed: Gresham Hain stood against the far wall, waiting for her. There was no sign of alchemy used on the door. He must've materialized into her home.

She snapped the door shut. "I didn't realize I'd extended an invitation," she said with more bravado than she felt. She tossed her keys into a waiting glass dish.

Hain said nothing. He slowly pushed away from the wall, watching her.

Marlowe buckled under his gaze, her own falling. There'd been days when she'd been proud to meet his stare with a glare of her own. "He was an alchemist," she said. "There was no way for me to have known beforehand, or I would've been prepared."

"Your job was to prepare for any possibility," Hain told her.

After Hain had adopted her from House Lune, he'd begun to train her in alchemy until, finally, he decided she was ready. He provided her with this town house and a monthly allowance and requested her assistance in small matters such as these every few months, always with an expectation of perfection. The pressure could be suffocating.

"I'm sorry," she said, unsure of what else he might want to hear.

"I trusted you to take care of this task."

"I still can," she insisted. "I'll be ready for him next time."

Hain stared her down as if he wasn't so sure, and this scared Marlowe, too, because she knew what would happen if Hain decided she was no longer useful. It wasn't often that he'd asked her to kill. She'd had to only three times before now: an older House Lune lord who seemed bent on convincing Alexander to outlaw alchemy altogether no matter Hain's threats, a historian from House Alder who'd wanted to alert the public about the existence of the Book of Source, and the singer. Marlowe wasn't sure why she'd had to kill that girl, but she'd done it without complaint, because if she didn't—if she refused and tried to escape Hain—Marlowe knew that he would have her killed, maybe by a Lune orphan just like Marlowe, living in another one of his town houses.

"Where is the boy now?" Hain asked.

She hesitated to speak the truth but knew there was no sense in trying to hide it. "He's behind some kind of energetic block," Marlowe said. "It's difficult to get a read on his exact location." She could see the boy whenever he stepped into Ramsay Thorne's office, but his trail ended there. She suspected a portal door was in use, taking him to a location she couldn't sense.

Marlowe had mastered remote viewing. It was a difficult form of tier-five alchemy, keeping enough control over one's own energy to leave their physical body but still remain in the physical plane. After memorizing another person's energetic signature, she could close her eyes and see where they were, the clothes they wore, and the food they ate. She'd sensed the boy, Ashen Woods, in the college gardens and on his walks through Hedge. It'd been easy for her to follow him and wait until he was isolated enough to attack.

"But he'll have to leave soon," Marlowe said quickly when she could feel Hain's growing anger. "I've been back to his apartment, and he left everything he owned behind. He'll return eventually."

Hain wasn't impressed. "*Eventually* is unacceptable."

She swallowed, hesitating to ask the question she'd wondered a few times now. "Why do you want him dead?" she said. "Why not just kill Ramsay Thorne? You want to stop her from finding the Book . . ." She trailed off, feeling the rising danger. Hain never liked being questioned.

"Thorne is too big a player in this game," he said. "I prefer to keep her alive and close. She could have her uses," he added, "if it comes time to needing someone to place blame."

Marlowe understood what Hain was implying: If he was ever caught with his experiments, and the Houses realized he had killed so many people in his hunt for the Book of Source, he would find a way to frame Ramsay Thorne instead. Marlowe could feel how it might work perfectly. There would be enough evidence that Ramsay had been searching for the Book, too, and she was already hated, her parents known to be mass murderers. It wouldn't surprise anyone if she followed in their footsteps.

"But we can't allow her to come any closer to finding the Book," Hain said. "I want the boy dead by week's end."

Marlowe nodded her understanding. She spoke quickly, hoping to placate him. "I've already begun to look into him further. Ashen

Woods doesn't have many records. He'd been in a juvenile detention center in Hedge—"

"What was his name?" Hain said, looking to her suddenly.

She hesitated. "Ashen Woods."

Hain had one day alerted her that, in his viewing of Ramsay
Thorne, the apprentice had found an assistant that she seemed
to think was her key to finding the Book, and so this assistant,
unfortunately, would need to meet an untimely end. That was all
the information Marlowe needed to begin her work. Hain hadn't
cared to know anything about the boy that he expected to die, not
even his name.

Hain's gaze narrowed with focus. Marlowe could feel his
storming energy, though she couldn't pinpoint what he was
thinking. She was surprised by his next words.

"Tell me more about Ashen Woods."

When Ash woke up in the morning, he frowned, confused—
until he remembered where he was and what had happened. It
was a Saturday, his day off from work. Usually, in his apartment
in Hedge, he would stretch and roll over and enjoy the feeling of
falling in and out of sleep before he dragged himself to his feet to
find something to eat. But he sat up in bed now, anxious.

Ash felt shy and like he was intruding when he ventured out
of the room and into the hall. White morning light poured in
through the window, making the gloomy corridor surprisingly
bright. Ramsay's house was cold, snow covering the mountaintops
and slicking the forest that stretched on into the horizon. The stone
floors were like ice as Ash hurried down the passageways, making a wrong turn and getting lost and needing to backtrack until
he knew where he was again. When he finally found the dining
room and connected kitchen, he found a half-eaten bowl of porridge and an apple core. Source, Ramsay lived as if she expected

a maid to follow behind her. Ash slipped into the kitchens and opened the cupboards of the pantry. Some forgotten bread had started to mold. If Ash was going to stay here, then he would need to find a grocery. He wouldn't feel safe wandering the wealthy neighborhood of Wynnesgrove or Kensington, but maybe there was a village near Ramsay's home that he could explore.

After he ate a soft plum for breakfast, he bathed and dressed, wearing a shirt over his binder and a pair of trousers he'd found in the room's wardrobe. The clothes were several sizes too big for him, but it would have to do. His only other outfit was still bloody and torn. It didn't matter. Ash was going to return to Hedge to check in on Tobin, and he'd stop off at his apartment and get his things, too. Ash felt lucky that he hadn't run into Ramsay. If she saw him, she'd inevitably ask about his plans for the day, and Ramsay would chastise Ash for wanting to go back, insisting that it was too dangerous. He rolled his eyes as he thought of what she would tell him with her usual condescending gaze.

He returned to the study. It was empty, though there were signs that Ramsay had been through the room, an empty mug on the table that was beside one of the chairs. Ash murmured the password, opened the door, and held his breath as he stepped into Ramsay's college office. He closed the door behind him again, then opened it and stepped out into Boylston Hall.

Though it was the weekend, the college still had a few students who wandered in their sweaters and cardigans. Ash caught one girl eyeing him and whispering to her friend, both bursting into giggles at the sight of him. He did have to admit he looked ridiculous in Ramsay's old clothes. She was at least one head taller than Ash, and he'd had to roll up the ends of the pants several times. Even then they were dragging through the mud.

He walked through the maze of buildings, thinking of Ramsay and wondering where she'd gone if she wasn't in the manor or her office, before he heard a voice calling. "You, boy—yes, you."

Ash turned, and for a moment, he forgot how to breathe. Gresham Hain stood before him on the path, coming out of the courtyard, holding a stack of texts. He glared down at Ash.

"You're a servant of the college, aren't you?" Hain said.

Ash clenched his jaw. It shouldn't have been surprising that his father didn't recognize him—the man had never seen a photograph of Ash, as far as he knew. If he never bothered to read his mother's letters, then Gresham Hain didn't even know that Ash existed.

"I'm assistant to the groundskeeper," Ash said when he found his voice again. It cracked slightly from the mixture of emotions that Ash wasn't sure he could untangle: nervousness, yes, and fear—but also anger, rage, disgust for this man who had taken advantage of his mother and left her to die. And curiosity, Ash had to admit to himself—shame for being happy that he had his father's attention for the first time in his life.

Gresham eyed him, as if thinking that Ash didn't look like a groundskeeper. "I require your assistance," he said. "Follow me."

Ash wasn't allowed to argue. Gresham could easily report Ash for insubordination and have him fired. And besides that, as much as Ash hated to admit the truth, he also *wanted* to follow his father. Ash couldn't ignore the little boy inside of him, excited that he was speaking to his dad for the first time in his life. He wanted to know what Gresham Hain was like. He wondered if he might even dare to tell Gresham who he was, just to see how the man would react.

He followed Hain in silence for several long minutes, across the lawn and into Vanderbilt Hall with its squeaky wooden floors and arched corridors. The classrooms were usually abandoned here, so Ash was surprised when Hain led him to an open door. It seemed as if Hain had taken over the room for himself as storage. There were piles of books and vials and jars of herbs and rusting alchemic devices that Ash had only ever read about but never seen with his own eyes: a frequency locator that looked like a small compass and could measure the energy of the person who held it, goggles that were claimed to help its wearer see nonphysical energies that visited this realm, a miniature sculpted map of the stars.

Hain gave Ash the simple order to begin organizing each object by groupings and labels. Ash stood by the threshold, looking from Hain to the room and back to Hain, unsure why he had been called here for such a strange job—but he knew he couldn't complain. He rolled up his sleeves and got to work, expecting that Hain would leave him there. He was surprised when the man only stood against a wall and watched.

"Are you new to the college?" Hain asked Ash, inspecting him as he worked. "I haven't seen you on campus before."

"I started here a few months ago," Ash said, rummaging through a box.

"Why this position?"

Ash was surprised by what felt like a sudden interrogation. He shrugged, unable to look at his father. "I'd wanted to attend the college," he admitted, "but I wasn't accepted. The position listing was posted, and I needed a job, so I applied."

"You wanted to study alchemy?"

Ash felt that the man's eyes were watching him too closely now. Was he suspicious, somehow, that Ash practiced alchemy illegally? He swallowed a bundle of nerves lodged in his throat. "Yes," he admitted, "but no point in pining after something you can't have, right?"

Hain gave a small smile. "I don't think so," he said. "If you had the opportunity to study alchemy, you would know that each and every single person can have anything we want. Desires are energy, already in existence. We only have to envision those desires and be willing to work to transmute them into our physical reality."

Ash wasn't sure how he felt, receiving a lecture on alchemic manifestation from his father, when his mother had wanted nothing more than Gresham Hain's help. "It's not always that simple,"

Ash said, unable to bite back his words. "It isn't alchemy when someone is born wealthy and given all they want because their ancestors stole their wealth, and someone who struggles to eat can't reach their goals because they're too busy working to put food on the table. Not everyone always has a leg up to their dreams."

"If you believe you're such a person," Hain said, "then it's inevitable that this will be your reality: someone who is unable to achieve what he truly wants because he has a chip on his shoulder about what the world hasn't yet given him."

Ash's rage sizzled through him, and to make it worse, it seemed Hain was watching him with a condescending smile as if he *knew* how much his words angered Ash and found this amusing. Ash was beginning to rethink his desire to meet his father. Maybe it would have been better to leave the man to his imagination.

"We're all meant to receive our desires," Hain said, smile fading as he eyed Ash. "And those who don't see this are simply given the roles of either helping others succeed or becoming blocks on the path because they did not have enough vision to make themselves the focus of their own life. I don't think you would want your only purpose in life to be the antagonist in another person's story, would you?"

Hain didn't wait for Ash to respond. His gaze flicked to Ash's hand pointedly, and Ash realized he was holding the frequency locator, its dial spinning and ticking. "Your frequency is higher than average," Hain said. "A shame, that you weren't able to study alchemy."

He left Ash with those words, closing the door behind him.

12

Ash left the college campus much later than he'd expected to; the task of sorting through his father's things had taken hours, maybe because he'd found himself lost in thought, ruminating on his father's voice and the man's words and the strange coincidence that Hain had approached him in the first place. Maybe it would've been better if the man hadn't. It'd been Ash's goal for so long, to meet his father—and now that he'd succeeded, Ash felt unexpectedly empty.

By the time he left, his hands were sore and his back ached. He still had the long walk to Hedge, and it was late afternoon when he made it to his apartment. He stomped up the stairs, then slowed down as he came to the landing. His door was cracked open. He took a deep breath, readying himself for a fight—but when he slammed open the door, no one was there.

His apartment was torn apart. His books were everywhere, papers ripped and scattered. The mattress had been cut open, stuffing spilling out. The shelves had been thrown to the ground. The picture frame with the only photo he had of his mother was shattered. He gingerly picked it up and slipped out the photo, folding it and putting it into his pocket.

"What the hell?"

He spun around, but it was only Tobin, stepping inside with wide eyes. "Source, Ash," he said, finally looking at his best friend. "Who the hell did you piss off?"

Ash shook his head. "I have no idea."

He knew why the alchemist had attacked him, but he didn't want to admit the reason to Tobin—not only because Tobin would say that Ash needed to stay away from Ramsay Thorne and alchemy, but because Ash hated to think what might happen if someone figured out that Tobin knew more than he should.

Tobin stood to the side as Ash grabbed a canvas duffel from his closet and began to pull out shirts and trousers. "You're leaving?"

Ash swallowed. He didn't think it'd be so hard to say goodbye. "For a little while."

"Where to?"

"I can't tell you," he said, stuffing the last of his socks into the bag and pulling the strings shut. "It's safer." Safer for Tobin, yes—but safer for Ash, too. He didn't know who might be listening in on their conversation. Ash threw the duffel over his shoulder, and his chest ached when he saw Tobin's expression. "But I can promise you I'll be fine."

"How can you promise that?" Tobin said gruffly. He swallowed hard, as if trying to hide the emotion in his voice. Their friendship hadn't been perfect, but they still cared about each other. Tobin pulled Ash in for a hug. "Check in with me if you can," he said. "Just so I know you're still okay, all right?"

Ash nodded. "I will."

He left, trying to ignore the fear that this would be the last time he saw Tobin.

✳

It was night by the time Ash returned to Ramsay's home. He was starving. He'd only had a plum for breakfast and a sandwich at the college, and he could feel that his energy was low. He stepped into the study, surprised to see Ramsay sitting in the chair by the fireplace, dressed in a black sweater and black trousers and a pair of slippers, hair pulled up in a bun and round spectacles on. A book broke its spine as it lay open in his lap. He'd seemed lost in thought and glanced up at Ash with concern when he stepped inside.

"Where've you been?" Ramsay asked. "I was waiting for you all day." He noticed Ash's bag, then said, "Did you go back home?"

Ash clutched his duffel. There was no point in hiding it now. "I needed some of my things," he said, closing the door behind him.

"What could you have possibly needed that was worth risking your life?"

"None of your clothes fit me, Ramsay." He demonstrated by holding up a hand, one baggy sleeve falling over his fingers. "See?"

Ramsay rolled his eyes. "Ah, yes, clothes—seems justifiable for your death."

"Don't pretend you actually care about whether I live or die," Ash bit back. "You only care about the Book."

Ramsay narrowed his eyes. "Yes, of course I care about the Book—but I also care about you, Ash. I wouldn't want to see you hurt or killed, whether you're helping me or not."

Ash didn't believe him. "Really?"

"Yes, *really*." Ramsay sighed, pushing himself up from the chair. "You should put your things down and get something to eat—if you're hungry, anyway. We have a lot of work to do tonight."

"Eat what, exactly?" Ash grumbled, crossing the room.

Ramsay's cheeks turned pink. "I went grocery shopping. You didn't seem happy with the pear last time, and—well, in any case, I hope I've bought ingredients that you like."

Ash blinked, unsure why he felt so amused by the thought of Ramsay wandering the aisles of a grocery store, filling his basket with tomatoes and cabbage. He also realized that Ramsay had gone just for *him* and felt a spark of pleasure and gratitude at the thought.

"I wanted to ask you what you'd like from the shop, but you'd already left by the time I woke up," Ramsay said nervously.

Ash outright laughed at that. "I left in the afternoon, Ramsay."

He shrugged with a frown and mumbled, "I hate waking up in the morning."

"Thank you," Ash said, managing a smile.

Ramsay nodded and walked past, Ash following him out into the hall. "You're welcome."

After Ash dropped off his clothing and had a quick meal of stewed chicken and vegetables—*so* much more delicious and filling than what he usually had—he met Ramsay in his library, where the apprentice claimed they would be more comfortable than in the study. Ramsay had changed into a loose white shirt and pants and stood anxiously in the center of the room as Ash entered.

"Have you been practicing your grounding exercises?" he asked.

Ramsay had given Ash a list of breathwork patterns and visualizations, images of himself with roots growing from his feet and into the dirt, encapsulated by stone, safe and untouched. He practiced every night before he went to bed.

"Yes," Ash said, trying to push down at the nerves as he remembered *why* he had been given these exercises in the first place. Ramsay and Ash would attempt to go to the higher realms again, and Ash had no real guarantee that he would return.

Ramsay seemed even more nervous than Ash. "I did more research," he said, "and I think it could be beneficial for us to practice an exercise that will connect us more as we attempt to reach the higher realms. It'll help you latch on to my energy. I could ground you if you begin to lose yourself again."

Anything that could stop him from being sucked into the chaos was preferable to Ash—but he thought it was odd that Ramsay had so much trouble meeting his eye. "What's the exercise?"

Ramsay took a sharp breath. "We sit and hold each other's gaze as we synchronize our breath," he said.

This on its own seemed monstrously awkward, something Ash would never willingly do—but he could tell there was more still. "And?"

"And," Ramsay said slowly, "we have to open ourselves to each other. Intentionally give access to our thoughts and emotions and—"

"Nope."

"Ashen—sorry, *Ash*," Ramsay corrected, "this would be incredibly beneficial."

"I'm not *opening myself* to you."

"It might be uncomfortable now, but when you're losing yourself in the chaos and need a reminder of who you are, *I* can provide that for you."

Ash could barely look at Ramsay. He bit back a groan, already knowing Thorne had won. He was starting to wish that he'd never agreed to any of this. The murder attempt and his trashed apartment and the need to go into hiding—that was all fine, when it came to searching for the Book of Source . . . but sharing his inner world with another person, much less Ramsay Thorne? Impossible. But Ramsay watched Ash steadily with a touch of desperation, and Ash knew that the other boy had a fair point. It would be embarrassing and uncomfortable now, but Ash didn't want to regret the moment he chose to tell Ramsay no and found himself trapped in the chaos forever.

"Fine," he said.

Ramsay let out a breath of relief. "Good. Let's sit on the ground—cross-legged, yes—and face each other."

Ash did as he was told. He felt strange, like he and Ramsay were preparing for something *else* that was intimate, and half expected Ramsay to say that it was time to strip off their clothes. He realized that they were, in a way, about to do something even more intimate than anything physical. Even when Ash had sex with Tobin, he still had emotions and thoughts that were his own, separate from his friend's—and in a way, that was what made the entire experience even more uncomfortable and unsatisfying. Though Ash and Tobin had shared a bed and touched each other's bodies, Ash had still closed himself off emotionally. He still hadn't felt safe enough to be vulnerable.

And now he would share that intimacy with Ramsay. He sat just a foot away from Ash and nodded with determination, a signal for them to begin. They spoke the words Ramsay instructed, their voices mingling. "I hold the intention to open myself to you."

Ash knew it wasn't enough to only say the words—he had to believe them, too. He forced himself to really, truly, fully feel that he could share every aspect of himself with Ramsay. They breathed in for three seconds, held for three seconds, and exhaled for six seconds as they stared into each other's eyes. Ramsay's were a dark brown, nearly black, and his pupils grew bigger the longer Ash held his gaze. Ash could feel the waves of vibrations begin. Ramsay's energy was a purple light dancing in front of Ash. He could *feel* Ramsay—his emotions mixed with Ash's, and it took a moment to understand why he suddenly felt so anxious, so nervous, so hopeful that this would work, and that everything he'd dreamed for so many years would become a reality—

The flashes of images began. A mountain bathed in pink light and rays shining through the surface of the ocean and endless fields of green and a black sun—

But Ramsay's presence was there, even stronger than the first time they'd reached for the higher realms. *Are you all right, Ash?* That same purple energy covered him, held him, reminded him to focus, to *breathe*—

The woman in the snow with pale skin and black strands of hair stuck to her cheeks looked like Ramsay, Ash realized. She had the same dark eyes rimmed by long eyelashes and the same smile that held surprising softness. She had left Ramsay on the frozen river, and the ice cracked, plunging Ramsay into the depths.

Ramsay gasped for air as he ran, feet crunching over fallen branches and dead leaves. He tripped over a root and flew to the ground. The laughter chased him. He scrambled to hide in a thicket of thorns, needles scratching his arms and legs. Blake called his name. "Don't be such a coward!"

The boy with kind brown eyes stayed with her in the gardens

until the sun began to rise, and even then, they didn't want to say good night. She'd forgotten her blazer, so he wrapped his own around her shoulders. He took her to his dorm room, where no one else would be able to find her, and she'd kissed him, as she had in the gardens a few times before, unbuttoning her uniform's shirt—but he'd shaken his head, whispering that he wanted to, Creator, he wanted to so much, but not then, not yet—

Ash stopped breathing. Ramsay had stopped, too. They stared into each other's eyes. It felt like Ramsay was searching Ash's for something. Ash could see that Ramsay's purple hues had tinges of red. The red that usually came from Ash's skin was closer to Ramsay's colors, too.

"Did it work?" Ramsay whispered. "Did you feel more grounded?"

"I think so," Ash said, voice hoarse. He'd remembered himself this time, at least—hadn't lost himself to the endless images of the higher realms—and the energy of chaos hadn't beckoned to him this time, either. "Were we still on our way to the higher realms?" he asked. "The visions felt more like memories this time."

Ramsay shook his head, as if trying to clear it. "I—yes, I think we were heightening our frequencies together, and we might've reached the realms eventually, but I—I saw clearer memories of your life this time, too."

Neither moved. They sat in front of each other, breaths hitched. Ash felt another energy also—one that grew in intensity the longer that he held Ramsay's stare. Ash could feel traces of Ramsay dancing along his skin. He felt hotter, suddenly, but he didn't look away.

"Your mother," he said, voice low. "I saw a vision of her again."

Ramsay nodded slowly. "Makes sense. I think of her a lot."

"She left you on a frozen river?"

Ramsay blinked and let his gaze fall to his hands. "No," he said. "That's a reoccurring nightmare that I have often. Almost every time I go to sleep, in fact," he admitted.

Ash didn't think it was possible to feel sympathy for someone like Ramsay Thorne. Maybe the exercise had worked after all. "Why do you have that nightmare?"

Ramsay's quick smile contradicted the pain in his eyes. They'd become wet, Ash realized to his horror. He hadn't meant to make Ramsay cry. "I'm sorry—"

Ramsay shook his head. "It's fine. I—ah—I think it was the exercise. It's heightened my emotions." Ash wasn't sure if this was true, but he didn't argue. "I've thought about it—tried to analyze the nightmare. I'm sure it's ripe with symbolism from my subconscious."

Dreams were another portal, a realm that the mind escaped to—and in this separate realm, the dreamer was often delivered messages from the higher realms and from their own subconscious. Maybe it was too intrusive of Ash, to ask about those messages, but Ramsay answered his question anyway.

"I always thought that my parents resented the responsibility to produce an heir," Ramsay said. "They would've preferred to spend their days and nights locked in their study, fulfilling their ambitions. I was a hinderance."

Ash didn't bother to deny the ache in his chest as he heard the pain in Ramsay's voice.

"My mother especially—sometimes, she doted on me, like it was an experiment to see if she could love me. Other times, I'm sure that she hated me."

"Hated?" Ash repeated softly. He couldn't imagine any mother hating her child.

"Yes." Ramsay swallowed, then sat straighter, entering the role Ash began to recognize was just that: a defense mechanism by taking on the identity of the astute alchemist. "The river I fall into symbolizes the lack of stability and trust I feel with other people because of my mother's inconsistent love; the ice that traps me is the fear, I think, that this is how I'll feel for the rest of my life, unable to make it to the surface again. And the blood—" he said, then stopped. Ash didn't need him to finish.

Ash had more questions. He wasn't sure how much Ramsay would be willing to answer, but the curiosity for the other boy's life was now overwhelming. Ash had wondered about Ramsay at times, but now he felt an almost desperate need to know him.

"I saw you running in a forest."

Ramsay's face reddened. "I was chased through the woods of Pembroke if I didn't manage to hide in my dorm room after dinner. I would try to skip meals, but the faculty insisted that I attend with the other students, and when I tried to sneak away, the others would follow. It became a nightly game for them to catch me."

"They chased and attacked you because of your parents?"

"I was an easy target. They wanted to feel justified in torturing another person for fun. My parents were the perfect excuse." Ramsay's bitterness stung Ash's heart.

"You didn't deserve that," Ash told him, but Ramsay only clenched his jaw, as if he wasn't sure that he agreed, so he said it again. "You didn't deserve to be treated like that, Ramsay."

Ramsay let out an impatient breath. "Yes, well."

It seemed like he would end the conversation there, so Ash asked another question quickly, the one he was most curious about of all. "There was also a boy," Ash said. "He was kind to you." Ash felt embarrassed as he remembered Ramsay unbuttoning her shirt. "He—ah—I saw the two of you together."

Ramsay seemed to pick up on what Ash meant by *together*. A deeper pain covered his eyes. "You saw Callum?"

"Who is that?"

Ramsay released a heavy breath, and it seemed he'd finally met his limit for the night. "A former friend, you could say."

"It looked like you weren't only friends," Ash murmured.

"You're right," Ramsay said, his voice cold. "We weren't only friends."

It was clear that this was all Ramsay would tell him. Ash wasn't sure if he wanted to know the answer to his next question. "And what did you see?"

Ramsay seemed even more uncomfortable now. "A woman," he said. "She seemed ill."

Ash's heart fell. "It was my mom."

Ramsay's voice softened. "Can I ask what happened to her?"

Ash hated that he could feel his own tears rising. He thought he'd gotten over his mother's death. Throwing himself into his studies, focusing on his goals of making it into Lancaster, receiving a license, and meeting his father—that had all been the distraction he'd needed these past years. He wasn't expecting to confront his grief for her now. "Lung disease," he said shortly. "She died a few years ago."

"I'm sorry, Ash."

Ash could feel the genuine empathy radiating from Ramsay, the warmth that tickled his skin and invited him to open himself to the other boy, to connect with him and trust him.

"I also saw you and a boy . . . together," Ramsay said with a quirked smile.

"Tobin? You saw me and Tobin?"

"Yes, that's the name you called over and over again."

Ash's face turned hot. "Source, I wish you hadn't seen that. That—ah—that isn't one of my favorite memories."

Ramsay's pitying smile suggested that he felt very sorry for Ash indeed. "I can see why."

Ash had a very strong urge to throw something at Ramsay. "You're one to talk," he said. "You didn't even *have* sex, so I don't know how you can be judgmental."

Ramsay raised a single brow and watched Ash long enough that Ash's blush returned as he realized that his assumption was wrong. This vision had only been one memory, after all.

He swallowed, embarrassed, and looked away, not sure if this was a conversation he could stand to have with Ramsay. "We're done for the night, aren't we?" Ash asked him, tugging on an ear.

Ramsay seemed on the edge of laughter, but rather than tease Ash more, he agreed. "Yes—we're both tired, so it'd be dangerous to attempt going to the higher realms now." He was obviously disappointed, but Ash appreciated that, regardless of how desperately Ramsay wanted to go to the realms and find the Book, he still considered their safety first.

They agreed to make their next attempt the following evening. Ash excused himself from the library, making his way back to his room, trying his hardest not to imagine Ramsay in particular visions that he had not seen.

13

Callum had been given instructions to Ramsay's manor. His own home had portal doors, as did most of the Houses, no matter their disgust for alchemy, so for all the summer before his last year at Pembroke, Callum would whisper the password *Snowdrop*, excitement buzzing through him at the thought of seeing Ramsay again.

Ramsay had been waiting for Callum in the sitting room. He'd gotten tea and a platter of biscuits, something Callum couldn't help but find adorable. Callum remembered the nights they'd begun to share, certain that the emotion that filled him was love.

"There you are," Ramsay said, rising to his feet with a smile. He'd been happier in those days, now that he'd finally escaped Pembroke. He'd worked hard to graduate from the school a year early. Ramsay crossed the room, hands reaching for Callum—and only stopped when Callum stepped away.

"I'm sorry," Callum had said, unable to meet Ramsay's eyes. He'd arrived at Ramsay's home with only one purpose. "We need to stop meeting."

Ramsay frowned, confused. "Is everything all right?"

Callum swallowed. "This has been too risky."

"What do you mean?"

"If anyone ever caught me—"

"No one would catch you, Callum. How would anyone catch you?"

"It'd be a disaster for my family."

Ramsay stilled. "A disaster," he repeated. "Because you'd be seen with me."

Callum stared blankly. "I need to choose my family. I hope you understand."

The silence that followed was awful. Callum chanced a glance up, and Ramsay's face was instantly etched into his memory. The mixture of surprise and hurt was heartbreaking, yes, but it was more difficult to watch the expression slowly transform into indifference. Maybe it had been even worse for Ramsay to be discarded by everyone around him and allow himself to trust Callum, to truly believe that he was accepted and loved by at least one person in the world, only to be betrayed by Callum, too.

"Was this all a game to you?" Ramsay asked.

"No."

"Was it a prank? Will you and Blake and Gavin all have a laugh at me now?"

"No, Ramsay—no, I just—"

Ramsay waited for his explanation, but it wasn't one that Callum could give. When Ramsay asked Callum to leave, he did so without another word.

※

Ash and Ramsay worked together every evening for one week, practicing the exercise of grounding themselves in each other's energy as they traveled higher and higher, closer to the realms, more memories flashing in their visions—thankfully none that were too scandalous, Ash wasn't sure if he could survive that—but still enough that Ash began to feel he knew Ramsay as well as he knew himself.

Ramsay's lessons continued, too, which she took just as seriously as their attempt to find the Book of Source, going so far as to give Ash a test, insisting that he sit down and answer each and every question. *What do the numbers three, six, and nine symbolize for Source manifestation? During the era of the Great War, which famed alchemist declared Source to be the Big Machine?* It took an hour, and Ash's fingers cramped. Ramsay even graded it, handing Ash the papers back with a 74 percent in the corner.

Ash groaned. "Is this seriously the test that you give your first-year students?" he said. "Don't you think this is ridiculously hard?"

"No, I don't," Ramsay said. "Lancaster is preparing its students for an even more competitive world."

Ash raised a brow. "Really? Don't all of you just—I don't know—go back to your family's Houses?"

"Some might," Ramsay said shortly.

Ash realized his mistake. "Shit. Sorry."

Ramsay took a breath. "It's fine. House Thorne is in its death throes, but once I atone for my parents, I plan to rebuild. But not everyone has to pledge to their family's House or the House that their family was historically loyal to."

"Which House would you pledge to, if you didn't have to be stuck with your family's?"

"You misunderstand me," she said. "I would gladly pledge myself to Thorne even if it wasn't my responsibility. I fit the House well. It was once a place of innovation, engineering, daydreaming of new ways to create technology using Source energy—"

"Okay, all right," Ash said, waving his hands around. "I get the point."

Ramsay smirked. "Which House do you plan on pledging to?"

Ash knew the answer: He'd wanted to pledge to Val, the same as his father—the House that explored all fields of science, alchemy included. But there was something especially vulnerable about admitting that Ash had dreamed of joining a House, knowing he never could.

"Who says I'm pledging?" Ash said.

"There wouldn't be any point in studying alchemy and receiving a license if it wasn't to join a House and rise quickly in its ranks."

"So you say. What if I just want a license so that I can practice my alchemy in peace?"

Ramsay gave an amused smile. "Because even without access to your memories, I would know you're too ambitious for that."

Ash glanced away. "Most people think ambition is negative."

"There you go again," Ramsay said, "caring about what I think."

"I don't care," Ash said, but something in his chest whispered that he was lying.

"And I don't believe that, for the record," Ramsay said. "Personally, I'm attracted to ambition."

Ash might as well have been set on fire. Ramsay couldn't have meant that she was attracted to *him*. Ash quickly spoke to cover his embarrassment. "Maybe I'd go with Galahad," he said. "I could become a food merchant. I'd never go hungry again."

He was joking, but Ramsay squinted, confused. "You don't need to study at a reputable college like Lancaster and earn a license to pledge to *Galahad*."

"Source, you're so judgy," Ash said. Ramsay ignored him. "Even the rich look down on each other, I guess."

"We have our rivals," Ramsay admitted.

"Who was Thorne's biggest?"

"Lune, without any doubt," Ramsay said. "The Val family was our greatest ally, and Lune opposed them. We'd answered to Val, originally, until our family became notable and—well—*wealthy* enough to form its own House with our area of expertise."

"I hadn't realized that's how Houses formed."

"Only the newer Houses," Ramsay said. "After the wars, the Kendrick, Adelaide, and Lune families answered to the Alexanders. From there, Houses began to form and branch out, all answering to one of the four main dynasties—Galahad to Kendrick, Alder to Lune, Val to Adelaide. This is basic history," she said. "Didn't you learn about it in school?"

"Didn't I learn about rich families and their Houses while I was in Hedge?" Ash said, brows raised. He was never one for the history or politics of the upper classes. Why should he care? "You're overestimating your importance, my friend."

"*Friend?* Is that what you think we are?"

"Well, we're not actively trying to kill each other," Ash said, joking again. "I think that means we're friends by default, doesn't it?"

Ramsay seemed to seriously consider this definition, head tilted. "Huh. Maybe it does."

※

Ash began to look forward to his time with Ramsay. He would spend his workdays in the college dreaming of the evening, wondering which lesson he would learn or what new memory of Ramsay's he would see. And even when they weren't working together, Ash found that he enjoyed the time he spent with Ramsay in the physical realm, too. Ash had convinced Ramsay to take eating more seriously after learning that her love of sugary meals generally meant she'd eat bars of chocolate or pies snagged from the college's dining hall before cooking a meal with any real nutrition. Chopping vegetables together, Ramsay grumbling about how much time it took, became a nightly event.

One afternoon, Ramsay took Ash on a walk around the grounds, explaining that the dead and frozen gardens had once been kept alive year-round by alchemy. "This manor used to be filled with plants, but the upkeep became too much," Ramsay said. She showed Ash the forest where she'd played as a child, collecting blackberries and wild mushrooms with her mother. From the outside, the Thorne manor was a two-story house of grayish-brown stone and intricate arches surrounding the windows and doors. The roofing looked like it needed patching, and there were crumbling statues of gargoyles perched along the edges.

Ash asked a question that had lingered in the back of his mind since he first came here to the Downs. "Why did you use Snowdrop as the password for the portal door?" he asked. He'd partly expected Ramsay to say that it was a reminder for her to stay focused on the goal of atoning for her parents, but her answer surprised him.

"I didn't set the password," she said. "It's as old as the manor itself. The Thorne family originated in the Derry Hills. We have a smaller lodge that overlooks Snowdrop. It's where my mother grew up."

Ash felt bad for questioning her and bringing up the painful past. It hit Ash, too, just how horrific it was that Ramsay's mother had sacrificed her own people.

Ramsay took him into the village that was a thirty-minute walk away from the manor, through the forest and down the mountain's path. There'd been a recent rain shower, from the looks of things, either washing away snow or freezing on the road, crystals crunching under Ash's shoes. Worn cobblestone curved through small stone buildings, a few shops and homes. It was almost evening, and not many people were around, but those who were gave the two such cold stares that it was more than clear that the Thorne heir and her new friend were not welcome. Ash understood why Ramsay's pantry was almost empty. He was even more grateful, realizing Ramsay had braved these villagers and shopped for groceries just for him.

✳

"What sense does alchemy appear as for you?" Ash asked curiously one evening as the colors danced around the room and faded away. The colors had been getting brighter and more palpable, recently. Ash wondered if this meant they were getting closer to reaching the higher realms.

They'd finished their synchronization for the night, staring into each other's eyes, which had become less uncomfortable with time. Ash had even started to feel at ease, as if looking into Ramsay's eyes was the same as looking into his own.

Ramsay had been in the middle of stretching her arms after she stood. She stopped, surprised by the question, and looked down at Ash, who leaned back on his hands, still spread out on the floor. "I hear music," she said. "Every vibration of alchemy is like the striking of a chord, and when I practice alchemy or another person performs it—well, it can be like an orchestration, sometimes, a complex song that's always in perfect harmony." Her smile was wistful. "It's beautiful to listen to. I wish you could hear it. Sometimes I'll perform a small bit of alchemy just to hear its song."

Ash felt warmer as he watched Ramsay speak. She had a glow whenever she spoke so enthusiastically. Maybe it was because Ash had spent so much time with Ramsay over the past week, learning more about her in three days than he'd learned about any other person in his life—or maybe it was the exercises, the two mingling their energies and Ash staring into Ramsay's eyes . . . but he knew he couldn't hide from the truth that he'd tried to push down again and again.

Ramsay sighed as she threw herself into a chair, legs over the armrest. "I have the first draft of my dissertation due."

"Do you need me to leave?"

"No, no," she said, already distracted and lost in thought. "Stay. I have to admit, it's nice having company as I work." Ash and Ramsay had started to spend their nights together in the study or library even when they weren't working on their synchronization or Ash's lessons, debating about the possibilities of alchemy or simply reading together in silence. She picked up her round spectacles from the nearby side table and slid them on, reaching for the work stacked on the floor beside the chair.

Ash cleared his throat and approached one of the library shelves, scanning for a book to read. He'd come several nights ago to see what books Ramsay secretly read for fun and was surprised to see old collections of children's fairy tales. Ash had flipped through one book and seen the oversized letters of Ramsay's handwriting as a child, attempting to spell out her name. It seemed she'd always had the habit of writing notes in books. "Aren't you excited to finish your paper?"

Ramsay blinked at him. "I already have. The issue is that I've written three drafts on three different forms of Source geometry, and I'm not sure which one to submit. What's so funny, Ash?"

Yes, of course she'd written three versions of hundred-odd-page papers. He shook his head, still grinning. "Nothing."

She rolled her eyes at him and picked up a notebook, flipping through its pages, presumably rereading one of her drafts. She knew so many tidbits of information, had entire calculations memorized, could recite some pieces of alchemic texts word for word, and—well, Ash didn't want to admit it, but he was impressed by her. She was a genius—this was more than obvious—but it was the passion she had for her studies that Ash loved. After spending so much time together, Ramsay's sarcastic voice was imprinted in Ash's mind, as was the excited gleam in her eyes as she spoke to Ash about various formulas and facts, debating the properties of power, so confident that she was always right, and it was infuriating that she always was—

Ash's warmth crept from his chest and up his neck. He chose a book on parallel-universe theory and sat in the chair opposite her. Though Ramsay had once angered Ash, he could feel the subtle shift in vibrations. She still annoyed him at times, but he almost felt magnetized toward her now. As he tried to study, he found himself needing to stop and reread passages several times because his mind kept drifting back to Ramsay again and again, glancing up at her and watching as she blew a strand of hair out of her face, swiping it away impatiently and tying it up—

She met his gaze over the rim of her glasses. Ash's face turned hot, and he looked back down at the book. There was simply no lying when it came to energy. Energy was the language of Source, of existence, and even if a person could say what they believed was the truth with their tongue, there was no denying the energy beneath their words. Ash could pretend that he didn't like Ramsay all he wanted, but he couldn't ignore his growing attraction toward her. He only hoped she wouldn't be able to sense his attraction, too.

Ramsay sighed. "It's no use. I'll just have to submit all three."

Ash snorted. "I feel sorry for your professors already."

Ramsay tossed the notebook to the side and pulled off her glasses, running a hand over her face. "Don't. It's only one professor, and he's a bit of an asshole."

"That isn't very nice, Ramsay."

She grinned. "I've never claimed to be nice. Besides, I'm his only student this semester, and he's so critical of everything I show him that I'm betting he'd *want* to see the three papers— more chance to mark every page in red. I don't even know why he agreed to work with me. No other professor would, given my family name. I suppose I should be grateful."

Ash wondered if he knew the professor, from the classes he'd looked at curiously through windows and open doors. "Who is he?" he asked. "Your professor, I mean."

She leaned her head back, eyes closed, like she meant to take a nap. "You probably don't know him. He's a little washed-up, honestly. He—his name is Gresham Hain—wrote some popular texts decades ago, but he hasn't produced any work since and still acts as if he's the most famous and powerful alchemist of the state, just because he's an advisor to House Alexander now."

Ash had stopped listening. He sat frozen, staring at Ramsay. Emotions vibrated through him, but he couldn't put a name to them. Shock, yes—anxiety, perhaps. Dread.

She opened an eye as if she could sense his emotions. "What is it?"

Ash blinked, looking away, unsure of whether he should tell her the truth. This was truly the most vulnerable subject of all. He swallowed, then said, "Hain is my father."

Ramsay certainly wasn't expecting to hear that, judging from the expression on her face. "Your *father*, Ash? Gresham Hain?"

He nodded, jaw clenched. "He abandoned me and my mom. She's dead, thanks to him."

Ramsay sat up, face serious with concern. "I thought you said she died of lung disease."

"She'd been a servant of House Lune, and he—my mom never said the words, but I think he . . ." Ash couldn't look at Ramsay, and Ramsay closed her eyes in the pain that flooded the air. "He took advantage of her."

"I'm so sorry, Ash."

"She tried to raise me on her own in Hedge. She got sick and couldn't afford healers. If she'd never met him, she wouldn't be dead." Ash also knew that he wouldn't be alive, but he wasn't sure if his life was a worthy exchange for his mom.

Ramsay shook her head. "Source—I've never liked him much, but if I'd known the sort of man he was . . ."

Maybe this was just another synchronicity, a cosmic joke—but Ash couldn't shake the feeling that something about this was wrong, not just a coincidence that could be overlooked. "Has he always been your advisor?"

"Only since the start of this semester. Why?"

"I don't know. Something feels off about this. It's too convenient that he's connected to both of us."

Ramsay met his eye. "Do you think he's after the Book, too?"

Ash remembered his father bringing him into the hall and asking ridiculous questions. "Maybe I'm being paranoid."

"Paranoid? No. You're being careful."

"Gresham Hain is exactly the kind of person who would want the Book's power."

"Yes, he is." Ramsay watched Ash curiously. "And aren't you, too?"

Ash's gaze snapped to her. "What the hell is that supposed to mean?"

She raised a brow. "No need to be defensive."

"Hard not to be, when you're accusing me of being power hungry."

"I'm not accusing you of anything," Ramsay said with her narrow-eyed gaze. "I'm only asking questions."

"You're always asking questions—Source," Ash said. In the silence that followed, he closed his eyes. "Sorry."

"It's fine," Ramsay said, but Ash hated how tight her voice had become.

It was hard to say the words aloud. "Yes," he finally managed. "I think there's a part of me that wants the Book's power, too."

Ramsay looked at him as if surprised that he'd admitted it. She paused, then asked, "Are you ashamed of that?"

"Shouldn't I be?"

"Do you think that the Book is immoral?"

"You're the one who wants to destroy it."

"To stop it from being used to harm others," she agreed. "But would you use it to hurt people? Maybe power isn't inherently good or bad," she said. "Just what you do with it. What would you do with all that power, Ash?"

Ash wished that he had a noble answer, but even if he'd told some lie about ending all wars or helping those who needed it most, Ramsay would've felt the truth hidden in the energy of his voice. "I'd finally be seen," he said quietly. "Respected."

This was his worst trait, Ash thought—the part of him he'd tried to hide from the world. And now, he'd shown even this to the one person who knew him the most. He expected a vibration of disgust from Ramsay, but she only watched him with hooded eyes.

"Is that important to you?" she asked. "To be seen? Respected?"

He took a deep breath. "Yes. By everyone who looks down on me, but especially Hain. It's what driven me all these years— wanting to attend Lancaster and even receiving my license," he admitted. "It's all because I wanted respect. I'd wanted to meet him," Ash said. "I don't know why. To force him to see me, maybe—to prove that my mom and I were worth more than the way he treated us—abandoned us."

"And will reading the Book for yourself change the way he treats you?"

Ash met her gaze. He could see now that she wasn't judging Ash—and she wasn't watching him like he was an experiment to be studied, either. He didn't think anyone had looked at him this way before. She only wanted to know the boy sitting in front of her. He'd never felt so bare.

"It would force him to, wouldn't it?" Ash asked.

"Maybe. But what if it doesn't change anything?"

Ash hadn't considered the possibility—receiving all the power of Source, just for others to still look down on him. "I don't know."

Ramsay seemed to ponder this for a moment. "Maybe you'd find a new motivation—a new dream." She paused, then added, "I'm sorry if my questions were prying."

"It's okay."

"I can't help myself, sometimes, when I'm curious."

"I know."

Ramsay hesitated. "I can admit a secret, too, if you'd like."

Ash's heart jumped at the chance. "That's all right—you don't have to." But Source, did he want her to.

She smiled as if she could tell. "The truth is," Ramsay began, "a part of me—a young, childish part—still hopes that my parents are innocent." Ash frowned as he watched her. She shook her head. "I know that the odds are small, miniscule, practically nonexistent . . . But when my father died, he pressed his thumb into the palm of his hand. I thought he was trying to send me a message, somehow. I thought he wanted me to know that he and my mom were framed."

Ash bit his lip. He didn't know what to say to this. He wished he could give her some hope—tell her that maybe, just maybe, this wasn't just a childish dream.

Ramsay sighed, not meeting his eyes as if she was embarrassed at herself. "You know that I can't let you read the Book, right?"

Something dug into Ash between his ribs. "I know."

"I have to destroy it—burn it. If you're not fine with that . . ."

Ash clenched his jaw. "A part of me isn't," he admitted. "But there's a larger part that knows you're right. It can't exist. No one should have that power."

They sat quietly for a moment, lost in their own thoughts.

"What do you think is written inside?" Ash asked her. "The Book, I mean."

Ramsay shrugged. "I've imagined ancient languages, or scripts from parallel universes scrawled on yellowed parchment with explicit instructions on how to reach your highest potential as an alchemist." It was exactly the sort of tome Ramsay would love to investigate.

"I pictured an older book, like a forgotten encyclopedia," Ash said, "with just one sentence written."

"What would the sentence say?"

"That's the thing," Ash said. "I don't know. No one could know. It'd be the secret of the universe, of Source—a single fact that would explain all of existence and chaos and . . ."

Ramsay met his eye. "I have to admit, it's a shame that we'll never know what's inside."

"I think I could do it," Ash said. He couldn't quite meet Ramsay's eye, his heart beating faster. "Find a new dream, I mean."

Her voice was soft when she answered. "I think you can, too."

14

Before they even began their work for the evening, Ash could feel it—could tell that, without any doubt, they were ready to reach the higher realms. He sensed Ramsay's vibrations as well as he could feel his own, her certainty and determination. They were rooted enough in each other, and with the right amount of focus, there was no other possible outcome. This was what they'd practiced and worked for and wanted desperately, and the complex equation of Source tipped in their favor.

The two sat and faced each other. There was no need to speak. They began their synchronized breaths, harmonizing effortlessly. Ramsay's memories began to flash through Ash's mind, and it was almost like seeing old friends he'd always known—Pembroke and Callum and Ramsay's mother and the river from her nightmare, always the river. This was what usually happened, but now there was something new Ash and Ramsay hadn't experienced before: the flashes of memories began to unfurl and deteriorate into fragments of color and energy and sound, the threads of the canvas too close to see the whole image. Those threads danced and weaved together to create patterns—Source geometry, Ash realized vaguely, what Ramsay studied and was now witnessing in its original form for herself—Ash could *feel* her excitement, and he was glad for her, overjoyed—

Focus, Ash.

Ash held on to Ramsay's words. The patterns weaved in and out, vibrating so quickly now that it was only a flickering light, as if Ash had begun to blink his eyes more rapidly than was humanly possible—and each time he blinked he saw a new place, a new reality, people he didn't recognize and voices in languages he couldn't understand and buildings that didn't belong to Earth, or at least not the Earth that he knew. Ash panicked. Heat grew, energy rushing faster than the speed of light. He was unanchored—no body, no senses, only chaos spinning through him, the tip of un-ending power—

He'd never been so close to chaos before—to feeling that he was becoming chaos itself. But Ramsay was here, too. Ramsay wouldn't let him go.

I'm here, Ash. Don't forget to breathe.

He blinked one final time, and when he opened his eyes again, he wasn't in Ramsay's library. It was a similar library, yes, he could see that from his peripheral, but it wasn't the same. Ramsay still sat opposite him. She was pale, shaking, as she held on to his gaze, just as he held on to hers, as if both were afraid of what would happen if they looked away.

"We did it," Ash said, voice hoarse and echoing.

She nodded, then took a breath and tore her gaze away from his. Ash dared to look, too. The library was as it had been in Ramsay's memories. The wooden floors weren't as scuffed and the wallpaper wasn't torn. It was like they'd gone back in time. But Ash knew that, where he was, there was no such thing as time. The rules of Ash's physical reality wouldn't fit here. According to the texts Ash had read, reaching the higher realms was like a state of lucid dreaming, visions spun through advanced meditation. Ash and Ramsay were sharing a dream while they were still awake, their physical bodies left behind in their plane.

The wallpaper's color shifted and voices echoed. Ramsay stood, as if she'd noticed something Ash hadn't and, mesmerized, raced to the door.

"Ramsay? Ramsay!"

She ignored him as she ran outside. Ash jumped to his feet also, following her.

"Don't you think we should be careful?" he asked with a hushed voice. He wasn't in his reality, but he and Ramsay could still be killed. If they died in this realm, there was a chance that the energy that gave them life wouldn't know the difference—their bodies in the physical plane would be abandoned, slumping over onto the library floor.

Ramsay either ignored or hadn't heard him. The voices got louder, and she followed as if hypnotized. Ash hurried after her, distracted by the shifts around him: paintings that faded in and out of existence, vines covering rotting wallpaper and the strong smell of dirt and mold followed by the scent of perfume. Ash wondered if they were seeing multiple realities coming and going. From the vantage point of the higher realms, they could see multiple possible universes. Ash saw the flash of a person before they vanished—saw another version of Ramsay a second later, storming past and unaware. Ash gasped and jumped out of her way, but he realized she couldn't even see them.

The Ramsay he knew hadn't cared to see another version of herself. She turned down a hall. The kitchen, usually falling apart, sparkled with wealth and was filled with cooks and servers who bustled and shouted before they disappeared and the kitchen blinked into ruin and rot, dirt scattered across the floor. Ramsay ran into the dining room and came to a stop. Ash caught up to her and saw what she'd been chasing.

Two people sat at the table. For a moment, servers pushed through the doors and more guests in their finery appeared, raising glasses in a toast from their seats, and they all disappeared—all except for the two who stayed at the head, watching Ramsay like they'd been waiting for her. Ash recognized them from Ramsay's memories. Angry purple bruises faded in and out around their necks. Ash felt Ramsay's emotion vibrating from her: The fear was so overwhelming that Ash could feel his breath shorten. He touched Ramsay's hand and she released a shuddering breath, tightening her grip around his fingers. His heart pumped, but he wasn't sure she was even aware that they were holding hands. Her eyes were glassy and wide.

"Are you okay?" he asked her.

She swallowed and blinked, then nodded. She let go. "Yes. I'm fine."

They walked inside together. Bright golden walls deteriorated, vines and roots like thick veins growing over the floor. It was dark except for faint light that filtered through a hole in a crumbling wall. Ramsay's parents watched her approach, staring with unblinking eyes. They faded, too, their skin showing the lines of muscle and bone beneath.

Ramsay's father spoke, though his mouth was closed, voice echoing. "Why are you here?"

Ash blinked, and the room had changed altogether. They were in a study, the same that Ash had spent so much time in with Ramsay—the same from her memories where she saw her parents sitting together, shutting her out as they closed the door. Her father sat at a desk alone now, frowning in concentration, papers surrounding him and open books stacked on top of one another. Ash could see where Ramsay had gotten some habits.

Silas Thorne barely glanced up at her. "You already know that you shouldn't be here."

Ramsay hesitated, then stepped farther into the study. "I need to speak with you. I need your help."

Ash felt like he'd intruded on something private. He hesitated near the threshold, but Ramsay looked over her shoulder at him so uncertainly that Ash walked closer and stopped at her side.

Her father gave Ramsay an impatient glance, much like he did in the memories Ash had seen. "Is that the only reason you came?"

Ash expected her to ask the question—the reason they'd worked so hard to come to the higher realms in the first place—but she hesitated.

"Why did you—" She swallowed. "When you were—when the execution . . ."

They were no longer in the study. They were outside, bright blue sky above and sun shining down. Ash spun around. They were surrounded by white buildings of ornate designs in what looked like a large courtyard. Kensington Square was empty, not a sign of another person in the entire city, except for Ramsay's parents. They stood on a galley, their hands tied together, ropes waiting around their necks.

Ramsay was shaking. Silas pressed a thumb to his palm. A clang rang out, their only warning before Ash pulled Ramsay's arm, turning her around so she wouldn't have to see—but when they turned, the scene had changed again. They were in what looked like an open field. Ash gasped, stepping forward, a bubble of air escaping his mouth. This must've been what the alchemists described as other worlds: The field of grass wavered back and forth as if under a sea, though Ash couldn't feel the water and could still breathe. Silas Thorne stood in front of them, hair flowing.

"What a childish hope you've clung to for so many years," he said.

Ramsay flinched, but she still spoke. "What message were you trying to send me?"

"Did you truly think we were innocent, Ramsay?" Silas asked.

Ramsay only repeated her question.

"You already know what I meant. Tell me yourself."

She swallowed. "To cover the palm's eye is to mean confusion, lack of clarity—"

"Chaos," Silas said.

Chaos exploded.

All realities and every particle in existence spun around them, and Ash saw it—the original spark, the energy of life, at the center of it all, the black orb that first emitted light, the black orb that grew until it was all Ash could see, sucked into nothingness, nonexistence—

Chaos dissolved.

They stood on a frozen river. Ash looked down. Cracks splintered beneath their feet.

Ramsay grabbed his arm. "Run—now!"

They raced across the ice, Ash's feet sliding, cracks forming with every step. Ash leaped from the river and onto the snowy bank just as the ice thudded beneath him, but when he looked back, Ramsay had slipped. She was clinging to the edges of the ice, seconds from being swept away beneath the waves. Ash threw himself forward, grabbing her hand and tugging her with all his strength, gritting his teeth—Source, he imagined for a moment what it would be like to return to the physical realm and find her dead on the floor beside him, and he grasped all the energy within his body as he yelled and dragged her onto the snow.

They lay beside each other, panting. She shook violently, dripping wet. "The first—time—I survived—that," she managed to gasp.

"You're going to freeze," Ash said. He sat up and closed his eyes, trying to imagine a coat, a sweater, anything she could put on, but there wasn't enough physical material, not like in his own reality. He cursed and began to strip off his own shirt to give her.

"What're you doing?" she said, shivering so violently that her teeth chattered.

"Giving you my shirt."

"You'll just freeze, too."

"I'd rather risk it," he said shortly.

Ramsay only shook her head and took a deep, calming breath. Ash felt the warmth of energy growing inside her. "You're forgetting we're alchemists."

"That isn't enough heat."

"I'll be fine. I grew up surrounded by ice. I've survived worse."

She turned slowly and took in their surroundings, looking

from the river to the edge of the forest they stood on. Ash recognized these woods from her nightmares. He also knew what those nightmares had been inspired by. On the other edge of the forest would be a lone town. Ash felt dread as he realized what Silas Thorne wanted to show Ramsay.

"We're in Snowdrop."

Ash looked at Ramsay, concerned. "Are you sure you want to do this?"

She shook her head. "No. I don't want to do this at all."

He knew what she left unsaid: She had no choice if she wanted to atone for her parents' killings. She needed to witness what they'd done for herself. She began to walk in determined silence.

Ash followed Ramsay along the path that cut through the thin gray trees. The freshly fallen snow was like powder, their feet sinking with every step, a light dusting left on their hair and lashes. There was a house on the edge of town, a thin line of smoke rising from its chimney. A man chopped wood and glanced at them, confused. There likely weren't many strangers who visited. A woman walked down the dirt road, holding a basket of clothes. Ash swallowed as he saw two children chasing each other, squealing. He wanted to warn them. Even if it was only a dream, a distant memory, it didn't feel right to let so many people die.

They came to the center of the town where there was a small market. People bustled about, unaware that anything was wrong—until someone looked up. They pointed, and others around them started to also, staring at the strange purple clouds that had formed. Ash saw, directly beneath the clouds that'd begun to spin, a woman and a man, heads bent together and holding each other's hands. There was an alchemic device between them and at their feet. Every few seconds, a thin bolt of electricity would strike the sky.

"It was the energy we needed," a voice said beside Ramsay.

Ash spun to see Silas Thorne standing beside them.

Ramsay looked from her father to the sky. "You can't blame me for hoping you were innocent."

"You misunderstood my meaning only because you wanted to," Silas told her. "That was always your greatest weakness." Ash watched as the storm grew stronger. People started to scream as gusts of wind ripped through the market. "You're willing to look away from the data, the proof that's right in front of you, to see what you *want* to. You're too soft."

There was an explosion. The force punched a crater in the ground, a hot wind igniting the fire that followed. Ash and Ramsay were thrown back, heat searing Ash's eyes. Ash landed in dirt that scraped his skin. He scrambled to his feet, breathing hard. Ramsay stood slowly, as if in awe—and Ash looked up to see what she had, too.

It was Earth, yes, but maybe an Earth from a different reality and a different time, a giant purple moon in the sky, so close that it looked as if it would crash into the planet's surface. There were towers on the horizon, but they looked like they'd been abandoned for centuries.

"We were not innocent, Ramsay," Silas said, standing beside them. He stared at the moon as well. "We knew exactly what we were doing. Your mother and I wanted to kill as many people as we could in one single moment."

Ramsay's voice was raw. "How could you think the Book would be worth so many lives?"

Silas turned to look at her. Ash swallowed a gasp. The man's face had begun to rot, red muscle beneath his skin smeared with dirt, empty eyes a light blue. "We believed that the energy of those lives could funnel into our purpose," he said. "And when we had the Book, we could bring the people back to life. That's what we were told."

"Told?" Ramsay said. She shook her head, confused. "Who would tell you that?"

Her father had disappeared.

They were in a library now, but it was unlike anything Ash had seen before. The halls, the shelves—it all appeared endless. Ash looked up, and there was no ceiling. The books and scrolls went on forever it seemed, farther than he could see. The walls were made of light stone, and the floor beneath them was red tile. There was a stained glass window near, allowing in dim purple light. Ramsay walked to a shelf and pulled out a book, looking at the cover and flipping it open.

"It's blank," she said.

Ash was unsure of where to look. The hallway they were in seemed to be never-ending, too. "Where are we?"

"I think I've heard of this library—but I thought it was only a myth . . ."

Ash realized he'd heard of this library, too. Alchemists claimed to have been told about the endless library in their meditations. The Akash was said to hold the answers to any question, the records of history across all universes and realities. If they really had made it to the Akash, then Ash could probably find a book about him—a book that would say what would happen in his own life, and how it would also end.

"Ask the book a question," Ash suggested, unable to ignore the surge of excitement.

Ramsay clenched her jaw for a moment, then said, "Where is the Book of Source?"

"Are you sure you want to know the answer to that?"

Ash turned to find Amelia Thorne. She walked closer to them, black heels clipping the tiled floor. Her white button-down blouse was tucked into black trousers. Ramsay looked so much like her mother, Ash thought—except for the coldness in Amelia's eyes.

Amelia glanced away from Ash dismissively, gaze landing on Ramsay. "You can see how searching for the Book of Source has brought nothing but loss, yet you do it anyway. I didn't raise you to be a fool, Ramsay."

Ramsay flinched like she'd been slapped. "I need to know

where the Book is so that I can atone for *your* mistakes." Her gaze was steady, but Ash noticed the tremble in her hands.

Her mother tilted her head. "And why is that?" she asked. "Do you think finding the Book will bring you value? Do you think that *atoning* will make anyone in that accursed city forgive you? *Accept* you? They won't," she said. "You already know that, but you choose to lie to yourself because you fear you have no other purpose in your meaningless life."

Ramsay stiffened but raised her chin. "I want to atone because it's the right thing to do."

"*The right thing to do,*" Amelia mocked. "I didn't raise you to *do the right thing*. I raised you to be intelligent and resourceful."

"You should be glad that she's willing to atone for you at all," Ash said, voice tight with anger, no longer able to bite his tongue.

Amelia's gaze cut to him. He could feel her energy—her iciness, her rage. It felt like an anger she'd held in her heart for each life she'd ever lived. He had to stop himself from taking a step back. She looked to Ramsay again. Her voice grew lower. "History sees us as the enemy now," she said, "but if we'd been successful—"

"At killing hundreds, you mean?" Ramsay said.

"—we would've been beloved, written into every child's text as the heroes of our state." Amelia peered at Ramsay. "Do you see how fickle these humans are, changing their minds about who is good and who is evil from one moment to the next?"

"Is that what you think you are?" Ramsay asked. "A *hero?*"

"You haven't even asked why we searched for the Book of Source," Amelia said. "It's easier for you to assume that it was our greed, rather than our selflessness."

Ramsay swallowed. "Why were you searching for the Book?"

"There are some who search for the Book out of fear," she said. "They want to oppress others in order to feel powerful."

"And you would have—what?" Ramsay asked. "Used the Book for good?"

"Yes," Amelia said simply. "I would've found the Book to help keep it out of the hands of those who would harm all alchemists. Finding the Book would have allowed this world to expand—to teach humans about alchemy so that we can evolve. The thought terrifies some," Amelia told them, "and they'll do all they can to ensure we don't see our own true power—to keep humans afraid and weak so that we'll gladly stay on our knees."

"You've said a lot of words," Ramsay said, "but I still don't understand why you murdered so many people."

Amelia's eyes narrowed.

Ramsay took a quick breath. "Father—he said that you were told to, as if instructed . . ."

Amelia's cold expression began to droop. Her skin rotted so quickly that her bones became powder, her clothes falling to the floor in a heap of dust. Ash blinked, shocked, and when his gaze followed what Amelia had been, he saw that the tile had become transparent. Beneath them was a drab sitting room, a flickering fireplace—and Amelia and Silas Thorne. Silas paced nervously while Amelia sat in a chair facing a man. It only took Ash a moment to realize that it was Gresham Hain.

"The energy exchange will be powerful enough," Hain insisted. "The deaths of so many in a single location would rip a portal into the higher realms."

"It wouldn't take just their deaths, I'm assuming," Amelia said almost lazily, legs crossed as she stared at Gresham.

"You would simultaneously need to focus on your intent, of course," Gresham said. "If you're in the center of it all, you could use the alchemic power to be transported."

"There's still no guarantee the answer is in the higher realms," Silas said, adjusting his glasses. "You've said it yourself—"

"An entire town," Gresham interrupted. "That's a lot of alchemic energy at your disposal. You can *demand* that you receive the answer you seek."

"And if it doesn't work?" Silas asked, wiping sweat from his brow. "So many people killed for no reason at all—"

"There's plenty reason," Gresham said. "To receive the Book of Source—the three of us together, Silas, we could balance the scales of alchemy."

"Yet you only want us to tell you the location of the Book," Amelia said, "and are insistent we don't read it ourselves."

"You wouldn't survive reading it."

"And you would?"

"Yes," Gresham said, and seemed certain of it. "I've been preparing for decades. I've learned how to funnel energy through my pathways so that my body isn't overwhelmed," he continued. "How have you prepared for reading the Book?"

Amelia's mouth pressed into a tight line, her eyes narrowing. "We are not servants nor messengers."

"No, of course you aren't," Hain said. "And if you're successful in finding me its location, and I read the Book as planned, I'll ensure that your House leads us in this new era."

"No," Silas said suddenly, and again, "no. We don't need to rule over New Anglia." He met his wife's eye and licked his lips nervously. "Funds, however—resources to continue our research . . ."

Gresham nodded. "Anything you desire—if you help me find the Book—is yours."

Ash let out a shaky breath. The tile faded into color once again, the scene beneath them disappearing. It didn't surprise him to learn now, without any doubt, that his father had searched for the Book of Source, too—but the fact that he'd instructed Ramsay's parents to kill so many was a blow to the chest.

Ash turned to face Ramsay, unsure of what to say but knowing he had to say *something*—

She was staring down at the closed book still in her hands. The pages had begun to emit a faint glow between the covers. She looked up at Ash. "She was always cruel," Ramsay said, "even as she gave me what I wanted."

Ash stared at the book as he stepped closer and offered Ramsay his hand. He wasn't sure what else he could give her now.

They'd worked tirelessly for this moment. Ramsay took it, fingers shaking, and squeezed his palm. Ash held his breath and, with his other free hand, opened the Book and turned to the first page.

They were in a dungeon. The only light was from the Book's glow. The floor and walls were stone. Ash's heart pumped. He heard footsteps echoing and a song, though he wasn't sure where the sounds came from. A voice declared that this world would burn, and only those who followed House Lune would be saved.

Ash realized where they were, suddenly, a simple knowing that appeared in his mind. "House Lune," he said. "The Book of Source is hidden in House Lune."

15

The moment the words left Ash's mouth, he felt a rush of heat searing through him. Images and colors filtered through his vision, and he searched for Ramsay's energy, grasping on to it the moment he did—

He opened his eyes. The first thing he saw was Ramsay's steady brown gaze. They breathed, staring at each other for a long moment, as if they couldn't look away even if they'd tried. Ramsay finally blinked and stood slowly, turning her back to Ash. She breathed long and hard, as if trying to control herself—but Ash could see the way her shoulders began to shake. He stood also, hesitated—then put a hand on her shoulder.

"Ramsay," he said, voice hoarse.

"I'm sorry," she said, wiping her cheeks impatiently. "I'm just— overwhelmed, I think."

"It's all right to cry."

"I didn't realize that seeing my parents again—speaking to them again—would be so . . ." She swallowed, rolling her eyes at herself. "I should've known that it wouldn't be easy." She shook her head. Ash could feel that she was trying to return to her familiar, nonchalant self. He didn't want her to. "It doesn't matter. We got the answer we needed."

A part of Ash wanted to prepare to leave for House Lune immediately—to rip apart the estate and find where the Book was hidden. He also wanted to know *why* the Book was there of all places, and if the Lune members knew that the Book was beneath their feet . . . But he let out a breath.

"This was a lot. Maybe we should rest, before we . . ."

Ramsay frowned as she met Ash's eye, an argument on the tip of her tongue. This was too important. Too much was at stake. He was surprised when she nodded instead. "Maybe you're right."

Ash suggested she go to her room. He went to the kitchens and heated up water and stocked a tray with bread and cheese and the last of the grapes. He wished he could've made them both a full meal, meat and carbs galore—he was starving now, his stomach grumbling—but he didn't have the energy, and he just wanted to be by Ramsay's side. He balanced the tray plus two mugs of tea and went to Ramsay's chambers, pausing at the threshold with full hands. He tried to imagine the door pushing itself open, but felt dizzy. Luckily the door swung open then, Ramsay staring down at him. The shadows under his eyes were deeper than before.

Ash realized he'd never seen Ramsay's chambers as he stepped inside. The room was a mess, of course. Piles of clothes were scattered across the floor and on the bed. But the balcony's drapes were open, allowing the sunrise's pink light to shine inside. They'd been awake all night.

Ramsay had changed into a more comfortable white shirt, top buttons open, with black pants. He sat on the edge of his bed and looked up at Ash expectantly when the other boy stopped in the middle of the floor, peering around for chairs.

"My sheets don't have fleas, Woods."

Ash sat down beside him, embarrassed and hoping Ramsay wouldn't pick up on why he was really uncomfortable. "Is ginger tea all right? I wasn't sure if you preferred this or peppermint—"

"Ginger is perfect."

Ramsay sipped the tea slowly, hands around the mug. Ash wasn't sure if it was an odd thought, to feel that his hands were beautiful—his fingers long, his knuckles ridged, as if he might have trouble fitting on rings.

Ramsay glanced at his fingers, then back at Ash. "Is there a reason you're staring at my hands?"

Ash's face burned. "No. Just lost in thought."

Ramsay peered over the edge of his mug as he sipped, staring at Ash as if he didn't believe him.

Silence filled the room. Ash swallowed nervously. Source, why was he so awkward with Ramsay now? "I should let you rest. I just wanted to make sure you ate something."

"No," Ramsay said, putting the mug down on a side table. "Please, stay." His eyes flicked up to meet Ash's own. Was it his imagination that it seemed like Ramsay was searching for something? "If you'd like to, anyway."

Ash hated how erratic his breath had become. "Okay."

Ramsay sighed, rolling his shoulders back, and picked up a piece of bread. "There's too much to process at once. My parents and Snowdrop and *why* they killed so many—and your father," he said, watching Ash again.

Ash had been trying to push the memory away. Gresham Hain had not only worked with the Thornes, but he was to blame for the massacre of Snowdrop, too. Emotion tangled in Ash's chest. "And now we know that he really was after the Book."

"And likely still is," Ramsay said.

"Does he know that you've been searching for it also?"

"We've never even discussed the Book. It's—Source, it's strange, Ash," he said. "This makes me rethink every interaction we've had. He never told me he knew my parents or worked together with them, and of course he wouldn't have admitted to pushing them to massacre so many people, but this—"

Suddenly, Ash understood Ramsay's fears about turning out to be the monster that his parents had been. Ash had always known Hain was selfish. He'd taken advantage of his mother and abandoned them. But this was another level of horror. If this man was his father, and Ash had Hain's eyes and ears, then what was to say he hadn't also inherited his capacity for evil?

"Are you all right?"

Ash looked up, surprised to see Ramsay's careful stare. "We

don't need to go to the higher realms anymore," he said. "You can stop reading my energy now."

"I can't help it. We're still connected." Ramsay added, "Besides, I've gotten used to it."

Ash bit his lip. "It scares me," he admitted. "My dad is a monster for what he did, and—"

"And you're nothing like him," Ramsay said.

"Aren't I?" Ash asked him. "I wanted to read the Book, too. I didn't want to use it to help other people. I wanted it because I was selfish."

"Then you're like every single other human being in the world," Ramsay said. "We're all selfish, Ash. You're just brave enough to see it."

Ash looked away, unwilling to believe Ramsay.

"You're selfish," Ramsay said. "And hot-tempered, and irrational, and you act without thinking, and you're infuriatingly always late."

"Source, tell me what you really think."

"And you're also kind," Ramsay said. "And curious, and surprisingly thoughtful." Ash met Ramsay's eyes and found that this time, he was unable to look away. "It's lazy to put a multifaceted human being, created from the alchemy of the universe, into a box of *good* or *bad*. No one is only one of the two."

"That would mean no one is good or bad, then. Even your parents. Even my father. And that can't be true."

"Why not?" Ramsay asked. "Harmful. They've all caused so much pain," he said. "But Hain revolutionized alchemy, changing the lives of so many for the better, and seeing my mom and dad again—I remembered the love they showed me at times, too. Believing that they are *evil* and we aren't—I think that's most dangerous of all. It means we'll surprise ourselves, when we end up causing harm as well."

"I don't think you or I will be massacring an entire town any time soon."

"No," Ramsay agreed. He said nothing else, sipping his tea with a frown.

"What will you do when you see him?" Ash asked. "My father, I mean."

"I don't know. I wonder if I should even return to the college. What would be the point, when I need to leave for House Lune?"

"Your work is important," Ash said. "You should make sure you can continue where you left off when you get back." Emphasis on *when*, Ash thought. "And I can let Frank know that I'm leaving, too."

Ramsay frowned, confused. Ash realized that Ramsay never planned on him joining for the second part of this adventure. He smirked at the thought of letting Ramsay go alone. "I'm coming," he said with a finality that was difficult to argue with.

Ramsay let out an impatient sigh. "You'd better not slow me down, Ash."

"*Slow you down?* Chances are, I'll end up saving your life."

Ramsay barked a laugh that seemed to surprise even him. Ash smiled, a familiar warmth growing. They sat in silence for a few long moments, Ramsay tearing off more bread and finally taking a bite.

Ash said, "What did they mean, that they wanted to use the Book to protect alchemists?"

Ramsay's sigh was more annoyed, but Ash had finally begun to learn that Ramsay's irritation wasn't always with him. "Probably an excuse—telling themselves it's for the sake of all alchemists, when really, it's just for their benefit."

Ash frowned, lost in thought. It'd seemed as if the Thornes and Hain had been speaking around something they all knew but wouldn't say aloud.

Ramsay didn't notice. "My parents were often lost in their delusions," he said, more quietly. "I just hope I won't follow in their footsteps."

Ash laughed at the absurdity. "You're *nothing* like your parents, Ramsay."

Ramsay glanced up at Ash with a softness that reminded Ash of a child's, hopeful after so many years of hurt. He blinked, walls back up again. "I'm afraid I might be like my mother especially."

"You do pace a lot like your dad," Ash said, and decided not to mention the breaking of books' spines as they were piled on top of one another, too.

Ramsay smiled, but Ash could see emotion beginning to well in his eyes. "Maybe I do pace a little."

Ash grinned. "A little?"

Ramsay smirked, but he looked down again, swallowing thickly. "My mother, though—I was a lot like her, especially when I was younger. Her superiority."

Ash frowned. "Did she always treat you that way, too?"

Ramsay sighed slowly, nodding. "Sometimes, I think that if my parents were still alive, and House Thorne was still in all its grandeur, I'd be just as awful as she was, treating everyone around me like they're nothing. I know how it feels to be on the receiving end. I don't ever want to be that way, Ash." He didn't meet Ash's eye. "I think back to the moments when we still didn't know each other very well, and I—Source, I'm sorry for treating you poorly."

Ash had to admit that Ramsay had his condescending moments and harsh tones, but he never showed Ash the level of his mother's icy rage. "It's okay," Ash said. "Besides, you were right. I could've tried harder to be on time."

Ramsay gave a soft, grateful laugh. "You were right, too. I am kind of an asshole."

"You're not," Ash said.

"I really think I might be."

"Even if you are," Ash said, "you're also the first person who's ever taken me seriously. And when you don't hide behind that mask, and I see the real you—you're warm, and funny, and eccentric, and . . ."

When Ramsay met his gaze, Ash's heart jumped. Desire

flooded him. He wanted to touch Ramsay, hold him—kiss him. Energy danced along his skin, and he knew that Ramsay could feel what he wanted. There was no use trying to hide it. Ramsay blinked as if surprised—but Ash could feel, too, that Ramsay had already known, had maybe even started to suspect the potential for these feelings when they first started to work together and their energy was on such opposite ends of the spectrum that they fit together perfectly—

Ramsay looked down. Ash, without thinking, had reached out and touched Ramsay's wrist. Ramsay clenched his jaw and pulled his hand away.

"Sorry," Ash breathed.

Ramsay wouldn't meet his eye. "Why're you attracted to me, Ash?"

Ash's mind went blank. Words weren't forming. "I—I don't know, I—"

"So you *are* attracted to me, then?"

Ash's embarrassment burned. "You already know that I am." Ash wasn't sure why frustration ticked through him now. Maybe it was because Ramsay still wouldn't look at him. "You probably have for a while. Why pretend that you don't know?"

Ramsay stood from the bed. "Source, Ash." He ran a hand over his hair. "You're right. I've known."

"Why haven't you said something about it before?"

"I needed to focus on finding the Book." Ramsay finally turned to look at him. "Besides, isn't it your responsibility to say how you're feeling?"

Ash bit his lip. "Has it only been me?" he asked. If Ash had felt how perfectly their energy meshed and felt a magnetic pull toward Ramsay as he learned all there was to know about him, unable to stop thinking about him, falling in love with him . . .

Ramsay swallowed.

"Have you felt the same way about me, too?"

"It sounds like you already know the answer to that question."

They waited in painful silence for one long moment, before Ash also stood from the bed and walked to Ramsay slowly, carefully. "I'm sorry," he said. "I didn't mean for you to find out—didn't want you to know at all, actually."

Ramsay turned away, then turned back, as if unsure where to stand. "You don't need to apologize. They're just feelings. It's not something either of us can help."

"Why does it sound like you don't want this?"

"Do you?"

Ash stopped in front of him. "I know what you'll probably think," he said. "I shouldn't let my feelings get in the way of our work. I tried to hide them. I promise I did."

"Yes," Ramsay said, nodding. "I know."

"If you don't want this, then I'll keep them hidden away," Ash said. "I haven't let them affect me at all."

Ramsay was shaking.

"But if you do want this . . ."

"Want what, exactly?" Ramsay said. His voice had hardened, but Ash didn't flinch away like he might've once.

He slipped a hand against Ramsay's palm. Ramsay froze, then held on to Ash's fingers. Ramsay closed his eyes. He was near tears. "The last time—Source, the last time I let myself feel this way . . ."

Ash took Ramsay's other hand. "I'm not Callum."

Ramsay nodded, squeezing his eyes shut now, lashes wet. He opened his eyes again and seemed caught by Ash's stare. He looked from Ash's eyes and down to his mouth. Ramsay hesitated before he leaned in, as if he'd been taken over by another energy and lost all thought and inhibition, and maybe it was *Ash's* energy that had influenced him, Ash's energy to do exactly what he wanted, when he wanted to—

Their lips barely touched. It lasted only a moment before Ramsay pulled away again, eyes wide with shock at himself—but the surprise quickly faded, eyes hooded with a desire that Ash felt, too. Ash grabbed a fistful of his shirt and pulled him closer, bumping their mouths together. Ramsay put a hand to his lip— "Source, Ash, are you *trying* to knock my teeth out?"—but Ash ignored him and tried again, kissing him more softly this time, thinking that Ramsay's lips were spicy from the ginger. They drew back, but for only a moment to breathe before their lips pressed together again, wanting more. Ash tugged him closer to the bed. They fell, Ramsay on top, Ash accidentally kicking the food to the floor.

"Such a waste," Ramsay muttered against Ash's mouth.

"Shit, sorry," Ash breathed, though he was too distracted to care. He licked Ramsay's lips, glad when they opened.

"You taste good," Ramsay said, licking Ash's tongue.

"Source, do you have to say something so embarrassing?" Ash asked as he arched up, wanting to feel more of Ramsay's body against him.

"Is that embarrassing?" Ramsay asked, genuinely curious. "It's just true. Maybe you're embarrassed because of your lack of experience."

Ash nipped Ramsay's lip in response.

"Ow," Ramsay said, jerking away with surprise.

Ash grinned as he sat up. "You talk too much while you're making out."

Ramsay narrowed his eyes. "Is that so?" He pushed Ash back down by his shoulders. Ash tried to roll him over to straddle him instead, but Ramsay pressed him down again, gasping when Ash rubbed a thigh between his own. They kissed harder and longer as Ash began to tug at Ramsay's shirt, threatening to rip the buttons.

Ramsay seemed to be straining with effort to not lose himself completely. He leaned over Ash, hands gripped into fists on either side of him. "Maybe this—this isn't—"

"You can't even get yourself to say the words," Ash said, biting back a laugh, kissing Ramsay's mouth, his chin, his neck and feeling a glint of pride at Ramsay's moan. "Do you want to stop?"

"No, of course I don't want to stop."

"Then why should we?"

Ramsay buried his face in Ash's neck, kissing his collarbone, hands reaching under his shirt, too. "Well, I *did* see a certain memory with your friend, and I wouldn't want a similarly monstrously awkward romp."

Ash gasped as if Ramsay had officially taken the teasing too far and was annoyed at the laugh that was building inside him. "You act like you're an expert."

Ramsay sat up, straddling Ash, and began to nimbly unbutton his own shirt. "You already know that I make sure to be an expert in everything I do."

Ash watched as Ramsay pulled off his shirt and tossed it to the side. Ramsay seemed pleased at the appreciation on Ash's face. He leaned down to kiss Ash again, pulling at the ends of Ash's shirt, too, before Ash sat up and let him strip it over his head. Ramsay paused, a hand on Ash's binder. Ash shook his head. "Not there."

Ramsay nodded his understanding and kissed Ash's ribs, his stomach. Joking insults were put aside. Ash wondered, briefly, if Ramsay might've had a point—that it was possible their relationship could become too awkward, and it was a *very* long journey to House Lune—but any concern was quickly tossed when Ramsay unbuttoned Ash's pants and pulled them down enough to kiss the inside of his thigh. Ash closed his eyes, hands tangled in Ramsay's black strands. Tobin had attempted the same but had used too much teeth, whereas Ramsay—he was surprisingly soft, gentle, and it seemed he knew how to use his tongue for more than sarcastic quips and verbal lashings. Ash hated that, in the end, Ramsay was right once again: He *was* somehow an expert at this, too.

And when he was done, and had made Ash properly curse Ramsay and Source and all of creation, he grinned up at Ash, looking entirely too pleased with himself. "Did you enjoy that, Ash?"

"Fuck you."

Ramsay laughed, sitting up—but as he watched Ash, his smile began to fade.

Ash sat up, too. "Not already beginning to regret that, are you?"

Ramsay let out a breath, leaning forward to kiss the corner of Ash's mouth, his lips. "No. I'm just scared."

"Scared?"

"The last time I had sex with someone, it didn't exactly end well."

Ash kissed Ramsay's cheek. "Callum really fucked you up, huh?"

"Isn't that what ex-boyfriends do?"

Ash let his hands roam over Ramsay's shoulders, his chest, down his stomach. "I wouldn't know. Tell me more about him."

Ramsay's breath hitched. "He was my best friend, before—ah, shit, Ash."

Ash began to kiss his abdomen, undoing the pants button and zipper. "Before?"

Ramsay's hand twisted in Ash's hair. "He let me think that we were in love."

"Did you? Love him, I mean?"

"You saw the memories." Ramsay didn't meet his eye. "I thought he was the only person in the world I could trust. And then even he betrayed me, too. He was the person who taught me that I can only rely on myself. No one else."

Ash had stopped, watching Ramsay as he spoke. "That isn't true," he said. "You can rely on me, Ramsay. I hope you know that."

Ramsay paused. He searched Ash's gaze before he nodded. "I think I'm starting to."

Ash grinned and kissed Ramsay's lips, then neck and collarbone. "Don't worry. I'll help you forget all about Callum Kendrick."

Ramsay only laughed.

*

Ash woke tangled in sheets. He looked around, confused, but only for a moment before he stretched with a contented sigh. Usually, when Ash acted without thinking, the consequences were disastrous—but this was one time he was glad he had. He realized that he was late for work, but this wouldn't matter much now that he would be leaving for weeks, maybe even months. House Lune was isolated in the Elder lands, inaccessible by train—and as far as Ash knew, Ramsay had no automobile or horse. They would need to take a train out of Kensington before they braved the wilderness on their own.

He sat up, tugging on the edge of the sweater he'd slept in, wondering where Ramsay had gone. His heart fell when he thought that maybe he'd returned to the college without Ash. Other bits of clothes were still scattered across the bedroom floor, along with the binder he'd tossed aside. The tray of food had been picked up, at least. Ash noticed that, on the nightstand beside the bed, there was a random collection of things—a forgotten mug of tea, a leather journal, and . . . He picked up the little blue hexagonal shape he'd created with a smile. The door opened with a click, and Ramsay strolled inside, shirtless. He smiled at Ash and made his way over.

"And you give me a hard time about waking up in the morning," Ramsay said, sitting on the side of the bed.

"I didn't realize you kept this," Ash said.

Ramsay plucked the shape out of Ash's palm and rested it back on the nightstand. "Of course I did. It's one of my prized possessions."

"What time is it?"

"Three in the afternoon."

Frank would be livid. "We were up all night," Ash said in defense of himself. "And we—ah—engaged in strenuous activity."

Ramsay's cheeks turned a pleased pink. At the reminder, his eyes fell to Ash's mouth. Ash smiled and kissed him—meant only to be a quick peck at first, but then becoming longer as Ramsay leaned into him, beginning to rest on top of him—

Ramsay sighed regretfully and pulled back. "We probably shouldn't. Not now."

Ash knew that he was right. They'd planned to begin their journey by evening and needed to get to the college to make their proper arrangements. "Maybe we can find a free moment later?"

Ramsay's smile was softer. He took Ash's hand. "That would be nice."

In the pause that followed, Ash wondered if Ramsay had begun to wonder the same thing Ash started to question: What were they to each other now? They'd gone from barely acquaintances to new friends and now to new friends who'd had sex with each other, and Ash had feelings for Ramsay, too—but did this mean they were in a relationship? It seemed like a precarious time to start a romance, searching for the Book of Source together and risking their lives in House Lune, but Ash could still feel in his heart that this was something he wanted—maybe even more so when he considered the danger they would face.

16

Ramsay said that they should leave within the hour if they wanted any chance of beginning their travels before sundown. Ash went back to his room and had a quick wash before he he tugged on his binder, dressed, and stuffed his clothes into his bag. He met Ramsay in the kitchen, and they shared a quick meal of eggs, bacon, and grapefruit—they would need the protein and vitamins. Ash sighed at the thought of Ramsay's newly stocked kitchen going to waste, but they had little other choice. Ash heaved his bag of clothes over his shoulder. Ramsay wore a coat over his vest and held luggage.

"Are you ready to go?" he asked.

Ash nodded. "Aren't you going to say goodbye?"

Ramsay gave him a strange look. "Goodbye to what?"

"The house," Ash said emphatically. "Who knows when you'll be back?"

Ramsay looked like he might laugh at Ash, but what else was new? "I've been on long trips before."

Ash remembered this well—and now he wouldn't be there to water Ramsay's office plants. "The house is consciousness, too."

Ramsay sighed, rolling his eyes, then took a breath. "Goodbye, house."

Ash stared at him blankly. "I can't believe you actually did it."

Ramsay seemed to contemplate strangling him. Ash swallowed a laugh. In a way, it was nice to know not everything had changed between them.

They walked through the study's door and into Ramsay's office, surrounded by the familiar stacks of books and papers on the desk and the jungle of plants. Ramsay said that he needed to go to the administrative department on the third floor to file papers of leave so that a replacement could be found for his class and he could pick up where he'd left off on his work if he returned.

"*When*," Ash interrupted to say.

Usually, Ramsay would try to find his professor, too—but in this case, it went unsaid that he'd avoid Gresham Hain.

"Do you think Hain would hurt you?" Ash whispered, concerned, as the pair left Ramsay's office.

"He never has before," Ramsay said. "But if he finds out that I'm leaving and figures out why . . ."

They strode down the hall side by side. Ash noticed the surprised double takes from students at the sight of the genius, infamous graduate apprentice speaking to the groundskeeper's assistant. Ash certainly wouldn't miss them.

"What if we're reading this all wrong?" Ash said, even as his instincts screamed otherwise. "Maybe Hain wouldn't harm you. He worked with your parents, after all."

"Don't be naïve," Ramsay said dismissively.

"I guess it's true that not much has changed," Ash muttered.

Ash turned away—he needed to put in his own leave of notice—but before he could get far, Ramsay grabbed his hand and pulled him back for a quick kiss. Ash blinked in surprise, his heart leaping. Two students who'd been walking nearby outright stopped to stare.

Ramsay didn't seem to notice or care. "I'll find you after," he said.

Ash blushed as he set off to find his own department's office. He already knew there was no chance his job would be waiting for him. He hoped that *when* he returned to Hedge, he'd be able to find work that wasn't on the docks. The office was hidden away in an abandoned hall, the room cramped. The woman at the desk hadn't remembered Ash's name, and when Ash said he would be traveling, she didn't even bother to look up from her paperwork.

"Fine," she said. "You're dismissed."

Ash hadn't expected to feel so melancholy as he made his way to the greenhouse, hoping he would find Frank there, disappointed when he didn't. At least Ash could say goodbye to his plants. He grazed a finger over the sprouts in their pots. He wasn't sure why he was so sad. He'd never loved this job at the college, and he knew this adventure with Ramsay was an opportunity. Some alchemists liked to think of the lives of humans as stories, each new chapter a symbol of their energy's evolution. This position at the college, watering plants and weeding gardens alongside a grumpy Frank, wishing that he'd had the chance to study alchemy . . . This was familiar to Ash. He knew what to expect. This expectation felt safe. But he couldn't live in safety, unchanging, for the rest of his life.

The door opened and Ash looked up, hopeful it'd be Frank—and pleasantly surprised when he saw Ramsay instead.

"I thought you might be here," she said, walking in and eyeing the rows of plants on tables.

Ash felt self-conscious, as if she'd walked into his bedroom unannounced and he had underwear scattered across the floor—but he also felt excited to show another piece of himself to her.

"Is this where you spend your days?" she asked, picking up a smaller pot of lavender and inspecting its leaves.

"For the most part," Ash said, leaning against a table. "Can you be careful with that, please?"

She put the pot down and made her way to Ash, lodging herself in between his legs, hands on either side of him. "I didn't realize you were so passionate about plants."

He blushed. "I'm not. Well, I wasn't," he corrected. "Once I got this job and started to learn more from Frank . . ."

She was nodding slowly, listening, though something *else* was clearly on her mind, too, evident by her growing smile. They needed to leave, but Ash couldn't help but grin as he leaned forward for another kiss, hands pulling her closer by her waist—

His mind registered that the door opened again, though his body was slower to respond. He only pulled away when he heard a voice.

"That's him, there."

Ramsay turned as Ash's head snapped up to look. Frank was at the door, not meeting Ash's eye, as he held it open for another person who strolled inside. Ash jumped from the table, palms up, already envisioning a shield—but the alchemist who had attacked him seemed on the edge of laughter.

"I've spent the past week searching for you, only to find you in the most obvious place of all," she said, "locking lips with *Ramsay Thorne* of all people."

Ramsay was tense. She looked from Ash to the newcomer. "Ash, who is this?"

"You can call me Marlowe," she said, striding forward with an extended hand. Ash pushed himself in front of Ramsay, and she stopped and raised a brow. "I'm not sure why you're being so abrasive," she told Ash, "when you're the one who nearly killed me."

Frank was stiff by the door. "Do you need anything else?"

"No, no," Marlowe said, turning to him with a pleasant smile. "But I suppose you want your sterling."

Frank refused to look at Ash as the boy froze. Marlowe produced a coin purse from her skirts' pockets and shelled out ten sterling into Frank's outstretched hand. Ten sterling, for knowledge of Ash's whereabouts—ten sterling, for potentially Ash's life.

"Frank—" Ash managed to choke out, but Marlowe turned to him with a cutting gaze.

"You can't blame him, can you?" she said. "You're a dangerous alchemist, injuring me and potentially so many others—"

"She tried to kill me—"

"—and, apparently, you never quite told him the truth about the alchemy you're practicing with Thorne." She lowered her voice to a stage whisper, palm hiding her mouth from Frank. "Don't worry. I explained everything over tea."

Ash tried to meet Frank's eye, but the older man only clenched his jaw, glaring at the ground. "She attacked me first, Frank, it was in self-defense—and Ramsay, she isn't—"

Frank interrupted, looking at Marlowe. "Our business is done, then."

Marlowe turned to him and shook his hand. "Thank you so much for your assistance."

Frank grunted a nonreply and hurried from the greenhouse, the door slamming shut behind him. He must've known that Marlowe wasn't making a friendly visit. Ash hadn't thought of them as close friends, but the betrayal stung all the same. He gritted his teeth, then turned back to Marlowe—but Ramsay had already raised her hand.

"So this is the alchemist who attacked and hurt you?" she asked, eyes focused on Marlowe even as she spoke to Ash.

"Yes," Ash said, raising his hand, too.

Marlowe only shook a finger at him. "I wouldn't practice alchemy here, if I were you," she said. "You'd be announcing to all of Kensington that you're unlicensed."

A shot of purple light seared the tip of Marlowe's ear. She gasped, finger touching her lobe and coming away with a smear of blood. "Why did you attack Ash?" Ramsay said, expressionless.

"An assault, without provocation, before a civilized conversation?" Marlowe asked. "I expected better of you, Thorne."

"You're joking, right?" Ash yelled.

"Answer my question."

Marlowe clenched her hand into a fist. "What if I said it isn't any of your concern?"

Ash felt fury twist through Ramsay. "If you've hurt Ash, then yes, it's my fucking concern."

She sighed, exasperated. "Source, I'm not going to attack him again."

Ramsay's eyes narrowed. "Forgive us for not believing you."

"Circumstances have changed."

"So, you'd like us to forgive and forget?" Ramsay asked. Another sear of light. Marlowe smacked a hand against her neck and pulled her palm away to show the barest trickle of blood. "If you don't answer our question, the next cut will be deeper."

"You wouldn't kill me," she said, staring at the blood on her hand. "Would you?"

"Yes," Ramsay said, steady enough that Ash believed her. "I would."

Marlowe met Ramsay's gaze, smile wiped from her face. "Well, I couldn't let Ash live if he was the key to you learning where the Book is hidden, could I?"

"And now?" Ash said.

"My orders have changed, you could say."

"Orders?" Ash repeated.

"Yes, orders—to escort you, Mr. Woods, to a private residence," Marlowe said, "where you will disclose the location of the Book of Source."

Ash swallowed. He tried very hard not to look at Ramsay, to not give away any information to Marlowe with his expression or vibrating emotions. "Why would you think I know where it is?"

"I know that you do," Marlowe said. "There's no other reason you would quit your job, and that you, Ms. Thorne, would put in a notice of leave." Her gaze dropped to the luggage waiting on the ground. "Why else would you suddenly decide to travel, if not to find the Book? You're coming with me today, Mr. Woods." Her tone seemed to add *whether you want to or not.*

Ramsay raised a second palm. "You're delusional if you think I'll let you take Ash."

"You don't need him anymore," Marlowe said. "Why fight for him? You could leave right now, unscathed. It'd even give you a head start to find the Book."

Marlowe might as well have punched Ash in the gut. He could barely look at Ramsay as she spoke. "I won't repeat myself."

"What would happen to you if you murdered me, Thorne?" Marlowe said.

Ramsay's hands were perfectly still, but Ash could feel the tremor of hesitation.

"You'd be hanged," Marlowe said, "just like your parents."

"It wouldn't matter."

"No? The end of the Thorne dynastic line, known forever as killers—"

"As long as I destroy the Book, I don't care," Ramsay said, but Ash could feel the energy beneath her words. Ramsay was lying to herself.

"I have no quarrel with you," Marlowe said. It became clear to Ash, then, that she'd been stalling, doing everything she could to avoid a fight—but he felt the heated energy growing in her now.

"Obviously you do, if you're threatening Ash."

Marlowe rolled her eyes. "Overprotective partners are so annoying. There isn't any need for a *dramatic battle*," she said, "but if you refuse to come with me, Mr. Woods, I won't have any other choice."

Ash met Ramsay's eye. The amount of time they'd spent together, harmonizing their vibrations, had its uses. Her eyes widened just as Ash took a deep breath and grabbed Ramsay's hand, twisting her around. He imagined a flash of red light, an explosion—felt the heat against his back and heard Marlowe's scream as she bent over with her palms pressed into her eyes—

"What're you doing?" Ramsay demanded. "Better to finish her off now, before—"

Ash clutched Ramsay's hand as he pulled her from the greenhouse, abandoning their bags, and raced into the gardens.

"Usually you're the one thinking shit through, not me," Ash yelled.

"I *am* thinking this through."

"You were going to kill her!"

"She'll kill *you* if I let her live—"

"And you'll be hanged if you do!"

They hurried onto the path that would take them back to Boylston Hall. Ramsay seemed to contemplate returning to Marlowe before Ash could stop her.

"Source, Ramsay, you'll be caught and executed and you won't be able to destroy the Book!"

Ramsay stilled. She slowed to a stop, breathing hard as she watched Ash. The timing couldn't have been worse. The bell must've rung seconds ago, and students were now streaming out of the buildings, chatting and laughing, for the most part unawares, though a few did crane their necks in the direction of Ash and Ramsay and the greenhouse, as if they'd also seen the flash of light.

"Remember what this is about," Ash said. "Finding the Book— burning it . . . Killing Marlowe won't help you. We need to escape."

The words that fell out of Ash's mouth were desperate. He knew that he didn't care about the Book as much as he did about Ramsay. He wouldn't be able to live with himself if she was hanged because of him.

Ramsay blinked, as if she'd been shaken awake from sleep and pulled out of a dream. They breathed, staring at each other. Ash suddenly wasn't sure what Ramsay was thinking. She finally gritted her teeth and her fists. "You're right," she said to Ash's relief. "I'm sorry. I let my emotions get the best of me."

They walked quickly, trying not to draw attention to themselves. Ash glanced over his shoulder, expecting to see Marlowe chasing after any moment. "Shit—shit, shit, what do we do? Where do we go?"

Ramsay stared forward. "We have to lose her. Head for the trains."

The train station was in the heart of Kensington. They'd need to make it all the way through Wynnesgrove and into the city. Even running, it would take them an hour.

"The trains are too far."

"What other choice do we have?"

Before Ash could answer Ramsay's demand, there was an explosion in the ground to their left, dirt and bits of grass and rock flying into the air. Ash spun around, arm shielding his face. Students around him screamed. When he turned, he saw Marlowe stalking toward them, hands outstretched, eyes swollen and red.

"I was only told to bring you alive," she yelled. Students had started to back away, most running. Only Ash and Ramsay faced her.

"Shit," Ash said. "Maybe we should've killed her."

Ramsay shot him a look. "Are you fucking kidding me, Ash?"

Marlowe clenched her hands into fists, energy glowing. "I wasn't told to bring you in one piece."

"What is the meaning of this?"

A professor had begun to march toward them, an older gentleman in a tweed jacket—but before he could get very close, Marlowe flung a hand at him. He soared through the air as if an invisible hand had picked him up and hurled him. She whirled back to Ash, rage glistening in her eyes. She held up one hand, fingers beginning to weave back and forth. Roots and vines grew from the ground around Ash's feet, twisting around his legs, tight enough that his bones might snap—Marlowe yelped as purple light sliced her arm, Ramsay's fists raised—

Ash was already tired from creating the flash, but he couldn't panic. He took a deep breath and imagined a knife of light, blade sharp enough to cut through stone—imagined it slicing through the roots and vines as if they were nothing but threads. He fell back to the ground, scrambling away as Ramsay pulled him up by his arm. Sirens wailed in the distance as they ran, Ramsay racing ahead—

Something hot hit Ash's back. He screamed and fell to the ground. Marlowe's attack had punched a hole in him, and it felt like his skin was on fire, his muscles burning. He saw Ramsay stop, looking back at Ash with wide eyes. She hesitated, then ran back to Ash's side. She pressed a cooling palm into his shoulder blade, but the pain seared through him.

"Source," she whispered, then looked up—Ash knew Marlowe had caught up to them. Ramsay looked back down at Ash. They only held each other's stares for three seconds, but it felt as if time had slowed. Ash felt Ramsay's vibrations—her anger, fear, uncertainty—and he felt, too, when the emotions stopped. It was as if a wall had risen. Her gaze became empty, with only a taste of regret.

He didn't understand what it meant yet—didn't realize what she would do. "I'm sorry, Ash."

He grabbed her wrist in pain. "It hurts—shit, Ramsay, please—"

She drew her hand away. She shook her head, swallowing thickly as she stood. Even then, Ash didn't fully understand. Even when she turned and started to run again, Ash didn't realize that she was leaving him behind. He clenched his jaw and fists, trying to breathe slowly enough to imagine whatever it was that had hit him being pushed out—

It wasn't enough to heal, but finally he felt it leave his body. He was still in pain, but at least now he could move. What looked like a hot piece of coal smoked on the concrete path as Ash stood, slumped, a hand to his shoulder. Marlowe faced him with cold determination. Ash looked around, still not fully believing Ramsay was gone, but it was starting to sink in now. Ash had felt her energy. He knew that she'd decided the Book was the priority, even if it meant Ash's life.

"It looks like your lover left you to die," Marlowe said. She didn't bother to sneer as she glared at him, walking closer, hands raised. The sirens were closer now, the campus around them abandoned.

"I hate that word," Ash muttered. He raised his hands, too, pain biting him. "*Lover.*"

A line of Marlowe's clones appeared. They surrounded him

as she walked to join the ranks. "Do you hear those sirens?" she asked. "Those are the Kendrick redguards. Would you rather wait for them to arrive? They'll arrest you and hang you by tomorrow's end. Wouldn't it better to stop this nonsense and come with me now?"

"If they hang me," Ash said, "then at least you'll hang beside me, too."

She gave a frustrated sigh. "Have it your way, then."

Marlowe and her clones raised their hands, but Ash moved first. He hadn't given himself the breath he needed, the moment to even consider what he wanted to bring into existence. There was only his fear, his anger, his pain—physical and emotional as he thought of Ramsay turning her back on him—and the chaos, always the chaos beckoning him closer. He heard the shouts and marching footsteps, could feel the heat of Marlowe's alchemy. He saw fire in his mind.

17

Ash woke in the back of a carriage. He swayed, sore, the wound in his back throbbing. His hands were cuffed behind him, making the pain even sharper. The redguard that sat on the other side watched with an empty expression. The red uniform was technically why they were known as the reds, but Ash knew it was really because they tended to inspire the same color to come from bodies, the uniform making it harder to see the stains.

The tinted window showed the white Kensington buildings they passed. Smoke gushed in the distance. Ash's heart clenched. He'd fallen unconscious and his memories were faded, as if they'd only been a dream, but the details were coming back into focus now. The explosion he'd imagined had engulfed Boylston Hall. The fire quickly spread, passing through the lawn and the dormitories, the offices and the library. Ash had burned down the college. He'd destroyed it, and Source, there was no way for him to know how many countless students and professors might've been injured, maybe even killed—

His breath tightened. He would be hanged. He knew that with certainty. Ash was going to die in Kensington Square, maybe in a matter of hours. He thought that, once he was close to death, he would feel regret or anger at not achieving everything he'd wanted to . . . But he was only numb. He felt nothing, except for tendrils of horror at what he'd done.

The carriage stopped. He could already hear the shouts, though he couldn't see the crowd that had formed. The red leaned forward with a black sack and yanked it on over Ash's head. He was wrenched up by his arm, the same that was connected to the wounded shoulder blade. He bit back a shout of pain as he was dragged into the sunlight. Ash could see the outline of the threads in front of his eyes but nothing else as he was pushed forward. The shouts got louder as he walked, and suddenly he was surrounded by them, the screams and demands for his death—

"Why does that boy still breathe?!"

"Hang the alchemist!"

—along with the questions that were yelled to him and the snaps and clicks of photographer's cameras. "What was your motivation?" one voice shouted above the rest. "Why did you attack Lancaster?"

He would be on the front page of the newspaper, Ash was willing to bet. *Unlicensed alchemist to blame for the destruction of Lancaster College.* His heart hurt at the realization that he would be used as proof that unlicensed alchemy was dangerous, as evil as House Lune claimed.

Ash was suddenly pulled into shadow, air much warmer than it was outside. A door shut behind him and his guard, muffling the voices that tried to follow. Shoes clicked on what sounded like tile. Ash tried to breathe, but it was difficult with the bag over his head and with his body overridden by pain. There was a stabbing ache in his chest, too, at the one subject he desperately tried not to think about. Ramsay, whispering that she was sorry. Ramsay, leaving him behind.

Ash tripped on stairs when he was shoved, yanked up by his elbow and pushed forward again. Another door opened, and he was tossed inside. Someone pressed down on his shoulder, and he fell into a chair. The sack was ripped from his head.

Ash sat in front of a large walnut desk. The room's red mahogany wall panels had inlaid golden designs, and the red tile of the floor had golden tones as well. A man stood with his back to Ash, peering out the window, perhaps at the crowd that had formed below. He was large—probably the tallest man Ash had seen, with an intimidating frame of muscle. He was also dressed in the redguard uniform, sword at his hip. His skin was a dark brown.

"Which group are you with?" the red said, back still to Ash.

"What?" Ash said, voice hoarse. "I—I'm not with a group."

The man turned to face Ash with a grim expression, gaze on the papers splayed across his desk. Ash felt a new flood of fear. He didn't make a point of learning about the House Heads, but Winslow Kendrick's face, as leader of the redguards, was well-known enough that even Ash knew who he was.

Kendrick pulled out his chair and sat, hands gripped together on top of the desk. "What was your motivation for attacking Lancaster College?"

Ash shook his head. "I didn't mean to. It was an accident."

He watched Ash coolly. "It was an *accident* that you used alchemy to cause a major explosion?"

Ash's breath was caught in his throat. "Was anyone killed?"

Kendrick's eyes narrowed. "There are three students in critical care with House Adelaide, but they will live." Ash's relief almost made him miss the rest of what the man said. "Luckily an evacuation had already begun, and those who were trapped in the buildings were able to use alchemy to escape."

They sat in silence for a few long moments, emotion welling inside of Ash—the relief was overwhelming, but so was the shame. Ramsay had always insisted that Ash needed to learn control and discipline. He wished he'd listened.

"Are you disappointed that you didn't succeed in killing anyone?" Kendrick asked Ash.

"What?" Ash shook his head. "No—Source, of course not."

"Why did you burn down the college?"

"I was attacked by a woman named Marlowe. I was acting in self-defense, and I—I lost control—"

"Are you referring to your accomplice?"

"Marlowe wasn't an accomplice. She was trying to capture me—"

"Tell me about Ramsay Thorne."

Ash's gaze snapped up.

"We've learned from the groundskeeper at the college that you were taught illegal alchemy by Thorne. Did he teach you so that you could attack the college on his behalf?"

"She," Ash said. "That's what she went by, still, when she . . ."

Kendrick stared emptily.

Ash dropped his gaze. "Ramsay was only doing me a favor. She taught me alchemy because I asked her to."

He wasn't sure why he was still protecting her when she'd abandoned him, but Ash also knew he couldn't risk telling the truth and speaking about the Book of Source.

"It seems that you were romantic partners," Kendrick said, glancing at a paper of notes on his desk. "Is that why you're protecting her?"

Ash wasn't expecting to lose his breath. He couldn't answer.

"Where is Thorne now?"

"I don't know," Ash said honestly.

"Do you understand why it's difficult to believe that?"

"I don't know where she is," Ash said again.

"Many are calling for your immediate execution," Kendrick said. This was no surprise to Ash, but his heart still pounded harder. "I'm inclined to agree, even if it's only to quell the city's growing rage. However," the man added, "I would be willing to consider a life sentence of hard labor if you gave us information on Thorne."

Ash wondered for a moment if he should admit that she'd eventually end up in House Lune—it didn't seem fair, that he would die because she abandoned him . . . But he also understood why she'd left. He knew that she needed to find the Book and ensure that it never landed in the wrong hands. This didn't do much to numb his pain.

"I don't know where Ramsay is," Ash said, this time with enough finality that Kendrick sighed as he leaned back in his seat with a vibration of disappointment.

"Sometimes I've wondered if I should've studied alchemy myself, even if only to force out the answers I need in these interrogations," he said, eyeing Ash. "But there are other methods."

Kendrick stood, watching Ash as if considering what he might do to cause the most pain. Ash tensed. There wasn't any point in attempting to fight back, not when he was in the heart of the Kendrick headquarters. He'd be easily overpowered and captured by redguards again, unless he attempted to set off another explosion and risk killing dozens, something he didn't want—and even then he was exhausted, didn't have enough alchemic power—

There was a knock. Kendrick's mouth tightened in anger as he strode past Ash and opened the door. Ash didn't dare turn around, but he heard the voices behind him murmuring.

"What're you doing here?"

"I've been afforded a questioning with the boy by Lord Alexander."

"You're using all your political chips. You'll run out eventually."

"Until then, would you mind if I used your office? Thank you, greatly appreciated—"

The door snapped shut. Ash saw, out of the corner of his eye, another figure walk into the room. He sat straighter when he saw his father stop behind Kendrick's desk. Instead of sitting, Hain stood behind the chair, hands gripping the back.

They waited in silence for a long time, long enough that Ash knew, then, that his father was aware of exactly who he was. Ash wondered how long Gresham Hain had known. He had a hard time looking away from the man's stare.

"You've burned down the college," Hain eventually said.

"I didn't mean to."

"Your energy suggests otherwise."

Ash frowned. He hadn't meant to destroy the college, and he never wanted to hurt anyone—but at Hain's words, it became harder for him to deny the glimmer of pleasure that had hidden in his chest. Lancaster had rejected him—had decided he wasn't worthy—and now it had been reduced to nothing but rubble and dust. Ash would've preferred that truth remain buried.

"Do you know who I am?" Hain said.

Ash nodded.

His father sighed, stepping around the desk to lean against its side. "You look more like your mother."

Rage struck through Ash. "Don't speak about my mother."

Hain's brow twitched. "You seem angry, Ashen—it *is* Ashen, isn't it? When, really, I'm the one who should be upset, I think. I've had my son hidden from me for eighteen years."

Ash wasn't sure he'd heard correctly, and once he processed the words, he shook his head. "You knew," Ash said. "My mom— she sent letters to you, begging you to help us, to help *her* when she got sick—"

Hain's expression grew cold. "There were no letters, and with reason. Your mother would've been a fool to contact me."

"You're lying."

He stood suddenly, walking to the window, peering down. "Samantha Woods was an . . . apprentice of mine, you could say. She ran away. She knew what happened to my apprentices once they deserted their positions." Hain glanced at Ash. "Though I understand now why she left. I would've forced her to get rid of you if I'd known."

Ash's hands tightened into fists behind his back. Heat wavered in the air around him, anger growing. Hain only turned, leaning against the wall, face shadowed. "I never wanted a child, in all my years," he said. "It was only when I grew older and was forced to accept I had no heir to carry on my legacy that I began to regret that decision. And now, here you are—as if you were delivered to me by Source itself."

"I'm not a gift, delivered to be your son," Ash said.

"No, perhaps not." Hain walked forward again, pulling out the chair and sitting at the desk. "But you certainly were delivered by Source."

It was clear that Gresham Hain hadn't come just to meet him as his father. It was ironic, that this was what Ash had wanted so badly once.

The man's voice and face were still. "Where is the Book?"

Ash didn't answer.

"Did Ramsay Thorne leave to find the Book on her own?" Ash flinched at Ramsay's name. It was enough for Hain to know that this was a painful spot that could be pressed. "She abandoned you," he said, "when you were planning to find the Book together."

"I don't know where the Book is."

"Yes, you do," Hain said. "And I trust that you'll tell me where it is willingly. I don't want to hurt you—you are my son, after all, and I can see that you have powerful alchemic potential. You're an asset to me, Ashen."

Ash shook his head, disgusted, unable to even look at the man.

"It saddens me that you don't trust me," Hain said. "I've had ample opportunity to have you killed and to kill you myself."

"Is *that* why I should trust you? Because you didn't kill me?" Ash nearly laughed.

"When it comes to the Book of Source? Yes."

There was a moment of quiet as Hain watched Ash make the connection. Ash frowned. "You're the one who sent that woman after me."

"Marlowe is my latest apprentice."

"Then you *have* tried to get me killed."

"Before I knew your identity, yes," Hain admitted. "When I learned who you were, my tactics changed. I easily could've killed you myself," he said, and Ash knew he was referring to that day Ash had helped Hain in Vanderbilt Hall. "And believe me, I did consider it. I hope that you can see this as a marker of trustworthiness. I kept you alive and risked losing the Book."

"I don't see that as a sign that I can trust you, no."

"Do you believe you're doing the right thing by helping Ms.

Thorne?" Hain asked, tilting his head to the side. "Do you believe that she has good intentions?"

Ash narrowed his eyes.

"If so," Hain said, "then you're more naïve than I expected. Did she lie to you, Ashen?" he asked. "Did she explain how she wants nothing more than to atone for her parents' deaths—that she wants to destroy the Book to ensure it never falls into the wrong hands?"

Ash's heart thumped at these words. He met his father's steady gaze.

"These are the lies she's perfected over time," Hain said, voice low. "I've heard her pity-inducing speech myself. She insists that her only purpose in life is to make up for her parents' mistakes. Yet when I study Thorne's motives, I see the truth."

"And what truth is that?" Ash asked, angry, yet also afraid of what he would hear.

"Revenge," Hain said.

"Revenge?"

"I've kept her close as my apprentice. I've watched her to see the sort of person she'd grow into. I knew her parents, and I felt it was my duty to keep an eye on her."

"Yes, we know," Ash said, finally feeling a bit of power. "And we know you were behind Snowdrop, too."

"An unfortunate accident," Hain said, unbothered. "Snowdrop never should've happened. I recognize that now. I couldn't see how my desperation for the Book affected my judgment, my senses. I plan to take accountability the moment I find it."

"And you want the Book so that you can take control of Kensington," Ash said. "The entire state, other nations. Isn't that right?"

"No," Hain said. "I have no desire for such a thing. I only want to protect alchemists—and protect us all from Thorne."

Ash shook his head, but something inside him whispered. What if Hain was telling the truth? Maybe Ash had believed all of Ramsay's lies because he had fallen in love with her.

"She wants *revenge*," Hain said. "She wants the Book's power so that she can attack the Houses. She wants to kill Lord Alexander for her parents' executions."

"You're lying."

"Am I? Is that what you sense right now, in this moment?" Hain demanded.

Ash closed his eyes, trying to force himself to breathe. It was possible that Ramsay had been dishonest all along, using him—and wouldn't it also make sense, why she'd left Ash behind?

"Thorne's capture is paramount to this state's safety," Hain said. "I'd like to believe that you'll offer her location to me freely. I'd rather not use other means to force you to tell me."

Ash glared at the tiled floor. "Why not? You've never cared about me before."

"I don't want to risk harming you," Hain said shortly.

Ash glanced up, wondering if this was a sliver of the man's fatherly affection. Hain had been the villain in Ash's mind—but maybe he was just as motivated by human emotions like love, too.

"I've already made a deal with Lord Alexander on your behalf. You'll be allowed to live, though imprisoned—and if you give us Thorne's whereabouts, and the location of the Book, you'll be pardoned."

Ash gripped his hands behind his back. Hain stood and walked across the room, opening the door and speaking to someone with a low voice. He walked back in, followed by Kendrick, who looked livid to have been kicked out of his own office. Kendrick glared down at Ash.

"I'm hoping we can come to an understanding," Hain said.

"And what understanding is that?" Kendrick asked.

"Lord Alexander has already agreed that the boy cannot be executed. He holds too much vital information."

"There's already a mob forming in the streets—"

"Lord Alexander has ordered that Woods be detained," Hain

said, ignoring Kendrick's interruption, "but I request another form of imprisonment, for his own well-being."

Ash frowned in confusion as the two men argued over him, Kendrick's hands clasped behind his back, as if to stop himself from strangling Hain. "I didn't realize that a prisoner's *well-being* was our priority."

"It is when we need him to cooperate. I ask that Ashen work for the state instead. You do have such a program, correct? Labor, in exchange for confinement."

"Yes, for minor crimes," Kendrick said, tone suggesting that Hain's request was ludicrous, "and usually meant for House members only."

"Exceptions are always made. We can even compromise further. Ashen can be given a personal guard that won't leave his side unless he's properly confined."

"You'd like me to now give manpower and resources to helping the terrorist who attacked the college? If word got out—"

"That sounds like an issue for House Kendrick."

Winslow Kendrick gritted his teeth. "The answer is *no*, Hain."

Hain stepped closer. "I think you're forgetting your position— the knowledge I possess. There are some headlines that would be even more noteworthy than *Hedge boy saved from execution*, I'd say."

Kendrick stiffened. He glared, face turning purple, as he looked from Hain and down to Ash. Ash glanced between the two. Maybe Marlowe was more than Hain's assassin, for him to have collected so many secrets and favors among the ruling Houses.

The redguard nodded stiffly then, turning for the door. "He'll be kept here overnight and assigned a guard in the morning," he said.

"Wonderful. Thank you, Lord Kendrick."

18

Ash learned that he was in the town house of House Kendrick, apparently the redguard headquarters in the center of Kensington. A guard was called for Ash, and he was hurried through the corridors where he passed sitting rooms and offices. Every now and then, a person inside would turn their head to watch as Ash was marched by, eyes widening and whispers following. Ash was taken up yet another staircase to a floor of private chambers.

The guard untied Ash's hands and practically tossed him inside, snapping the door shut and locking it with a click. Ash stood in the center of the room, rubbing his wrists. It reminded him of the room he'd stayed in at Ramsay's home—a pinch of hurt at the thought of Ramsay, he tried to push that aside—but the rooms were nothing alike, not really. The only similarity was the size of the beds and the fact that there was a connecting bath. The sheets were maroon, and the wallpaper was a bright ruby red. The bath and sinks were copper. Ash gingerly pulled off his shirt as it stuck to his wound, hissing when he tried to twist around to see the reflection in the mirror above the sinks. It was a nasty pink burn that was already infected.

He moved slowly, sorely, as he filled the bath and stripped his clothes and binder and stepped into the lukewarm water. His wound stung enough that he began to cry, and once he started, he couldn't stop. The physical and emotional pain blended. The regret that he'd caused so much damage, the looming threat that he could still be executed, and Ramsay—Source, he could hardly think about Ramsay. He didn't believe his father. He refused to believe that Hain was right. But even if he was lying about Ramsay's motives for the Book, nothing could undo the fact that she'd left Ash behind. He loved her. He'd thought she'd felt the same.

*

There were no windows, and there wasn't a clock on the wall, so Ash had difficulty keeping track of time. He didn't know if it was still day or if it'd become night. It didn't matter. Either way, Ash couldn't sleep.

When he got tired of lying in bed on his stomach, in too much pain to lie on his back, he finally sat up, folded his legs under him, and breathed. He closed his eyes. He'd made it to the higher realms before. He would try again—and if he made it, he would be able to ask the Akash where Ramsay was hiding—

It was no use. He felt a flicker of energy, but he and Ramsay needed each other to reach the realms. Alone, there was no chance he would succeed. Besides that, there was a familiar fear that chained him to this plane. He wasn't sure he would survive the chaos without Ramsay's whisper, telling him to focus.

Ash sighed in frustration when another idea came to him. He'd never attempted remote viewing, though he'd read about it enough times. It was tier-five alchemy, something that needed decades of study to pull off successfully, but Ash was desperate. He closed his eyes and tried to concentrate. He vaguely remembered the steps he'd read in texts about imagining and *feeling* the energy of the person he meant to find, allowing images and smells and tastes to come to him—

Ash was in too much pain and was riddled with too many emotions to focus. He groaned and curled up on the bed. A sob threatened to break through, but along with the heartache was a recognizable rage. It was starting to sink in, finally, that Ramsay had betrayed him. He'd helped her reach the higher realms. Without Ash, she wouldn't have even *known* where to find the Book of Source. For her to leave him behind—and after they'd kissed and held each other and . . .

There were the other whispers he tried to ignore, too. What if Gresham Hain was right? What if Ramsay had been the Thorne everyone said she was all along?

＊

Ash never fell asleep that night. He was in too much pain, too uncomfortable, too anxious that the door would open and he would be killed in his sleep by a Kendrick guard that didn't agree with Lord Alexander's mercy. When the door *did* open again and a guard stood at its threshold, Ash sat up in bed, ready to defend himself. But the guard only placed a tray of food on the ground and closed the door again.

It was a bowl of steaming porridge, Ash's only clue that it was morning. He wasn't hungry, but he forced himself to eat because he didn't know if he'd need the energy later. After a full night of feeling sorry for himself, Ash felt power filling him. He wouldn't sit in House Kendrick, awaiting his fate. He'd escape the first chance he had. He would travel to House Lune on his own, and he would find Ramsay.

And then?

He stopped eating, staring at the bowl of porridge. What hurt more than anything, he realized, was that—even when she had betrayed him, abandoned him—he still loved her. He still wanted to help her. He still wanted her to be safe.

His back's wound burned, and he was just thinking that he might not survive the infection anyway when the door opened again, this time by a healer wearing the pale blue uniform of House Adelaide. She was silent and grim as she stepped inside, followed by yet another guard who stood by the door.

"Any injuries?" she asked, voice clipped. Ash had the feeling that she was healing him against her will.

"Yes. My back."

She motioned at him to stand, and he gingerly got to his feet. He could see the healer's bright yellow energy that glowed from her hands as she traced them along his arms and his neck. He glanced up and saw that the redguard was watching him. Ash blushed as he realized the guard was looking at the binder around his chest. The redguards and House Kendrick were conservatives. This guard likely didn't have much experience with an alchemist who shifted genders like Ash.

"What're you staring at?" Ash snapped.

The red, surprisingly, gave a blushing expression as well, his gaze falling. Ash raised a brow. He thought that the guard would've sooner hit him across the mouth. "Your binder," he said. "It's stained with blood."

Ash flinched. He was already in a vulnerable position, and he didn't like this guard's attention on his chest on top of it all. "Why the hell do you care?"

"Would you like me to have it washed for you?"

"Fuck you," Ash replied.

The red blinked at Ash but said nothing else.

There was a sting of pain on Ash's back, followed by a cooling sensation. Images of flowers and yellow sunlight danced through his vision. The healer pursed her lips, as if she didn't think Ash deserved her loving energy, and maybe she was right.

"I did the best I could," she said to the redguard, "given the circumstances."

It didn't hurt anymore, and from what Ash could see when he twisted around, the wound had become nothing more than a purple scar. "Thank you."

She ignored him and left the room without another word. Ash expected the redguard to follow, but he stayed by the door, arms crossed. The guard had dark brown skin and black curly hair cropped short. He was exceptionally tall—tall enough that he might have to duck his head to enter some rooms, with broad shoulders and large muscles. Unsurprising, for a redguard. He was also young, Ash noticed, maybe only a couple of years older.

Ash said, "Are you going to stand there all day?"

The red shrugged, as if he hadn't noticed the sarcasm, though there was an annoyed twitch in his cheek. "Yes, I suppose that's the point of being your guard."

So this was the guard that'd been assigned to him. The other boy didn't seem too bright, if Ash was going to be honest—he assumed not many redguards were—which was good, in the end. He'd have a higher chance of a successful escape.

The guard eyed Ash silently.

"Does being my guard also mean staring at me like a creep?" Ash asked.

The guard's face had become carefully blank. "Apologies."

Apologies? Kensington assholes always spoke like a silver spoon was stuck in their ass.

"I didn't mean to stare," the red continued. "I'm curious, I guess—surprised that such a small person could cause so much destruction."

"Size doesn't matter. I could still put you down."

The guard let out a startled laugh. "Do you always have such an awful attitude?"

"Only when I've been locked up for a night with a hole the size of a fist in my back."

"You're more aggressive than I would've expected for a prisoner."

Something about this boy annoyed Ash terribly. "Oh, I'm sorry—am I supposed to bow? Kiss your feet?"

The guard smiled as if he found Ash amusing. This only pissed Ash off more. "That won't be necessary," he said. "You should let me have an attendant wash your binder. We'll be leaving soon."

Ash looked down at his flattened chest. He hated that so much was unknown. "And go where?"

"I don't know if anyone explained this to you, but your punishment is through labor," the guard said. "You're to be my scribe."

Ash's heart fell. "Isn't *scribe* just a kinder way of saying *personal servant?*"

"Not at all," the guard said. "You only need to take notes for me throughout the day. It's easy work, considering."

"I'd rather stay locked in here."

The boy sighed. "That's something we can agree on, but my father expects me to watch you, so I will."

"Father?" Ash repeated. Only then did he make the connection. "You're a Kendrick?"

The boy nodded with a small smile, as if he now wondered if Ash was the slower of the two. "My father wouldn't risk you with just anyone. He asked me and my brothers, and I was happy to volunteer."

Ash stared. He should've seen it before. The boy in front of him had grown. He was no longer the tall, awkward, gangly thing from Ramsay's memories and dreams. "Callum?" Ash managed to breathe.

Callum tilted his head, practiced smile still on his face. "I'm sorry—have we met?"

"No," Ash said quickly.

Callum's eyes squinted with suspicion. Ash saw echoes of Winslow Kendrick. "Then how do you know my name?"

It would be too strange to say that he recognized Callum from Ramsay's past. "I've heard of you," Ash confessed.

"Then why did you seem so surprised?"

The red was sharper than Ash had given him credit for, he had to admit. "I was told stories about you," Ash said.

He was damned persistent, too. "From whom?"

Ash hesitated. "Ramsay."

Callum's face fell. For a moment, Ash saw a glimmer of the boy who was more familiar—gentle, vulnerable. But it lasted only a second. Callum's expression was wiped clean. "I wondered if she might've said something to you. When I saw in the interrogation report that you two had worked together, I thought . . ."

He didn't finish his sentence. Callum clenched his jaw. "I'll have an attendant come for your binder and prepare you a fresh uniform. We leave within the hour."

✳

A scribe, it turned out, *was* different from a servant. Ash didn't have to help Callum into his coat or buckle his boots, but he was still expected to stand near, a leather notebook and pen in hand. "Remind me to pass on condolences to Lord and Lady Val when they visit tomorrow morning," Callum said as he opened the town house's front door, "and, oh, put in a note to have the house manager change my drapes, too."

Ash, for likely not the last time, considered spiking the pen through his eyeball.

He chased after Callum as the older boy walked into the heart of Kensington. Ash had never been so deep in the city before. He could even see the manor of House Alexander standing tall several streets away. The buildings curved with the road, glowing white under the gray sky. Horses and carriages and a rare newer automobile passed. Ash had been given a scribe's uniform, at least, so he wouldn't stick out in his torn and stained clothes. It was a plain white button-down with a maroon tie and gray slacks, along with a pair of old black brogues that'd been found for him by the butler. Tobin would've died with laughter at the sight, Ash thought with a pang. He found himself uncomfortable as wealthy socialites nodded and greeted Callum with the respect expected for a House heir, their gazes sliding over Ash. He could practically hear the gossip begin.

Ash was quick on his feet, but Callum's long strides were hard to keep up with.

"Can you slow down?" Ash said. Callum didn't respond and kept his pace. This irritated Ash. "Hello? Kendrick? I'm talking to you. Source. I'm putting way too much effort into staying your prisoner. I should just let myself fall behind and escape—"

The redguard came to an abrupt stop. "I consider myself to be a patient person."

Ash looked to the left and right and left again. "Okay. And?"

"And it's a gift, truly it is, that you're managing to wear my patience thin before we've even made it to lunch."

"Thank you."

Callum shook his head and continued walking—but he'd slowed down a little, at least. He was quiet. Maybe he felt as awkward as Ash did. Ash was grateful the other boy didn't force small talk, but he could feel his own curiosity growing. It almost felt like Ash knew Callum as well as Ramsay had, an old friend that Ash hadn't seen in years—or like a character from a story come to life. He hated that his energy was so drawn to the other boy.

When Callum broke the silence, Ash jumped, surprised. "The interrogation report," he said. "It mentioned that you and Ramsay had worked together on an alchemic project."

"Yeah. So?"

"What was the project?" Callum asked, looking at Ash with a frown.

"I didn't realize the interrogation had continued."

"Believe me," Callum said, "you would know if this was an interrogation."

Ash snorted. "Is that a part of redguard training? Practicing lines that sound intimidating? I'm terrified."

"How long did you work with her?" Callum asked after a moment.

Ash sighed. It was hard to imagine, but it'd only been a couple of weeks since he'd first been caught practicing alchemy in Ramsay's office. "Why do you want to know?"

Callum shrugged. "Just curious." He fell back into silence once again.

Source, Ash certainly related to that. Questions built with every step, but his curiosity was replaced by dread when he finally realized where they were headed.

A stone fort was near the docks of the white city, where old battlements still stood. The fort had been used over a century ago during the Great War, but it had another use now. While Lancaster College was notable for the practice and study of alchemy, McKinley College was well-known for the prestigious training of redguards—and not just any reds. It was a military school, teaching guards how to become captains and commanders. From what Ash had heard, the school was even more selective in its students, with only ten accepted every year. It made sense that a son of House Kendrick would attend.

They reached the fort's entrance, an old drawbridge over a dry canal. Inside, students ran one-on-one combat drills in a courtyard, grappling and wrestling one another to the ground, wearing thin red shirts and shorts, despite the cold.

"Hey, Kendrick," one boy called as Callum and Ash passed. "Heard you got a new dog."

The dog, apparently, was Ash.

Callum laughed along with the other students, but he didn't stop walking. Ash, however, did. He turned to face the boy who'd spoken. "What the hell did you just call me?"

The laughing faces of redguard students stilled before their expressions turned to anger.

"Looks like you need to train your dog, Kendrick," the same boy called.

"I'm not a fucking *dog*, you piece of—"

A hand pressed against his shoulder, pushing him forward.

"A muzzle, maybe," the student called after them.

"Don't say another word," Callum told him.

"That asshole—"

"Is the first son of the Galahad family."

"Why the hell does that matter? He can't speak to me like that—"

"He shouldn't, no," Callum said. Ash looked at the older boy in surprise. "But talking back will only make things worse."

Callum guided Ash across the courtyard and into the shadow of an empty entry hall. It was bare except for its stone walls, a long corridor peppered with doors to classrooms. Ash shook him off, and Callum finally paused, watching him.

"Has anyone ever told you that you stare too much?" Ash said.

Annoyance ticked in Callum's jaw. "You're proud."

"Yes," Ash agreed.

"You don't take insults well."

"Should I?"

"You're also looking for an excuse to fight."

Ash tilted up his chin.

"I'm only going to say this once: For your safety, you need to rein that defiance in. You're not in the slums of Hedge—"

"I'm sorry, the *what* of Hedge?"

"You're a prisoner—"

"Go fuck yourself—"

"—of the *Kendrick*," Callum said, voice low. "Insolence isn't tolerated, and your punishment will be painful and swift." He stood straighter. "And I'd rather not administer it." Callum spoke with a steady gaze and voice. Maybe that's what frustrated Ash more than anything else. The other boy seemed so unbothered.

They were quiet for a long moment, watching each other. "You know," Ash finally said, "I think you might have to quit the redguards."

It was clearly bait, and Callum sighed as he took it. "And why would I have to do that?"

"Because this is the second time this morning that you've cared," Ash said with a mocking smile. "A proper redguard wouldn't give a shit."

Callum turned on his heel and kept walking. "Despite popular belief, redguards have an ability to care."

"Not sure Ramsay would agree," Ash said.

Callum spun around. The emotion that tore through his face rooted Ash to the spot.

Callum blinked. "It seems you have a gift for pushing buttons, too," he said. And with that, Callum turned on his heel. "Please walk faster. I'm already late."

19

McKinley College didn't only teach hand-to-hand combat drills. Callum opened the door to a classroom with five desks, two students sitting at each. Ash realized that Callum's simple red shirt, buttoned to his neck, and maroon trousers weren't a fashion choice but another uniform of the college. Ash was surprised to see that there were six other scribes standing along the wall, too, taking notes on the professor's lesson while the actual students whispered to each other with soft laughs.

The professor seemed to be a commander himself, judging by his uniform's badges. He was an older man with a bent back, which he turned to the students as he scrawled dates on the board. "Late today, Mr. Kendrick," the professor said. The whispers and laughter hushed as heads turned to look at Ash and Callum standing in the doorway.

"My apologies," Callum said with a charming smile. He strode into the room as if he owned it—and, well, maybe he did. "I had a delay."

Clearly, Ash was the delay. He followed Callum inside and stood against the wall as the other boy took a seat near the front of the room. It seemed word had spread that Callum's new scribe was the prisoner who had attacked Lancaster, judging by the cold stares Ash received.

This was confirmed by a lazy hand rising into the air. "Excuse me, professor," a girl with yellow hair said. "I don't feel comfortable with a dangerous alchemist in the room. Shouldn't he be jailed so that he won't distract us from our studies?"

Callum turned in his seat to look at the girl with a practiced smile. "Dangerous?" he repeated. "Mr. Woods is outnumbered by ten redguard trainees and a retired commander. We've learned multiple strategies in this very classroom—flanking, defensive maneuvers, attacks that constrict breathing. Don't you think we'd be able to subdue one alchemist?"

Ash's skin tightened with every word. He'd never been in a battle with a group of reds, and he preferred to keep it that way. For every person Ash had to fight, it'd take more imagination and alchemic power, spinning around in circles to keep his eyes on all his enemies, desperate to control his panic with less time to think and react before, as Callum suggested, someone slammed Ash in the gut or neck, making it hard for him to breathe. Ash was willing to bet that he would struggle against even just one trained redguard student, much less ten of them. Ash could've attempted another explosion, but he didn't want to risk so many lives again.

Callum continued, glancing around at the other students. "How can we claim to be protectors of the state, declare that unlicensed alchemists are our greatest threat—and then be unable to handle just one?"

It seemed for a moment that Callum had won the argument, but another boy toward the front of the room grinned. "Say what you like, Kendrick, but this single alchemist brought down half of Lancaster within seconds, from what I hear. He could destroy this classroom with all of us inside easily, no matter our training." The boy turned to the professor. "Which is why all unlicensed alchemists should be hanged, starting with this one."

Ash's hands clenched. It wasn't a pleasant feeling, listening to someone make a case for his death. He opened his mouth to speak, but Callum's gaze cut to his.

"Hanged?" Callum repeated, on the edge of laughter, though his eyes weren't amused. "Don't you think that's a little extreme?"

"I suppose you prefer giving a terrorist freedom as a scribe?" the boy sneered.

Callum shrugged. "It's what Lord Alexander requested," he

said. His words were met with silence, but he continued. "Do you disagree with Lord Alexander's ruling?" Still silence, but Callum seemed to be the sort of person who enjoyed soaking in his victory. "We're Kendrick redguards. We're sworn to uphold Lord Alexander's decrees. Maybe it isn't the best way start to our careers, publicly arguing with the Head of our state."

The other boy had nothing more to say. He cleared his throat and sat straighter, facing forward. The professor, who seemed used to debates, also turned back to his board unceremoniously. "The Battle of Westfields, between the Alexander and Lune families . . ."

Ash stood silently against the wall. Whispers began again, students turning to glare at him. Callum met his eye, and Ash hated that the Kendrick's gaze was somehow comforting.

※

Ash followed Callum to two more classes, one on battle strategy and another on leadership technique, both of which Ash fell asleep for even while standing on his feet. Lunch was served in a large dining hall, where servants and scribes alike stood along the walls, not allowed to touch the food. The roasted lamb chops and shepherd's pies smelled incredible, and Ash's stomach grumbled in complaint.

He stood a few feet behind Callum as he came to a table where he was greeted eagerly, one boy even getting up and offering Callum his seat. Ash snorted. It seemed that this was where the royalty of the military college sat—and that Callum, as the Kendrick son, was the king. Callum laughed easily and smiled graciously whenever someone leaned in to kiss his ass, and he gave just the right amount of a smirk when a girl suggested that they find time for a *study session* later that day (something Ash very strongly hoped he wouldn't have to join).

Ash watched Callum through his lashes. This version of Kendrick was the same boy from Ramsay's memories, too, as he sat with his friends in Pembroke, too afraid to openly talk to her. An amiable prince of Kensington, the severe son of Kendrick, the quiet boy who heals hands when no one else is looking . . . Callum had so many versions that Ash wasn't sure which was real.

When lunch ended, Ash followed Callum out into the courtyard. An older woman with a patch over her eye, referred to as Professor Rake, called for the trainees to begin their drills. Ash stood with the other scribes and watched as Callum partnered with a boy, the same who had argued with him in class—Edward, Ash had heard him called throughout the day.

"Begin," Rake shouted.

Edward hadn't fully waited for the word to leave Rake's mouth when he rushed forward, ready to knock Callum to the ground. Callum was tall, limbs long—but apparently he'd learned control of his body in the past few years. He stepped to the side swiftly, then again when Edward aimed a kick at his side.

Ash watched with little interest, then squinted and looked closer. Sky-blue light had begun to glow from Callum's skin. Ash blinked in surprise. Callum probably didn't know it, but he was using second-tier alchemy—ironic, seeing that most of House Kendrick believed that alchemy needed to be outlawed altogether. Callum was so focused, his mind so still, that energy radiated from his core—and it showed. He was only nineteen, but he fought with the grace of a trained master. A halo shined around Callum's head as he dodged Edward's attacks. Ash didn't want to admit it, but Callum was magnetizing. He couldn't look away.

Edward became more frustrated, yelling as he kicked and punched, then gave one final leap at Callum—

Ash had barely blinked when Callum's foot slammed into Edward's gut. Edward fell to his knees, gasping.

"Point—Kendrick," Rake called.

Callum sighed, running a hand over his hair, and it was then that Ash saw a glimpse of what might've been the real Callum. He wasn't pleased that he'd won. In fact, it seemed like Kendrick had no interest in fighting at all. He bent down, offering Edward a hand, but it was slapped away as Edward stood, face red with anger.

Callum waited at the side for his next partner. Ash had a feeling that he would win again and again—had no doubt that Callum was the best fighter there. Maybe that's what was expected of him. Ash wondered how Winslow Kendrick would feel, knowing that his son was practicing alchemy, whether he meant to or not.

                                        ✳

By evening, Ash was beyond exhausted and wanted nothing more than to fall into bed, any bed would do—but Callum's day didn't end with his classes. Ash followed Callum through the maze of brick streets, stopping when they reached a white town house. A butler opened the door, and Ash followed Callum down a golden hall and into a sitting room with garish design, bright green floral wallpaper clashing with the orange and red sofas and drapes.

Ash wavered on his feet against the wall where servants stood, noses in the air as they ignored him. There were only ten or so other people in the room. Callum sat on the other end with two others. A phonograph played soft crackling music. Whiskey was served. A couple laughed as they danced, clearly drunk. A boy lay sprawled across a sofa, smoking a drug Ash had never seen before. Haze filled the air. Every guest seemed so assured in their power, their wealth, their charm. Some leaned into one another, as if they would disappear to find a room at any moment. Ash didn't know which House hosted this gathering, and he didn't care. He wasn't in the mood to watch spoiled House heirs drink and fondle one another.

Ash dreamed of making it to a room where he could rest his eyes and feet and begin to plan his next steps. He wouldn't stay imprisoned until some House lord finally convinced Alexander to hang him. He needed to figure out how to escape Callum. He would get out of Kensington immediately—start his journey to House Lune, where he would find Ramsay—

"So, he has to follow you everywhere you go?"

Ash looked up. One of the guests had sauntered over to Ash, eyeing him. It was the same who had called him a dog earlier. Ash stilled as he realized that the boy was from Ramsay's memories, too. He'd been a student of Pembroke, another of her former friends—Gavin, Ash thought his name was. Gavin wasn't as tall as Callum, but he was close, and he had more muscle, too.

Callum's smile was tight. "Yes. A bit of a pain, if I'll be honest."

Ash glared. The feeling was more than mutual.

"Doesn't seem like much of a punishment," Gavin said, stopping in front of Ash. "For everything the alchemist's done, I mean."

Conversations had died down, heads turned. Callum stood from his seat also. Ash hated that he felt a jolt of relief. "It's the punishment Woods received from Lord Alexander himself."

But his earlier arguments didn't seem to affect Gavin. "We wouldn't be in contempt of Lord Alexander if we gave him a punishment of our own. I doubt anyone would make a fuss if the terrorist showed up with a bruised face and a broken bone or two."

Callum's legs were long, yes, but it was as if he'd crossed the room in only three strides. "I would prefer if you didn't," he said. He stood beside Ash and smiled down at Gavin. "It'd be bothersome to deal with his injuries. We'd have to call on House Adelaide, which has given enough resources to his health already."

"You almost sound like you're trying to protect him, Kendrick," Gavin said, eyeing Callum. The room was now silent as everyone watched.

"I'm fulfilling my duty."

"It wouldn't be the first time you sided with an alchemist."

Ash saw a flurry of emotion on Callum's face before he forced a smile. "I've never sided with an alchemist."

"No. Just had your fun with one."

"I don't know what you're implying—"

"Thorne," Gavin said. "You two were close in secondary, weren't you?"

Callum swallowed. Gavin knew his friend's weak point, and he wasn't afraid to exploit it.

"That was before her parents—" Callum started, then said instead, "That was before Snowdrop."

"There was a rumor going around that she'd snuck into your dorm."

"Thorne hadn't done anything wrong."

"She's wanted in the Lancaster attacks, too," Gavin said. "Seems she's no better than her parents after all."

"I ended my friendship with her, just as you did."

Ash gritted his teeth. Even now, Callum still lied, too afraid to admit that he'd continued their friendship in Pembroke—that he had not only had his fun with her as Gavin claimed but had *loved* her.

"I don't know, Callum," Gavin said, grin growing. "You were so reluctant to join us when we found ways to punish Ramsay before. Just like you're reluctant to beat the shit out of this alchemist now."

"It seems unnecessarily cruel," Callum said.

"You're the son of Kendrick," Gavin said, "and you're worried about *cruelty?*"

Callum seemed at a loss for words. He wouldn't look at Ash. Ash was afraid that this was it—Callum Kendrick would finally give in because it was clear that his reputation mattered more than anything else. He would be willing to watch Gavin beat Ash to death if it meant his name and standing wouldn't be questioned. Hell, maybe Callum would even throw the first punch.

Luckily for Ash, the host lazing on the couch, blowing out a haze of smoke, spoke. "Lay off them, Gavin. Isn't there something more interesting you can do?"

Gavin glared at the boy, but he only laughed and sat up to offer the rolled-up drug to Callum, who put up a hand with a tight smile.

"No, thank you," he said. Maybe it was the battle-strategy

classes that helped him see he needed to retreat. "It's late. I should get going."

Ash and Callum were silent as they left, stepping out into the purple evening, the sun setting earlier in the winter months. The buildings of Kensington had yellow lights that glowed against the white walls. "It seems that being your prison guard also means being your bodyguard," Callum said after a moment.

Ash's anger at Callum's lies and his lingering fear mingled as they walked. His heart still pounded. He glared at the ground. "Why did you help me?"

"Did you not want me to? I could take you back if you like."

Ash shook his head. "Did you volunteer to guard me because of my relationship with Ramsay?" He took Callum's silence to mean yes. "Why did you end things with her?"

Callum swallowed. "It isn't easy to openly associate with alchemists in this society."

"But *you* studied alchemy, too," Ash snapped. "In secret, at Pembroke—you let Ramsay teach you alchemy, right?"

Callum stopped, frozen.

"You can't use alchemy as an excuse for hurting her when you practiced alchemy, too."

Callum glanced around, as if to ensure no one else was near, then lowered his voice. "Did Ramsay tell you that?"

Ash let out a frustrated sigh and kept walking. "Source, your entire life is an act."

But Callum took two long strides to catch up with Ash, stopping in front of him. "You have no idea what it takes to survive my world. It's nice, I suppose, to live however you want, but I have a responsibility to my House and family—"

"However I want?" Ash repeated. "You have no idea what my life is like—"

"And you know mine so well?"

"I know you're living in luxury while your family forces people like me to live under your damn feet, so don't—"

"I think you're forgetting your position," Callum said, voice growing louder. "I am your guard, and I'm much kinder than another that might've been assigned to you."

"Oh, yes, you didn't let your friend *murder* me, congratu-fucking-lations!"

Callum worked his jaw back and forth, speechless. Ash was proud to have finally shut him up. They stood in silence for one long moment. It was only then that it occurred to Ash that he and his guard were arguing in the middle of a Kensington street.

"I'm trying to help you, in case you haven't noticed," Callum said, voice softening as if he'd realized the same.

"If you really wanted to help me, you would let me leave."

"Are you trying to be funny?"

"No, I'm not."

Callum paused. "I can't do that."

"Let me guess—because of your *responsibility*, right?"

"I could've left you to one of my brothers. You would've been found dead by now if I'd done that."

"Maybe you should have. Would've been a mercy, not to deal with your bullshit."

Callum stared blankly at Ash. "I can't imagine how you and Ramsay ever managed to work together. I'd assume she'd sooner kill you."

Ash didn't like Callum speaking about Ramsay like he still knew her. He didn't think Callum had the right. "Do yourself a favor and stop imagining, then."

Callum nodded slowly, as if it was truly sinking in how difficult it would be, guarding a boy like Ash Woods. "I thought I would try to help you," he said, "even as you disrespected me again and again."

Ash looked away with a small laugh.

"But don't mistake my kindness to mean I'm someone you can treat however you like," Callum said. "I am, after all, still a Kendrick."

"Yes," Ash said, anger pulsing. "I know. That's the problem, right? That's the reason you're lying to the entire world—"

"I'm not *lying* about anything—"

"What's worse, you don't even realize you're lying to yourself." Callum's gaze narrowed, but he didn't speak.

"You have a shit ton of versions of you," Ash said. "Do you even know which *you* is real? Do you fancy yourself to be the good guy, Callum?" He kept speaking, even as Callum finally turned away from him and started walking. "Do you think you're a hero, volunteering to guard me?" Ash called after him. "You're not. The truth is that you're too scared to do the right thing. You're too scared to go against your family—your House—"

Callum swung back around, anger glistening in his eyes, but Ash kept going. "So you just cower and do as you're told and tell yourself that at least you're not as bad as the rest of them. Well," Ash said, with the biggest smile he could muster, "fuck you."

It seemed the Kendrick boy was so infuriated he was trembling, even as he managed to keep his expression wiped clean. "Do you think my life is easy? It's not."

"I don't give a shit," Ash said.

"Don't you think I wish I were like my brothers? Able to just follow orders."

"Just let me go," Ash said. "That's all you have to do."

"No," Callum told him. His voice sounded pained. "I'm sorry, but I can't."

Callum continued walking. For a moment, Ash debated following him—but if he ran now, he'd only be caught. It didn't matter, he decided as he fell into step behind his guard. He would escape the Kendrick town house that night.

20

Ash was deposited in his bedroom by Callum without another word. The moment the door closed and locked behind him, Ash fell into the bed. He would need the sleep, since he'd likely be awake for the rest of the night.

He woke up groggily when the door opened again and a tray of soup with bits of vegetables slid onto the floor. He assumed that these were the leftovers from the Kendrick family's dinner, which meant that it was probably about seven at night. After he ate, he sat and closed his eyes. Ash never would've been able to count the passing time so easily before Ramsay, but the patience she'd taught him was useful now. He breathed, counted, forced his mind back to the task at hand again and again—and the moment it was what he hoped was midnight, and Ash knew he'd have a better chance of escaping the town house and Kensington altogether, he opened his eyes.

Ash went to the door and pressed his hand onto the knob. He sensed the inner workings of the lock's grooves, then shook out his hands and took a deep breath. The fact that he'd been meditating already for hours meant he had an even closer connection to Source, so it was easy to force a flare of energy into the grooves, unlocking the door with a click.

He pushed open the door slowly, sticking out his head. The reds hadn't bothered to put a full-time guard outside his room. It amused him that they thought a lock would be enough to keep him imprisoned. He closed the door again, slipping through the hall and halfway down the stairs. He heard voices and paused. On the floor below, a woman swept past with a servant following closely behind. "Find out how many guests were invited to Eleanor Adelaide's gala last season—I want ours to have at least twice the amount . . ."

Ash waited until the voices faded, then hurried down the remaining steps, across another hall, and to the last staircase. A servant was just turning the corridor when he made it to the entryway—no, of course it couldn't be so easy to just *escape*, but Ash threw open the door and raced out into the streets anyway. There was a shout behind him, yells that followed. He sprinted around corners and clambered over walls and stole through alleyways, and even when he couldn't hear the shouts anymore, Ash didn't stop running. He wasn't even sure *where* he was going until he reached the edges of Wynnesgrove. The smoke had cleared, at least, but Ash thought that he could still smell the burnt college in the distance. There was a stitch in his side, and his knees were weak. He was just beginning to slow down when he heard the sirens in the distance. He wondered if Hain would be able to argue for his life a second time.

Anyone he passed walked quickly, heads bowed. Ash ran, slowed to a jog with a hand pressed into his side, walked as quickly as he could, then forced himself to run again until he finally reached the iron bridge. His heart flooded with relief. Now that he was in Hedge, he could finally *breathe*.

He'd need supplies for the trip. A coat, at the very least, to brave the wilderness and mountain trails before he reached House Lune. He wouldn't bother going to his apartment. It was probably boarded up by now, and it'd be the first place the reds came knocking. But he had one other place he could turn to.

Tobin lived in a wooden apartment complex several blocks away, rooms stacked on top of one another, sometimes shared by dozens of people who had nowhere else to go. Ash climbed the stairs where laundry was hanging from lines and made it to Tobin's door. He knocked, fast and hard, and wouldn't stop until the door flew open.

Tobin stared down at Ash as if he'd come back from the dead. "Ash?" he said. "What're you doing here? What the hell happened?"

Ash took a step forward to go inside. "I'll tell you about it—"

But Tobin put out an arm, stopping Ash from entering.

Ash paused in surprise, then looked up to meet Tobin's eyes. Ash had misread his best friend's expression. The shock held some disgust. He took a step back.

"You attacked people, Ash?" Tobin said. "Burned down the college?"

"I—no, I didn't—"

"Do you know what people are saying about you?" Tobin asked. "They're saying you're like the Thornes. You attempted another mass murder for alchemy."

"Source, Tobin, that's not true at all." But Tobin still didn't move his arm. Ash shook his head. "You'll believe gossip you heard in the streets over me?"

"You've been pulled in so deep by alchemy, you can't even see how it's changed you."

"And you've been pulled in so much by fear that you can't see how you've been manipulated to hate."

Tobin shrugged, stare cold. "I don't see that as a bad thing. Hating alchemists who want to kill a bunch of innocent people? Seems like the right side to be on, in my book."

"I'm not like that, Tobin. And the way you're talking, you sound like the Lune followers who'd be just as willing to kill innocent people, too. As long as they're just alchemists, right?"

Tobin gripped his hand against the door's threshold. "I'm not going to report you," he said. "That's the one thing I'll do for you, all right? One last thing I can do, in memory of our friendship."

Ash swallowed. He could feel his anger breaking down into heartache, but he refused to cry in front of Tobin.

"But you need to get the hell out of here," Tobin said, "because

if a red catches you and strings you up, I'm telling you now, Ash—
I'm not doing anything to help you."

※

Ash didn't know where to go. He walked through Hedge until
he reached the docks. There was a glow of light in the distance,
turning the sky gray. Dockworkers would start arriving within
the hour. Something in him screamed to forget Tobin, to get out
of there, to leave while he still had the chance. He could gather
supplies on his way to House Lune. But this betrayal had rocked
through Ash. He'd never felt more alone than he had in that moment.

He sat on the concrete edge, feet dangling over the gray water.
He looked up only when he heard footsteps. He didn't have the
will to fight, and was glad when Callum didn't seem set on fighting him, either.

"How did you find me?" Ash asked as the other boy stopped
beside him.

"Reds questioned a few people. Someone saw you walking toward the dock. I said I'd come alone."

"Are you going to have me executed?"

"It'd be a lot easier than arguing for a life you seem hell-bent on
throwing away," Callum said.

Ash looked back at the ocean. "Are you in trouble for letting
me escape?"

Callum sighed. "Yes. My father—well, it doesn't matter, and I
don't think you really care, anyway."

"You're right. I don't."

"Then why ask?"

Ash shrugged. Maybe he'd cared more than he let on. He was
surprised when Callum sat down beside him, allowing his boots
to dangle over the water's edge, too.

"Why did you run away?" Callum asked.

Ash played with his hands, staring at the old scar on his palm. "I wanted to find Ramsay."

"Redguards across the state are searching for her now," Callum said. "What makes you think you can find her, when hundreds of others haven't?"

Ash knew where she was going, but he wouldn't admit to that. "Everyone thinks that she's evil—that I am, too, just because I'm an alchemist."

"There are a lot of assumptions about alchemists in Kensington."

"Is that why you hide that you learned alchemy, too?"

Callum clenched his jaw. "I ask that you keep that to yourself."

"There's a lot that you want to hide, isn't there?"

"I don't have to explain myself to you."

"You're a coward."

"Surviving isn't cowardly," Callum said. "And I don't know what Ramsay told you, but you don't know me well enough to judge me. You don't know anything about me."

"I know that you abandoned Ramsay."

Callum's mouth snapped shut.

"I know that, when she needed friendship the most, you hid her away like you were ashamed of her—that you wouldn't admit, and still won't admit, that you loved her."

Callum stood and took several long steps away from Ash, his back turned. He took deep, slow breaths. Ash watched him, unimpressed with Callum's display of emotion. If he really cared so much, then he wouldn't have been able to hurt Ramsay again and again.

Callum finally spoke. "I've been thinking about what you said."

"You're going to need to be more specific."

"About thinking I'm the hero, I mean," Callum said softly. "And you're right. I want to believe I'm a good person, but . . ."

Ash waited.

"What do you think it takes to change?" Callum asked him.

"I'm not in the mood for a philosophical debate."

"I think about changing," Callum admitted. "All of the time. I think about how different I'd like my life to be—the sorts of things I would do or say to become the person I want to be instead."

"Okay. So?"

"I've realized that thinking and daydreaming aren't enough," Callum said quietly. "It's action that matters." He paused. "You said you wanted to know why I volunteered to be your guard."

Ash narrowed his eyes. This was the most honest Kendrick had been with him since they'd met.

"Truthfully, I don't know why," Callum said. "Maybe a part of me wanted to feel closer to Ramsay again. I wanted to feel like if I helped you, then I was somehow making up for how I treated her. Fuck."

"Shit, Kendrick. Didn't think you knew how to curse."

Callum turned to look at him again. "I suspect that you know Ramsay's true location," he said. "My father suspects the same."

"And?" Ash said, though his heart started to hammer. Hain wasn't in the town house with them, watching the redguards' every move. He wouldn't be able to stop the Kendricks from torturing the truth out of Ash.

"And—Creator, I . . . I wondered, maybe, if we could work together to find her."

Ash froze. He stared at Callum, his brain catching up with what the other boy had said. "Work together?"

"We could help her."

Ash didn't trust a word that was coming out of his mouth. "Is this your plan to get me to admit where Ramsay is so that you can arrest her and deliver her to your father? You need a better plan, one that isn't so obvious—"

"No!" Callum shouted. Ash jumped at the outburst. "No," he said again. "I know I've made mistakes with Ramsay, but I can't—I won't betray her. Not again."

"I don't believe you," Ash said. "You love your life too much. You wouldn't give it up for her."

Callum outright laughed. "You think I *love* my life?"

"You talk about it enough," Ash said. "Talk about your *responsibility* to your House—"

"Can't two things be true at once?" Callum said. "I've learned how to survive. I play by the rules. And I hate every second of it."

Ash watched Callum as he took a breath.

"You were right. I've been afraid—*terrified*. But I think . . . maybe I could find the courage to change."

"If you help me find Ramsay," Ash said slowly, "you'd be giving up everything. You could be arrested for helping a fugitive alchemist."

At his words, Callum practically began to wither. Ash was certain he would change his mind. Callum swallowed, not meeting Ash's eye as he stared at the sea slapping against the dock. "I've been weighing my happiness for the past few days, since Ramsay escaped Lancaster," he said. "I've imagined myself with the life I have now, staying on the expected course. Ramsay would be captured and executed, and I'd try to ignore the pain I would feel at her death. I would graduate from McKinley and become a commander, leading a unit of the Kendrick redguards. I would marry whoever provides a strong alliance to House Kendrick, most likely Charlotte Adelaide. I'd have children, and I would act as my father did, beating them into submission to ensure they understand their purpose as the heirs of Kendrick. And all along, for the next several decades of my life, I would try to forget Ramsay and ignore the heartbreak and shame I feel when I think about the fact that I stood by as she died."

Ash watched Callum closely. "Or?"

Callum seemed to waver. "Or I could live the life I've always wanted to." He met Ash's eye. "I could do everything that terrifies and thrills me. I could escape Kensington, help Ramsay—and we could leave the state together, maybe, if she'll have me. We could find peace. I don't even know what that life would look like, but maybe that's where freedom lies—not knowing what will happen. Just following happiness."

Ash blinked, gaze falling. This was a similar dream Ash had started to have as he lay tangled in Ramsay's bedsheets, kissing her and thinking that he wouldn't mind if this was what the rest of his life looked like. Ash didn't want to believe Callum, didn't want to trust him—but energy didn't lie, and this entirely too-tall Kendrick boy was more softhearted than he ever wanted to let on. He was still in love with Ramsay.

"I think I've made my choice, honestly," Callum whispered. "Even though it scares me to admit, I would rather die than stand by at Ramsay's execution. I already know that I'll try to save her when they sling the rope around her neck. I'll be punished, and she'll be killed anyway. I would rather take a risk and change now, before that happens. And so you have a choice now, too," he told Ash. "Either I let you go, and you escape and become a fugitive of the state—inevitably captured, maybe executed . . . or you stay. You act as my prisoner, you play by the rules, and we work together and do things my way. It might take longer," Callum said, "but we can help each other. We can find Ramsay together. It's your choice, Woods. It's up to you."

Ash pressed his mouth together, turning back to the ocean. The sun was rising higher now. Any moment, the sky would turn red and dockworkers would appear, maybe Tobin with them. If Ash was going to escape Callum and the state, his moment would be now. But he also knew Callum was right. Ash wouldn't make it far on his own.

He nodded. "Okay. We'll work together."

21

The walk back to the town house seemed longer somehow. The awaiting redguards ran to Callum and Ash the moment they were spotted—it seemed they were ready to fling Ash to the ground—but Callum held up a hand. "It's all right," he said, but before he could get out another word, Winslow Kendrick stepped out of the town house's front doors. The reds surrounding them stood straight, holding a fist over their hearts. It seemed Kendrick was already on his way out. He yanked on black gloves, barely sparing his son a glance.

"He's agreed to comply," Callum said. He stood straighter, too, but Ash could hear that his breath had quickened.

His father stalked closer, but Ash realized he was only heading for the waiting carriage. He treated Ash's capture like a quick chat over morning tea. "How are you sure he isn't lying?"

"Because I promised he'd have a front-row seat to Ramsay Thorne's execution if he tried again."

Ash flinched. It scared him a little, that Callum knew exactly what he'd use against Ash to crush him.

"And what will his punishment be now?"

The question seemed like a test. Callum's shoulders were stiff. "No meals for one day," he said.

Winslow's gaze narrowed. He finally looked at his son. "The boy ran away. That demands twenty lashes, at the very least."

"Normally, I would agree," Callum said. "But given that Woods is protected under Hain and Lord Alexander, I thought—"

Winslow turned on his heel and slammed a fist into Ash's gut.

Ash gasped, breath torn from his throat, and landed on his knees. "Then hit him where the bruises can't be seen," Winslow said. Ash's hands shook with the effort to stay down. He'd agreed to play by the rules. "Take care of it."

The redguards saluted Winslow again as he continued to the carriage. The guards glanced at Callum and Ash, but moved on to their own duties, too. They were alone. Callum stood over Ash, staring around to see if anyone was still watching.

"Are you all right?" he asked beneath his breath. The concern in his voice sounded genuine, at least.

Ash struggled to his feet, ache spreading. The man had known exactly where to hit to cause the most pain. "Your dad's a fucking asshole. You know that, right?"

Callum's clenched jaw was his only response.

As they walked the empty corridors, Ash asked, "You won't really whip me, will you?"

"No—Creator, of course not. But . . . if you could do me a favor, and act like you're in pain for the next few days—limping and wincing whenever you move . . ."

If it meant getting out of a beating, Ash was more than happy to oblige.

※

Three days passed. Ash tried to force himself to get used to his new routine, but by the third night, he knew he would never adjust to a life among the Houses. It was ironic that, once, he'd so badly wanted to prove that he was worth their respect—and maybe a part of him still wanted their validation. But he could see more easily now how impossible that would be, when the House members looked down on one another so much already. In the dining hall of McKinley, Ash overheard students plotting to frame another for cheating on a test to have them expelled, just because they had accidentally bumped into each other in the hall. At a luncheon Callum had to attend, Ash listened to a member of

House Galahad whisper that his greatest joy in life was destroying the careers of his enemies with salacious rumors, to which Callum only smiled. The catty, political gossip hidden behind polite laughter, everywhere he followed Callum, was more than Ash could take.

"How do you put up with this fake bullshit?" he muttered to Callum one evening as he sat on a plush sofa. Callum had asked Ash to come to his chambers. The room with dark red wallpaper and mahogany floors was an entire suite with its own sitting room, a bed on a platform and a balcony facing the city.

"By joining rather than fighting," Callum said. He walked up to a mirror and peered at it as he unfastened his collar. "There's no winning against it."

"Why am I not surprised?" Ash said.

"You'd probably do the same if you were raised as I was."

Callum flopped onto the sofa beside Ash, stretching and yawning, his shirt unbuttoned enough that Ash knew he'd be considered scandalous by most members of his high society. Callum had told Ash to have patience these last few days, and Ash had tried his best, following Callum up and down as the other boy promised he would listen out for new updates and information on Ramsay. Finally, today, Callum made a grand performance of ordering Ash up to his room to help him write an essay for class, and Ash bit down on the excitement that he was sure Callum had learned something new.

"Well?" Ash said. "What did you find out?"

Callum sat up straighter, rubbing his face. "Ramsay was last seen in Kensington Station." Ash bit his lip. She'd probably made it out of the city, then. "But we've lost track of her since. And you're sure that you don't know where she's headed?"

Maybe Ash shouldn't be so harsh with Callum for his fakeness. He'd decided not to tell Callum about House Lune or the Book of Source. He trusted Callum enough to know that the other boy wanted to help Ramsay, but Ash still wasn't convinced that Callum's methods wouldn't hurt Ash, other alchemists, and maybe even ultimately Ramsay in the process.

Ash shook his head. "No. Like I said, we'd decided to leave the city, but we didn't agree on which route to take yet."

"That seems odd for Ramsay, is all. She was never the type to leave things up to fate."

Ash's breath always became a bit tighter whenever Callum referred to how well he'd known Ramsay. He swallowed. "Was she always so—ah—rigid?"

Callum laughed. "That's certainly a word for it, yes. She had a set way of working, and anything outside of that was unacceptable."

"And punishable by death," Ash said, grin growing. "If I was ever late for a meeting, she'd threaten to murder me."

Callum's laugh faded. "Creator, she hated it whenever I was late."

"But, no matter how *rigid* she is, every room she walks into becomes a disaster."

Callum threw his head back with another laugh. "I pointed that out to her, once."

"And you're still breathing without assistance?"

"She told me that messiness was a mark of genius because it showed she wasn't tethered to this physical reality."

"What bullshit."

Callum's smile softened as he watched Ash. It seemed there was something he wanted to say, even if he wasn't sure how to say it. "You must've spent a lot of time with her, for her to be angry that you were late, and for you to know what her rooms look like."

Ash swallowed. The energy coming from Callum was muddled. It wasn't jealousy, not completely—a longing, maybe, more melancholy. "We did end up spending a lot of time together," Ash admitted.

"Did you feel—" Callum paused and cleared his throat. "I understand if it isn't any of my business, but I heard that you'd been romantically involved, and—"

"Yes. I love her."

"*Love*, not *loved?*" Callum asked. "Even when she betrayed you?"

"You still love her, don't you?"

Callum nodded. "Yes."

The silence grew between them, and Ash wasn't sure he could deal with this tension for however long he'd have to be around Callum. Ash sighed, arms crossed. It was better to tackle the issue head-on rather than wander their way around it.

"How did you fall in love with her?" he asked. He'd seen the memories of them in the gardens, in Callum's rooms, but he'd never seen their past from Callum's perspective.

"We hated each other at first," Callum said.

"Ramsay said she didn't like you, but *hatred* seems to be another level."

"It was because of the House alliances, built by views on alchemy."

Ash was sure he would regret his next question. "How so?"

"The Val and Thorne families have a political alliance against the Great Houses," Callum said. "House Kendrick's strongest relationship is with House Alexander—we've always served as the seconds-in-command, though House Lune hopes to replace us. The Adelaide family is caught in the middle of the two sides. Healers have used alchemy almost as long as the Val family has studied it, but even the Adelaide can be conservative at times. They speak of alchemy as a gift from the Creator and believe that alchemy shouldn't be used freely. My family's official position agrees."

Ash had been right. "So, because your family believes that alchemy is evil, you hated Ramsay when you first met her."

Callum didn't seem to notice Ash's hardened voice. "Yes—and she hated me even more. But we were only twelve when we met at Pembroke. We were acting as we'd been trained to by our parents. It took about a year for me to realize that I enjoyed her company. She was quick-witted and surprisingly funny, and her passion for learning anything and everything drew me to her." Callum's gaze had warmed as he spoke. "I'm not sure why she decided I was worth spending time with, but we became friends."

Ash knew why. He remembered Ramsay's surprise at Callum's softness, the kindness she could see he tried to hide, the sympathy she felt for him as she realized he was caught in a lie, trapped by the responsibility of his family's name. She hadn't realized that this lie would be the same that undid their relationship.

Ash looked away. It was strange, knowing so much about the boy. "How could you turn out so differently from the rest of your family?" he asked.

"Ramsay," Callum said. "It's thanks to her. She wasn't supposed to—Creator, we both would've been expelled if we were caught—but she showed me how beautiful alchemy could be. She changed me."

"Did she teach you how to heal also?"

If Ramsay had been in the room, Ash was certain she would've given him a murderous glare. He would've liked to give himself one, in fact. Callum almost answered automatically, but then he paused and frowned, looking at Ash again. "How did you know I'd learned healing?"

Ash stared at the hands he played with in his lap. "Ramsay told me."

"She must've told you a lot about me."

"You could say that."

"Why do I have the feeling that you're lying to me, Ash?"

Ash felt a flicker of pleasure that however he felt about Callum Kendrick, the moment he'd told the other boy that he wanted to be called Ash, not Ashen, he'd immediately listened. Ash sighed, shifting in his seat. "I wouldn't say I'm *lying*, exactly." Just omitting the truth.

"Just omitting the truth?"

Ash's gaze flicked up to meet Callum's. "Are you sure you don't still practice alchemy?" he asked.

Every average human being could pick up on the energy of others, sense emotions or know when another person was lying, perhaps—but it wasn't common for a person to repeat someone else's thought word for word.

"I think I would know if I did," Callum told him.

"But you just said exactly what I thought."

Callum shrugged. "That isn't alchemy, is it? I've done that since I was a kid, though I try not to. Other people find it annoying when I finish their sentences."

"Does the thought appear in your mind, almost like it's your own?"

Callum frowned. "Sometimes. But like I said, I'm not practicing alchemy. That's just how I am."

Ash knew that Callum believed he was telling the truth. Sometimes there were naturally talented people like Callum whose energy allowed them to practice second-tier alchemy without needing study. Callum must've been able to feel the energy of others so strongly that he could even translate those emotions into thoughts. Source, the boy was a natural mind reader, and he didn't even know it.

"Why did you stop practicing?" Ash asked him.

"I ended my studies when I stopped seeing Ramsay. Practicing on my own wasn't as rewarding, and—well, it only made me miss her more."

Ash rubbed his brow. "You'd do well as a trained alchemist," he admitted. Especially healing. Healers needed to be able to feel others' emotions, since physical pains and even injuries and diseases were a manifestation of emotional energy. To heal the physical, the emotional energy needed to be healed first.

"Which truth are you omitting?" Callum asked. His gaze was gentle, but the small crease between his eyes was a clear sign that he wouldn't let the topic go.

Ash pushed his tongue into the side of his cheek as he tried to find a good way to put this—but, well, there wasn't much of a good way, was there? "Ramsay showed me a shit ton of her memories, and you starred in most of them."

Whatever Callum was expecting to hear, it certainly wasn't that. He sat back in surprise, head tilted in confusion. "What?"

"We were—uh—practicing, I guess, a form of alchemy, and the side effect was seeing each other's memories, so—"

"Which memories did you see?" Callum demanded with a frown. Ash could see that he felt violated, and honestly, Ash would've felt the same.

Ash bit his lip. "Only a few. I could name them."

"Please do."

"The time you followed Ramsay into the garden in Pembroke, after her parents were executed and you healed her hand."

Callum's eyes filled with pain. "What else?"

"The—um—well, the time you brought her to your dorm room." He added quickly, "Nothing happened. Except—well, kissing—"

Callum buried his face in his hand. "Creator. What else did you see?"

Ash hesitated longer this time, long enough that Callum looked up. "I saw when you told Ramsay that you didn't want to have a relationship with her anymore. That it was too risky, and you needed to choose your family over her."

At this, Callum's expression dropped completely. He swallowed thickly, looking away from Ash. The silence stretched on, and Ash realized the other boy was struggling to force down emotion. Ash never would've thought he'd live to see a Kendrick cry, but it seemed that Callum was, after all, very different.

"That was the hardest day of my life," Callum managed to say.

"I'm guessing it was harder for Ramsay."

"I know that it's easy for you to judge me from where you sit," Callum said. "But you have no idea what sort of responsibility I face."

"You're willing to throw that responsibility to the side for her now, aren't you?"

Callum hesitated for a second before he nodded, jaw clenched. "Yes. Because I've come to regret what I did more than anything else, and I know I'll never be happy anyway, and—"

"So it's just your happiness you care about," Ash said. "Your desire for happiness made you treat Ramsay like shit."

The Kendrick boy's eyes shined as he stared at Ash. A flurry of anger seemed to rip through him. But in the end, he only looked at the hands he had clenched in his lap. "You're right," he said.

Ash raised his brows. "I am?"

"There's no excuse for it. I never should've treated her the way that I did," Callum said, "when she was and still is the most important person in my life."

It hurt Ash to hear how much Callum cared for Ramsay, though he wasn't sure why. Maybe because Callum showed Ash he would never know Ramsay as well as Callum did; maybe because Callum reminded Ash of the love he had for her and had also lost.

Callum watched closely, as if he'd felt Ash's emotions. Shame stabbed Ash, but Callum only smiled. "I don't mind that you love her, too," Callum said. "I'm glad you do, in fact. Ramsay's faced so much hatred for what her parents did. She deserves more love."

Well, now, Ash just felt bad for feeling jealous. He let out a small self-conscious laugh, rubbing his neck. "Right. Yeah."

"I—well, it might not be any of my business, and I understand if you'd rather not answer me, but—"

"Just ask the question, Kendrick."

"I'd like it if you called me Callum instead," he said.

Ash hesitated, then nodded. "Okay. Callum."

"I think you know more than you're letting on—and that's okay," he added quickly. "I hope you'll trust me enough to tell me the truth eventually. But if you're hiding something that Ramsay might do to hurt herself or—or others . . ."

Ash frowned. "Do you think Ramsay would hurt other people?"

"The Ramsay I know would never hurt anyone," Callum said.

"But I also haven't seen her in two years, and there's one thing I've learned from being a guard of House Kendrick: If you treat a person like they are a criminal long enough, eventually, they might start to feel like they have no choice but to be exactly that."

"You do think she could hurt other people, then."

"Do you?"

Ash wanted to say no with all his certainty—but he also knew that Ramsay was desperate for the Book, and she'd wanted to kill Marlowe, too. Even if she'd convinced herself that it was for the good of everyone, would she be willing to hurt or even kill to get to the Book first, before someone like Hain did? And there was the lingering fear, too—the fear that his father was right, and Ramsay had only planned to find the Book of Source so that she could take revenge against the Houses.

"Maybe it doesn't matter," Callum said. "We both know what we want. To find Ramsay—to save her. I know who Ramsay really is at her core. I know that she can remember, too, even if it's with our help."

It was getting late. Ash expected Callum to dismiss him and was surprised when instead the Kendrick boy asked if he would like to stay awhile.

"You want me to stay?" Ash asked. "Really?"

Callum shrugged. "Why not? I enjoy your company."

Source, Ash wanted to hate Callum. He *should* hate a son of the redguard family, shouldn't he? But maybe this was how Ramsay had felt, too, in her early days of Pembroke. Maybe she'd also begun to see that, no matter how much she wanted to, she couldn't force herself to hate Callum Kendrick.

It took Ash several long moments to say what he would next, even as his mind had already decided it was the right thing to do. "I know where Ramsay is going," he said.

22

Ash decided to attempt another remote viewing. He'd told Callum that Ramsay was going to House Lune—well, he'd written it down and quickly thrown the paper into the fireplace, he was more paranoid than ever that Marlowe or another alchemist was watching his every move—but Callum still wasn't convinced that this was enough information to begin their journey.

"We still don't know how she decided to travel to—"

"Don't say it, not out loud," Ash said.

"Right. Sorry." He rubbed the back of his neck. Ash could tell that Callum still didn't fully believe that the Book even existed. When Callum read Ash's quick note about the Book and House Lune, he'd frowned. "Is this a joke?" he asked. And when Ash shook his head, Callum said, "But it isn't real. It's just a myth."

Ash was glad Callum had thought so. What would House Kendrick do if they learned the Book of Source existed? "It doesn't matter if it's real or not, does it?" Ash had asked him. "This is where Ramsay is going, so that's where we need to go, too."

Ash was relieved that Callum hadn't been angry with him for keeping the secret for so long. If anything, Callum seemed grateful that Ash trusted him enough to tell him the truth. He only hoped he wouldn't regret telling Callum.

The older boy took a breath. "So the two of you had no plan on how you would travel to—well, you know . . . If she took the train from Kensington Station, she could've gone to three locations: Ironbound, Riverside, or Glassport in the Westfields."

"It's like I said, we'd planned on traveling to Riverside."

"She would've known you'd be captured and interrogated,

Ash. And besides, when she arrived at the station, the timetables for that day only had one train leaving for Riverside an hour later. She could've hidden for that hour, yes," Callum said before Ash could interrupt, "but there was a train leaving for Glassport fifteen minutes later, and a train to Ironbound she could've jumped on just as it was leaving the station. Those are three separate directions." And there was still the chance, of course, that Ramsay hadn't even left Kensington at all—that she was still hiding somewhere in the city. "We need more information."

Ash had groaned in frustration, but he knew Callum was right. If Ramsay had gone to the city of Ironbound, in the opposite direction of Lune in her desperation to escape, then it'd take her weeks to cross the mountains and arrive in the Elder lands—but Ash couldn't imagine that she'd ever willingly get on a train that'd take her closer to the Derry Hills. There were little isolated villages in the mountain ranges, Snowdrop being one of them.

Riverside was the closest city to House Lune, but it would still take her at least a week of walking along the river that cut through the villages and farmland, as long as there were no delays. The Westfield's forests wouldn't make the journey easy, either.

If Ash could manage to successfully remote view and get a sense of Ramsay's location, then he could at least tell Callum where they should go to find her. But there was another reason Ash knew Callum hesitated: The other boy was still afraid. No matter how much he wanted to help Ramsay—how much he wanted to *change*—his fear made him freeze. Ash couldn't afford to lose time, and if he successfully remote viewed, Ramsay's location would be too much for Kendrick's many excuses.

Callum asked to watch. "I'm curious," he said, but he looked so much like a child who'd been caught stealing cookies that Ash had to bite back a laugh.

"It's okay to look at alchemy," Ash said. "You aren't doing anything wrong."

Callum played with the end of his shirt. "It's a little difficult to make myself fully believe that, when I was taught my entire life that alchemy is evil."

Ash was impressed by Callum's self-awareness. "Well, maybe I can help you see that alchemy isn't a sin."

Callum blushed. "I'd like that."

The Kendrick boy sat in his bedroom's lounge, upright on the sofa like an overexcited schoolboy. Ash had gotten used to sitting on the floor when practicing alchemy, thanks to Ramsay. He closed his eyes and breathed.

He tried to sense Ramsay's energy. He imagined her purple hues, untouchable yet warm—envisioned her dark eyes and long lashes, remembered what her fingers had felt like against his skin. But there was a pinch of pain. He flinched, then sighed in frustration.

"It's no use," he said, opening his eyes.

Ash was surprised to see Callum gazing at him intently, as if studying him. He blinked when caught and looked away, embarrassed. "Why didn't it work?"

"I don't know," Ash murmured, feeling awkward now, too, though he wasn't sure why. He scratched a cheek. "I'm following all the steps, but this is tier-five alchemy. I just don't have enough alchemic power." Whenever Ash had an explosion of alchemic power in the past, tapping into chaos, it'd always been because of a buildup of emotion, usually rage. Ash wasn't sure if anger would be the trigger to give him the energy he needed now.

Callum leaned forward, elbows on his knees. "Well, if alchemic power is the problem," he said, "I have some that you could borrow."

Ash snorted. "You want to lend me energy?"

Callum gave a shrug. "Why not?"

Ash frowned now, seeing that the Kendrick boy was serious. "I'm not sure it would work."

"We could at least try."

"It'd leave you feeling drained."

"If it's for the sake of finding Ramsay, I don't mind."

Ash bit his lip. He hated to accept help like this from a Kendrick—it was almost humiliating, for an alchemist to depend on alchemic power from a redguard—but Callum was right. This was for Ramsay. "Do you know what to do?"

"No, but you can show me."

Ash stood carefully, as if afraid Callum would change his mind if he made any sudden moves. He took a few steps and stopped in front of the other boy. Ash knelt and took Callum's hand, ignoring Callum when he startled, his skin burning hot. Maybe it was the energy that constantly radiated from his body. Ash felt Callum's pulse nervously skip. Callum was surprisingly self-conscious, too, it seemed—yet another trait he'd hidden well from the world.

"You have to put your left hand over your chest, like this," Ash said, demonstrating with his own. "Then close your eyes and focus on the sensation of energy. For an alchemist, it's easy to know what our energy feels like since we've had so much practice, but you—"

"I can sense my own energy," Callum said shortly.

Ash raised a brow. "Then focus on pushing it through your right hand." He pressed Callum's palm against his own collarbone. Warmth spread from Callum's fingers and into Ash's skin. "As I'm using alchemic power, it'll become mine."

Callum nodded, determined. Ash took a deep breath. Maybe this really would be just the push he needed to find her. He tried again, crossing his legs beneath him. He closed his eyes and breathed, focusing again on Ramsay, her hair and her skin and—

Ash gasped. A new energy charged through him, rushing in his veins. Light-blue color glowed even beneath his eyelids, and it felt so soft, so comforting, that Ash almost wanted to release all thought and feel swaddled in nothing but this energy—release all fear and feel, for once, that he was safe.

It took willpower for him to remember his goal. He could practically see Ramsay in front of him now, her smirk as she leaned close—and then, there, he did see her. She wore a black coat, a hood up so that her face was shadowed. She crunched through a cobblestoned road, melting snow piled along the sides, a horse and carriage clopping past. There was a mixture of apartments and warehouses against a gray sky, made so by clouds and smoke, factories off in the distance.

Ash opened his eyes. He was on his back. He frowned, confused, as he peered up into Callum's face. Callum leaned over him, a hand on his shoulder. He'd been speaking, though it was only now that his voice reached Ash's ears.

"Are you all right?"

Ash frowned as he sat up with Callum's help. "Yeah—I'm fine."

"Creator, you scared me—you suddenly fell over—"

Ash met his eye. "I know where she is."

Callum's hand gripped his shoulder. He helped Ash to his feet, and the smaller boy crossed the room to a desk where pens and parchment waited. He scrawled out the city's name, letting Callum look at it briefly over his shoulder before Ash tore out the page and walked to the fireplace, tossing it into the flame. Ramsay had been desperate to leave Kensington Station and had jumped onto the train leaving for Ironbound, even if it meant taking her closer to Snowdrop.

"It looked like she was in the outskirts," Ash said.

"I don't understand. Why hasn't she left yet?"

"She's probably waiting for the redguard patrols to die down, and besides that, it's a long journey. She might be taking time to prepare." A part of Ash longed to dream that she was also still in Ironbound because she was waiting for him, hoping that he would figure out where she was and meet her there—but Ash knew better now. She wouldn't risk so much just for him.

Callum sat on the sofa again, frowning as if he was lost in

thought, while Ash chewed on his lip and began to walk back and forth across the room. It seemed it was another habit he'd picked up from Ramsay.

"Creator, Ramsay used to drive me crazy whenever she paced," Callum murmured. "You can think just as well seated, can't you?"

Ash ignored him. "We need to leave. We can catch her if we take the first train out in the morning."

Callum shifted, crossing his legs and his arms. "I'm not sure that's wise."

Ash stopped in his tracks. "What? We finally know where she is, and you don't think it's wise to go after her?"

"We will, Ash," Callum said, "but we need to be strategic about this. We can't just run flailing into fire."

"Fuck your battle strategy. If we wait too long, we'll lose our chance."

"We need to be patient," Callum said stubbornly. "If we act without thinking, we might lose her *and* face even greater consequences."

Ash paused. Ramsay had told him something very similar once, and no matter how she'd betrayed him, she'd turned out to be right.

Callum continued. "We need time to prepare, and besides, my family's annual gala is tomorrow night."

Ash squinted at Callum. "You want to delay finding Ramsay for a *party*?"

"No," Callum said slowly, as if struggling to stay patient himself. "I'm expected to stand beside my family. If I don't, my absence will be noticed, and I'll be presumed missing. Guards will be on the lookout for me. We'll have a more difficult time leaving Kensington. If, however, I leave after I make an appearance . . ."

Ash frowned. "People will still notice that you're gone, won't they?"

"Not necessarily. I only see my father when he gives me an order or reprimands me, and my mother is always busy with her events. My brothers have lives of their own. I can go weeks without seeing my family, sometimes."

Ash wasn't sure why he felt compassion. Maybe it was the shine in Callum's eyes that reminded Ash of the young boy he'd seen in Ramsay's memories. Maybe it was the energy that Ash could feel, energy that Callum couldn't hide: his loneliness—the longing to be accepted by his father and not be surrounded by empty friendships.

Callum rubbed the back of his neck. "Even if it takes them a few days to realize I'm gone, that's still a few extra days we can use to escape." He stood from his seat. "We can use tomorrow to prepare, and leave that night after I've shown my face. Agreed?"

Ash still wanted to argue, but he couldn't find a sound enough reason. He sighed. "Agreed."

※

It was luck that Callum didn't have any classes the next day. That morning, Callum had Ash follow him through Kensington Main Street, filled with tailors and stores for hats and shoes. The Kendrick boy made a great show of handing his new scribe bags of clothes and coats and winter boots—all outfits that he'd bought for Ash.

Ash had tried to insist that Callum was doing too much. "I'll be fine," he whispered as Callum bought him a large wool scarf inside a small boutique. Callum paid for the scarf at the register with a thank-you. "Really, I will."

"I'd rather not risk you freezing to death" was Callum's only reply as he held open the door, waiting for Ash to walk through first, his hands full with bags.

"I didn't realize you cared," Ash muttered. He hadn't meant for Callum to hear, and was surprised when the other boy paused outside the shop, the door shutting behind them.

"Why wouldn't I?"

He asked the question so seriously that Ash had no choice but to blush and duck his head as he walked past. "Redguards don't have an ability to care, remember?"

Callum followed. "I do care about you, Ash."

"Why?" he asked, stare focused on his shoes. "It isn't as if we're friends."

"Maybe not yet," Callum said, keeping up easily with his long strides. "But we are working together, and besides that, I—well, I would like to be. Friends with you, I mean."

Callum had such a simple way of discussing his emotions and desires that Ash felt self-conscious. He didn't answer, glancing up from his feet only when Callum spoke again. "Is that something you'd like, too?"

"Does it matter what I want?"

"Yes, of course it does," Callum said. "And if you'd rather not be friends, then I'll respect that. You only need to say the words."

"You care an awful lot about what your prisoner wants." He struggled with the bags, heaving them up, then blinked in surprise when Callum plucked most of them out of his hands. "I don't exactly look like a servant if you're carrying the bags."

"You're not a servant, remember?" Callum said. "You're my scribe."

Ash swallowed as they walked in silence for a moment. "Maybe we can be friends one day," he finally said. "But I don't see how we can now, with me as your prisoner, and you as my guard."

And there was the other bit that Ash was too nervous to say out loud. He wasn't sure how he and Callum could ever be friends, when both loved Ramsay, hoping she would love one of them in return.

※

They reached the Kendrick town house. Ash was used to the glares he received now. Any guests who happened to be in the house would stare as if they'd come just so that they could catch a glimpse of the prisoner who'd destroyed Lancaster.

Ash followed Callum up the stairs and to the redguard's chambers.

Callum sat down heavily on his sofa with a sigh. "I have to start getting ready for the gala," he mumbled to himself.

Ash sat on the other end of the sofa, watching Callum curiously. "There's something I've been wondering . . ."

"Yes?"

"Does anyone else know that you use alchemy when you fight?"

Callum sat up as if electrocuted. "What? I don't use alchemy to fight. Creator, don't say something like that—I could be expelled from McKinley if anyone thought I did."

It was as Ash thought, then. Callum was such a naturally talented alchemist that he didn't even know when he used alchemic power. "Well, maybe you don't use alchemy purposefully," Ash said, "but you do use it."

Callum frowned now, leaning back again as he watched Ash. "Go on."

"Every human being uses alchemy," Ash explained, "when we breathe and feel emotion, for example—but it doesn't take a lot of alchemic power to do basic things like that. We need more alchemic power to—say—create something using our imagination, or to heal another person's wound."

"And my fighting?"

"You're drawing more alchemic power than the average person would," Ash says. "You're skilled and you're strong, and your alchemy enhances that."

"I've sometimes wondered myself," Callum admitted with a murmur.

"Wondered?"

"It's difficult to describe. I could feel myself—heating, maybe? My energy getting stronger. To think it was alchemy all along. If anyone finds out . . ."

Ash stared down at his hands. "I have to admit, I'm jealous. You're such a natural that you don't even have to think about it."

"If I tried to learn another skill besides fighting, I'd need to think about it more," Callum said. Ash wondered if the other *skill* Callum imagined was healing.

"That's true," Ash said. "I'm more of a natural at creation alchemy, but when it comes to fighting . . ."

Callum quirked a smile. "Do you want to learn how to fight?"

"No—no, I was only using that as an example."

"I could teach you a few moves," Callum offered. "It could be helpful on our journey. What if you need to use self-defense?"

But the thought of Ash attempting to flail against Callum mortified him. "No, I'm fine. I've always been a fast runner, and I've held up well against other alchemists in the past."

"Those are *alchemists*," Callum said. "Redguards are trained against alchemy. We have strategies to overwhelm and outrun, attack before you can make your move or wait until you've used up your power and strike when you're weak. If you faced even three redguards, you wouldn't stand a chance."

Ash pouted. "I did burn down half of Lancaster, you know."

"That's true," Callum said, standing and offering a hand. "But you were also caught and arrested and made my prisoner."

Ash sighed as he took Callum's hand, allowing the Kendrick boy to pull him to his feet.

"First, you should be aware of your position. Your stance should be widened, like this."

Ash tried to follow Callum's instructions, but he felt off-balance and awkward with his hands up in fists.

"Never poke your thumb out like that," Callum said, taking one of Ash's hands and moving the thumb so it was tucked beneath his clenched fingers instead. Ash flushed. "You can break your thumb that way."

"Is your skin always so burning hot?"

Callum considered. "I've never noticed. Now, hit my hand."

Ash looked at Callum's outstretched palm.

"Go on," Callum insisted.

Ash took a deep breath, bit his lip, and hit the palm. His knuckles stung. "Source!" he said, turning away and flapping his hand back and forth. "Are you made of steel?"

"Come on, don't stop there."

"I'd rather fight using alchemy, thank you."

Callum grinned. "Let's at least attempt one sparring match."

"Has it secretly been your plan to kill me all along?"

Callum laughed now. "I'll go easy on you, Ash, I promise. Shall we?"

Ash sighed and put up his hands, ready to fight—and paused when Callum began to unbutton his shirt. "What're you doing?"

The other boy barely glanced up at Ash as he unfastened the buttons at his wrists. "I can't fight in this. It's not my sparring uniform."

Callum didn't seem to think there was anything odd about stripping off his shirt in front of Ash. Maybe this is what the redguard students did at McKinley. Ash tried not to look at Callum, but it was hard not to. It was even more apparent that the Kendrick boy's body was made mostly of muscle. His arms were thick, his chest round, his stomach with a hint of the abs that were beneath a solid frame. It made sense that the more physical body there was—more muscle, more fat—the more ability there was to store alchemic power, too. It was hard to believe that this was the same lanky boy from Ramsay's memories. Source, there was no way around it: Callum was undeniably attractive.

Ash glanced up to meet Callum's eye and realized that Callum had stopped, noticing Ash's stare. Callum blinked in surprise. Ash's face grew very hot, and even hotter still when he remembered just how easily Callum could feel another's emotion, to the point of sometimes hearing thoughts. Ash hoped that Callum hadn't heard this particular one, but from the way Callum looked at Ash now, the odds weren't favorable.

Callum cleared his throat. He began to pull his shirt back on. "You're right. Maybe the timing isn't the best. The gala and all."

"Yes. Right."

Callum rubbed the back of his neck. "I need to get ready."

"I should go, then."

"Yes, okay. I'll escort you downstairs."

"No need," Ash said quickly. "I'll go right to my room." Ash tried not to run. When he closed the door, it took everything in him not to slump to the floor.

23

Ash would've loved nothing more than to hide in his chambers for the rest of the night, if not the rest of his life—but, humiliatingly, he was still expected to stand at Callum's side for the gala. A worker brought by a white button-down and slacks, a slightly elevated version of his usual uniform. When Callum knocked on his door nearly an hour later, the redguard's careful smile hid any awkwardness. Usually Ash was against fake bullshit, but he was grateful that Callum had decided to pretend the earlier incident simply hadn't happened at all.

"I won't stay long," Callum promised Ash with a low voice as they walked down the hall and the stairs. "I'll make the rounds, make sure I'm seen, and then we'll go." The last train was leaving for Ironbound at midnight. They'd need to be quick if they wanted to make it.

The party below was already in full swing, from the sound of laughter and clinking glasses. Ash followed Callum to a golden ballroom where guests had already arrived and stood in small groups. They were dressed in finery and wore tight smiles. Stringed music drifted through the air. Ash hated that the music reminded him of Ramsay.

He felt self-conscious as he walked several steps behind Callum, doing his best to ignore the turning heads and whispers. As Ash shuffled farther into the room, someone caught his eye. He nearly froze as his father raised his chin, inspecting Ash for a moment, before turning away to continue speaking to the gentleman by his side. Ash tried to swallow his quiver of fear as he followed Callum.

He looked up in surprise when Callum pressed a warm hand against his arm. "Are you all right?"

Ash glanced at his father, but the man acted like he wasn't there. "Yes," Ash lied.

Callum frowned like he didn't believe him. "We'll leave soon, okay? Stay close." Ash hurried to keep up with him, feeling that Hain was aware of his every move.

Callum paused every now and then. "Ah, Lord Quintrell—yes, it's wonderful to see you, sir. Madam Huxley, you seem to be faring well—how you manage to stay aglow in such dreary weather escapes me."

Ash wanted to roll his eyes at Callum's performance, but he had to admit the youngest Kendrick was in his element, a dazzling actor on the stage that was his life. Ash never would've guessed that Callum hated any of this.

There was a group in the center of the room where people buzzed closer and closer. Winslow Kendrick stood beside Lady Celia Kendrick, her warm-brown skin glowing. On Lord Kendrick's other side was a man who looked like an older version of Callum, only with eyes that were much more frigid, and beside him was yet another clone, and another—four brothers in total, Ash realized. He hadn't known Callum was the youngest of so many. He better understood now the pressure Callum must've felt to get in line and do as expected.

Ash stood several feet behind Callum as the lady of the House made a show of kissing Callum's cheeks and welcoming him into the circle. All the while, Ash looked up across the room at Hain again and again, wondering why his father was there, hoping the man didn't have something insidious planned. But Hain only ignored Ash, his back turned.

"I think it's reprehensible," a gentleman in the circle murmured, just loudly enough for Ash to hear.

It appeared the elder Kendrick heard as well. "I agree," he said, "but it's unfortunately out of my hands, with Lord Alexander's orders."

Lady Kendrick stood with a straight back. "And is there any word that the college will rebuild?"

"Yes, of course they will," another man said. "They haven't much choice. Lord Val will need more pledges to sustain the House, and he has Alexander wrapped around his finger."

"I think you'll find that Val has lost quite a lot of standing lately," the eldest of Callum's brothers said. "His cousin's death was too suspect."

"Didn't another alchemist of House Val go missing almost a year ago now?" a woman asked. "Randall Pierce, I believe his name was. There've been calls to investigate Lord Val in Sir Pierce's disappearance as well."

"And now this latest incident," Lady Kendrick said. Ash's heart and fists clenched.

"It was an alchemist's attack against other alchemists, at least," Callum's second-oldest brother said. "The Lune can't use the attack to insist alchemists are a danger to society as easily as they could with the Thornes."

"A shame," Winslow Kendrick said. "Sometimes I wonder if Alexander has had alchemy performed on him without his knowledge. He refuses to see how alchemists continue to threaten this state." Winslow looked his way, eyeing Ash openly, as if picturing the noose around the boy's neck. "They've been given too much freedom. An alchemist, attacking a college of alchemy? This should give us more concern, not less. They're willing to attack even their own. How will they act toward everyone else?"

The doors opened, and servers holding platters of appetizers made their way through the room.

"You, boy."

Ash stared at his feet and only looked up when he felt energy pointed in his direction. Winslow Kendrick raised his hand impatiently at Ash. "Fetch me a glass of wine."

Fiery anger built inside him. He wasn't a *servant* to be ordered around, and *most certainly* not by Winslow Kendrick. But the longer Ash stood, refusing to move, the more heads twisted toward him with murmurs that Ash couldn't quite hear, though he could feel the rising anger all the same. Disobedience, if shown within House Kendrick, was always met with harsh discipline. Winslow Kendrick met Ash's eye, as if he considered changing his mind and executing the boy with his own hands, right then and there.

Before the Head of the House could say anything else, however, Callum stepped forward, standing in front of Ash. "He is my scribe," Callum said. "Not a servant."

The silence was heavier now. Ash noticed that Callum stood very still as he faced his father, as prey might when facing its predator. The silence stretched for so long that Ash was sure it would snap, when finally, Winslow Kendrick spoke.

"Yes, of course," he said. "My mistake."

The conversation didn't easily start again. There were whispers, an uncomfortable "excuse me" and "ah, is that Madam Galahad—one moment, I must say hello." Callum turned to Ash, as if bent on taking this moment to leave the group as well—to leave the town house and the city altogether, Ash hoped.

"I need some air," Callum said, not meeting Ash's eye as he swept past. Ash tried to keep up with the other boy—it appeared that what he had done, what he had just said, was now catching up with him, and he looked like he would be sick.

Neither noticed that Callum's father had followed them. With little warning, the man gripped Callum's arm and tugged him into a servant's hall, shoving Callum against the wall.

"What—stop! Let him go!" Ash said, running forward to help Callum—even he wasn't sure what he would do against a man like Winslow Kendrick, not without a death wish—but Callum held up a single hand, staring at his father.

Lord Kendrick gritted his teeth. "You dare disrespect me?"

Callum seemed to struggle not to wince in pain. "No disrespect was meant, sir."

"You will not embarrass me," he said, twisting his hand harder, "or this family's name."

"Yes, Father. I'm sorry."

Winslow seemed satisfied. He released Callum, eyeing him with a twinge of disgust before his gaze fell on Ash. "I should've had you killed when I had the chance," he said. "But corrections can always be made." He knocked past Ash, back into the main room.

Callum adjusted his collar with trembling hands, staring at the ground.

Ash wasn't sure how to comfort him. "He can't treat you that way."

Callum smiled. "You truly don't know what life is like among the Houses." He took a quick breath. "It doesn't matter. This is a good excuse to leave. Everyone will assume I've gone to hide in my room in shame."

Ash wouldn't argue with that. They walked out of the hall, striding through the gala, past the guests who watched them go. Whispers of the confrontation had likely already made the rounds. They were close to the doors, so close to freedom, when a voice called.

"Mr. Woods."

Ash turned.

His father stood several feet away. It was like he'd waited by the doors, knowing Ash would try to make an early exit. "Can I ask for a moment of your time?"

It should've been an easy answer. Ash should've come up with a quick excuse. *No, I'm sorry—Callum has ordered me to follow him.* Anything would've done, really. But old habits died hard, and Ash had an eighteen-year-old habit of wanting to meet with and speak with and be acknowledged by his father. Ash stopped, silent, unsure of what to say.

"Sir Gresham Hain," Callum said with a glowing smile. "It's been some time."

"Yes, yes," Hain said impatiently, his eyes still on Ash.

"I hear it's you I have to thank for my new scribe."

Hain's gaze flickered to Callum. "I trust he's been useful."

"Greatly. In fact, I'm in need of his assistance now. If you'll excuse us—"

"This will only take a moment," Hain said. He stepped away, down the empty hall, confident that Ash would come. Callum looked at Ash expectantly, but Ash already knew his choice. They would be early for their train if they left now, sitting in the station and hoping they wouldn't be recognized. They could spare a few minutes.

"I'll meet you in your chambers," Ash said over his shoulder to Callum, before he turned to follow his father.

⁕

Hain found an empty sitting room for the two. It looked like the sort where House members would sip tea and gossip about meaningless nothings, but it was dark and empty now. Hain went to the fireplace and sparked a flame with a flicker of alchemy, poking at the embers with an iron rod. He was silent for long enough that Ash struggled not to squirm nervously in his seat. He couldn't ignore his own energy. He felt like a child hoping for his father's approval.

"How have your days been, serving Callum Kendrick?" Hain finally asked, though he still didn't turn to face Ash.

"The best of my life," Ash said sarcastically. "I've always longed to be a prisoner of House Kendrick."

Hain finally turned to look at Ash. "You must've gotten that cheekiness from Samantha."

"Don't say her name," Ash said. "Don't speak about her at all."

Hain strode across the room and sat on the opposite sofa, crossing one leg over the other. The only source of light was the flickering fire. "You seem to have the wrong impression of me and your mother," he said. "Samantha Woods was dear to me. She was the most talented of all my apprentices. The most powerful, when it came to alchemy."

Ash gripped his hands together. His mother had hated alchemy. It made little sense that Samantha had been an unlicensed alchemist all along, even as she told Ash to stay away from magic. He wasn't sure where Hain's lies ended and where the truth began. "My mom didn't know any alchemy."

"Is that what she told you?" Hain said with a small laugh. "Her specialty was creation alchemy. She would've been the strongest creation alchemist on record in the state if she'd been licensed. She would've easily become my successor as an advisor to House Alexander. I needed to keep her power a secret, of course—she was more valuable to me when kept anonymous."

"You pretend that you cared about her, but you only cared about how useful she was."

"Isn't that all anyone cares about?" Hain asked. "Yes, sure, people learn to love one another eventually. I'm not such a cynic that I'd argue with that. But would you care for a stranger without wanting something from them first?"

"Are you trying to convince me that you loved her?"

"I was shattered when she left," Hain said. "She abandoned me, betrayed me, without even a note to explain." He paused. "I think you might know the feeling well."

It took everything in Ash not to explode at his father. "What do you want?"

"You already know the answer to that—and I already know that you won't tell me where the Book is, not willingly, not yet. I won't waste my time or energy on that tonight."

"Then why am I here?"

"I wanted to spend time with you," Hain said simply. "You're my son."

Ash couldn't deny the warmth that spread through him, even

as he managed to bite out his next words. "Sorry, I'm having a hard time believing that one."

"Is that so?" Hain gave the smallest of shrugs. "You are a talented alchemist with potential, and you are, technically, my heir. I'm curious about you, Ashen. I want to know if I can shape you into a boy who can carry on my legacy."

"Your legacy?" Ash repeated with a laugh. "Your legacy of murdering hundreds, you mean? Your legacy of stealing girls from House Lune and taking advantage of them? Your legacy of leaving them to die?"

His voice had risen as he spoke. Hain watched Ash quietly, tapping a finger against a crossed leg. "What is your definition of power?" he asked Ash.

Ash hated the man, Source, he hated him more than he could bear. He blinked away the tears that had risen. "What? Why're you asking me that?"

"I'm curious," was all Hain said.

Maybe Ash was more similar to Hain than he wanted to admit. Curiosity had motivated Ash many times, too. He took a breath. "Power is alignment to Source," he said, remembering the lesson he'd received from Ramsay. His classes felt like they'd been ages ago now. He surprised himself by continuing. "At least, this is what respected alchemists say. But they were born into privilege. They don't know what it's like to be hungry, to run from the redguards, to have their ability to practice alchemy taken away."

"Do the complaints you've listed affect your connection to Source?" Hain asked him.

"Yes," Ash said, anger growing again. "Yes, of course it does. While rich assholes get to sit around sipping tea, I'm struggling to survive. I don't get to have the same peace of mind required to align to Source."

"That sounds like an excuse."

Ash would've liked to strangle his father. "Maybe someone

should mug you and take all of your things and leave you to die out in the street. We'll see how connected to Source you are then."

Hain laughed. "That fiery temper is certainly your mother's." He ignored Ash when he tried to interrupt. "I would like to suggest that, if you are in true alignment to Source, you'll be guided as needed—and from what I can see, you have been."

"You need some fucking glasses, then."

"Have you not learned alchemy from a professor of Lancaster?" Hain said. "Have you not received, in this very moment, valuable guidance that some students would be willing to pay thousands of sterling for?"

"You're overestimating your own importance."

"You don't see the gifts of Source when they're handed to you."

Ash swallowed. Hain watched his son carefully for a few moments. He uncrossed a leg and leaned forward, elbows on his knees, still staring at Ash as if he could see something in Ash's energy field that Ash himself could not.

"This is the truth of Source that no one wants you to know," Hain said. "Source is always helping you—always giving you what you want, whether you're aware of what you've asked for or not. The destination of your path in this lifetime is up to no one but you, as long as you can admit what it is you truly desire."

He leaned back suddenly, as if satisfied with what he'd found in Ash. This only made him uncomfortable. Anything that pleased Hain couldn't be good.

"There are many in this state who want you to think of Source as the Creator," Hain told him, "a force outside of yourself, rather than one you contain. They use the idea of the Creator to oppress. Most don't realize they're being manipulated to fear."

"You're talking about House Lune," Ash said, hating that he could understand his father.

"Yes," Hain said, "and House Kendrick, and even at times House Adelaide. As you can see, the Great Houses are swayed in one direction, and it won't be long before House Alexander follows. When I speak of my legacy, Ashen, I speak of needing someone who will help me balance the scales."

"Isn't that what House Val is for?" Ash said. "House Alder and House—"

He paused. He had almost said House Thorne. Hain's careful stare suggested he knew what Ash was going to say, and in that moment, Ash realized he'd already proven his father's point. House Thorne was dead, Alder ill-equipped, and Val was politicized against by the most powerful of the Houses. The war against alchemy was already won.

"As the fear grows, so does the desperation for control. The very fools who fear alchemy are the ones who don't align to Source. If they did, they'd see there's nothing to fear when humans discover their own power and potential. We can't force the Great Houses to practice alchemy—but we can work together, Ashen, to leave behind a legacy I would be proud of, no matter the cost."

Ash felt like he'd been enchanted by a spell as he listened to his father, thinking that the man was right—he made sense, yes, of course alchemy needed to survive the fear that House Lune spread . . . But at these last few words, Ash pulled back. "Cost?" he said. "Killing, you mean."

His father studied him. "Sacrifices will be made. The enemies of alchemy can't be allowed to live. If that means destroying New Anglia and starting again, that's a price I'm willing to pay."

So now Ash knew what his father would do if he got his hands on the Book. Ash closed his eyes and breathed. "I don't think our alignment to Source would mean wanting to destroy an entire state and murder so many people. Do you?"

Hain tilted his head slightly. "I don't think that we can ever assume what another person's alignment to Source means." He stood abruptly, surprising Ash. "Enjoy the rest of the gala, Ashen. I look forward to seeing you again soon."

Ash wasn't sure if his father meant this to sound like a threat.

⁕

Marlowe pulled her coat closer to her neck, ignoring the odd looks she received for her expensive furs. The streets were busier here than in Kensington, horse-drawn carriages clopping down the road and people pushing past with scowls. Marlowe could feel the energy she'd followed for days now. Hain's orders had changed, though she didn't fully understand why. His focus had been on Ashen Woods, not Ramsay Thorne.

Marlowe had escaped and hidden after the attacks on the college, and had been unsurprised to find Hain waiting for her in her sitting room the very next day. "Now that Woods is in our possession, he could be helpful to locate the Book. Even more helpful than Thorne."

She could see the familiar coat's hood farther down the street, ignorant to her existence. Marlowe had put up an unseen shield of energy around her so she wouldn't be detected. She had to continuously think of this shield, and it was quite draining, but Hain's orders had been clear: Do not let Ramsay Thorne out of her sight; and, once Thorne was isolated enough, kill her.

"Couldn't it be useful to let her live?" Marlowe had asked, not for Ramsay's sake, but for her own—killing was a nasty business. "I could follow her to the Book's location." And hadn't Hain wanted to keep her alive in case he needed to place blame?

But it seemed Hain was more concerned with how close she was to finding the Book now. "I won't risk her finding it before you have a chance to stop her," Hain said. "Kill her. Woods knows where the Book is, even if he pretends not to. He's our key."

24

Ash found Callum waiting in his chambers. The other boy sat on his sofa, already changed into travel clothes, workman leather boots that had not a spot nor scratch and a hooded cloak over his gray sweater and trousers. It looked like he was trying very hard to wear clothes that would help him fit in among the gruff Ironbound crowds, but he had absolutely no idea how the average person dressed. Ash would've normally found this amusing, but he struggled to push his father from his mind.

Callum picked up on Ash's mood immediately. "Are you okay?" he said, and when Ash didn't answer, he asked, "What did Sir Hain want?"

Ash realized that Callum still didn't know that Gresham Hain was his father. He didn't think that now was the time to talk about it. It was already after ten o' clock, and the last train they planned to take would start boarding within the hour.

"Nothing," Ash said, turning his back to Callum as he began to unbutton his shirt. Callum had helpfully laid out one of the outfits he'd bought for Ash, and there was a duffel bag waiting with his other new belongings.

"Isn't that strange?" Callum asked. "First, Sir Hain requests your pardon, and then he asks to speak with you . . ."

Ash tugged off his shirt with frustration, pausing in surprise when Callum appeared behind him, helping to slip it off over his shoulders. Ash blushed, remembering their earlier incident, and turned to the couch to pick up the thick, slightly oversized sweater that Callum had bought him. Normally he would've taken off his binder after wearing it all day, but there was little time now, and he wasn't comfortable exposing his chest anywhere near Callum, even if the other boy wasn't looking.

"I think I deserve to know what's going on with you and Hain," Callum said as Ash pulled on the sweater. His tone was sharper than usual, but then again, Callum was also about to aid in his own prisoner's escape. Maybe it was understandable that he was on edge. "We're supposed to be working together, Ash. I'm about to rip my life apart. I don't think there should be secrets between us."

"No one asked you to rip your life apart," Ash muttered. He sighed. "Can you turn around, please?" he asked, glancing over his shoulder.

Callum turned around.

He unfastened his pants. "Gresham Hain is my father."

"What?"

Ash knew Callum had whipped around again. He glared at Callum over his shoulder. "Turn around!"

"Creator, sorry," Callum said, spinning so that his back faced Ash once again. "Gresham Hain is your dad?" he repeated with a lowered voice. "Well, it makes sense now that he'd save you from an execution."

"He's after the Book, too," Ash said. He pulled on his new pair of trousers and strode over to Callum, picking up his duffel. "He wants to get there first. My father isn't a nice man, Callum."

"I can relate."

"Mine will kill to get what he wants."

"Is this a competition for worst dad? Mine *has* killed."

"My dad will destroy the state and murder thousands of people if we don't stop him."

"You've won, then."

Ash pulled the duffel strap over his shoulder. "We have to make sure that doesn't happen."

❋

The last tendrils of the party continued below. Callum suggested they used the servants' halls to sneak out of the town house. "They'll be too distracted with the gala, hopefully," he said as they hurried down the stairs and the corridor. Callum opened a mahogany door at the end.

"Callum?"

Callum turned. A man was walking up the last of the stairs—one of Callum's older brothers, Ash realized, one who had been called Edric. He looked to be in his late twenties, only slightly shorter than Callum, but broader still.

He slowed down as he stepped into the corridor, taking in the situation and coming to a conclusion he didn't share out loud. "What're you doing?"

Callum took a sharp breath, stepping in front of Ash, blocking Edric's view. "Nothing," he said—not a good response, clearly they weren't doing *nothing*. Callum seemed to realize the same and added, "I wanted to go for a walk and get some fresh air."

"Dressed like that?" Edric said, walking closer, voice soft. "And with bags packed?"

Ash's heart thundered. It was possible that Callum could be so intimidated by his brother that he'd give up completely right then and there.

Edric stopped a few feet away from them. "It seems to me that you're about to leave."

Callum was frozen, caught—it was clear to Ash and maybe his brother, too, that he didn't know what to do. "I—well, I—"

"Does Father know you're leaving? Has he authorized this? It's suspicious, Callum, that you're sneaking about and taking your scribe with you."

"It isn't—you needn't concern yourself—"

"Yes, I do," Edric said. "As we're both responsible to our father and House Kendrick, it's absolutely my concern if my youngest brother is about to do something foolish and ruin our family's name."

Callum pushed Ash back with a hand. "Let us go. Pretend you haven't seen anything."

"You're already a disappointment to our father," Edric said. "Don't do something you'll regret now."

Callum stiffened. "Please, Edric, you don't have to—"

"Do you think your last name protects you? He'll disown you—perhaps more, if he ever lays eyes on you again."

Callum's shuddering breath frightened Ash more than anything. It'd be so easy for the youngest Kendrick to change his mind.

"Return to your chambers," Edric said. "I'll pretend this never happened. I'd rather avoid putting this stress on our father now. This can be a secret between us."

The silence ticked on, Ash tense. He wanted to believe in Callum, but Ash had been betrayed enough times now, by all the people he'd thought he could trust. It wouldn't be a surprise for a Kendrick to betray him now, too.

Callum looked over his shoulder at Ash, his eyes frightened. "I'm sorry," Callum said. Ash's heart sank.

Callum turned around and kneed his brother in the gut. Edric gasped, but he recovered quickly, slamming a fist into Callum's ribs. Edric wasn't one of the McKinley students in training. He was a stronger opponent. They grappled with a shout, Edric knocking Callum into the wall with an echoing thud.

"Shit, shit," Ash cursed. The noise would only bring more people. His mind spun as he tried to imagine Edric bound by rope, but he was too breathless and panicked for alchemy.

Callum managed to wrap an arm around his brother's neck, but Edric grunted, pushing Callum off—

Ash pulled back his arm and punched Edric in the nose. The two both shouted in pain, blood now streaming down Edric's face. Callum blinked at Ash in shock, but his body moved on its own. He threw Edric to the ground and hit the temple of his head with the side of his open palm. The older brother slumped into a heap.

Ash winced and looked at his fist. His knuckles throbbed.

Callum reached for his hand as if he wanted to check the injury, but there was movement on the stairs, voices—"The yelling came from here—"

Callum snatched his bag and tugged on Ash's shoulder, opening the servants' door. They closed it, leaving Edric behind, and rushed through the thin shadowed halls. There was a stone staircase that Callum barely fit inside, squeezing around one corner and the next. A servant girl squeaked when Ash pushed past, and Callum shouted his apologies. They made it to the bottom floor, and Callum pulled on Ash's arm, leading him to the final door.

They burst out into the night.

"This way," Callum gasped, turning a sharp corner. They came to a wall in an alley. Callum helped Ash up, then threw the luggage over the wall and pulled himself up, too, landing beside Ash on the other side.

"You have a lot of experience escaping from your house," Ash huffed as they ran through a maze of alleyways, skidding over freshly fallen snow.

"I've snuck out a few times," Callum said, voice unshaken even as he ran.

They reentered onto a bustling street. Callum pulled up his hood, and Ash wrapped the scarf around his face. They walked as quickly as they could without bringing attention to themselves. A couple of redguards on patrol passed by without a glance. Word hadn't spread yet that a prisoner had escaped with the youngest Kendrick son's help. Ash glanced up at Callum, but his face was too shadowed for Ash to see his expression. He wondered what Callum must be feeling. It was what he'd feared doing all his life—choosing his freedom over his family.

"You don't regret it, do you?" Ash asked.

Callum looked down at him, enough light falling across his face now for Ash to see that he'd begun to cry. "No," he said. "I don't."

＊

Kensington Station was a domed building near the sea with a tangle of tracks woven beside it, various bridges heading for the mainland. The ceiling was painted a cerulean blue, as if to inspire the sky to change from its hazy gray. Wooden benches were filled with waiting passengers. There were ten minutes before their train departed. Callum bought tickets, staring hard at the ground as he and Ash received suspicious glances from the clerk, but they weren't stopped from making their way to the train.

"First class?" Ash said as he looked at the ticket Callum gave him. "I thought we were trying to fit in."

"We need some privacy," Callum said. His voice was stilted, expression stiff. Source, Ash hoped that Callum wouldn't change his mind.

They boarded the train and walked past the rows of passengers, some speaking excitedly while others slept or read a newspaper. Ash tightened the scarf around his face. A week before, the newspaper had shown photos of him with a black sack pulled over his head, but he was still nervous he'd somehow be recognized as the dangerous alchemist.

They reached the first-class car. The seats were sectioned off by private rooms with two cushioned benches in each. Callum slid open one of the doors and shrugged off his coat, then stacked his and then Ash's luggage above them on the overhead rack before falling heavily into his seat. Ash sat gingerly opposite him, unwrapping his scarf with his good hand. His other hand had started to swell.

Callum sighed. "Let me see."

Ash pulled his hand back. "No. It hurts."

"I know. Let me take a look at it."

Ash hesitated, then held out his hand. Callum took it softly, carefully, spreading it out on his palm. Ash hissed, and Callum glanced up at him through his lashes.

"I don't think it's broken. Just badly bruised. Still, we should ice it, and you shouldn't move it too much."

Ash hated being treated like a child. He pulled his hand back again. "Ramsay would've been able to heal it."

"Yes, well, Ramsay isn't here."

"I wasn't trying to suggest that I prefer Ramsay to you."

Callum took a deep breath. "If I still remembered what she taught me, I could try . . . But it's been some time, and I don't want to risk hurting you further."

"I know. It's fine," Ash said. The train's engine started, a gentle rhythm. The whistle blew. "Are you all right?" he asked.

Callum swallowed. "It's what I knew would happen once I left," he said. "Being disowned by my family, I mean. I think I just wasn't expecting it to happen so soon, so quickly. I imagined that they'd discover me missing in a week or so—that they would slowly realize I hadn't been kidnapped, and maybe in about a month official word would spread that I left on my own accord. I thought I'd be disowned quietly, without having to see my family at all."

Ash had once read that Source would sometimes come to people as tests. If a person declared that they wanted a new way of life, then a chance such as Callum's would come to him. It was the opportunity he'd needed to break free from his family, finally, to do exactly what he pleased.

"I'm grateful," Ash said. Callum looked up skeptically. "I mean it. You didn't have to come. You knew what it would mean, but you did it anyway. Thank you."

Callum's gaze softened. "I should be thanking you, too," he said. "For that punch, I mean."

Ash snorted.

Callum managed a smile. "It was pretty good, even if you hurt yourself. You even tucked your thumb."

"What can I say? I'm a fast learner."

"Yes, apparently." Callum watched Ash for a moment. The train jerked forward and began to move slowly. The snow had begun to fall harder, white clumps sticking to the window. "And I'm grateful, too," he said, "that you're here. I wouldn't have had enough courage to leave without you."

Ash's face and chest warmed. He began to carefully inspect his hand. "You're welcome," he said.

25

A conductor came to check their tickets, and shortly after, someone pushed a cart to their door, offering tomato soup and crackers, frowning at their covered faces. The trip lasted well into the night, Ash unable to see through the dark except for when there was a glittering town in the distance, white snow floating past the window. It was his first time outside of Hedge and Kensington, and he was curious to see the world beyond the two cities and their neighborhoods—but he couldn't fully enjoy the moment as he thought of Ramsay again and again. It'd been almost two weeks since she escaped from Lancaster, two days since Ash had seen her in his remote viewing. Anything could've happened since.

He was sure he wouldn't be able to sleep with so many thoughts racing through his mind and was surprised when he jerked awake to pale morning light. Small towns passed by outside the window before they were replaced by white pastures of snow, the gray ocean's coast on the horizon. They were close to Ironbound.

Callum appeared to have stayed awake all night. He stared out of the window. "Good morning," he said. "How did you sleep?"

"Like shit." Ash noticed that Kendrick still wore his hood over his face. "Did you keep that on all night?" he asked, moving his bundled scarf from his shoulder to his lap. It'd acted as a comfortable pillow, but he had no use for it now.

"Yes," Callum said. He glanced at Ash. "You should put that on, too. Someone could see us."

Ash opened his mouth to argue, but fell silent when he saw the serious look Callum gave him. He must've learned how to give the *fall into line and obey my command* glare in military school. "Don't you think you're being too paranoid?" Ash mumbled. Still, he wrapped the scarf around his face and neck again.

"No. When I think about what will happen if we're caught, I don't consider myself too paranoid at all."

"To be fair, only one of us will be executed," Ash said. "You might be disowned, but you'll still have your life, at least."

"There's no proof that only one of us would be killed."

Ash quieted at Callum's words. "Your family wouldn't kill you."

"It'd be easy to announce my disownment publicly and quietly have me killed to ensure I don't bring more dishonor to the Kendrick name."

"But it's your *family*," Ash said. No matter how cruel the Houses were, no matter how punishing Winslow Kendrick seemed, Ash couldn't imagine that the man would kill his son.

Callum met Ash's gaze. "You mentioned that you'd seen Ramsay's memories."

Ash hesitated. "Yes. It was because of our harmonization techniques."

"What if I wanted to give you a memory of my own?" Callum asked.

"You'd do that? Why?"

"I don't think you'll ever fully understand me unless you can see for yourself how ruthless my family can be. It'd be useful, too," Callum said, "for you to understand who is now chasing us—who wants to kill you."

Ash's curiosity grew. "I've read about alchemists purposefully sharing memories," he said. "It'd require full energetic permission—you can't just tell yourself that you want me to see. You have to truly mean it."

"I do. I want you to see this."

Ash sucked in a breath and got to his feet. He sat down next to Callum, suddenly too shy to look at the other boy. "Then think of the memory. Hold an intention of sharing it with me. I only have to touch you, like this." Ash put a hand on the back of Callum's, glancing up to be sure it was all right. Callum nodded. "And I'll focus on the intention of seeing the memory you share with me."

"Let's begin."

＊

It started like a dream, not too differently from the memories Ash had seen with Ramsay. Flashes of color, scenes, and voices that were jumbled and made little sense, until finally he felt he'd landed. He sat in a dining room of red-stained paneled wood. Two of Callum's brothers happened to be at the Claremont estate, along with their father. Business had called them away from Kensington. Callum stared down at his plate while his brothers spoke with gleaming smiles, something that, though he was seventeen, Callum hadn't yet mastered. Callum wondered what it was that his brothers and father had that he did not—how they were able to convince all the world that they were worthy of respect, how they were the sort of person who could command a room just by walking into it.

There was a thud. Callum gasped and saw a bird fall from the window, a smudge on the glass. He scraped his chair back, intent on running downstairs to help it—

"Sit down," his father snapped.

Callum blushed. He sat back down. Edric watched Callum with a disappointed sigh, while Culver bit back a laugh.

"I'm sorry," Callum mumbled. "I only wanted to help."

"You are a Kendrick," was all his father said.

Callum knelt outside the manor of beige stone, overlooking the garden and its courtyard, hands cupped together. Callum stood, head bent. A squirming bird was in his palms. It had a broken wing, but it could live if he managed to remember what Ramsay had taught him—Creator, it still hurt to think about Ramsay now that she had officially graduated early and left Pembroke, but Callum thought, too, with excitement of the nights he'd managed to sneak through the portal door and to the Thorne manor. His heart beat harder as he thought of the nights they'd spent together in her bed, a great consolation now that he could no longer see her every evening in the school's gardens.

Ramsay had told him that, in order to heal, he needed to be empathetic. He had to recognize that this reality was only an illusion, and that each and every being was a part of the same energetic field of existence known as Source. Callum, in fact, was also this bird.

Callum closed his eyes, trying to focus on the love he had for it—but still, the bird only squirmed in pain. Its wing didn't heal.

"What're you doing?"

He spun around. Edric stood behind him, hands in his pockets, chin raised with a genuine confidence that couldn't be taught or learned. Though he was only twenty-three years old, Edric had quickly risen in the ranks as a commander. As the second oldest, he would be the right-hand man of their eldest brother, Culver, once he inherited the title of Head from their father. Edric was everything Callum was expected to be, and everything Callum was not.

Edric strode over and inspected the injured bird. He plucked the bird from Callum's hands before Callum could protest and snapped its neck. Callum gasped, heart sinking, as Edric tossed its body into the bushes.

"You'll need to be a little more careful than that," Edric said, leaning against the railing and looking out over the acres of fields, the blue sea in the distance. "You're seventeen now. This is your last year at Pembroke before you join McKinley. Father would be disappointed to see such . . . ." Edric paused, searching for the right word, then said, "softness."

Callum clenched his jaw. It was only luck that Edric hadn't realized what Callum had truly been doing: Attempting unlicensed alchemy would've earned him a harsher response. "Not much will have changed, then."

Edric offered Callum a pitying smile. "Softness has its uses," he said. "There needs to be a balance in the world, after all. Just—"

"—not when we're the sons of Kendrick." Callum stepped on a feather that had been left behind.

Edric nodded his agreement, eyeing Callum closely.

Callum ducked his head. "I only wish I knew what I need to do to change into a person who meets his expectations." He hesitated, glancing at Edric. "To be powerful—not just pretend to be, or try to be, but actually be powerful."

His brother seemed to take in everything that Callum said. "The only thing you lack is confidence," Edric told him. "You are a son of Kendrick. You already have the power you seek, everything that you require to become the person our father needs you to be."

"Then why doesn't it feel that way?" Callum asked, a touch of desperation in his voice.

"You'll be met with challenges," Edric said carefully. "You only need to know, without any doubt, that you are able to face those challenges." He turned away, clapping Callum on the shoulder as he started to leave. "Don't worry. You'll have plenty of opportunity to prove yourself. To show us all how powerful you can be."

"I'm not even sure I know what power means, sometimes," Callum said, before he could think better of it.

Edric stared at Callum expressionlessly before he released a small laugh, placing a hand on Callum's head as he used to do when they were young. "You've always liked to ask questions," he said, and Callum wasn't sure if Edric saw this as a weakness or a strength. "Come with me," he said to Callum over his shoulder as he walked away. "Father wants to speak with you."

Callum forced himself to bite back his fear and follow Edric. They walked into the Claremont manor and down a hall and then another, through the maze of corridors, lights growing dimmer with every step. They walked into a hall that ended with a closed door for a room that Callum had always assumed was a private study of his father's. When he was young, Callum had sometimes heard shouts and screams of pain come from this room and had learned to avoid it. The screams weren't unexpected. The

Kendrick manor was old, and many old buildings had souls of the dead, lost and unable or unwilling to return to the Creator. But as they approached the room, Callum could feel the hairs on his arms stand.

Edric whispered a word and opened the door without knocking. He gestured for Callum to enter. The rusting scent of burned iron and the smell of salt and mildew was so strong that it made Callum dizzy. When his eyes adjusted to the shadows, and he saw the sticky reddish-brown stains on the ground, he realized that he wasn't smelling burnt iron at all. His stomach twisted. Edric shut the door behind Callum, shoulders back and head raised, but even his older brother couldn't hide the quick quiver of nerves in his vibration, something Callum had learned he was quite good at picking up on since Ramsay had begun to teach him alchemy.

"What is this?" Callum gasped, staring up at his brother. "Edric?"

His brother didn't speak. Edric only waved a hand forward. Callum took a shaky breath, and he began to walk.

They were in some sort of dungeon, that much became clear as they passed the bars of cages, chains hanging from the ceiling. There was a sliver of a window that let in gray light, and Callum could also see that they were no longer in Claremont or his family's mansion, from the silhouette of city buildings and warehouses. He could be anywhere in the state. He reached the end of the dungeon's hall and almost jumped when he saw his father standing in the middle of one of the cells.

He wasn't alone. Another man was seated in a chair, hands bound behind his back. A black sheet wrapped the man's head and was tied shut around his neck, but Callum could still see he was crying from the shaking of his shoulders and his low moans. "Please. Please."

Callum was going to be sick. He looked from the man and to his father, whose cold eyes watched Callum's every movement and response. Callum usually would've wanted to do what he could to put on a performance to earn his father's respect, but now—

"What is this?" he said. His words sounded too loud.

Winslow Kendrick glanced down at his prisoner. "We are currently in the dungeons of Hedge. This man is set to be executed tomorrow. Death by hanging."

The man's moaning grew louder.

"I spoke to the executioner, and an arrangement was made."

Callum began to shake his head, taking a step back.

"There is a long-standing tradition in House Kendrick," his father said, "to prove your strength, your loyalty, and your duty to your family before you come of age."

"By *killing* someone?" Callum said, his voice hoarse. The man shuddered.

"By taking the life, yes," his father said, hands behind his back, "of a person unworthy of living. We are the House of order. The House of discipline. This is a tradition that we've all performed."

Callum looked at Edric and could see from the coldness that had shuttered his brother's eyes that it was true. Before Edric turned eighteen, their father must've brought him into these dungeons, too, and ordered him to kill another person, along with all their brothers.

He shook his head. "No," he said. "No. I can't—"

His father took one long stride forward and backhanded Callum. Callum's head snapped to the side, his cheek and nose and lip stinging. This, he wasn't surprised by. This, Callum practically welcomed. At least it was familiar, almost comforting in the face of the horror he was expected to commit.

Edric mirrored his father's stance, hands behind his back. "It's better if it's done quickly, Callum. Thinking about it only makes it worse."

The man flinched. "Please," he choked. "I beg of you."

"You knew," Callum said to Edric, betrayal clogging his throat. "You knew he was asking for me to come here and murder—"

"It isn't murder," Edric corrected calmly. "It's an execution. House Kendrick is in charge of executions, of order and justice for all the state of New Anglia. How can we command our soldiers, our redguards, to execute and kill others in the name of our House without knowing the full weight of what it means to take a life ourselves?"

Winslow was not as patient. He turned to a wall where rusted weapons waited, drawing a dagger. He marched to Callum and thrust the blade into his hands. "If you do not kill this man," he murmured in his son's ear, "then I will kill both him and you."

Callum knew that this was no idle threat. He could feel how his father would rather Callum be dead than be a son who was unwilling and unable to fulfill this duty. Callum wasn't sure how it'd be done, but he could imagine it easily enough: a poisoning, maybe, that could be blamed on a sudden illness. Callum, thrown from a cliff by his family's own guards, a tragic accident where he fell while he was out riding alone.

Winslow stepped away from Callum. His brother and father watched him silently, waiting. Callum looked down at the blade in his hands.

***

Ash didn't want to see the killing. He yanked his fingers away, shaking.

"Do you see now?" Callum asked. "Do you see why it wouldn't be so surprising, if—" He seemed unable to finish his sentence.

Ash had a harder time looking at him now. He nodded.

"And now I've also shown you something that you didn't know about me before," Callum whispered.

"You didn't have a choice," Ash said softly. "And the man—he was going to be executed anyway."

"He died by the unskillful hand of a seventeen-year-old. He deserved a swifter death, no matter his crime," Callum said, his voice hardened. "I'd been so fearful before that moment, but afterward—when I saw how far my father was willing to go—I forced myself to play the role of the perfect son. And even that I couldn't do."

"That's when you told her, isn't it?" Ash asked. "That's when you ended your relationship with Ramsay."

Callum swallowed. "I was afraid that, if my father discovered us, he would punish me—have me kill Ramsay myself, maybe, before he killed me, too."

At least Ash could better understand Callum now, even if he'd hurt Ramsay. Ash slipped his hand over Callum's palm unthinkingly, only wanting to comfort the Kendrick boy who, despite himself, Ash had truly begun to think of as a friend. "I think that Ramsay would appreciate knowing why."

Callum looked down at their hands with some surprise, but the soft smile he gave Ash when he looked back up was genuine. He squeezed Ash's hand. "Yes. I agree."

Ash blushed, pulling his hand away again. A conductor's voice announced that they would be pulling into Ironbound Station within the hour. They were one hour away from Ramsay—from finding her, from helping her. Ash's nerves pumped. He was an hour away from demanding an explanation from her, too.

26

Ironbound was similar to Hedge. There were warehouses and docks, smoke soiling the air, and frozen streets filled with people who knocked past with glares. Ash wished he'd fought harder when Callum had insisted on buying new clothes. They got more than a few stares for the quality of their cloaks and shoes as they left the station, luggage in hands. Ash was sure he'd heard someone mutter that they should go back to Kensington.

"Does anything look familiar to you?" Callum asked, ignoring the looks they received. "Did you see her on any of these streets?"

Source knew it wouldn't be that easy. "I think that she was farther away from the center of the city—the buildings were more spaced out," Ash said, searching for anything recognizable. "But I don't know for sure."

Callum nodded with only some impatience, though Ash didn't think it was directed at him. It'd been a long journey. "Well, it won't do us any good to stand here all day. Let's at least find an inn. We can get some ice for your hand and wrap it."

Ash narrowed his eyes at Callum, annoyed that he'd stepped into redguard-commander mode. "I don't want to waste any time. We should start looking for her now."

"We don't even know where to begin, Ash. It's better to attempt another remote viewing once we're settled," he said. "We can try to pinpoint where Ramsay is hiding so we'll at least have an idea of where to search."

Ash hated that Callum was right. "Fine."

They wandered the streets until Ash was forced to approach a man smoking against a wall and ask where the nearest inn was, scarf carefully hiding his face.

"Closest inn is the Scarecrow, a few blocks down," the man said gruffly, eyeing Ash. "But the best inn for avoiding reds is the White Pig."

Ash wondered what'd tipped him off. It was a risk, admitting to this man that he didn't want to be found by redguards, but he asked for directions nonetheless. He and Callum made their way through the maze of brick apartments and warehouses, closer to the outskirts of the city and the docks, salt lingering in the air. The roads were slippy with ice. Ash imagined Ramsay walking through these roads on her way to the market, perhaps wanting to hunker down in Ironbound for as long as possible before patrols relaxed and she moved on. The sun had risen higher now, but the gray clouds made the sky dim. Ash shivered as he pulled his scarf tighter around his cheeks. He was grateful when Callum seemed to notice and stepped closer, blocking the icy wind from hitting him.

The White Pig was hidden in an alley, easily missed. Ash and Callum had to double back around twice before they finally saw the small swinging sign above the door, letters faded. Inside, it seemed like nothing more than an ill-lit two-story pub. There was only one patron in the corner. The innkeeper stood behind the bar's counter and glared as if unhappy to see customers. Ash needed to do a double take, the man reminded him so much of Frank—but Frank was just slightly taller and thinner, and this man was a bit younger.

"One room, please," Ash said when they approached. Though Callum would be the person paying, he didn't see any point in wasting the coin.

The bartender stared hard at Callum, and then down at Ash. He made an assumption with a sneer. "This inn isn't a place for a romp in the sheets. You'd have better luck on South End."

Ash wasn't sure who was more mortified in the silence that

followed, him or Callum. Ash stammered and stuttered, unable to find the right sounds to form the words *no, Source, you're mistaken*, but Callum stepped forward.

"You've caught us," he said. Ash whipped his head up to gape at Callum, aghast, but Callum only put on a polite smile. "South End isn't to our tastes. We'd prefer to stay here." He dropped his coin pouch on the counter with a clink.

The bartender watched Callum like he didn't believe the Kendrick boy for a moment, but coin had a way of swaying people's minds. "As long as you don't bring any trouble."

"No one should come looking for us, but if they do—well, I'm willing to pay a little extra now for you to say we went to South End, like you suggested."

The bartender's sneer grew as he reached for a key behind the counter. "Rich boys have plenty of extra coin on their hands, eh? In my day we'd find an alley and be done with it."

Ash suppressed a disgusted shiver. Callum gave a tight smile. "Yes, well, my lover is a little too precious for that."

Ash swallowed back a gag. All this, plus the word *lover*, was too much to bear.

"Oh," Callum added as if he didn't notice that Ash was about to be sick on the floor, "and could we have a cup of ice, please? Need to find ways to keep the love life interesting." He *winked*.

The innkeeper only muttered an indifferent nonresponse and handed Callum a cup and a key as Ash tried very hard not to die on the spot. As the two made their way up the stairs and to their new room, Ash could hardly look at Callum. He wasn't sure why the conversation below mortified him so much. He wasn't a prude. But when he thought about how Callum had sensed Ash's attraction . . .

Ash hadn't been physically attracted to Ramsay, not at first—she was pale and thin and had appeared fragile before Ash learned how resilient she really was—but as Ash got to know her, the more he began to care for her and the more his attraction grew.

But Ash's physical attraction to Callum had been instantaneous, and he was horrified to admit to himself that his attraction had only grown the more time they'd spent together. Callum's softer personality might've annoyed Ash, once—he preferred Ramsay's biting sarcasm—but Ash knew that the boy had officially won his friendship. Ash cared about Callum.

They stomped up the creaking wooden stairs and down the musty hall. There were voices in a room they passed, a muffled shout. Callum slid in the key and unlocked the door with a click, pushing it open. The room reminded Ash of the apartment he'd left behind in Hedge. There was a single bed that he wasn't sure would fit Callum, much less both of them—one would have to sleep on the floor—and a wooden wardrobe was pushed up against the wall. An open doorway showed a sliver of the bathroom's molding tub, providing enough evidence that Ash wouldn't want to spend more time in there than necessary. A tiny window let in very little wintery gray light, and the bulb's chain that Ash pulled didn't make the room much brighter.

Ash sighed with relief as he dropped his bag, but he paused when Callum didn't follow him inside. He turned around, then smirked when he saw the expression on Callum's face.

"Doing all right?" he asked.

Callum hesitated. "This is the room?" he said.

"Careful, Kendrick. Your *spoiled House heir* is showing."

Callum glanced around uncertainly as he stepped inside, also placing his bag down and closing the door behind him. He went to the window and stared at the alleyway below, then up at the sky— likely for some sort of redguard strategy, figuring out the best way to make a quick exit, perhaps. "I don't mean to sound spoiled. I'm just surprised, is all."

"I guess anything less than a bedroom the size of most people's apartments would be surprising."

Callum seemed satisfied with whatever he found at the window and shrugged off his cloak while Ash unraveled his scarf with one hand, still gingerly holding up the other. The bruising had gone down, but it still stung to move his fingers. Callum stepped closer—not too hard to do, the room was quite small anyway—and inspected Ash's knuckles.

"It's getting better, but it could still use a proper icing. May I?"

Ash stared at the ground so that it wouldn't appear that he was flustered as Callum dumped the ice into a handkerchief he pulled from his bag.

"Why did you pack a handkerchief again?"

"A gentleman never knows when he'll need one," Callum said. It was hard for Ash to tell if the other boy was joking or not.

Callum took Ash's hand. He tied the handkerchief around Ash's palm twice so that the ice rested on top of the cloth that was bundled against his knuckles. The cold seared his skin for a moment before it went numb. Ash glanced up at Callum. The older boy frowned with concentration, working with a level of care that reminded Ash of the way he'd touched his seedlings and plants in Lancaster. Callum looked up, meeting Ash's eye, and Ash dropped his gaze again.

"You really would make a good healer," Ash said, more to cover up the uncomfortable silence.

"Do you think so?" Callum asked. He let go of Ash's hand, checking his work. "Most people would disagree, I think, given my last name."

"Most people like to make assumptions without really knowing anything at all." Ash hesitated. "I made assumptions about you, too, before I really had a chance to get to know you."

Callum rubbed the back of his neck as if he was nervous now. Ash wasn't sure the room was large enough for them and their awkwardness. "I did the same to you, I suppose," Callum murmured. He cleared his throat. "I'll get us something to eat from the pub."

"What?" Ash said. "No. I want to begin the remote viewing."

"You'll need my energy to be successful," Callum said, "and

right now, I don't have any because I'm hungry. I'll be quick. You can take the opportunity to wash up, if you like."

Ash agreed with a sigh. He had to admit he was starving, too. Callum left, locking the door behind him, as Ash went into the bathroom and pulled off his clothes and his binder, struggling with one hand. The tub's water was lukewarm at best for a few moments before it became ice-cold, so Ash was quick to scrub down and dry off with the inn's threadbare towel. He realized as he tried to pull his binder around his chest again that it was impossible without both hands. Another reason to feel uncomfortable as he shared a room with Callum, then. Ash's chest was small, like the rest of his frame, but it had made him uncomfortable the moment it began to grow. In his dreams, he always had a flat chest, like Ramsay's, and the flashes of memories he received from past lives had been bodies with flat chests, too. These things hanging from him felt like extra appendages that simply didn't belong.

The only thing that Ash found strange was that there was *another* appendage that his past lives also tended to have, swinging between their legs, but he didn't miss that at all. He rather liked his anatomy below the belt, the extra hole that most men didn't have. He enjoyed how it'd felt when Ramsay had touched him there, licking and kissing and using her fingers. Ash wondered, for only a moment, how it might feel for Callum to make his way between Ash's legs, too.

It was a strange and unnecessary thought. He pushed it away almost angrily as he tugged on the sweater, grateful at least that it was baggy enough to hide his chest, and yanked back on his pants. He opened the bathroom door and was surprised to find that Callum was already back, hunched over two plates of what appeared to be stale bread.

"I didn't hear you come in," Ash said, running a hand through his wet curls.

Callum blinked up at him, as if startled by something, though

Ash didn't know what, then stared hard at the plate. "This was all they had."

Ash flopped onto the floor and picked at the bread. "Aren't you going to wash up also?"

"I did last night before we left."

It was obvious that Callum simply didn't want to wash in a bathroom that was below House standards. As capable as Callum seemed, it appeared he'd have a more difficult time on this journey than Ash expected.

No matter. "Let's begin."

※

The flicker of images that flashed through Ash's mind were difficult to untangle. Brick row houses like many he and Callum had seen on their walk to the inn alone, much less across the entire city; the gray ocean from the busy docks and an empty square with a dead tree standing in its center. Ash and Callum left the inn and began their search through the city streets, watching for the images Ash had seen. Whenever they saw a redguard, Ash's nerves pumped, certain that they'd be ordered to stop, grateful when they continued unscathed each time.

The two walked for hours until Ash's feet ached and his cheeks stung in the cold. His injured hand throbbed. He was so frustrated he could scream. When they reached the abandoned square, Ash lost his last sliver of hope. He'd imagined that Ramsay would be waiting for them beneath the tree. He walked up to it and saw a faded plaque beneath, reading that this had been the hanging tree of Ironbound criminals for over a century. He imagined that Ramsay had been here, maybe only hours ago, before she'd moved on.

"Fuck!" he shouted, kicking the tree's trunk. He stopped only when Callum put a large hand on his shoulder.

"Take a breath," he said. He looked pointedly at some passerby who had turned to them, alarmed. Attacking a city monument was certainly a way to be caught by the reds.

Ash did as he was told, taking in a slow breath and releasing it. He remembered how he and Ramsay had shared so many similar breaths, too. "How can you be so calm?" he asked.

"You're assuming that I am," Callum said with a small tired smile. "I'm frustrated, too, Ash. But there isn't much we can do now. Let's go back to the inn, and when we've rested, we'll have an easier time figuring out our next steps."

They were silent for the entire walk, lost in their own thoughts even as they marched back up the stairs and opened their room's door. Ash sat on the edge of the bed as he kicked off his boots, defeated. He knew it'd be difficult to find Ramsay, but now it felt impossible. They'd have better luck screaming her name in the streets, hoping she'd eventually shout back, *Yes?*

Callum pulled off his cloak and shoes also, picking up both his own and Ash's and lining them up by the door. Maybe that was something he was trained to do as a red, too. "Don't give up after one day. We'll find her."

Ash didn't meet Callum's eye. It seemed Callum was getting better at reading Ash's emotions the more time they spent together. "I think that's partly why I'm on edge, too," he admitted.

Callum gave him a curious look. "Why?"

Ash didn't mean to be so vulnerable, but maybe he hadn't realized how close he'd started to feel to Callum. It was hard not to trust the other boy after the memory he'd shared with Ash— difficult to not want to share a part of himself, too. "Because then I'll have to figure out how to feel both happy and relieved that I've found her, while also angry and betrayed that she left me behind in the first place."

Callum sat at the head of the bed, resting his back against the wall, legs crossed. He considered Ash. "I can see why that'd be difficult."

"It'll probably be complicated for you when you see her again, too," Ash said, a little more stiffly this time. He glanced up at Callum. "Right?"

Callum nodded slowly, frowning at something over Ash's shoulder. "Yes, you could say that. I know how I feel about her. I know that I want to apologize, explain myself, and promise that I'll never hurt her like that again." He met Ash's eye. "But I don't know how she'll react to me. She might reject me. Creator, I'm not sure what I'll do then. I've given up everything with the hope that she'll forgive me."

Ash tried to bite down on the curiosity that grew, but it wasn't much use. "You really must love Ramsay a lot, to be willing to risk so much."

"Yes. But you know what it's like to love Ramsay, too."

Again loomed the threat of the unspoken rivalry between the two—but Callum didn't seem concerned as he adjusted his legs, stretching them out behind Ash with a contented sigh. Ash could see now how Ramsay would've fallen in love with Callum. His kindness and patience and comforting gaze and hands—his hands were large and rough, but his touch was always careful and soft. Ash had never seen any memories of Ramsay and Callum sharing a bed, but he was curious about that now, too. He knew how Ramsay was when she pressed Ash down into the mattress with a smirk, but how did Callum hold another person? How did he hold Ramsay? How would he hold Ash?

Ash glanced up, feeling Callum's stare. In the few seconds of silence, Ash realized that all his emotion and perhaps the thoughts that went along with them were on full display. He froze, unsure of what to do or say, unable to look away from Callum's steady gaze. Usually, he'd pretend nothing had happened at all, maybe make some sorry excuse as he threw back on his shoes and left the room—but it felt like there was no sense in hiding it now, not when Callum watched him the way he did, eyes hooded.

"If you're attracted to me, Ash," Callum said, "why won't you just say so?"

Ash forgot how to breathe. He blinked, finally looking away at the hands he held together in his lap. "I don't know what you mean."

"There isn't any point in lying about it, is there?" Callum's smile was only slightly amused. "Even if I couldn't feel your emotions, it isn't hard to notice the way you look at me."

Ash was bewildered by his straightforwardness. The shared quarters were already uncomfortable enough. In the name of Source, why would Callum say any of this? Why couldn't he have gone on pretending he hadn't noticed? They wouldn't be able to return to any semblance of normalcy now. They'd be too embarrassed to look at or even speak to each other. And still Callum only watched Ash, waiting for his response.

Ash took this as a challenge as he turned to face Callum fully. "Fine," he said. "Yes. I admit it. I've found you attractive from time to time. It's nothing I could help because believe me, if I could control it, I wouldn't be attracted to you of all people—but I am, so here we are. Now, go ahead. Laugh all you want."

"Why would I laugh?"

"Isn't that why you interrogated me about it?" Ash said. "Because you think it's funny?" He could see no other reason.

"No," Callum said plainly. "Not at all. The way you feel isn't funny to me."

"Then what was the point?" Why couldn't he have shown Ash some pity and let it go?

"I just wondered why you didn't say anything, when you've been so open about everything else you feel," Callum said. He finally looked away from Ash. "And I decided it might be a good chance to tell you that I've begun to feel the same."

Ash, for the second time in as many minutes, forgot that air was necessary. He opened and closed his mouth, then said, "I'm sorry, what?"

Callum gave a small laugh now, though more at himself. "I'll admit, I hadn't considered it until I realized you were attracted to me the other night, but once the thought formed . . ." His smile faded and his gaze reached Ash's again. "I'm tired of hiding how I feel. I have too many regrets, pushing away what I want because I'm afraid."

"What about Ramsay?" Ash asked.

"I've learned from my mistakes with her," Callum said. "I've wasted so much of my life suppressing myself for the sake of my family. I'm attracted to you, Ash. I don't want to hide that from you or myself. I don't want to hide anything that I want anymore."

Ash wondered, vaguely, if Callum only said that now because he'd lost everything. Maybe he'd become unhinged without even fully realizing it. Ash related.

"Maybe," Callum whispered. "But even so, that doesn't change the truth."

Would it really hurt to welcome a distraction like this? Even if it did, Ash had stopped thinking several minutes ago now. He crawled forward, careful not to hurt his hand as he leaned onto his knees, one on either side of Callum's leg, who waited with a smile that quivered with nerves. At least Ash wasn't the only one scared.

"This isn't a prank?" Ash whispered.

"No. This isn't a prank."

"You won't regret what we've done the moment it's over, will you?"

Callum's smile faded as he hesitated. "I can't promise how I will or won't feel," he eventually said.

Somehow, this was good enough for Ash. He pressed his lips to Callum's, adjusting so that his knees were now on either side of the other boy's lap. Callum satisfied Ash's curiosity, finally, resting his hands on Ash's back. Heat radiated from his palms, as if inviting Ash to melt into him. There was a firmness in his grip, plainly used to being in control as he guided Ash closer. He raised a surprised brow when Ash smirked against his mouth and pushed back.

"Don't tell me that awful attitude follows you into bed, too," Callum murmured, though he didn't seem completely displeased.

"No, of course not," Ash said sarcastically, grinding deeper into Callum's lap and glad when he let out a small gasp. "I'm always respectful and will gladly follow every little order you give me."

Ash found it interesting that, even as Callum picked up Ash by his waist and tossed him onto his back, he still managed to be gentle, as if he was handling something precious to him. Even as he pinned Ash's wrists, he seemed to be aware of the bruised knuckles, careful that they weren't pushed too tightly into the mattress as Callum kissed Ash's mouth and his cheek and his neck. Callum pulled away as he tugged his own shirt over his head, smiling down at Ash all the while as if he knew how much Ash's heartbeat had sped up at the sight. He kissed Ash again, more softly than before. This made Ash uncomfortable—he wasn't used to gentleness, like he was someone that needed to be shown tender love, and he didn't think that Callum *loved* him anyway, not as he did Ramsay.

"You're in your head," Callum murmured, mouth lingering over Ash's stomach.

"You're not reading my thoughts, are you?"

Ash felt Callum's smile against his skin. "A little hard not to, when you're shouting them at me."

"It isn't fair that you know my thoughts and I don't know yours."

"I can share them with you, if you like."

Ash gasped as Callum's hand trailed under his thighs. He could feel sparks of energy tracing along his skin. "Tell me."

"I'm thinking that I'm scared," Callum murmured, kissing Ash's abdomen.

"Scared?"

"Worried that this is a mistake."

Ash frowned. "That's reassuring."

"I'm also thinking that I'm tired of being afraid," Callum

added, leaning forward to kiss Ash's jaw and neck. "That I wish I could let myself be free to do as I please."

"And what do you want to do, exactly?"

Callum sat up and gazed down at him, breath shallow. "I think we're even now."

Ash stared up at him. He wanted to let go, too—let himself enjoy Callum's warmth and touch. "You're right," Ash admitted. "I am in my head."

"Stop thinking. Focus on my hands."

Ash didn't think he'd be willing to do as he was told, but he was glad when he did, gasping at the energy that moved over his thighs, his waist and abdomen, reaching underneath his sweater—

Ash sat up so abruptly that he almost knocked into Callum. Callum pulled back immediately, alarmed. "Are you okay? Do you want me to stop?"

Ash had forgotten that he'd taken his binder off. "I—uh, I don't like my chest to be touched."

"Understood." Callum watched him, waiting as if he knew there was more to be said.

Ash wanted to keep going, but he felt uncomfortable at the thought of Callum seeing his bare chest. But he also didn't want to keep his sweater on—he was already overheating and, shit, it was humiliating that his discomfort with his own body should get in the way now—

Callum put a hand on Ash's, playing with his fingers. "Tell me what you need."

Ash bit his lip. "Usually, I'd have my binder on."

He was grateful now that Callum could hear his thoughts. He didn't need to say anything else as the other boy nodded. "Where is it?"

Ash stood and went to his duffel, pulling it out. Callum got up from the bed and told Ash to turn around. Ash did so and pulled off his sweater. He shivered when he felt a soft touch on his back, Callum putting a hand beneath his rib.

"Tell me if it's too tight," he said, lacing up one side.

"Have you put binders on many chests before?" Ash asked, only half-jokingly, though Callum's confidence made him wonder.

"No," Callum said with some amusement. "But I was trained to bandage." Callum continued to lace up one side of the binder, then the other. "It was a short seminar," Callum continued, "only in case of emergencies during battle. I learned that it's dangerous to compress the chest too tightly."

He finished tying the last of the strings. "Will that do?" Callum asked softly, kissing the back of Ash's neck and his shoulder.

Ash turned, kissing Callum's mouth again, even more eagerly now than before. He pulled Callum by the front of his pants, both falling back onto the bed, grinning as Callum leaned over him. He would let himself enjoy this, Ash decided. He wouldn't let himself worry about whether this was a betrayal to Ramsay. He wouldn't let her enter his thoughts with every kiss and touch.

27

Snow had fallen high enough to reach her knees, but luckily a path had been cleared through the field. Smoke drifted on the breeze, a gray haze that covered the sky. A door opened, warmth from a fireplace touching her skin. A woman greeted Ramsay— she didn't know who Thorne was and didn't have the faintest idea that there'd been an attack on a college. Ash couldn't hear what either said as the door closed behind them.

He opened his eyes. Callum stared back into them intensely.

"Did you see anything?" he asked.

Ash closed his eyes again, frustrated. "Yes, but—Source, it's confusing. I could sense that she was still near the city, even if I couldn't see it, but there was a field and a cabin, too."

"Ramsay's already left Ironbound, then?"

"Factories were also nearby, I think. There was smoke."

"She must be on the outskirts now. There's a mining town at the base of the mountains," Callum said. It didn't surprise Ash that he would know something like that. It'd probably been Callum's responsibility to learn about small towns and villages near major cities as a commander in training. "The smoke could've been from the drills."

Ash stood without another word. He had a hard time looking at Callum as he grabbed his bag. "Then we should get going," he said. "Before she moves on again."

"It'll take about half a day to travel there," Callum said.

It was still morning. The sun had barely risen. "Even more reason to leave quickly, then," Ash said. "We should try to get there before dark."

Ash and Callum were quiet as they packed. Ash was annoyed that, after they'd had sex, Callum had been the one to continue meeting Ash's eye with a pleased smile, leaning in for kisses as they lay together in bed—well, as Ash lay on top of Callum, anyway, since there hadn't been enough space for them to lie down side by side. Callum acted as if everything was perfectly fine and he had no regrets at all. But Ash felt confused and frustrated by his confusion.

He wasn't ashamed of sex. His desire and pleasure didn't embarrass him. But he couldn't stop thinking about Ramsay, either—couldn't help feeling like he'd betrayed her, even while he was still angry that she'd left him behind. And, within the same breath, he also somehow felt betrayed by *Callum*, knowing that the other boy had slept with Ash while still loving Ramsay.

Ash caught Callum staring. "You're not in my head again, are you?"

"I don't hear thoughts every minute of every day, you know," Callum said as he shrugged on his coat. "I don't have enough control over it."

"Good," Ash said, and turned away as he closed his duffel. "I'm not in the mood for an invasion of privacy right now."

Callum didn't reply. Ash wondered what this meant for their relationship. Were the two now friends who had sex with each other, like Ash had been with Tobin? Did Ash care about Callum in the same way that they both loved Ramsay, too? It was a confusing mess of thoughts and emotions that Ash couldn't begin to untangle.

He'd just wrapped his scarf around his face when a hand clasped his own. Ash paused, releasing a breath.

"Is everything all right, Ash?" Callum asked softly.

"No," Ash said, "but there's no point in talking about it now. We need to find Ramsay."

"I think it's better to talk this through," Callum said. "It doesn't help for us to be uncomfortable and distracted. That could put both us and her into danger, ultimately."

Ash bit his lip as he forced himself to turn and face Callum. "I'm confused, is all," Ash said.

"Confused about how you feel about me?" Callum asked.

Maybe it'd been a lucky guess, or maybe Callum was more in tune with Ash's emotions than he'd realized. It angered Ash that it felt like he didn't have a free thought of his own, protected from Callum's ability. "Yes," he admitted, frustrated. "And confused about who we are to each other now, and what this means for how I feel about Ramsay, and—"

Ash had rambled on without meaning to, but he stopped himself before he could admit the most vulnerable part of all. But Callum only watched him steadily, waiting, perhaps even already knowing what Ash would say. He forced himself to continue.

"And confused about how you feel about me, too."

Callum nodded, unsurprised. "Our friendship is new, Ash, but I know that I care about you," he said. "I want to let our relationship and my feelings for you grow."

"And what relationship do we have now?"

"I hope that we're friends."

"Friends who have sex with each other?"

"I would like that," Callum said, voice hoarse, "if you would, too."

After last night, it'd be difficult to pretend that he didn't want the same. "I do," he said after a moment. "But what about Ramsay?"

Callum took in a steadying breath. "I love her, like I've loved her for years."

"You sound defensive, Kendrick."

"Not defensive. I'm only speaking the truth."

"And you know that I love her, too. You can't pretend you don't give a shit about that."

Callum looked away. "Why do I get the sense that you're trying to pick a fight with me, Ash?"

Ash swallowed. "Better to get the fight out of the way now, isn't it?"

"You're assuming that we have to fight at all."

"Don't we?" Ash said. "We both want Ramsay."

"I don't know how Ramsay will react when she sees me again," Callum said. "To be fair, you don't know how she'll react to you, either. She could reject me and want you. She could reject you and want me. She could reject us both."

Ash's breath tightened. He could imagine Ramsay choosing Callum and leaving Ash behind again. Callum had been the love of her life, after all, long before Ramsay had even met Ash. And then? Callum spoke pretty words now, but what if he realized he wanted Ramsay and only Ramsay, and the two both abandoned Ash? It seemed to be the story of his life, to be left by the people he loved. The odds suggested it would only happen again.

Callum continued. "I don't think it's fair of us to consider what Ramsay does and doesn't want without her input."

Ash groaned. "Source, I hate when you sound so reasonable."

But maybe Callum was right. Maybe it wasn't fair of Ash to decide what Ramsay would do—and maybe it wasn't fair to Callum, either, assuming that he would choose only Ramsay when Callum probably didn't even know what he would do himself.

"How're you so unbothered by all of this?" Ash asked, but the other boy only laughed.

"Do you think I'm unbothered? Really?" His laugh faded, though an uncertain smile lingered. "I'm just as scared as you are, Ash."

They looked at each other for a long moment before Ash reached for Callum's hand, who let him take it with some relief, looking at Ash's fingers like he considered kissing them. "I suppose we'll just have to see what happens."

※

Ash was eager to leave, but Callum insisted on stopping by the innkeeper below and making several orders of dried fruit and meat. "We don't know how long we'll be traveling," he said, "and we don't know where we'll find our next meal."

When they finally left the inn, Ash wasn't sure if it was only his imagination or if there really was a sudden rise in the number of redguards on patrol. The two ducked their heads and changed streets and blocks several times, Ash's nerves growing tight in his chest.

After avoiding the fifth patrol, Callum murmured, "Word's likely spread that you escaped with me. Either someone recognized us on the train to Ironbound, or there's been a patrol increase in all major cities." Either way, it was clear that they needed to keep their heads down.

They made it to the station without being stopped. Along the street were rows of horse-drawn carriages and bored drivers who chewed on tobacco and only became animated when a potential passenger walked past. There was one driver who sat at the very end of the row, head nodding as he fell asleep. He appeared to be younger than Ash by a few years, and when Ash and Callum approached, he eyed them warily.

"Good day, sir," Callum said. "I have a question for you."

The boy stared back at him, indifferent.

"What would you do if a fight were to break out in front of you, here and now?"

The boy snorted. "Depends on what I'm paid to do."

"And if you're paid nothing?"

"I'd mind my own business and go back to sleep."

It was good enough. "There's a mining town on the base of the mountains outside of Ironbound," Callum said.

"But that's Dunsbrow," the boy said, as if he'd told a bad joke.

Callum extracted his coin pouch and gave the boy a handful of sterling. "That's half now. I'll provide the other half when we arrive at the town."

The boy counted the sterling, and when he reached one hundred, he looked up at Callum and Ash with suspicion. Maybe in that moment he realized who the increase in redguard patrols was for, but he finally nodded his head at the carriage. Callum and Ash clambered inside, closing the door. The carriage smelled like wood and cleaning solution, the purple cushions on the seats worn and stained. Neither complained as the boy pulled on the reins, and the horses began to clop forward, the carriage rocking back and forth.

Ash stared out the window at Ironbound, glad to be leaving. Though he'd grown up in Hedge, he was starting to think that he didn't have much of a heart for cities.

He looked up to find Callum watching him. Callum didn't seem to care he'd been caught. He gave a small smile.

"Don't start to gaze longingly at me," Ash said.

"Is that what you think I was doing?"

"Why else would you be staring at me?"

"I was imagining what we could do the next time we share a bed."

Ash blushed, rubbing the back of his neck. "You're pretty bold, you know that?"

"I've been told."

They were silent for a few long moments before Ash found himself curious. "Is Ramsay the only other person you've had sex with?"

Callum appeared shyer now. "No. McKinley isn't as conservative as you'd think. I've had my fun, especially after I told Ramsay I couldn't see her anymore. I was desperate to distract myself."

This didn't surprise Ash. He thought Callum was confident in bed, with a strong sense of what to do and how he liked to touch and be touched. It seemed everyone had more experience than Ash when it came to sex.

"And you really don't feel guilty?" Ash asked.

"Why would I?"

"I can't stop feeling like I've betrayed Ramsay."

Callum frowned. "I don't think we've done anything wrong. Neither of us have an agreement with Ramsay to be in a relationship with only her."

"That's true, I guess."

"And it isn't as if we should only feel attraction and love for one person. I've never understood it, this expectation that people should only love one other at a time. Isn't that what alchemists say?" he asked. "Energy is infinite, and love is energy, so love has the potential to be infinite, too."

Ash grinned as he shook his head. "Spoken like a true healer," he said, and at Callum's confusion, he explained. "That's the main premise that goes into healing, from the texts I've read—the idea that healing requires love, and we can all love one another, if we choose to. They say that in order to heal, you need to first believe that love is limitless."

Callum looked pleasantly surprised at this, happy that he'd passed the first requirement in becoming a healer. Ash felt himself brighten at Callum's excitement. It was funny how Kendrick could go from being a calm redguard one moment, to a boy guiltily eager about alchemy the next. It only made Ash more interested in Callum's little hypocrisies. He thought of Callum's memory—his gangly younger self cupping the bird in his hands—and imagined him now, still wanting to heal small things.

"How much healing did Ramsay teach you?" Ash asked, forcing himself to look back out the window.

"Only little cuts and things of the like. We never got very far into the subject."

Well, Ramsay's main interest had never been healing. She'd focused on the mathematics of alchemy, so it made sense that she wouldn't be the best teacher for it. Ash wouldn't be much better. He only knew the theory he'd read from texts. But still, a part of him wanted to see that excitement in Callum's eyes again.

"I can teach you some more," he said, glancing back at Callum. "If you'd like."

There it was. The shine brightened and grew with Callum's smile. It looked like he wanted to suppress it, knew that this didn't fit his carefully constructed self, but he couldn't fully hide his enthusiasm as he nodded. "Thank you, Ash. Yes. I'd like that very much."

∗

Ash fell in and out of sleep on the ride, opening his eyes now and then to see that the city had fallen away to smaller neighborhoods and scattered towns, until finally all evidence of humans disappeared into rocky fields. The Derry Hills were in the distance, and it seemed the mountain range wasn't getting any closer no matter how much time passed. Ash felt his frustration growing. Ramsay might've moved on again hours ago.

"I want to try another remote viewing," Ash said. Callum offered his hand, and Ash closed his eyes, fighting through the fatigue.

Maybe it was because he was physically closer to Ramsay, but he was able to connect with her energy much faster than he had before—could sense her almost as if she was in the carriage right beside him—

She stumbled into the snow. Drops of red fell, crystallizing in the ice. Source, she couldn't stop there—she wouldn't make it if she did. She forced herself to her feet, pain splintering through her. The river from her nightmares waited, its waves frozen.

Ash opened his eyes. The pain that had ripped through Ramsay now spread through his chest and abdomen as a dull ache.

Callum must've felt Ash's panic. "What is it? Creator, Ash, what's wrong?"

His eyes had teared up. "It's Ramsay," he managed to say, though it was harder to push out the next words. "She's injured. I think she's been attacked."

Whereas Ash tended to freeze in moments like this, Callum

stepped into his commander role. "Where on her body was she injured?" he said, voice tense.

"It was hard to tell."

"Is she still in the cabin?"

"No—no, she was running in the snow. I saw a frozen river." The same river, Ash realized, that was outside Snowdrop.

When Ash told Callum that she'd gone to the site of her parents' killings, Callum only nodded. "Did you see her attacker?" he asked.

"No, Source—I didn't see anything else."

"Okay," Callum said calmly, unaffected by Ash's frustration. "It'll be all right. We'll find her and help her, and she'll be fine."

Ash thought that Callum was being unreasonably optimistic. They'd barely made it to Dunsbrow, much less the journey on foot that would take them to Snowdrop—but Ash also knew there was no point in giving in to his fear now. It wouldn't help Ramsay. All he could do was knock on the carriage window and ask their driver to move faster.

28

When smoke appeared in the distance, the driver stopped on the path. "I'm being paid to transport you," he said, "not risk my life."

Callum paid the boy his coin, and he and Ash watched as the carriage started the journey back into the city. They began their trek through the snow and ice. The sun was going down, the sky red. Dunsbrow had been a smaller village of scattered houses in a wide field, a few climbing the slope of the hills, but nothing was left now but the blackened skeletons of burned houses, embers still glowing in and out with every breeze. Ash smelled a faint rotting that reminded him of the bodies that hung by their necks in Hedge.

"Source," he said, voice hoarse. "What happened?"

Callum frowned, hand out to prevent Ash from walking closer. "An attack. There wasn't any resistance, from the look of things. It was probably an ambush."

"But who would ambush a town like this?" Ash asked. Anger welled in his chest. "The people . . ."

"No sign of any survivors," Callum said. He was monotone, as if reading an official report. "The bodies have already been taken away, probably buried in a mass grave."

There was only one reason why Callum would know so much about this attack. "The reds did it?"

Callum didn't answer him. "We shouldn't linger."

"Makes sense," Ash said. "House Kendrick, murdering the same people they're supposed to protect. Why aren't you more upset about this?"

"You don't think I'm upset?" Callum said, swinging to him. "Of course I am. But right now, my anger isn't going to help Ramsay."

Ash let out a heavy breath. Callum was right.

Callum turned, squinting at the sun and mountain range. "Snowdrop should be six miles east from here."

"Do you have entire maps of the state memorized?"

"Yes," Callum said, crunching away and leaving Ash to follow. "You said that Ramsay was injured. She might've been hurt in the attack. That means it's probably been more than five hours, if she's made it to Snowdrop."

Ash's heart clenched. Ramsay could be dying alone, if she wasn't dead already. "We need to hurry."

It wasn't easy to run in the snow. Ash was normally quick, but his feet were used to the solid pavement of Hedge. His boots were soaked and heavy, his feet numb and cold as ice. Ash found it hard to breathe. The steady rise in the slope was not steep, but as they went higher, the air thinned. His duffel dragged down his shoulder.

When he slipped a third time, Callum grabbed his hand.

"Here," Callum said, falling to one knee. "Climb on my back."

Ash's face heated. "What?"

Callum met his eye. "Get on my back. To be frank, you're slowing us down. We'll be faster this way."

Ash hated to admit that Callum was right, but he put his pride aside for Ramsay. He climbed onto Callum's back, grateful for the other boy's heat. Source, he was like a furnace even then. It was hard not to remember the previous night, Callum's hands searching Ash's skin.

Callum's firm hands gripped Ash's legs as he continued the climb. Callum was now carrying his own bag as well as Ash's and Ash himself, but he moved with sure feet, beginning to jog and then flat-out running, breath steady. Ash realized he was racing the setting sun. Once it was dark, it'd be too dangerous to continue. They'd have to set up camp, risking frostbite and Ramsay dying of her injuries over the course of the night.

The sky turned a dark purple. Animals howled in the distance. Ash could feel Callum's thudding heartbeat against his chest. He'd already been running nonstop for over an hour, and as scared as Ash was for Ramsay, it wouldn't help any of them if Callum collapsed, too. Ash was just about to suggest that they stop for the night when he saw it. The frozen river looked exactly like it did in Ramsay's memories and nightmares. Callum didn't stop running even as he crossed, clutching Ash to his back tighter, no sign of the ice cracking. He only slowed down and finally stopped when he reached the first of the houses. Ash slid down from his back as Callum leaned forward, breathing hard, hands on his knees. Ash squeezed his shoulder gratefully. It went unsaid what his job was now.

The village had been abandoned since the attack so many years ago. Its remains were familiar to Ash. He recognized where the market had once been and where laughing children had chased each other down the path. Some of the homes on the outskirts had survived the explosion. The gray wood panels were rotting and falling from the walls, drifts of snow piling high around the remains that crumbled. There weren't many left standing to check, and when Ash found one with a door open and drops of blood outside, he paused, for a moment afraid of what he would find inside.

Callum stopped beside him. Ash took a slow breath in and exhaled as he pushed open the door. It was one room, walls splintering. Some spots of the wooden floor had decayed into dirt. The person who had once lived here hadn't owned much: a table and two chairs and a round iron stove. Ramsay lay in a corner of the room, huddled on the floor. She breathed heavily, red soaking her shirt as she shivered.

Ash and Callum ran to Ramsay's side. Ash's shaking hands

reached out, too afraid to touch her, but Callum pulled at the collar of her shirt, ripping it open and exposing her flat chest and the gash that ran from her collarbone to her ribs.

Callum looked up at Ash, eyes intense with focus. "Can you heal her?"

"I can try."

Ash took a deep breath. It was easy, at least, to think of the love he had for her. He remembered the nights they'd spent together, harmonizing their vibrations, and concentrated his energy on the wound. He gasped as he felt a sharp pain in his own chest. Ramsay's gash began to close, skin stitching together, but it wasn't enough. Another pump of blood gushed out, flesh beneath pulsing. It was a miracle that she'd survived this long, and it was clear that she wouldn't live much longer.

"Help me, Callum," Ash said, voice ragged. He took Callum's hand and pressed it to his own chest.

Callum had asked to learn healing, but this was a high-stakes first lesson. He sucked in a breath. "What do I do?"

"Think of how much you love her. Direct that love to the injury."

They sat silently as they worked. Within seconds Ash felt the bright blue light of Callum's energy flow through him. Calm washed over him and, it seemed, Ramsay as her clenched eyes relaxed. Her breath wasn't as labored. It was as if she recognized Callum's light and felt comforted by it. The wound closed until it was little more than a deep cut.

"Source," Ash said in relief, on the verge of tears.

"We should still clean and bandage her."

Callum took charge as he told Ash to collect water, pointing to a pot that was stacked with other dishes near the stove. Ash hurried outside to scoop up snow and brought it back to Callum, who had already begun to rip apart a nightshirt from his luggage. Callum dipped the cloth into the snow and pressed it to Ramsay's chest. She grimaced, cheeks flushed. Callum asked Ash to hold her up as he wrapped strips of fabric around her chest and back, compressing it tightly.

"We'll need to change the bandages every few hours," he murmured as Ash lay Ramsay back down again. She was in and out of consciousness now, her eyes opening and closing again. Ash wasn't sure if Ramsay even knew he was there. He pressed a hand to her cheek, then looked up to see Callum watching. Callum looked away quickly, swallowing, and Ash let her go.

Ramsay didn't wake up for the rest of the night. Ash couldn't sleep, no matter how exhausted he was. He gathered the driest wood from crumbling houses and sparked a fire with his alchemy, remembering with a pang how Ramsay had been the one to teach him how to control a flame.

Callum sat beside Ramsay, checking the pulse in her wrist and patting her feverish skin with cloth and melted snow. A blanket had been pulled from Callum's bag of supplies and wrapped around her. Ash rummaged through his own bag, searching for a sweater that could be draped across her, too.

"Ash," Callum said with a soft voice. "We've done all we can for her. Sit down for a moment. Relax."

He reluctantly did as he was told, sitting opposite Callum and watching Ramsay's faint breaths. Ash realized it hadn't fully hit him yet that they'd found her and that she was right there in front of him. She was paler than usual, but she had the same long eyelashes and nose, the same pinch between her brows, and tumbling black hair. The flurry of emotion that Ash had been trying to avoid enveloped him. There was relief that she was safe, anger that she'd betrayed him, and through it all, love that he couldn't ignore. Fear that she wouldn't survive, despite all they'd done.

"Are you all right?" Callum asked. Ash looked up and realized that Callum was watching him as closely as Ash had been watching Ramsay.

"Can't you tell for yourself?"

"I'd rather hear it from you."

Ash chewed on his lip. "I'll be fine," he said, suddenly too shy to open up to Callum now. "I just want to focus on making sure Ramsay will be okay, too."

Callum nodded. It looked like there was something else he wanted to tell Ash, but he didn't say anything more.

※

Ramsay stirred when white sunlight began to shine through the windows. She'd been waking up for a few seconds before falling asleep again all night, but this time, her eyes stayed open. Ash had been half-asleep himself, watching her from a spot against the wall, expecting that she'd fall unconscious again—then sat up when Ramsay stared up at the ceiling and turned her head to look right at him.

"Ash?" she said, voice gravelly.

Ash scrambled to Ramsay's side just as Callum opened his eyes, too. He'd fallen asleep on the floor across the room.

"Are you okay?" Ash asked, tense. "How're you feeling?"

She squeezed her eyes shut like she was still in pain. "Like shit." She tried to sit up, but Ash put a hand on her shoulder. "Source, what happened?"

Callum got to his feet slowly, uncertainly, and stopped moving when Ramsay turned to look at him.

She stiffened. "What—"

Callum swallowed. "Hi, Ramsay."

Ramsay looked back and forth between Ash and Callum like she thought she might still be asleep and this was only a fever dream—or maybe a nightmare. She blinked as she tried to sit up. Both Ash and Callum reached out to help her, but she raised an impatient hand. She looked down at her bare chest and the pinkened strips of cloth.

"What're you doing here?" she said, voice hard. Ash wasn't sure who she was asking. Maybe them both. "What happened?"

"You were injured," Callum began hesitantly, as if he didn't want to admit how close she'd been to dying.

Ramsay frowned, confused, and Ash couldn't blame her. She hadn't seen Callum in years, and to wake up to find him and Ash together . . .

"Where am I?" she asked.

Ash bit his lip. "Snowdrop."

Ramsay put a hand to her head. "I'd made it to Dunsbrow." She looked up, eyes wide. "Source, the town—"

Ash swallowed. "There'd been an attack."

Ramsay struggled to get to her feet. Callum put out a hand. "You might not have enough strength to stand yet—"

She pushed his arm away, stumbling. She glared at Callum, eyes burning. "Were you with them?" she demanded.

"With who?" Callum said, uncertain.

"Ramsay, you're confused."

"The reds," she said.

Ash met Callum's eye. "What happened in Dunsbrow?"

She let out a sharp breath and seemed like she'd finally met her limit. Ash and Callum both reached forward and took her arms before she could fall, helping her back onto the floor. She glared at the ground, breathing hard. Ash dipped a chipped bowl into a second pan meant for drinking water. Ramsay took the bowl, fingers trembling.

"I was hiding in the town," she said. "The patrols in Ironbound had grown, so I decided Dunsbrow would be a safer choice. The reds gave no warning. They marched in and declared the people were guilty of hiding a fugitive. Source, no one but the innkeeper knew I was there, and she didn't even know who I was."

Pain filled Ramsay's voice. Ash wanted to reach for her hand.

"I hid in my room," she said. "I didn't think they would burn everything to the ground just to find me. The guards didn't care who they killed." She looked like she wanted to cry. "I'm not any different from my parents after all. Another town was destroyed because of me."

"No," Callum said. Ash looked at him, surprised by the roughness in his voice. "That isn't your responsibility to bear. That's mine—my family's and the redguards' who attacked innocent people in the first place."

She didn't seem to believe him. "What're you doing here, Callum?"

He hesitated. "It's a long story. Maybe we should let you rest—change your bandages and—"

"No," she said. "Tell me now."

Ash and Callum exchanged looks, but after a breath, they began their story. They described Ash's punishment of being ordered to follow Callum, the friendship they'd built, and the decision to help Ramsay together. There were other details, too, that Ash and Callum silently agreed to skip.

"You told him about the Book, Ash?" Ramsay said, incredulous.

"I trust him," Ash said without hesitation.

She shook her head. "You *trust* Kendrick?" she said. "After knowing him for two weeks?"

"That's about how long I knew you, too," Ash reminded her. "And Callum hasn't left me behind just yet."

Ramsay clenched her jaw and looked away. "How did you find me?"

"I remote viewed and saw the river," Ash said. "I knew that you were hurt and that you'd made it to Snowdrop."

Ramsay stared at the two as they fell into silence. "I don't believe you," she finally said, gaze sliding to Callum. "There isn't any reason you'd be here unless it was to deliver me to your father."

"I know that it's hard to believe—"

"Yes," she said emphatically. "You're right. It's hard to believe that you'd ever want to help me. You never gave a shit about me."

"That's not true, Ramsay."

"You pretended you did," she said, eyes narrowed. "I still don't know why. Because you were bored, or thought it was funny—"

"Creator," Callum breathed. "You were never a joke to me."

"But either way, you decided your family was more important."

"I wanted to help you—"

"You don't care about anyone but yourself and your responsibility to your family name. You would kill me yourself if it meant you'd earn your father's respect."

"I wanted to make sure you were safe, because I—"

"You chose House Kendrick." She was shaking—maybe from both the cold and her anger. "So, please—go back to the fucking redguards where you belong, and stay the hell away from me."

She'd begun to cry. She wiped an eye with her shoulder impatiently, looking away. Callum swallowed, then stood from where he'd knelt beside her. "Okay."

Ash's heart thumped. "Wait—Callum—"

Callum had already crossed the room to his bag.

"Ramsay," Ash said, "you don't know what you're saying—"

"Yes, I do," she told him. "I don't know what Callum told you, but he can't be trusted." She spoke over him when he tried to interrupt. "I've spent years with Kendrick at Pembroke, and he's a lying coward."

"That was two years ago," Ash said. "Are you the same person you were two years ago? He's grown. He's changed."

She clenched her hands and teeth, eyes welling. "Source, Ash, why would you bring him here?"

"I needed his help," Ash said. "I'm glad that I did. You'd be dead by now if it wasn't for him. I'd probably be dead, too."

Ramsay flinched, brows stitched together. Callum had stopped, bag slung over his shoulder as he listened, staring hard at the ground.

"Give him another chance," Ash said softly. "We need him."

Ramsay shook her head, but she didn't speak. She didn't insist that Callum leave. This was enough for Ash. He gave Callum a pointed look and raised his brows expectantly when the older boy still hesitated.

Callum sighed and slid his bag to the ground. His voice was quiet when he spoke. "I'll give you some space," he said, crossing the room to the door.

"You don't need to go outside," Ash said. "You're not in exile."

"I think I need some space, too." He paused, hand on the wood. "I really am sorry, Ramsay." He pushed it open, stepping outside, and closed the door behind him.

Ramsay grimaced. Ash wasn't sure if it was from emotional or physical pain. He stood with the chipped bowl, frowning as he dipped it into the water pan again and brought it back to her. There was so much he wanted to say—so much he needed to ask her—and he wasn't sure where to begin when the feelings of betrayal clouded it all.

She took the bowl with a thank-you. She sipped for a moment, then sat back and breathed. "If I'd known you were bringing Callum, I wouldn't have bothered to wait."

Ash frowned. "You waited for me?"

She released a small breath. "Yes, Source—of course I waited for you, as long as I could. Why do you think I'm still here and not halfway to House Lune?" Ramsay met his eyes again uncertainly, and now Ash wasn't sure what to believe.

"I thought you were just waiting for the right moment to leave. You didn't have a problem doing that at Lancaster."

Ramsay looked away. At least she seemed ashamed. "I made a mistake at Lancaster," she said. "I realized that quickly."

"A mistake? Is that how you'd describe leaving me to die?"

She clenched her jaw for a moment. "I heard you were House Kendrick's prisoner. I thought you'd try to escape, so I stayed in Ironbound for as long as I could. I tried to use our connection to send you images of where I was, hoping you'd figure it out. I didn't know what else to do."

Ramsay sending Ash visions helped to explain why he'd succeeded in remote viewing at all. "You could've stayed with me in Kensington," he said. "You could've fought by my side instead of abandoning me."

She was silent for a long time, gathering her thoughts or her lies, Ash wasn't sure which. Finally, she said, "I'm sorry. I panicked. I imagined us both captured, neither able to help the other. I pictured Hain finding the Book before me, using it to destroy the state—and I thought I'd made a decision for the greater good. I thought I'd acted selflessly, putting my feelings for you aside. I realized as soon as I got on the train that I was wrong."

Ramsay reached for Ash's hand, and though anger seared him, he let her take it. He felt warmth ease through him. "All I can do," she said, "is apologize and promise to never leave your side like I did again."

Ash stared at her hand and the long fingers he'd missed. Energy didn't lie. Ramsay truly did care for him.

"You still need to earn back my trust," Ash said.

She squeezed his hand. Her eyelids were blinking shut as she whispered. "Anything . . ."

She needed to rest. Ash stood to add more wood to the dying embers in the stove. By the time he turned back around, Ramsay had already fallen asleep again.

*

Ash found Callum sitting on an abandoned workbench outside. Ash hoisted himself up to sit beside him, rubbing his hands together and shivering in the cold.

"Where's your scarf?" Callum asked.

"Inside," Ash said.

Callum sighed and pulled off his sweater so that he only wore a shirt, handing it over.

"No, that's okay—"

"Just put it on."

He hesitated, then took the sweater and tugged it on over his head. He positively drowned in the thing, but he was grateful for the heat that still emanated from the wool. "Source, you really are like a furnace."

Neither spoke for a moment.

"She's hurt, Callum," Ash said. "She just needs time."

"You heard her. She doesn't want me here."

"You haven't even explained why you ended your relationship with her yet," Ash said. "Don't you think she deserves to know?"

Callum snorted and shook his head. "Is that your attempt to manipulate me into staying?"

"Depends. Did it work?"

Callum laughed, but his smile faded. "The Ramsay I knew won't give a shit about my explanation," he said after a moment. "When she gets like that—when she's made up her mind—it won't matter what I do or say. She won't forgive me."

"You don't know that for sure," Ash said. "Weren't you the one who said we can't decide how she'll feel?"

Callum sighed and leaned back, staring at the gray sky. It looked like more snow was coming. "I'm surprised," he said.

"About what?"

"That you're working so hard to convince me to stay."

A tangle of emotion erupted in Ash's chest. "Why is that surprising?" he asked, though he already knew what Callum meant.

"Aren't you happy?" he said. "Ramsay didn't choose me."

Maybe this was what Ash would've thought himself, once. If he hadn't gotten to know Kendrick more—hadn't shared a bed with him in Ironbound—maybe he would've been glad for Callum to leave. He looked away. "No, not really. That's not how I feel at all."

"Then how do you feel?"

Ash flashed a smile. "You already know, don't you?"

"It's hard to tell right now, to be honest."

"Try a little harder, then."

Callum considered Ash for a moment. Ash felt Callum's warmth as the other boy's face grew soft. He took Callum's hand, playing with his fingers.

"I want you to stay," Ash said. "We need you, yes—but even if we didn't . . ." He swallowed. "I want you to stay, okay?"

If Ash didn't know any better, he'd think that Callum was blushing. He nodded. "Yes. Okay."

※

Callum insisted he was fine waiting outside a little longer. "I want to gather my thoughts," he said, so Ash returned the sweater and went back inside to stay with Ramsay.

She was still in and out of sleep, though when she woke up she kept her eyes open longer each time. Soon, maybe even by the next day, she'd be strong enough to leave Snowdrop, and they could continue on to House Lune.

Ash was grateful Callum had insisted they buy food from the inn. Even what they had wouldn't last long. The jerky was too tough for Ramsay to chew, so Ash mashed the dried fruit with water the best he could. He held a spoon to her mouth.

Ramsay snatched it away. "I can feed myself," she said.

"Glad to see you haven't changed too much," Ash muttered. He made himself comfortable beside her, biting into dried meat. Now that he knew Ramsay was safe, he was starving.

He felt a buzz of energy and looked up to see her watching him. She'd reached out, as if to test their connection. Ash was relieved that the bond he and Ramsay shared from their harmonization hadn't faded away—that he could still feel her, and she, him.

"I've missed you," Ramsay murmured. "It's a little hard to believe you're here in front of me again."

"Me, too," Ash said, smiling at the fact that they'd had the exact same thought.

She paused, then said, "It seems like you two got pretty close these past couple of weeks."

Ash blinked at her. "Yeah. I guess we did."

"You've never had any love for redguards," she told Ash, "and yet you don't seem to mind the House heir of the redguard family."

Ash hesitated. "Callum's proven himself different."

"How so?"

"He saved your life, Ramsay. If it hadn't been for him—"

"How do you know this isn't another trick of his?"

"You're letting your fear get the better of you," Ash said. "The priority is finding the Book, right?"

"Yes, but if Callum betrays us—"

"You have no evidence that he plans to," Ash said.

Ramsay didn't answer.

"Callum has the entire state's map memorized. He'll know where he's going, and he can protect us against reds if they show up again. If you really want to find the Book, maybe it's better to put feelings aside and let Callum come with us."

Ramsay let out a heavy sigh. Ash couldn't stop himself from grinning. He knew he'd won. Ramsay glared, nudging him weakly with a knee, though a small smile met her lips, too. "Don't be so smug."

The door opened before Ash could reply. Callum stepped inside, stomping off snow at the threshold's entrance. Ramsay looked away but didn't say anything as Callum stopped in front of the two.

"Can I speak with you, Ramsay?"

She inhaled sharply and still didn't respond. Ash glanced from Callum to Ramsay uncertainly. He stood to give them space but felt a tug on the back of his sweater, Ramsay pulling him back down again.

Callum took a breath. "I've regretted the way I treated you in the past," he said. "I've regretted it all. I wanted to apologize to you, to take accountability for my mistakes, and to tell you the truth, finally, like I should've done two years ago."

"And what truth is that?" Ramsay said.

Callum clenched his jaw. "I ended our relationship because I was afraid for our lives."

Her gaze narrowed. "What?"

"I thought that if my father found out, he'd have one or both of us killed."

"It's true," Ash whispered. "He opened himself—showed me the memory."

She shook her head, confused. "Why would you think that?"

Callum described what he'd done—the execution in the dungeons of Hedge. It sounded like he was listing facts, though Ash could see the shame that trembled through him. Ramsay's breath tightened as she listened.

"I realized my father's cruelty has no limit," Callum said. "I was afraid. I decided to get in line. You were right—I was a coward."

Ramsay's hands gripped into fists. Ash wondered if she regretted those words now, listening to Callum's story.

"But not anymore," Callum said. "I've left my family. I've been disowned. I've lost everything."

Maybe it was because Ash had gotten to know Callum so much more that he was able to tell that the other boy was struggling to push down the emotion that threatened to well up as he spoke.

"And I would do it again," Callum said, "because I've realized I'd never be happy living under my father. I wish I hadn't ended things with you. I wish I'd told you the truth, then—that I loved you."

Ramsay looked up at Callum at this. Coldness still filtered her gaze, but Ash could tell she sensed Callum's sincerity, too.

"It's been years," Callum said, "but in some ways, I still do."

"That's ridiculous," she said. "Why would you even tell me that?"

"Because it's the truth, and I promised myself I would be more honest from now on," Callum said. "I know that you probably don't feel the same way, but I don't mind. I want to help you, Ramsay."

"Why?"

"To make up for how much I hurt you in the past," Callum said. He looked at Ash. "And because I wouldn't forgive myself if anything happened to either of you."

Ramsay glanced at Ash, too.

"And besides," Callum said, "it sounds like this Book is pretty important. I wouldn't mind making sure it didn't end up in the wrong hands."

Ramsay didn't speak for a long moment. Ash wasn't sure if it was because she was still tired or if it was because she had so much to process.

Callum ended the silence with a low voice. He leaned against the table, arms crossed, staring at the floor. "I can be an asset," he said. "We're all acting for the safety of the state, and I have the most experience in combat and survival training. If you allow me to stay at your side, I can ensure you'll find the Book."

"And I—" Source, Ash realized he wasn't much of an asset at all in comparison to Callum, but he continued anyway. "I will gather snow."

Ramsay snorted, then laughed, even if it looked like she didn't want to.

"You heighten your chances with me," Callum said, speaking in emotionless-commander mode, though Ash knew that was Callum's defensive shield.

It was difficult to argue with him. Ramsay clearly knew that he was right, even if she wanted to find a reason to reject him. But it was no use. Ash knew she'd realized that if she truly wanted to find the Book—to keep it out of the hands of Hain and other alchemists who would use it to kill—then she would need both Ash and Callum at her side.

She sighed, closing her eyes.

※

She could see them in the little house they had huddled in— watched as they gathered their things and left the abandoned village. Hain had told her he'd seen his son and the redguard searching for Thorne in Ironbound in his remote viewings and had given her the orders. Marlowe followed the three, unnoticed— paused in the shadow of the trees and watched as they got comfortable in their new home. She watched when the Kendrick heir sat outside for some time, staring up at the sky, and when Woods joined him. And Marlowe knew her opportunity was coming. It was almost time.

29

The three marched through the snow and ice and trees, up the crumbling path. Ramsay was well enough to walk, and he said they'd be more comfortable in his family's cabin. "We can gather supplies before we keep moving."

Ash imagined Ramsay as a child, holding his mother's hand as she led him back to their winter home after spending an afternoon in Snowdrop. Ramsay checked that the old energetic barriers were still in place, creating new protections for good measure, before opening the door. The house was much smaller than the Thorne manor. It was a single story, its stone sturdier than the houses that crumbled below. It had two bedrooms and a living room that also had an iron stove and a dining table. It had many more resources and supplies than the abandoned homes below: old furs that didn't immediately deteriorate when touched and even hunting gear. Callum suggested that they spend the night hunting and gathering dry wood in case they needed to make camp in the mountains.

Ramsay glared at Callum as he sat at the wooden table, chewing on dried fruit. "We won't be traveling through the mountain passage," he said.

"What?" Ash said with a frown, sitting opposite Ramsay. "That's the only way to the Elder lands from here."

Ramsay was more hesitant now. "It's not. There's a portal door connected to my father's childhood home in the Westfields."

"Your family really loves portal doors," Ash muttered.

Ramsay ignored him. "It's even closer to House Lune than

Glassport." Glassport was near the border and the neighboring state Caledonia, miles away. "It'll be faster from there."

Callum stoked embers in the stove. "And a much easier journey, too."

Ramsay straightened in his seat, gaze planted on the ceiling. It seemed even though he'd agreed to let Callum come, he didn't like having to acknowledge the other boy's existence.

"Given the time it'd take to climb through the mountain passage, along with the danger of the cold . . ."

"But the Westfields will be crawling with reds by now," Ash said.

"There will be patrols, but redguards won't expect us to be on the other end of the state. They'll focus on Ironbound and the Derry Hills," Callum said. "It's concerning we still haven't seen any sign of them after the attack on Dunsbrow. They might be deeper in the mountains, waiting to ambush us. I agree with Ramsay. We better our chances in the Westfields."

Ramsay didn't seem to appreciate being agreed with by Callum. He tapped an impatient finger on the table's surface. "We leave tomorrow at first light."

✳

Ash was glad to find a greater use. While Ramsay was forced to stay in the cabin and rest, and Callum found a rusting axe to begin chopping wood, Ash stepped out into the thin dead trees that stood between the cabin and the village below. There wasn't much evidence of life, and he wasn't convinced he'd find any animals to hunt—but when he heard a faint scampering, he zeroed in on the energy of the animal and took in a deep breath, imagining small arrowheads, made from red light—

There was a squeal. A white hare lay dying in the snow, squirming until it stopped moving. Ash's heart hurt for the animal, but he remembered a passage he'd read in a text. There was no true death, and in a sense, as Ash was grateful to the animal for sustaining his body, the animal was also Source, choosing to die by Ash's hand so that it could become a part of Ash and experience life in a new form. This was what Ash told himself as he picked up the rabbit by its hind legs, but it didn't do much to help his guilt.

He took a step back to the cabin when he heard another rustle. He paused, focusing his energy again, searching for the second animal. When he didn't find anything, his nerves ticked higher—but maybe it'd just been his imagination. Ash had barely gotten any sleep last night, and it was starting to show.

Ash heard raised voices before he even reached the house. Ramsay and Callum's shouts were muffled until he opened the door. They were both on their feet, Ramsay red in the face, Callum with a hand in the air. "You have no right to say that, Ramsay—"

"The hell I don't," he yelled. "After what you did to *me*—"

"You don't get to decide how I feel about him—"

It took them both a moment to realize that Ash was there. Callum turned to look at him, eyes wide. Ash wondered if he should simply turn right back around again. Ramsay sighed, annoyed, swiping a hand through his hair.

Callum swallowed in the silence, then took a breath and stepped forward, reaching for the rabbit. "Well done, Ash," he murmured.

"What were you fighting about?" Ash asked, looking from Callum to Ramsay and back to Callum.

"It's nothing."

"So, is that it, then?" Ramsay said at Callum's turned back. "Pretend we weren't talking about Ash and hope the problem goes away because it's too hard to deal with? Looks like you haven't changed much after all."

Callum closed his eyes for patience, then walked the rabbit to the table, reaching for one of the hunting knives he'd found. Callum held the rabbit to the wood, dug the knife into its side, and began to tear its skin. "I'm not ignoring anything. I'd just prefer to talk about this when we're calmer."

"No, you want to have the conversation when *you're* ready, on your own terms."

"I'm allowed time to process my thoughts and feelings," Callum said, stiff. "I'm allowed time to calm down, before I say something that I regret."

Ramsay sneered. "What? Too afraid to let Ash see another side of you? Understandable. You've done so well at hiding it."

"I don't want to do this right now."

"Why?" Ramsay asked. He gestured at Ash, who still stood by the door. "Because Ash is here? Obviously, you two have already shared so much with each other. Why not this, too?"

"You're being unreasonable in your anger, Ramsay, as usual."

"Fuck you, Kendrick."

Ash dared to speak. "Ramsay, maybe we should all take a breath—"

"Just how close are you two now?" he asked, meeting his eye. There was a flicker of hurt in his gaze.

Ash didn't want to say that he and Callum had shared a bed, but it seemed he didn't have to. Ramsay never did let much slip past him.

Ash hesitated. He met Callum's steady gaze. "What's going on between me and Callum—we—"

"It only took two weeks for you to replace me, then."

"I didn't *replace* you—"

"Or maybe Callum has pulled you into his game, too," Ramsay said. "Maybe it's fun for you, pretending to care about me while the two of you have a laugh because I actually dared to believe you."

Callum stopped his work on the rabbit, hands pressing the table and head bowed.

Air caught in Ash's throat. "Ramsay, you've been hurt by everyone around you," he said, "so it makes sense that you think I'm out to hurt you also. But you couldn't be more wrong. I care about you. And Callum does, too." Ramsay shook his head, but Ash continued. "Why else do you think we would risk our lives to come here?"

"It doesn't matter what you say now," Callum said, as he picked up a rag, wiping off his hands. "He's already made up his mind that you and I are plotting against him."

"Not helping, Callum."

"Because, yes," Callum said, looking at Ramsay now, "of course it makes sense that I would give up everything—my entire life— just for an elaborate *prank*."

Ramsay seemed too angry to speak. He walked to the door, threw it open, and stormed out of the house, slamming the door shut behind him. Ash had never seen Ramsay so angry before, even when they'd had their arguments and spats.

"Why would you say that?" Ash demanded.

"What? Is Ramsay the only one who's allowed to be angry? I must've missed that memo."

"He's hurt," Ash said. "You're the one who hurt him."

Callum took a breath, a hand against his head. "And I'm trying to do what I can to make up for that—but, Creator, saying that I don't care about you, that I'm just taking advantage of you . . ."

Ash hesitated, chewing on his lip. He stepped to Callum's side. "He's angry, so he's trying to upset you, too."

Callum met his eye. "I thought I was prepared to accept his rejection. I didn't realize it would hurt this badly."

Ash swallowed. He wanted to comfort Callum—whether as friends who had sex with each other or as friends who were starting to fall in love, he wasn't sure. "I'm sorry," he said. He touched Callum's fingers.

Callum met his gaze, and Ash felt the other boy's energy, his familiar steadiness and the color of bright blue skies, even if it was dimmed by his frustration and hurt. Ash didn't think much of it when he stood on his toes, leaning forward for a kiss.

"Maybe we shouldn't," Callum whispered. "That'd just complicate things between you and Ramsay, too."

Ash leaned back, disappointed. "Aren't you the one who said you don't see any point in forcing yourself to love only one person?"

Callum's smile managed to break through. "Yes," he said, "but that doesn't mean you shouldn't move carefully. You might end up losing him, too."

Ash had just turned away, thinking he'd refill the buckets of snow, when there was a faint thump that echoed like a muffled explosion in the distance. Ash frowned at Callum. They both headed for the door, Ash swinging it open. The sunlight bounced against the white snow, shining into his eyes, before he saw a line of smoke rising from the trees. Ramsay wasn't anywhere in sight.

Both began to run. There was another explosion, a stronger crack that made the trees around them shudder. Ash saw him first—Ramsay had fallen to one knee, a cut over his brow, stream of blood leaking into his eye as he winced, a hand up. Marlowe walked closer, spears made of embers spinning around her. Neither noticed Ash or Callum. Marlowe raised a hand, and the spears flew at Ramsay. Ramsay clenched a fist and a gust of wind blew them off course—all except one, aimed for his neck. Ash didn't think when he threw up his hand. The spear veered into a nearby tree, exploding into flame before it crackled out of existence. Ramsay looked up, eyes wide.

Marlowe turned, too, surprised—then sighed with rolled eyes when she saw who it was. "Ashen Woods. Source, do you ever *not* get in the way?"

Ash ran to Ramsay's side, helping him to his feet. "Are you all right?"

"I'm fine," he said with gritted teeth, though he didn't look it.

"Who is this?" Callum said, voice low, as he stepped forward, watching Marlowe carefully, already beginning to size her up.

"Callum Kendrick," Marlowe said lightly. "Aren't you supposed to be in Kensington? Oh, that's right—you've become a traitor to your own family, the redguards, *and* the entire state. I suppose no one will make too much of a fuss if I happen to kill you, too."

"As you can see," Callum said, ignoring her, "you're outnumbered and outmatched. You'd do well to surrender."

She laughed, flipping red hair over her shoulder. "Is that right?"

A twitch in her smile was the only warning they had. Her hands unclenched at her sides and beams of golden light shot in all directions. Ash threw himself and Ramsay to the ground, while Callum rolled and landed on his feet, ready to spring forward. He charged, swinging a fist at Marlowe, but she danced out of the way, a handful of fire reaching for Callum's face, blocked by Callum's arm. Ash shot red arrows of light at her, but she turned in time with an outstretched hand, a sharp wind cutting the arrows down. Ramsay followed, shadows pulling themselves from the dirt and ground, snagging Marlowe's ankles and twisting around her knees. There was a flinch of panic on her face before she closed her eyes and bright light shined from her skin, shadows fading enough for her to jump out of their reach. She didn't look up in time to see Ash and what was in his hand. It slid into her stomach and out her back. She gasped, frozen. Ash let go, and the blade of light disappeared.

She coughed, red spraying, then fell to one knee. "Well, fuck," she said, then fell forward into the snow.

The three stood over her, breathing heavily. Ash was the first to move. He ran to her side, turning her over. Marlowe's breath was shallow, her gaze unfocused, eyes welling from the pain. She wouldn't have long.

"How did Hain know we were here?" Ash asked.

Callum's voice was behind him. "Why did she try to kill us?"

Ash shook her shoulder. "Marlowe—stay with me. What does Hain want with the Book?"

She looked at Ash, squinting in confusion. "I should've run."

Ash frowned. She was too out of it, too close to death. He looked up only when Callum knelt on her other side, a hand to the wound that was below her rib.

He met Ash's eye. "We should heal her."

Ramsay stood over them, arms crossed. "No, the fuck we should not."

"She doesn't need to die."

"I'm not going to make the same mistake twice. I should've killed her in Lancaster."

"You claim to hate the cruelty of House Kendrick but then refuse to show mercy?"

"She works for Gresham Hain," Ramsay said, voice rising. "She'll try to kill us again, as many times as he orders her to."

Callum swallowed, looking at Ash. "We can't leave her to die like this. I swore to myself I'd never take another life again."

"I'll do it," Ramsay said, raising his hand and stepping forward. "Move aside. This isn't about you and your redemption. This is a case of kill or be killed."

"We can heal her and leave. She won't know where we've gone."

Callum met Ash's eyes pleadingly. Ash felt a twist of uncertainty as he looked down at Marlowe. She was frowning, staring at him with surprising lucidity now—but Ash's mother had done the same, illness fading so much that it seemed she'd suddenly healed, laughing with Ash and telling him how much she loved him before she passed in her sleep later that night.

"I'm sorry," Marlowe said, voice soft. Ash had heard of people admitting to their regrets when close to death. He was uncomfortable that she did so now. It reminded him that she was human. "I didn't want to hurt you or Ramsay."

"Then why did you?"

She shook her head, tears falling. "I didn't have a choice. He would've killed me if I didn't do what he said. He would've killed me, and no one would've known or cared."

Something inside of Ash ached. He was afraid to ask his next question. "Why do you work for Gresham Hain?"

Marlowe grimaced, eyes squeezed shut. She didn't answer him, but Ash knew. It was clear now—obvious that she was forced to work for Gresham Hain, just as his mother had been, too. It felt like Ash was looking down at his mother again as she struggled to breathe, hand tight around his own.

Ash looked up at Callum. "Let's heal her."

Ramsay cursed behind them.

Ash ignored him. He took Callum's hand and pressed his fingers to Marlowe's wound. For a moment, he wasn't sure that he would be able to find love for Marlowe—but after a moment, he realized he didn't need to. He only needed to think about how Marlowe was just like his mom: likely another orphan, maybe also of House Lune, her freedom taken away as she was forced to work for Gresham Hain. He felt his love for his mom. He usually tried to push the pain away, because it could be so overwhelming, his grief—but he welcomed it now and let his love flow through his body.

When Ash opened his eyes, he saw that Marlowe stared up at him. For a moment, he was afraid it hadn't worked—but she blinked and sat up.

"You're too much of a fool to really be Hain's son," she muttered.

Ramsay leaned against a tree behind them. "If you attack us again, I promise you, I'm not listening to these two. I'll kill you myself."

Marlowe ignored him as she watched Ash. "You won. Why would you heal me?"

Ash wasn't sure he could even begin to explain how close he felt to Marlowe in that moment, so he didn't answer her question as he stood, dusting the snow from his knees. "You don't have to go back to Hain," he said.

She glared at Ash. "You don't know Gresham Hain like I do."

"You could come with us," Ash offered, ignoring Ramsay's sputtering protests. Even Callum raised a brow. "You could help us find the Book."

Marlowe only snorted, shaking her head. "I have a strong sense of self-preservation. It's what's helped me survive all these years."

She met Ash's eye. "I know a failed mission when I see one. Hain will win, and you will die, whether by my hand or his."

Ash clenched his jaw. "If that's what you want to believe, then there isn't any point trying to convince you."

Callum left for the house and returned with rope. Marlowe would eventually have the alchemic energy to break free, but the battle and near death had left her exhausted enough to give them a head start. He tied her hands with multiple knots and swung one end of the rope over a branch so that she was forced to stand with her arms in the air.

Ramsay watched coldly, arms crossed. "You're both so fucking soft," he said.

Ash didn't reply. He turned to follow Ramsay as he began to walk through the forest, Callum close behind.

30

The three scrambled to pack, throwing their things into the bags they'd brought, carrying wood and bundles of fur in their arms.

When they were ready, Ramsay closed the front door and whispered, "Hyacinth."

Ash blinked in the yellow sunlight. The air was so full of dustings of pollen that the breeze itself shimmered gold. He appeared to be in the crumbling remains of a house. He stepped through an empty threshold that still stood, though only half its wall remained. The floor had sunken and rotted away completely to dirt and grass, and vines and moss twisted over the stones.

Ramsay stepped through also, Callum following, and answered their unasked question. "The house was practically abandoned after my father married my mother," she said. "They'd use the portal door for its convenience when traveling, but they never bothered with the upkeep. I think my father was embarrassed that he wasn't from a wealthy House."

As they stepped over chunks of fallen stone, Ash saw a wooden table covered completely in green as if it'd been made by the fields. He stepped out of what appeared to have once been the front door and looked at the expansive fields surrounding them. He couldn't even see the forest they'd have to pass through. It'd be a long trek to House Lune—and he wasn't entirely sure that Ramsay and Callum would make it without killing each other first.

Callum had returned to commander mode. "Stay here and let me scout ahead," he said. Ramsay looked ready to argue, but

Callum said, "I just want to make sure there haven't been any signs of patrols. I'll only be a minute."

Ash agreed, glad to put down the heavy bag. He plopped to the ground, petals and yellow pollen flying into the air. Ramsay sighed but did the same, sitting beside Ash and glaring at the grass. Callum turned on his heel and jogged into the distance.

"He's much faster than he looks," Ramsay muttered, thinking the same as Ash. She met his eye briefly. "Why have you worked so hard to defend him?"

"I haven't, have I?"

"You're constantly arguing on his behalf. You're always on his side."

Ash bit his lip. "Are you jealous?"

"Source, Ash, of course I'm jealous."

"I still feel the same way about you," Ash told her. "You know that, don't you? Nothing has changed."

"Only the fact that you're screwing Callum Kendrick, too."

Ash wasn't sure how he'd found himself in his mess. "You and I—we never decided we were exclusive, and you'd abandoned me at Lancaster—"

"So it's my fault that you decided to move on?"

"I haven't moved on," Ash said. "What will it take to convince you of that?"

She looked right at him. "End whatever the hell is going on between you and Callum."

Ash lost his breath for a moment. He shook his head. "I can't do that. I'm sorry, but I can't."

She looked away. "That was a quick choice."

"I'd rather not choose at all."

She sighed, rubbing a hand over her face. "Source," she murmured. "How did I end up competing with Kendrick for you?"

"Maybe you don't have to compete at all."

"Well, I'm definitely not sharing you with him."

"You're talking about me like I'm an object that can be passed back and forth."

Ramsay sucked in a quick breath and clenched her jaw. A long moment passed before she murmured that she was sorry.

Ash was frustrated, but he was glad to have a moment alone with her now, too. He swallowed nervously, playing with a blade of grass between his fingers. "I've missed you, Ramsay," he said. "I was so angry and hurt but—I missed you more than anything else."

She leaned forward and kissed Ash, as if she'd been waiting for just this moment to finally touch him. He couldn't help but smile as she pulled away, her fingers finding his hand.

"I've been jealous of Callum, too," he said.

"You shouldn't be," she said. "I don't have feelings for him."

Ash hesitated. "Don't you?"

In that moment, Ash and Ramsay could both feel her tangle of emotions: There was anger and bitterness and jealousy, yes, but she couldn't deny the thread of love, too. She'd loved Callum for years. It wasn't easy to simply decide not to.

"It isn't fair that I'm still trapped by my feelings for him," she said.

Ash swallowed a pang. "It's understandable, isn't it? He was your best friend. Your first love."

"You're not helping, Ash."

They both fell into silence as they watched Callum begin to make his way back, off in the distance. He jogged into earshot. "We're clear," he said as he reached them again, eyes fastened to the ground as if he knew he'd been the topic of conversation.

✳

It'd been just two days ago that Ash had walked up and down through Ironbound, searching for Ramsay at Callum's side. Now he saw that this had been only a taste of what was to come as they walked through the green fields, meadows, and pastures, interrupted now and again by single houses, most of them abandoned and falling apart. After the first hour, Ash's feet began to ache. After the third, his knees felt like they'd give out at any moment. After the sixth, he could barely pick up his boots. They took short breaks every now and then for Callum to run ahead and ensure they were still safe, but somehow, stopping only made the pain worse.

Ramsay wasn't faring much better. She ignored Callum's questions. "Are you sure you're all right? Maybe we should rest." When she stumbled in exhaustion, Callum grabbed her arm before she could fall and insisted that they stop for the evening.

"The sun is about to go down anyway," Callum said as Ramsay snatched her arm away. "We should focus on setting up camp."

They'd crossed into the Yarrow Woods. The thick trees were covered with green moss, roots dancing out of the rich soil. Ferns unfurled and little white mushrooms grew from fallen branches and dead leaves that crunched beneath their feet. Patches of dappled golden sunlight fell through the canopy. Even if he was in pain, Ash couldn't help but enjoy the beauty of the forest. It felt like he could breathe for the first time in weeks.

Callum searched for a clearing before he declared their home for the night, a spot beneath a wide tree. Ash dropped his bags and sat gingerly, body aching and feet stinging. The three were quiet as Callum bustled about, working to unpack sheets and furs and gather wood to start a fire. Though they weren't in the mountains, the temperature was quickly dropping. Callum crouched over a pile of wood and tried to use a flint against a rock, but Ramsay impatiently flicked a finger and sparked a flame.

"Thanks," Callum murmured, but Ramsay ignored him.

Callum was, surprisingly, a talented-enough cook. He insisted Ash and Ramsay relax while he bustled about the fire, murmuring to himself that he wished there were spices, and questioning if he should forage for mushrooms. Ash hated the uncomfortable silence as they ate cooked rabbit and drank the melted ice from the mountains. He agreed that love was infinite and that he shouldn't have to choose between Ramsay or Callum. His love for Ramsay felt exciting and explosive, full of debates and kisses with bites. Callum's love felt steadier, firm hands and gentle smiles and patient disagreements. Ash couldn't toss his feelings for Callum away, even if it was for Ramsay. He wanted them both. He feared that there was a future where this couldn't happen.

The sun went down. The air was cold enough that Ash could see wisps of his own breath in the flickering campfire. The three silently agreed that they were too tired and tense to speak. Callum chose to sleep on the other side of the fire wordlessly, while Ash shivered beside Ramsay. He was grateful when she turned to him and pulled him closer, their chests pressed together, Ramsay sighing as one leg slid in between Ash's. He felt warmer now, at least, even if he started to squirm, remembering the fun they'd had in Ramsay's bed. Ramsay smirked against his neck—but her smile dropped when Ash pulled away.

"Can I ask Callum to join us?"

"What?" Ramsay said, though from her tone she'd clearly heard Ash just fine. "No—Source, he can't *join us*."

"He shouldn't be alone," Ash whispered. "It's unfair to him."

"I don't care."

"You two do know I can hear you, right?" Callum called over the fire.

Ash sat up. "Good. Come over."

"It sounds like Ramsay doesn't want me to."

"You'll lie on one side of me, and Ramsay on the other."

Ramsay bristled. "I don't want him so close to me."

"You're being childish. It's freezing. I don't want to wake up in the morning and find that Callum's frozen to death."

"Do you *see* him, Ash? He's built like a bear. He'll be fine."

Callum didn't speak throughout the argument. Ash frowned at Ramsay, her face lit by the embers of the fire. He could feel that, beneath her anger, she was afraid. She was worried that if she let herself lie down so close to Callum, she wouldn't be able to ignore her feelings for him. Ash put a hand on hers, hoping she would sense his silent promise to her that she was safe.

Ramsay sighed, closing her eyes. "Yes. Fine. Callum can join us."

She pulled her hand away and lay down again, this time her back to Ash. Callum still hesitated. He only stood, bringing his furs, when Ash pulled open his own sheet as an invitation. Callum knelt beside him, murmuring a thank-you. It took a moment for the three to settle again. Ash lay an arm around Ramsay's side, and though she was stiff, she let him snuggle his chest into her back. Callum wrapped his arm around Ash's waist, giving a content sigh. They all squirmed and shifted for a few moments before they stilled, breaths slow.

31

None of the three spoke in the morning when they woke up and untangled their arms and legs from one another. Callum kicked dirt over the fire's remains, and Ramsay found a stream to wash his face in and returned, running his fingers through wet strands. "Source, what I wouldn't do for a bath . . ."

Ash bundled their things into the packs the best he could. It was strange, this new tension—like sleeping beside one another had been its own conversation that'd lasted the full night, and too much had still been left unsaid.

Callum seemed to agree. "Ash, can you give me and Ramsay a moment alone, please?"

Ash's brows raised. "Yeah—sure—"

Ramsay looked at Callum like he'd lost his mind. "No," he said, and pointed a finger at Ash. "Don't you dare go anywhere."

Callum turned to Ramsay with a frown. He seemed to have done a lot of thinking over the course of the night. "I'd like to get some emotions out into the open."

"I don't care what you want."

"You don't have to say anything. I'm only asking you to listen."

"That'll be an issue, since I can't stand the sound of your voice."

"We're on this mission together, and I think it'd be better if—"

"I didn't even want you here in the first place, Callum!" Ramsay's voice grew louder. "You don't have the right to speak to me, not ever but especially not now. We're supposed to be focused on finding the Book."

"That's *why* I want to speak to you," Callum said, "before we arrive at House Lune. You've always been one to push your feelings aside, Ramsay—"

"Don't act like you know me—"

"—and pretend they're not there, but your emotions haven't gone anywhere just because you're ignoring them. They could be even more distracting and dangerous if you don't look at them now."

"You don't get to tell me about my feelings when you're the one who fucked me up in the first place!"

Ash swallowed heavily. He wondered if he should give them space like Callum asked, but he was nervous to leave the two alone. At least here, he could break up the fight.

Callum clenched his jaw. "I've gotten pretty good at sensing the emotions of others around me," he said, voice low. "I can feel how furious you are with me. I can feel how much you hate that you still love me—"

Ramsay turned to leave.

"Ramsay, stop—"

Callum held up a hand before Ash could say anything else.

"I'm sorry," Callum said. "There's so much that I want to say, and Creator—if you would just let me speak . . . You don't have to answer. You can still feel as you do now and hate me for the rest of our lives. But please—I'm begging you to listen."

Ash looked nervously between them. Ramsay was still, silent, and looked very much like he wanted to hit Callum—but finally he found a rock and sat, legs crossed. He opened his hands, a gesture for Callum to begin, even as his face was twisted in anger and heartache.

Callum looked at Ash. "Please, just give us some time."

Ash swallowed and nodded. "Okay."

He looked up in surprise when Callum walked over, taking his hand and squeezing it. "You're still wanted," he said, bending over to Ash's ear, making him want to lean into Callum even more. "I just think that Ramsay and I deserve space for our issues, too."

Ash knew that Callum was right. They'd had their own relationship, after all, years before Ash knew either of them. He agreed with a nod and walked farther into the woods until he found a root to sit on. He'd barely gotten comfortable when shouts echoed through the trees. Ramsay was yelling, though it was difficult to pick out what he was saying, and Ash felt like he wasn't meant to be listening anyway.

It was some time before the shouts quieted. Ash wondered if Ramsay had killed Callum. Either that, or Ramsay had started to kiss him instead. Jealousy and curiosity mixed, but Ash forced himself to sit, hands clenched and knee jiggling up and down, until he heard quick footsteps. He looked up just as Ramsay stormed past without a word. Ash stood just as Callum called his name.

"Are you okay?" Ash asked as Callum caught up with him.

Callum took a quick breath. "Ramsay listened. He said he needs time to sort out his feelings. That it would take time to trust me again."

Ash nodded, and they began to walk side by side. Neither tried to catch up to Ramsay, when it was clear he wanted space from them both.

*

It was another full day of walking to House Lune. They stepped carefully so that they wouldn't trip over rocks and roots. They slid down a slope and jumped over a trickling stream. Ash had lost count of the passing hours when he climbed up the other side, took several more steps, and saw that the forest had come to an end.

The ground sloped down into a field that stretched into the distance, and on the horizon, he saw it: House Lune didn't look

like any of the other House manors Ash had seen. Its estate walls
were so high that it was better described as a fortress. Towers
pierced low-lying clouds. A small village with lines of smoke surrounded it. Ash's nerves built. How were they going to have any
chance of finding the Book inside a place like that?

"If there was ever a chance to change your minds and turn back
around," Ramsay said, "it would be now."

Both Ash and Callum kept walking without hesitation, and it
wasn't long before Ramsay followed.

✳

The estate of House Lune was like a mountain in the far distance, never getting any closer. It was half a day before they
reached the outskirts of the scattered village, and even then,
the House's manor seemed a mile away. The road was muddy.
The houses were made of white stone and straw-thatched roofs.
The closer the houses were to the manor, the larger they became, the roads twisting up a hill to where the fortress rested.
Ash was surprised to see that the paved road led to a gate that
was open, people dressed in the white robes of House Lune
walking in and out. Maybe Lune didn't feel any need for closed
gates. There wasn't anyone in the state foolish enough to attack
them.

"How is Lune the only of the Houses that doesn't make members pay a tax," Ash whispered, "but they're still among the
wealthiest?"

"Isn't it obvious?" Ramsay said, eyes also on the manor ahead.
"They use fear. Fear of the Creator, fear of their House—people
will throw coin at them if it means they're safe from hell."

Ash remembered his father's words. House Lune didn't want
anyone to learn about their own power—that they were all the
Creator, all fragments of Source. It chilled Ash to think that
House Lune had kept the Book hidden away all this time. Did the
members even know it was behind their walls? What would they

do if they learned it was—and what were they willing to do to the alchemists who tried to find it?

Callum said they needed to find an inn. "We're already gathering too much attention as it is," he said.

Ash realized that he was right, from the glances sent their way. He'd heard that people made pilgrimages to House Lune and hoped that the villagers assumed that's what they were doing— but the three didn't look like the average Lune follower, with Ramsay's bored and shadowed expression and Callum's hulking frame and Ash's tendency to look like the sort of person Lune would rather string up than allow into their walls.

It wasn't difficult to find what appeared to be the village's only inn. The innkeeper gave them all a strange look when they requested only one room. Ash suspected that Ramsay would've preferred separate chambers, but Callum's coin purse was a lot lighter these days.

The room was more spacious than the one Ash and Callum had shared in Ironbound, at least. The window let in plenty of light, and though there was only one bed, there was a sofa beside a flickering fireplace and a table where they could take their meals. The adjoining bathroom had a tub that beckoned to Ash. He dropped his bag in relief and sat on the sofa while Ramsay created his usual energetic protections, eyes closed and murmuring beneath his breath. Callum made his usual inspections, too, much more thoroughly this time as he checked the window and the door and even under the bed.

Ramsay stood in the middle of the room, arms crossed. "And now?"

"House Lune has few defenses," Callum said, sitting on the edge of the table. "As you could see, they have the gates open to visitors. Most of the chambers are closed to the public, but they allow followers into the courtyard and its gardens."

"Then it's easy to get inside, at least," Ramsay said. He started pacing, even though his legs must've been aching.

"Easy to get into the public areas, yes," Callum said. "But trying to get into the restricted rooms will be impossible without being questioned."

"Can't we just pretend to be members?" Ash said. "We can insist that we live there." The building was so large that he couldn't see how anyone would be able to say that they knew every face.

"We'd need uniforms. They'd be able to take one look at us and see we don't belong."

"We could try to steal them," Ash said. From the blank stares, he realized it was an unhelpful suggestion.

"Even if we aren't immediately caught and arrested and likely executed once they realize who we are," Ramsay said, "I think it'd be quite difficult to ambush a House member, tie them up in our inn, and attempt to take their place. Don't you agree?"

"All right, fine," Ash said, rolling his eyes. "It isn't a good plan."

"And besides, none of this even begins to answer the question of where to start looking for the Book itself," Callum said, frowning thoughtfully.

"Could we attempt a remote viewing?" Ash asked Ramsay.

"I've already tried several times," he said. "There're too many energetic barriers and protections blocking the Book from being seen."

Someone must've put those blocks into place. Someone had to know that the Book was in House Lune. "When we were shown the Book, it looked like it was in some sort of underground chamber," Ash said. "There were footsteps and voices above us."

"That's true. We should focus on the lower chambers, if we manage to get inside and start our search."

Another idea came to Ash, then—maybe because of his own experience following Callum around Kensington, maybe because of his own work at Lancaster where he was treated like a servant anyway. "What if we worked there?"

He received blank stares again—this time, more confused than anything else.

Ash nodded. "Why not? We could work at House Lune. A manor that big? They must have domestics. They wouldn't question why we're in the restricted halls if we look like we're busy and we keep our heads down."

Ramsay stopped pacing. He seemed unhappy to admit that this wasn't such a bad plan. "How do you know they're even hiring?"

"A place like that is always hiring, as long as they're barely giving any pay."

Callum sighed, rubbing the back of his neck. "I don't know, Ash. Dignitaries and officials from different Houses visit one another often. What if a House Kendrick member visits, and one of us is recognized?"

Ash hesitated. "Well, you and Ramsay might be recognized as House heirs," he said, "but I wouldn't be."

"You want to go into House Lune, alone, as a servant?"

"I could try to gather information, at least," he said. "Wait for an opportunity and search for the Book."

"It's too dangerous," Callum said.

"This entire situation is dangerous. Trying to find the Book is dangerous. It's not any safer with you there, holding my hand and insisting that you protect me."

Callum clenched his jaw and, annoyingly, looked at Ramsay of all people. The two had what appeared to be a silent conversation, wordlessly agreeing that they would never let Ash put his life at risk without them there to make sure he was safe.

He stood from the sofa. "Can either of you think of a better plan?"

Ramsay sighed loudly, still looking at Callum, before he finally met Ash's eye. "It's worth a try."

"But you need to promise not to do anything reckless," Callum said. As soon as the words left his mouth, he seemed to realize who he was speaking to. Ash grinned, and Callum sighed. "At least agree to wait before you throw yourself into a life-threatening situation. Find us first."

"I'll do my best," Ash said, but he knew full well which option he would choose if it came to finding the Book or waiting to ask Callum for permission to make a move. Callum seemed to realize this, too, from the concern pinching his brows.

"We don't even know if this plan will work," Ramsay said, slightly dismissive, maybe to push aside his own worry. "Let's at least see if Ash will be hired as a servant first."

32

The sleeping arrangements had been more complicated than Ash expected. There was only enough space for two people on the bed, and though Ramsay and Callum were no longer in a constant fight, they obviously wouldn't be able to sleep right next to each other. Ash could've slept beside either Ramsay or Callum, but he didn't want to choose.

"Ramsay, I think that you should sleep on the bed," Callum suggested after they'd eaten and washed. "You're still weak after the attack."

He rolled his eyes but didn't bother to argue. Callum could be stubborn when he entered redguard-commander mode.

"I'll sleep on the floor," Callum said. "I'm used to it, thanks to my training."

Ash rubbed the back of his neck. "I'll take the sofa," he said.

The three were exhausted as they shuffled about the room. Ash wrapped himself in sheets on the couch. The moment he closed his eyes, he felt a piece of his energy escape into his dreams. He saw a frozen river and his father standing in the center of Snowdrop and heard his mother's screams—

He thought he was still asleep when he heard the low murmur of Ramsay's voice. He shifted. The lights were off. The silver light of the moon cast shadows in the room. Callum stood by the window, leaning against the wall. Ramsay's back was to Ash as he rested against the sill, whispering. "It isn't that easy."

"Do you miss how things were?"

"Not when it'd all been a lie," Ramsay said. After a pause, he added, "Sometimes. Not the sneaking back and forth, though."

Callum glanced at Ramsay like he wasn't sure he was allowed to look at him. "I think about the night on the fields a lot. Do you remember that?"

Ramsay seemed to surprise himself when he laughed. "I wish I didn't."

"Did you know there was a rumor that you'd come to my dorm?"

Ash rested his head back down again, staring at the ceiling as he listened.

"Really?"

"Gavin told me. Creator, I hadn't realized they were talking about me behind my back."

"Is it a rumor if it's true?"

Callum gave a low laugh. "Maybe not."

There was a long pause. Ash could practically feel both Ramsay and Callum's heartbeats.

"Do you think there's a chance?" Callum asked him softly.

Ramsay took a long moment to respond. "Maybe," he eventually said. "I don't know yet. Let's wait to see if we survive first."

Ash frowned. It wasn't any of his business what they spoke about, but he hated that he felt left out. He listened to their low murmuring voices, every now and then interrupted by Ramsay's surprised, soft laugh. Maybe it wasn't so unexpected that Ramsay had begun to forgive Callum. His sincere apologies would soften anyone. And they'd been best friends, too, after all, even before they'd fallen in love.

Melancholy followed Ash into the next morning. He became very aware that, while he was in House Lune, Ramsay and Callum would be in the room alone. With a bed. Ash was embarrassed by it, but he couldn't deny the jealousy that flourished in his chest.

Callum frowned at Ash as he got ready to leave. The air in the room was tense enough as it was, with Ash about to risk his life. "Are you all right?" he asked.

Ash shrugged, eyes downcast. "Sure," he said. He added, "Nervous, I guess."

Ramsay had been right when she'd said that they couldn't allow themselves to be so distracted. Here he was, worrying about Callum and Ramsay and where he would fit in their relationship, when he was so close to finding the Book.

Callum buttoned up Ash's shirt while Ramsay watched as she stood by the door. It was obvious that neither wanted to let Ash go.

"If you sense any sort of danger," Callum said, "you should leave immediately and return here at once."

"And as tempting as I'm sure it'll be," Ramsay said, "don't do anything foolish. Unnecessary risks will just reduce your chances of success."

"You're acting like I'll storm into the House and start shouting to every person I see that I'm there to find the Book," Ash grumbled.

Ramsay's quirked brow suggested she wouldn't put it past him. She didn't seem to think much of it when she leaned forward and kissed him on the mouth. Callum finished adjusting Ash's collar and apparently didn't want to be left out as he angled Ash's chin upward and kissed him, too. The moment sank in, and all three looked away from one another. Ash fumbled with the doorknob and let himself out, turning when Callum called for him to be careful, unable to help a smile at the sight of the two of them crowding the doorway just to watch him go.

*

Ash didn't want to admit to himself just how nervous he was, but the moment he was on his own, walking through the village and closer to the manor itself, nerves rose into fear. His mother had never spoken about her experiences in House Lune, before she'd been taken by Hain—but he realized he would be going to the place where she'd spent years of her life.

The muddy road with scattered houses gradually became busier, people bustling back and forth. A few wore the white robes of Lune. Ash's heart pumped harder. He'd always avoided Lune followers in Hedge, never sure when they'd become a mob screaming for his death. Now he was surrounded by them as he willingly walked right into the heart of Lune itself.

There was a redguard, too, standing by. Ash's walk slowed with shock before he sped up again. Redguards were in most major cities and towns, but he didn't expect to see one here. Had the Kendrick realized he and Ramsay and Callum had made it out of the Derry Hills and come to House Lune? Ash ducked his head when he passed, relieved that the guard only stared through him.

The road became paved with brick as it led up toward the manor. The entrance had low light. The floors were a warm mosaic, the walls covered in a golden design of blooming lilies. Two staircases rose on either side of the hall, and directly in front of Ash was an archway that opened to what looked like a garden, gray light shining from overhead. It reminded him of the Lancaster greenhouse he'd spent so many of his days in, with a pinch of nostalgia. There were even trees, a pathway that led through the flowers, and benches where it seemed followers could sit and pray. In the center of that garden was what appeared to be a large courtyard.

"Hello, traveler."

Ash jumped. He turned to see a stern, elderly man. He was bald, but he had a beard of white, and there were bluish spots on his pale skin. His eyes scanned Ash. Even with his treatment in Lancaster and as a prisoner in Kensington, Ash had never felt so small under a person's gaze. The stranger wore white robes, though there was a floral design stitched into its fabric, with a rope of red tied around his waist.

Ash gave a nervous nod. "Hello."

"You seem to have come a long way," the man said.

"I have."

"Where are you from?"

What were the chances that this man had heard of the attacks on Lancaster College by an alchemist from Hedge? "Ironbound," Ash lied.

"Ah, that's far indeed," the man said, smile frozen onto his face. "Usually, we don't have city folk here in the Elder lands. Our visitors are generally humble people, traveling from Riverside or the Westfields."

"I hope that you're willing to make an exception."

The man tilted his head. "Did you come to make your praises to the Creator?"

It was Ash's chance. "Yes," he said, and tried to put just the right amount of emotion into his voice. "I felt called to come here. Everyone I know in Ironbound has lost their way, and I don't want to follow their path."

This seemed to quell some suspicion in the man, at least. He raised his chin as he inspected Ash. "It's easier to lose your way in cities, I believe," he said. "There are too many people who celebrate . . . *differences*."

The man would have likely seen Ash, Ramsay, and Callum as *different*. "I hoped to start a new life here," Ash said. "Closer to Lune and the Creator."

"We welcome you, then." The man spoke as if he was in a play himself and he had no choice but to recite those lines.

Ash hesitated. "It's just—I came without anything," he said. "Only the clothes on my back. I've run out of money, and I have no food."

The man watched Ash expressionlessly. "You gave up so much to journey here, and all because you heard the Creator's calling."

"I wondered—hoped—that there might be a job for me. Maybe in the kitchens, or scrubbing the floors?"

The Lune member sighed, more impatient now. Ash wondered how many came through these doors asking for help, only to be sent away with nothing but a prayer.

"I work hard," Ash added quickly, "and I don't complain. I only ask for food and a place to rest my head. Being close to the Creator in a place like this would be payment enough."

The elder eyed Ash for a few moments, before finally he said, "This is all that the Creator expects of us. Sacrifice as a show of gratitude, in exchange for his unconditional love."

Ash bit back disgust. He wasn't sure how sacrifice could ever be an exchange for unconditional love. Conditions had been placed for another person to be worthy of the Creator—conditions that, conveniently, gave wealth and influence to House Lune. The hypocrisy of it all angered Ash. But still he nodded, head bent as he had seen some of the followers do.

The man snapped his fingers at a girl near Ash's age passing by. She stopped, eyes fastened on the ground. "Take this boy to Mistress Davies. Let her know I've authorized him to begin work however she sees fit."

"Yes, sir," the girl said, still refusing to look up from her feet. The man turned and walked away from them without another word.

The girl moved so quickly that it took Ash effort to keep up with her. She hurried away from the garden, up the stairs, and down a corridor. The walls and floors were made of some sort of white stone, and the ceiling consisted of pointed arches. Ash stared around, wondering where he would begin his search for the Book. He would need to figure out a way to sneak downstairs again and search the hidden chambers beneath the manor.

The girl first brought Ash to a room with shelves of uniforms. She threw white pants and a white robe at him. "Be quick about it," she said, her back to him. Ash changed out of his clothing and was dismayed when it was all thrown into a bin, but he knew better than to complain.

She brought him down creaking wooden stairs and to a kitchen filled with attendants who hurried back and forth. Mistress Davies stood in the center of it all, shouting orders. There were tables where attendants chopped vegetables. The smell and sight of platters of fresh bread, meats, and fruit made Ash's stomach grumble. His last meal had been dinner at the inn with Ramsay and Callum. He'd been too nervous to eat porridge that morning.

Mistress Davies didn't seem pleased to be handed a new attendant. She impatiently assigned Ash to cleaning pots. There was a tub of water where he and three others knelt, scrubbing until his arms ached, his fingers pruned. The other three ignored Ash altogether as they gossiped, not that he minded. He chewed on his lip as he tried to figure out how, exactly, he'd be able to get out of the kitchens and begin searching for the Book. He doubted he'd be able to simply walk out, his absence unnoticed for the hours that he searched.

"Mistress Davies is in an even fouler mood than usual," the girl to Ash's right muttered.

"She's probably stressed. There's going to be a big dinner tomorrow night," a boy said, annoyed. "An alchemist is being welcomed."

Ash's skin went cold. He paused his scrubbing, looking up.

"But why would an alchemist come here?" the boy to Ash's left whispered. "I thought they were the enemies of Lune."

"They are," the girl said, and judging by the disgust on her face, they were her enemies, too. "They should all be burned, as far as I'm concerned."

Ash's heart sank. He looked down at his hands and continued scrubbing. He'd already known he was hated by complete strangers, without them even knowing him, but it always hurt to see the evidence of that hatred for himself.

"Apparently, he's some political figure. An advisor to House Alexander."

Ash stopped again. "What did you say?" He received odd looks, but he didn't care. "Gresham Hain is here?"

The girl frowned. "I don't know the alchemist's name," she said, with a tone that implied that Ash shouldn't have known, either.

They went back to work. Was it really that surprising his father would be here? Maybe Hain had somehow broken through Ramsay's protections and managed to trace Ash all the time that he and Callum and Ramsay thought they were safe in the Westfields. Maybe he'd figured out that the Book was hidden in House Lune on his own.

All the more reason to get away from the kitchens and begin his search. Ash was just starting to think he might need to use alchemy to spark a small fire and cause a distraction when he heard the clanging of bells. The sound reverberated through the halls and the floors. The attendants around him sighed as they stood as one. He frowned up at them, confused.

"What's going on?"

One looked down at him as if he wasn't very bright. "It's time for Head Peterson Lune to lead us in afternoon prayers."

Ash hesitated, then stood, too, joining the line that formed. He walked through the maze of halls, trying to memorize the direction in case he needed to run for his life later, looking into the open doors to see where people had been boiling white sheets and robes. The halls collected what seemed to be dozens of attendants who filed up the stairs and to the gardens. Ash's heart clenched as he watched rows of small children led from rooms by people holding their hands, too. His mother had been one of those children, once.

The House members had gathered at the front of the courtyard, from what Ash could see ahead. They all stood to face the very man who had welcomed Ash that morning.

Source, he'd been greeted and hired by the Head of House Lune itself. Something bit at Ash—there were no coincidences in this universe, only parallels and cosmic jokes.

Peterson Lune started a speech about his love for the Creator, something Ash's ears immediately blocked out. He couldn't stand to listen about the Creator when he knew House Lune cared nothing about the words they preached. He wondered if there was a chance he could sneak away when the man declared it was time to raise their voices in song. Those around Ash began to do just that, singing a slow hymn that seemed to have no purpose other than to make Ash want to fall asleep on his feet—

A thought struck him.

The vision he'd received with Ramsay in the higher realms showed the Book of Source not only underground, but with the sounds of footsteps and music . . .

His gaze fell, slowly, to the ground beneath his feet. He and Ramsay had asked the Akash where the Book was hidden, and it was as if the library had already known that Ash would find himself right there, at that moment—that he would be able to realize what the thuds of footsteps and the voices in song meant. The garden was large, but it was possible, wasn't it? That, at that very moment, the Book of Source was directly beneath his feet.

He felt like he walked a thin rope and was near the other end where a platform waited. He could try to teeter, taking his time, and risk falling at any moment—or he could simply leap.

The afternoon prayers ended. The attendants moved to line up again. It was as they walked through the corridors that Ash slipped into another hall. He could feel the startled stare of the person who'd been behind him, but he ignored them as he hurried down a series of creaking stairs. Even in this hall, he could hear the footsteps and muffled voices above.

There was a door, amber colored, shining in the flickering torchlight. Ash swallowed as he stepped closer. He could open the door to find the Book of Source itself. Even as something in him whispered it wouldn't be so easy, he placed a hand on the knob and tried to turn it. Locked, of course, and it was an ancient knob, not as easy to push energy through to force open—but maybe if he closed his eyes and tried to get a sense for the alchemic makeup on the knob, he could convince it to become undone—

The lock clicked. Ash's breath shuddered as he pushed open the door and stepped inside. There was no light. He opened one hand and held up his palm, allowing energy to glow bright. He shined the light around the room, at the molding stone walls—

There was a groan. Ash jumped. His light shined across a person. This person was sitting in the middle of the room on a wooden chair—no, not sitting, but chained to the ground and the chair itself. He was naked, and the man's face and body were bloody and bruised, several open and infected gashes on his legs and arms. He groaned again as he looked up, his eyes so swollen, he could barely peer at Ash through them.

"You—" the man rasped.

Ash shook his head slowly, horror crawling through him. "What the hell is this?"

"You—you're not of Lune."

Ash looked over his shoulder as if he expected guards to appear any moment, all of this a trap to sniff him out and capture him. "Who are you?"

"Please," the man said. "Please, help me. Unchain me."

"Why are you here?"

The man was stiff. He sniffed the air, and his eyes brightened, crazed with desperation. "You're an alchemist."

"I don't know what you're—"

"Don't lie to me, boy. I smell it on you. You've performed alchemy, haven't you?" The man almost seemed near laughter. "Don't worry. I'm an alchemist, too."

Ash's heart sank. He wanted to step forward to unchain the man, to help him and free him—but if he did, he knew he wouldn't get out of House Lune without someone noticing. He'd give up any chance of returning to find the Book.

"What happened?" Ash asked.

But the man ignored his question. He murmured to himself, as if he'd forgotten Ash was there altogether. He was delirious.

"And if another alchemist has come, then there's only one reason why they're here—all of this would be for naught—"

Realization dawned on Ash. "Did you come here to find the Book of Source, too?"

As soon as Ash spoke, he realized he should've been more careful. He was certain that, for Ramsay, speaking openly about the Book would fall under the *foolish* category.

The man's eyes grew cold as he met Ash's gaze again. Ramsay had been right that there were other alchemists after the Book, then. They'd focused on Hain so much that alchemists she hadn't even known existed had been even closer to finding it.

Ash whispered, "Do you know where it is?"

"Why should I tell you that?" the alchemist spat.

"You've seen it, haven't you? You know where it's hidden."

The alchemist suddenly laughed. "Do you know they've tried to destroy the Book?" he asked as if sharing a joke. "They've even forced me to use alchemy against it. Tortured me into trying. Nothing on Earth is powerful enough to destroy the Book of Source."

Ash paused. This was Ramsay's only goal, her entire reason for seeking the Book. To hear that it was impossible to destroy made Ash's heart sink for her. But Ramsay wasn't the average alchemist. Maybe where this man failed, she'd find a way to succeed.

"If you tell me where it's hidden," Ash said, "I can help you. I can free you."

The man was quiet for a long while. He seemed to consider as he stared blankly at Ash. "Free me first," he said, voice suddenly rough. "And then I'll tell you where it is."

Ash wasn't sure what to do. The part of him that had sympathy for this man wanted to free him just because it hurt to see another human being bound and tortured. Another part would do almost anything to find the Book, even trust another alchemist who might not have good intentions. But something else whispered inside of him. This man was a rival. Ash knew what rival alchemists were willing to do to find the Book first. This man could attack Ash as soon as he was set free. Ash needed to slow down. He needed to think.

Ash hesitated long enough that the alchemist's confidence seemed to dim. He slumped, his fate clear. "I'll come back," Ash said, though he wasn't sure it was a promise he could keep.

The alchemist began to plead with him, but Ash stepped outside quickly again, shutting the door behind him. He released a shaking breath. Was this another cosmic joke sent by the universe? Two parallel lives colliding, one who had questions about the Book of Source, and another who wished desperately for help, and also happened to have all the answers.

33

Ramsay opened the door before Ash even stopped in front of it. Her face was etched with worry, and when he walked inside, Callum stood from the bed, also concerned.

"You're late."

"Are you all right?"

"Did anyone suspect you?"

"What happened?"

Ash frowned, not sure why he was so annoyed. The Lune uniform made him feel like something was crawling beneath his skin. He started to yank at his top.

Ramsay and Callum both stepped forward, Ramsay pulling the robe from Ash's arms and handing it to Callum, who folded it and placed it on the sofa.

"Well?" Ramsay said, voice soft.

Ash stood in the center of the room in nothing but his binder and his pants. He realized he must've looked lost. "I was allowed in for work," he said.

"Hence the uniform," Ramsay said, a bit impatiently.

"I overheard other attendants," Ash told them. "They said the advisor to House Alexander is coming tomorrow."

He was met with silent shock, interrupted only by Ramsay's curses.

"Is there any chance at all that it's just a coincidence?" Callum asked.

"There are no coincidences," Ramsay told him. "Hain's either figured out that we're here, or that the Book is—or both."

Ash continued his story, describing how he'd slipped away and found the locked room beneath the gardens. He took a breath. "I thought the Book would be inside, but I found an imprisoned alchemist instead."

He'd moved to sit at the table, hands around a mug of tea that Callum prepared for him while he spoke, using tea bags from their duffel of supplies while Ramsay heated the mug with her palms. Callum sat opposite him. Ramsay paced as she listened, but at the news of the alchemist, she stopped.

"He'd been beaten and tortured," Ash said. He hesitated, then added, "He claimed to know the Book's location."

"Source," Ramsay murmured. "Well, we always knew we weren't the only ones searching for the Book . . ."

Ash stared into the lavender tea. He'd never told Callum that lavender was his favorite, but the boy still somehow knew. "What do you think I should do?"

"Leave the alchemist to his fate," Ramsay said without hesitation. "He's probably just bluffing when he says he knows the Book's location—and even if he *does* know, why would he tell you if he wants it for himself?"

"But this is our only lead right now."

She swiped a hand through her hair. "So let's find a better one."

"We can't afford to wait. Hain is arriving tomorrow," he reminded them. "What if he finds it before us?"

Ramsay hesitated. "He might not know where it's hidden yet."

"And that's a risk you're willing to take?"

Ash looked at Callum, expecting that he'd agree with Ash instead, but he only leaned back in his seat, his brows pinched together. "You don't know this man or his motivations. He could hurt you, Ash, and Ramsay and I wouldn't be there to help."

Ash felt frustrated with them both. "This is the closest we've come to finding the Book. It wasn't in the underground room, like the Akash showed us," he told Ramsay. "It could be anywhere in House Lune now. There's no way I can search the entire manor on my own, even if I work there for months." And in the race against Hain, he likely didn't even have a day to find the Book before his father did.

Ramsay seemed to realize this, too. She bit her lip. "Better than getting yourself killed."

"Don't you think I can protect myself if he does attack?"

"We'll find another way," Callum told him.

Ash clenched his hands around the mug. "The Akash showed that specific room, just for me to find an alchemist inside," he said. "There must be a reason for that. I'm supposed to help him."

"You're forcing meaning where there's none to be had," Ramsay said, voice rising. "If you free the alchemist, he will *kill* you, Ash—"

"We don't know that for sure."

"Well, that's reassuring."

"We knew this would be dangerous when we left—"

"You're not going back," Ramsay said.

"What?"

"You're not going back to House Lune."

Ash stood out of his seat. "But I've finally found a way in—"

"We shouldn't have let you go alone in the first place," Ramsay said.

Callum frowned silently, listening to the argument, only glancing at Ash apologetically when Ash gave him a pleading stare. "She's right."

"Well, of course you take her side—"

"Oh, come on, Ash," Callum said with a heavy sigh.

"We can regroup," Ramsay said. "Figure out a better move than getting you killed."

"Like what?"

"We could go to the higher realms again."

"We got all the information the higher realms are willing to give."

"I can ask my parents where the Book is specifically hidden—"

"If they didn't tell you before, why would they tell you now?" Ash shook his head. "I need to free the alchemist."

"I already said no, Ash—"

"You aren't in charge of me, able to give me orders—"

"*I* am the one who wanted to find the Book in the first place, so, yes, I would say I'm in charge—"

"You wouldn't have even gotten here without me!"

Callum stood. Ramsay and Ash were breathing hard, glaring at each other. "Let's take a breath."

Ramsay rolled her eyes and turned on her heel, walking to the window, while Ash sat back heavily in his seat.

"Ash," Callum said, "Ramsay is right. It's too dangerous."

"But—"

"Redguard patrols began. We saw them earlier from the window." Ash frowned, remembering the red he'd seen before. "My family must suspect that we're here, too."

"Even more reason to find the Book as quickly as possible, then, and get the hell out of here."

"We discussed," Callum continued, "and letting you return isn't a risk either of us is willing to take."

Ash crossed his arms. "Sounds like you've already made up your minds about what I'm allowed to do, then."

"Ash—"

"I'm not your prisoner still, remember? You can't order me around anymore."

Callum walked to his side and placed a hand on his shoulder. Ash sighed. He didn't want to accept the light-blue energy that began to wash over his skin, slowing his speeding heart, pouring water on a flame. "We'll find another way."

It had never been clearer to Ash that there *was* no other way—but he could also see there was no use in arguing with two of the most stubborn people in the entire state. He clenched his jaw but still nodded, pretending to agree. While Callum and Ramsay had both already made up their minds, Ash had made his own decision, too.

He played along. When Ash and Ramsay sat and breathed in harmony, they realized that their ability to reach the higher realms together had faded. It would take at least another few days of practice before they'd be able to propel each other upward again. Ash did his best to pretend he was disappointed, too, and nodded when Callum said they'd find another way.

When it was late enough, Callum suggested that they get some rest. "We'll have clearer heads in the morning."

Ash knew there was a chance this would be the last time he spent a night with either of them. "Would it be okay if we slept in the same bed?" he asked. "The three of us, I mean."

Callum and Ramsay both hesitated, then looked at each other. Ramsay ran a hand through her hair. "All three of us?"

Callum seemed embarrassed, too. "I don't think we'll all fit."

"Can we try?"

Ash did his best to hide his true thoughts from Callum—to focus on anything but *tomorrow* and *the Book* and *possible death*. Callum must've still picked up on something, though. He frowned at Ash. "Yes. All right. I'm okay with it, if Ramsay . . ."

Ramsay clenched her jaw. "Fine."

It took a lot of maneuvering and annoyed sighs from Ramsay before Ash found a spot sprawled across them both. Callum was at risk of slipping off the bed, and Ramsay was cramped against the wall, but it was comfortable, somehow. Ash leaned a cheek against Callum's chest and listened to him breathe while one leg slid beneath Ramsay's thigh. The lights were off. Only embers of the fireplace flickered across the room, putting the three into warm shadow. This helped to dim some of the embarrassment, at least.

The silence was unbearable. It was obvious that none of the three could sleep. Ash wasn't sure if it was his imagination, the other tension that grew.

"I'm a little jealous of you two, to be honest," Ash murmured.

Callum frowned. "Jealous? Why?"

"I heard you talking last night," Ash admitted. "You both have a history," he said. "You get to whisper inside jokes."

Ramsay frowned at the ceiling. "We have inside jokes, don't we?"

"No, we don't have any inside jokes."

"Would you like to make one now?"

"I'm not sure inside jokes work that way, Ramsay."

She rolled onto her side, facing Callum and Ash, Ash's leg caught between her thighs now. "You're overthinking things. Which is, you know, rare—"

Ash swatted her arm.

"—and maybe should be celebrated—"

Ash tried to swat her again, but she grabbed his hand at the last second, intertwining their fingers.

"Do you think *inside jokes* show how much I care about you?"

Callum's heart sped under Ash's cheek. "I care about you also, Ash. You know that."

"Is this a competition for saying how much we care about him?" Ramsay said.

"What? No—"

"You only said you care about him after I did."

"Does that mean it isn't true?"

He heard their words, but Ash didn't want to let himself believe them. He was still afraid that he'd let himself fall so completely in love with both Ramsay and Callum, only to be left behind. But maybe now, it didn't matter. Maybe now, when he didn't know how much time he had left, Ash needed to live exactly as his heart desired.

"What's strange is that I actually want to see both of you together also," Ash said. "I want to see you happy. I'm just afraid of where I'd fit with you."

Callum tilted Ash's chin so that he'd look up at him. "I wish you could feel our emotions right now, because then you wouldn't worry about any of this. You'd feel how much we both love you."

Ash leaned forward and kissed him. There wasn't much thought involved. Ramsay's fingers tightened around his, and Ash pulled away to kiss her, too. He hadn't meant for the kiss to linger as long as it did, Ramsay leaning closer, hand letting go of Ash's to run up his arm and down his back. He was vaguely aware that Callum watched them. The moment Callum put a hand into Ash's hair, he pulled away to kiss Callum's cheek, his mouth, gasping as Ramsay didn't seem to want to let go of him yet, following to kiss the back of his neck. Ash hoped to Source that whatever happened next between the three of them wouldn't split them apart.

Ash had a strange feeling in his chest when he pulled back from Callum to see the other boy watching Ramsay. Callum waited silently—for a sign, for permission, for anything, it seemed. Ramsay didn't speak for one long moment. She stared at Callum so expressionlessly that Ash couldn't tell what she was thinking. He was surprised when she leaned forward and kissed Callum. It was so quick that Ash might've blinked and missed it. She pulled away again, making the same thoughtful face she did when analyzing an experiment. She leaned forward and kissed Callum again— more slowly this time, murmuring something that sounded a lot like *fuck it* against Callum's mouth.

Ash wasn't as jealous as he thought he'd be, watching them kiss each other. Instead, he felt a burst of happiness. This was the first kiss they'd shared in two years, when they'd both been so in love with each other. Ash's heart started to speed even more, to see Callum's softness as he kissed Ramsay, as if he now knew how it felt to lose her, and he'd never take another moment with her for granted again. Callum gasped when Ramsay nibbled on his lip and gasped again when Ash kissed his neck.

The three discovered a rhythm. There were times when their hands and mouths were almost frantic, fingers reaching beneath clothes, and Ash wondered just how far they would go. There were moments when the kissing gave way to sighs, fingers tracing over skin. Eventually, they slowed until they were all lying on the bed in a tangle of limbs, Ash's head on Callum's chest while Ramsay spread out on top of them both. They were silent, breath and heartbeats languid, as if the realization of what they'd just done had settled.

"Maybe I've been thinking about this all wrong," Ash mumbled.

"Isn't that generally the case?" Ramsay laughed when Ash pinched her leg.

Callum shifted beneath Ash. "Thought about what wrong?"

"This," Ash said. "Us. I thought about our *situation* as me having a growing relationship with Callum, and me having a relationship with Ramsay, and you both having a relationship with each other. Maybe it's that, too," he said, "but I think we might also have a relationship with one another. The three of us. If you would like that, anyway," he added, voice soft.

Callum smiled as he nestled a hand into Ash's hair, drawing him closer for a kiss. "I'd like that very much."

Ash smiled against his mouth, then tensed as he noticed Ramsay's silence. He turned to look at her just as she sat up. She ran a hand through her hair, pulling it back, wrapping strands into a loose bun. Callum put a hand on Ash's, signaling for him to wait.

"What're we doing?" she asked as she sat on the edge of the bed.

"What do you mean?" Ash said. He thought it was pretty clear what they'd been doing.

"Pretending that we can be together?" she said. "We're on the run from the Kendrick, and Hain—"

"You're assuming this will end badly for us," Callum said.

"How can I not?"

Callum reached a hand for Ramsay's, and she sighed and let him take it. "You could be right. We could be found and killed.

But I'd rather have these moments to think back on. It's the only thing that'd give me peace as the rope is placed around my neck."

Ash understood Ramsay's fear. He felt even guiltier, knowing that in the morning before either could wake, he would slip away and return to House Lune on his own. The embers in the fireplace died down, leaving the room dark. Callum's breaths eventually slowed, and Ramsay stopped tossing and turning. Ash tried to force himself to get some sleep, too. He didn't know how much energy he'd need the next day, when he went to the alchemist and offered his help.

He thought about how angry both Ramsay and Callum would be with him. He'd lied to them. There was a chance that he would die alone. But Ash knew he had no choice. This was beyond him—beyond Ramsay and Callum, too. He couldn't let his father find the Book first.

Ash wondered what death would feel like. Would it be similar to reaching the higher realms? Some alchemists claimed that death was the ultimate release—the shedding of the physical body, an explosion of joy and love as the person's energy returned to Source. Ash wondered if, when he died, he would care about the fact that he'd left so much behind—if he'd have any regrets. He would never become a licensed alchemist if he died tomorrow, wouldn't prove his worth to his father and all the Houses and everyone who looked down on him. He would die a criminal, a low-level alchemist, a joke and topic of idle gossip. He'd never be able to share his love with Callum and Ramsay again.

No, Ash didn't want to die at all. There were still too many adventures to be had, too many dreams to come true. But that was the point of *sacrifice*, he supposed as he closed his eyes. Giving up what he wanted for a cause greater than himself.

34

The alchemist looked up with an unblinking stare as Ash closed the door behind him.

"You came back," he said. "I didn't think you would."

Ash was silent as he began his work. The chains were complex, and it took longer than usual to imagine a blade sharp enough.

"Is that creation alchemy?" the man asked, sounding impressed despite it all.

Ash managed to cut through the chains at the man's feet first, and then sawed through the chains around his wrists, aware that the stranger could use his free hand to grab Ash by the neck. When Ash was finished, the alchemist stood slowly, gingerly. Ash tossed him one of the uniforms he'd snagged, and the man murmured a thanks as he clothed himself. Ash's guard was up as he watched the man carefully, waiting for the moment he spun, ready to attack—

"What's your name?" the alchemist asked.

He felt no need to lie. Ash didn't think he would go running to the redguards any time soon. "Ashen Woods, though I go by Ash." He paused. "You?"

"Randall Pierce."

Ash had heard that name before, at the Kendrick gala as he stood by Callum's side. "But—but you're the alchemist that went missing," he said. "How long have you been trapped here?"

"I'd purposefully vanished," Randall told Ash. "Left society, hoping I'd be forgotten as I searched for the Book. It's easier to find success when others' minds aren't on you."

Ash stood straighter. "I freed you like I said I would. Now it's your turn to hold up your end of the bargain."

Randall hesitated. "I think it'd be easier if I showed you the way to the Book instead."

Ash's eyes narrowed. He didn't like the game this man played. "That isn't what we agreed on."

"You wouldn't be able to access the room without my help," the alchemist insisted. "Allow me to come with you."

Randall's endgame was obvious. He would kill Ash the moment they found the room. Ash wasn't sure why Randall didn't just try to kill him now. Maybe the man figured it'd be better to have another alchemist on his side for the journey, in case they were found and attacked by guards. It was even more likely that Randall would want to use Ash as a shield, throwing the younger boy at their enemies while Randall attempted to escape.

"Fine," Ash said. "Lead the way."

*

Ash was confused when the man placed a hand to the stone wall. Randall breathed, and Ash watched as the wall crumbled into dust, showing dirt and roots. Randall took another deep breath, and there was a pulse of energy that began to press a hole into the dirt. He was carving an underground tunnel.

It was a technique Ash had only read about. Demolition alchemy was tier four and required the imagining of the unweaving of alchemic bonds, understanding the properties of the object to turn it to dust.

"I need my full palm to touch the surface to activate all of my energy points," Randall said, as if he could hear Ash's silent question of why he hadn't destroyed his chains. "They knew this and were always careful to position my hands in a way that I couldn't fully touch a surface."

Ash was nervous to ask his next question. "Does that trick work on human bodies, too?"

Randall only smiled at Ash, as if he fully meant for the boy to learn the answer to that soon. Ash kept a decidedly wide berth between them as Randall worked. The minutes ticked on, dirt crumbling at their feet into smaller particles. The effort seemed to be depleting Randall quickly. His skin shined with sweat in the light Ash held in the palm of his hand, and his limbs started shaking. It seemed that the pure motivation of finding the Book kept the alchemist going.

The last bit of dirt crumbled away. They stood in front of a wall of stone. Ash could feel, from the stiffness in Randall's shoulders, that this was it. The might of the moment felt heavy on Ash, too. There was too much energy in the air, too much excitement and dread, in knowing that the tool to grant any one person all the power of Source was on the other side of a mere wall. For a fleeting moment, Ash wished that Ramsay was here with him. It was what she'd wanted, what she'd worked for, and it seemed unfair that she wouldn't be the first to see the Book. But Ash would bring it to her, he thought to himself. Whether he would have enough strength to not open the covers and read its words was another question.

Randall gulped down air while Ash stood several feet behind him. Randall could try to kill him now, before he opened the room. It felt like they both sat at a chess table, Randall carefully considering his next move. His breathing calmed, and he stood so still that Ash began to ready himself to attack first.

But the man raised a hand against the wall. The stone fell apart.

There was no light in the room. It took Ash a moment for his eyes to adjust, even with the white ball of light in the palm of his hand. He saw the stone graves and tombs, the holes in the wall that held busts and carvings and various treasures.

"Are we in a crypt?" Ash said.

He'd barely finished speaking when something heavy lashed out at his head. Ash ducked just in time. Randall breathed hard as he swung what looked like a vase. Ash scrambled back and threw up embers of light that blinded Randall enough for Ash to jump to his feet.

"Decided I can die now since there aren't any guards to fight?"

"You're smarter than you look," Randall said.

Ash backed away. "You should've used your demolition alchemy on me. Letting me live long enough to defend myself was a bad move." He was just stalling, edging closer to the nearest tomb so that he had a defensive wall to hide behind.

"You need to be lying still, unfortunately," Randall said, following him, eyes glimmering. He meant to knock Ash unconscious and then kill him. "But I'll take care of that."

Ash clapped his hands together. The light went out, but he could still see the outline of bright red dancing along Randall's skin. Ash aimed and shot a bolt of sharpened light, but Randall threw up a hand and *caught it*, laughing as he readied to hurl it back at Ash before he could think to put a shield around himself—

There was a creaking. A door opened, and the crypt flooded with white light. Ash squinted, confused, as there were footsteps. His eyes adjusted enough to see Peterson Lune stride inside. Randall's eyes widened, but he'd frozen—he tried to take a step back, but too late. Peterson grasped his arm without expression. There was an explosion. Red and bone and bits of flesh scattered. There was a sharp ringing in Ash's ears. He gasped, wiping red from his eyes—gagged as he realized *what* was on him—and struggled to get back to his feet, his heart pounding as Peterson turned to him next. Ash raised his hands to defend himself.

Peterson only eyed him. "Did you really think I would let two alchemists on the premises of House Lune reach the Book of Source?"

Ash's hands were shaking. He surrounded himself with a white shield—it was only now sinking in that the Head of House Lune knew alchemy and was powerful at that—

"Lower your hands, boy," the man said. "Why would I kill you?" His smile gave Ash chills. "You're too useful."

"An alchemist," Ash managed to say, breathless. They were the only words that would find their way to his lips. "You're also an alchemist."

Peterson only pointed a finger. A rope appeared from the air effortlessly, binding Ash's hands behind his back. Ash was too shocked to fight it. The truth was sinking in more with each second that passed. The hatred that had been shown to alchemists, the people who had been strung up by their necks in Hedge because of Lune followers—

"How can you claim alchemy is evil," Ash said hoarsely, beginning to find his voice again, "when you—"

"Alchemy may not be evil," Hain said, "but human beings are. My family works to keep peace and control."

Ash was stunned as the man pushed him by the shoulder, forcing him to walk. "It isn't your place to decide—it isn't anyone's right—"

Lune led Ash up a series of steps. "Rights? If humans weren't subdued, there would be no order. They need to be told what to think and how to live—and who to hate. It's easier for them and their small minds to exist in an infinite universe."

They marched out of the crypt and into a stone hall. "Do you see how quickly they all jump at the chance to hate others?" Lune said with a slow smile. "To believe that they are more worthy than another in the eyes of Source?"

"You believe that people are evil," Ash said, "but you're only seeing a reflection of who *you* are—"

Peterson slapped Ash across the face. Ash was useful, apparently, but not so useful that he'd remain untouched.

"Why haven't you just read the Book yourself?" Ash said, voice shaking with anger. Lune shoved his shoulder again, pushing him farther down the hall. "Instead of hoarding it here all these years."

Peterson seemed in a genial-enough mood to humor Ash. "Alchemy is not a sin, but it's unnatural for any one human to have so much power. Humans aren't meant to be on the same level as the Creator. The Book of Source should not exist."

"So you—what, keep the Book in your manor, using it as bait for any alchemist who comes? Kill them, before they can find it?" Ash had no proof, but he could only assume that the man had placed some sort of alchemic barrier around the crypt and maybe the entire manor so that he was alerted when another alchemist of the higher tiers stepped onto its premises. Ash realized the man must've known exactly what he was from the very beginning.

But it seemed Peterson had finished answering Ash's questions. "Word has spread out of Kensington," Lune said. "Sir Gresham Hain has an odd fixation on the boy who attacked Lancaster College. I don't know why he's used so much influence to keep you alive," the man said, "but I'd be surprised if he was willing to lose you now."

It was a political game, then, and Ash was the pawn. "Doesn't it worry you that Hain is here?" Ash said, speaking quickly. "I could tell him the Book is in the crypt if you gave me to him—"

Peterson Lune only laughed. "Hain must suspect that the Book is in my family's home," Lune said, "but he wouldn't dare to stride through these halls however he wishes. He would ruin his standing if he attempted to steal from House Lune."

Lune was underestimating Hain. He didn't know Gresham Hain's ambitions, didn't realize that the man didn't care about Kensington politics when it came to the power that the Book of Source offered him.

"He doesn't care about losing his *standing*," Ash said quickly. "He'd kill you if it meant finding the Book."

Lune laughed again, a low chuckle that suggested he found

Ash and his antics amusing. Either he was in denial, or he over-estimated his own power. Desperation rose in Ash. He needed Peterson Lune to see—Source, to understand just how danger-ous his father was—

An attendant standing farther down the hall straightened with surprise at the sight of Ash bound and covered in red but said noth-ing as he bowed his head and opened the door he stood beside.

Ash was shoved inside. The room was much different than the rest of the Lune manor. It was small, with dark wooden panels and paintings covering the walls and a heavy mahogany table that had been set for a small dinner. Gresham Hain sat on the other end of the table. Marlowe stood at the wall behind him.

Lune pointed at the ropes that bound Ash, then at the chair and the table. The chair scraped itself out, and Ash was pulled into the seat. The chair pushed itself back in. Lune sat at the head of the table with a smile.

"So glad you could join us, Sir Hain."

Ash hated that his heart sped up with fear at the sight of his father. Hain barely looked at his son. His eyes were fastened on Lune. He didn't seem surprised that the head of the Lune fam-ily was also an alchemist. Maybe this was common knowledge among the elites of Kensington. Maybe it was one of the many secrets Hain had collected to gain political favor.

"Thank you for welcoming me," Hain said.

An attendant brought a bowl of water. Lune dipped his hands inside, washing them clean of the blood that covered them from touching Ash. "Would you like your friend to join us?" Lune asked, gesturing at Marlowe.

Marlowe was silent and still. Ash's heart pinched when he no-ticed there were faded bruises on her cheek and nose, bruises that she hadn't received in her fight with him.

"No," Hain said. "Marlowe eats little. She'd prefer to stand."

Lune shifted in his seat as if Marlowe made him uncomfortable, but he said nothing else about her. "As you can see," Lune said, gesturing at Ash, "I have something valuable to you."

"Yes. I do see that."

Ash wanted to scream at Lune. Ash's only value to his father was to deliver the location of the Book. The door opened, and attendants carrying platters of food walked inside. Stewed lamb and roasted vegetables were placed on the table. The attendant who filled the wineglass in front of Ash did so without looking at him or his bound hands, swallowing nervously. They were all silent until the attendants bowed their heads and left the room, closing the door behind them.

"What do you want in exchange?" Hain asked.

"You've maintained a particular influence over Lord Alexander," Lune said. "He refuses to see the importance of greater control on alchemy."

"We already have the tier laws. Alchemists require licenses."

"Alchemy should not be a practice for citizens of this state."

"Illegalize alchemy altogether?" Hain said. "Don't you believe that takes away people's basic rights?"

"For the good of all."

"And when you've successfully made alchemists the official enemy of the state," Hain said, "and you're able to use the peoples' hatred of alchemy as a game piece to grow your political power with Alexander, what will be your plan? Will you attempt to replace Kendrick as the most favored House in Alexander's eyes?"

"I'm not entirely sure what you mean," Lune said, not bothering to cover his knowing smile. "But we've discussed long enough. Go to Lord Alexander and renounce your advisements to protect the licensing rights of alchemists. I'll give you the boy, and you can both leave House Lune safely."

Hain nodded his agreement. "That sounds reasonable to me."

The fact that Hain did not fight or argue further was enough evidence of his plans. He would never hand Lune so much power just for Ash's life.

"I only ask one more thing of you," Hain said.

"What is it?" Lune said, more impatient now that their game was over.

"Allow us a room to rest in before we begin our travels back to Kensington. It'll be a long journey, you understand, and we'll need the energy."

To Lune's credit, he did at least hesitate, glancing uncertainly at Ash. Ash stared back at him, willing Lune to see past his own ego—but he only nodded.

"Fine. I'll have a room prepared for you shortly."

35

Hain clenched a hand painfully around Ash's arm as he dragged his son through the halls of Lune. An attendant opened a door for them, and Hain shoved Ash inside. Marlowe followed with her eyes downcast, silent as she closed and locked the door behind her.

Ash nearly stumbled and fell. He turned, his hands still tied behind his back as his father entered after him, glancing around the chambers lazily. It was more modest than any of the House rooms Ash had stayed in, without any decorations. Everything was white. There were two cots standing against opposite walls, but Ash could see from the expression on his father's face that they wouldn't be sleeping in House Lune that night.

Hain snapped his fingers at Marlowe without looking at her. She produced a handkerchief, and his father wiped his hands of the gore that covered his palms after touching Ash. He dropped the cloth to the ground.

"Where is it?" Hain said, meeting Ash's eyes.

Ash swallowed. He raised his chin and didn't speak. Hain's mouth twitched. He stared at Ash, and Ash could feel Hain's energy—saw an icy-white glow from his skin as Hain tried to break into Ash's mind and force the answer from him. Ash concentrated on a mental shield, impenetrable—Hain would not get the answer, not from him.

"You had me chasing you across the state," Hain said, voice even colder than it had been when he'd spoken to Lune. "I've been patient with you, Ashen. I saved you from execution and gave you the greatest life of comfort I could manage. Your repayment was running away to find the Book on your own."

Still Ash didn't speak. He hated that he'd begun to shake. His father hadn't been willing to harm him before. Ash wasn't sure that was the case now.

"Tell me where the forsaken Book is," Hain said, "and I'll spare your life."

"Finished pretending to care about me already?" Ash said, proud that his voice only trembled slightly.

"I did care for you," Hain said. "I cared for what our relationship could've been as father and son. You would've been the perfect heir. But you've disappointed me."

"Sorry to be such a disappointment," Ash said as sarcastically as he could. "But I haven't been totally useless, have I? You wouldn't have even known the Book was here in Lune if it weren't for me."

Hain narrowed his eyes.

Ash managed a grin. "You act like you're the most powerful alchemist who's ever lived, but you couldn't even find the Book without an unlicensed alchemist's help. What—did Marlowe follow us again? And even after we let you live?" he asked her. Marlowe's gaze fell.

"Marlowe did excellent work for me," Hain said. "She realized that you used a portal door out of Thorne's house in Snowdrop. If you'd wanted to ensure you weren't followed, you should've been more careful. Traveling with Thorne and the Kendrick boy, for example—that was a mistake."

Ash's skin went cold.

Hain considered Ash. "Did you think that they'd stay hidden?"

"Where are they? If you touched them—"

Hain laughed. "It isn't me you need to worry about. The Kendrick redguard found them on their own a little before noon."

"You're lying."

"It was quite the spectacle," Hain said. "Winslow Kendrick himself arrived. He slapped his son across the cheek and had him taken away in shame. Thorne, of course, was arrested, to be executed in Kensington."

"You're lying to me!"

"Would you like to see for yourself?" Hain offered, head tilted. "I can share the memory with you."

Ash was unsteady on his feet. He struggled to breathe now, tears rising, and he couldn't—*wouldn't*—cry in front of his father. Hain rolled up his sleeves, circling Ash now, as if searching for the most painful place to begin his interrogation. "What would you have done once you found the Book of Source?" Hain asked him.

Ash swallowed.

"Would you have read it?"

"No," Ash whispered.

"I believe you would have," Hain said. "You're my son, after all. And I can see it in you. Your ambition."

"I'm not a fucking monster like you."

"Is that what I am?" Hain asked with a surprised laugh as he looked at Marlowe, who forced a small, quivering smile of her own. "Here I am, trying to save the fate of all alchemists, and I'm a monster for it?"

There wasn't any warning. Hain snatched a handful of Ash's hair, ripped his head back, and put a searing hand to Ash's neck. Ash screamed. Ash screamed like he never had before, the pain was so blisteringly white-hot that he didn't even process how much pain he was in until the scream had torn from his throat. And still through it he remembered the shield—he couldn't let the shield down, not for a moment, couldn't let himself think of the Book or Randall—

Hain released him. "Randall?"

Ash fell to his knees with a jagged, pained breath, sure that his neck was covered in boils even if he couldn't see them.

"Tell me where the Book is, Ashen."

Ash's voice was hoarse. "Fuck you."

Hain bent over and squeezed Ash's cheeks with one hand, the same searing pain flashing through him. Ash tried to pull free. He was ashamed that he sobbed on his knees at his father's feet—ashamed when he looked to Marlowe pleadingly. "Help me—Marlowe, help—"

Marlowe stared at the floor as if unable to watch. His father didn't only resort to alchemy. He landed a kick in Ash's ribs. Ash groaned, rolling over and curling up on his side. Hain sighed, running a hand through his white hair, muttering about his piece of shit of a son. Ash saw Hain's feet walk away. He sat on the edge of the bed.

"Maybe another method would be more useful," Hain said, as if talking to himself. "It takes so much energy, so much power, and I wouldn't have liked to risk it—but now, when I'm so close . . . It won't matter how weak I am, when I'm only moments from holding the Book."

Ash forced himself to sit up, trying to glare at his father and not look as afraid as he felt. Hain stood and took his time walking until he stopped in front of Ash. "Yes. Let's try this instead."

He pressed a finger to Ash's forehead.

*

Ash opened his eyes slowly. He sat up. He was in bed. It was a bed he'd woken up in for most of his life, but it felt unfamiliar, somehow—its plushness, the soft sheets. His chambers were large for a town house of this kind, looking out over the Kensington streets. The glistening white manor of House Alexander was in the distance.

He'd be late for class, he realized. He got up and dressed in his Lancaster uniform, his white button-down and plaid pants and brogues. He wasn't sure why he felt so off, somehow, as if there was something he'd forgotten, or as if he was still dreaming. Maybe he was coming down with something. There'd been a nasty bug going around his first-year class.

He hurried down the stairs, turning into the dining room. His mother smiled at him as he paused to kiss her cheek, then sat opposite her at the table, where an egg and a cup of tea waited for him. Samantha was beautiful, with her brown skin and thick black hair pulled into a fashionable bun. She wore a robe over her nightgown, but she'd put on her pearls. She likely had another luncheon or some sort of charity gala to attend.

"Running late today?" his mother said warmly.

"I'm not sure why I overslept."

"Really?" she said with a small smile. "Staying up all night reading your texts had nothing to do with it?"

Ash wasn't sure why his chest ached at the sight of her smile. She smiled at him as she always did, even as he knew she wasn't happy. She did her best to hide it from him, but Ash heard the yells late at night when he was supposed to be asleep, the same shouts that were sprinkled throughout his childhood. Ash had begun to hear the rumors when he was just a boy—how his mother had once been an orphan living on the streets, but she'd been so talented at alchemy that she received a scholarship to Pembroke itself, a boarding school for magic, the same that Ash had attended. Samantha was now one of the most powerful alchemists of the state, but her past haunted her, and she was never given the same opportunity as others around her.

Ash only had half his boiled egg and a sip of his tea, but the clock on the wall showed just how long he'd overslept. "I should get going."

His mother nodded, but halfway through telling him to have a good day, she began to cough. Ash's hands tightened. Why? It was just a cough.

"You should take care of that," he said.

She waved her hand dismissively. "I'll see you when you're home."

It was strange, this foreboding feeling that his mother was wrong.

*

He made his way through the maze of Kensington and into Wynnesgrove and arrived at the entrance of Lancaster campus. There were the familiar crowds of students who passed, some raising a hand with a smile in greeting. Ashen Hain wasn't a House heir, but his family name was prominent enough, well respected among the inner circles. Ash had a group of friends among the students who were practically royalty, and his girlfriend, Sophie, was a cousin of the Galahad family. He received top marks and, within his first year, had already been offered an apprenticeship with several of the most beloved professors of Lancaster. Ash wasn't sure, then, why he was so unhappy. He had a life that many dreamed of having—had opportunities that so many would never see. Source, why did he still feel so empty?

Ash walked through Boylston Hall until he reached his seminar's classroom. The tables faced the front of the room, where the professor was nervously organizing handouts. The moment Ash stepped over the threshold, Professor Thorne looked up, eyes narrowed.

"You're late, Mr. Hain."

Heads turned, the other students staring at Ash.

Ash bit down on his teeth. "I overslept."

The heads swung back to look at Professor Thorne.

"That isn't a viable excuse."

The heads turned back to Ash once more.

Ash shrugged. "Nothing would be a viable excuse for you unless it was a pardon written and signed by Lord Alexander himself."

There were snickers around the room. Professor Thorne's cheeks pinkened. Ash felt a stab of guilt, but he pushed that aside as he walked to his usual seat. Ramsay Thorne had always acted arrogantly just because he was already an apprentice professor. The entire Thorne family was obscenely arrogant, in fact, and entirely strange.

Ramsay tried to regain control of the class as he stood from his desk with papers in his hand—which he then promptly dropped, ears turning red as he bent over and scrambled to pick them up. The laughter grew. Ash and his friends had enjoyed quite a few laughs at Ramsay Thorne's expense, but maybe Ash really was under the weather today. He couldn't understand why he felt so badly for the young professor now.

※

When the bell rang, Ash was supposed to have a free period, which he would've generally spent in Giddings with Sophie and his friends—but a student dropped a note in his hand. Ash sighed, thanking the messenger, and walked down the hall and up the stairs to the top floor of Boylston. He knocked on a door, waiting until he heard permission to enter.

He walked into the headmaster's office. His father stood at the window, looking out at the campus, turning only when Ash closed the door and sat on one of the two chairs waiting in front of the large desk. Gresham Hain didn't bother to smile at his son. He watched Ash closely.

"You don't remember," he said, "do you?"

Ash squinted in confusion. His father often called on him so that he could give Ash private teachings and reminders that he'd sour the Hain name if he didn't remain at the top of his class—but this was more cryptic than the usual lecture. "What do you mean?"

Hain almost seemed amused as he walked around to sit on the edge of his desk in front of Ash. "It can be like a dream sometimes," he said, "entering into parallel realms. It takes skill to realize that you're only sleeping."

Ash blinked in confusion, unsure of why he felt a rush of dread—

He stopped breathing. Blood flooded from his face.

Hain's smile grew as he watched Ash.

"How did we—" Ash stood, looking around as if expecting a hole where he could jump through the fabric of the universe. "What're we doing here?"

"Calm yourself," Hain said. "I pulled our consciousnesses into a parallel realm. It isn't much different from visiting the higher realms. Our bodies are unconscious, waiting for our energy to return."

Ash was shaking. Everything he'd seen—his *mother*—hadn't been real. No, that wasn't quite right. Even worse was that they *were* real. There was a universe where his mother was still alive, and where Ash had everything he'd ever wanted, and still was not satisfied.

"Well?" Hain said. "Don't you want to know why I brought you here?"

Ash's gaze snapped to his father with a glare. "Got bored of torturing me in House Lune, so you wanted to torture me here instead?"

"This is the world we would see," Hain said, "if alchemists weren't used as political pawns, the target of hatred. Isn't it interesting?" he asked Ash. "All the changes this world benefits from."

Ash's hands clenched. His mind raced. His mother would still be alive. Alchemists didn't need licenses. There'd been more students at Lancaster—more people willing to learn alchemy. And there was probably more he hadn't seen, so much more that could change. But not everything was perfect. His heart sank as he thought of Ramsay.

"You think that I act selfishly," Hain said, "when the truth is that I only dream of what our world could be."

Hain reached forward. Ash jerked away, but too late—his father had touched Ash's head again. Ash watched as the universe around him shifted, patterns of light twisting and fading. He no longer sat at the headmaster's desk. He stood on blackened soil, soot falling from the sky. Hain wasn't in front of Ash anymore. Ash frowned, looking around. The sky was dark, a fire's red glow in the distance. Sirens called. There were faded screams.

Ash was where Lancaster had once stood, but it didn't look like the college had been freshly destroyed. It looked like the school had been burned down already for decades. Ash frowned as he stepped over the rubble, walking toward the neighborhood, unsure of where he should go, what he should do, *how* to wake up from this nightmare—when he heard a voice behind him.

"There's another one!"

He turned. Two guards ran toward him, though they wore white uniforms instead of red. One guard stopped running and pointed something at him. It looked like a metallic stick, as far as Ash could tell, but there was a sudden blast and smoke. A sharp pain hit Ash's leg. He shouted and fell, looked at the blood that streamed from him. It didn't seem like alchemy, but he couldn't tell what else it might be—

The two guards ran at him, the other pointing a shorter iron stick at Ash's face. He threw up his hands to defend himself, and another blast rang, the dirt beside Ash exploding. Bits of rock hit his cheek, and he screamed as there was a ringing in his ears.

A guard snatched Ash's hand, yanking his arm behind his back. The other guard rushed forward, pinning him as he struggled to break free. One of them stuffed a ball of fabric that had a chalky residue in his mouth, clamping a leather mask around his nose and mouth and forcing it shut. The chalky powder closed Ash's throat. He felt like he was drowning. He could barely breathe to keep his heart pumping, let alone use alchemy. His eyes watered and he made muffled protests, begging them to let him go—

A guard dragged him out of the rubble of Lancaster and into a street that had once belonged to Wynnesgrove. The neighborhood was burning. Even Kensington in the distance was gushing smoke. Ash was thrown onto the concrete beside a line of others who'd been arrested. They were silent, bruised and beaten. The man beside Ash was unconscious, blood dripping from a cut over his brow. Ash squeezed his eyes shut, trying to focus on breath, the little wisps of air that managed to make their way to his lungs. He heard another pair of guards speaking only a few feet away.

"We've already met the quota," one said, sounding bored. He lit a cigarette with a match. "We were only ordered to bring in at least fifty."

"Lord Alexander wanted any found to be brought for public execution."

Ash looked up at the voice, his heart sinking. Callum stood in front of him—but, Source, it wasn't *his* Callum. This was the version Callum had always been afraid to become—the Callum who was obedient to the Kendrick, killing all of his own desire to be the responsible son his father expected.

Callum glanced at Ash, maybe feeling his stare, and only gave Ash a cold glare before he looked away again.

Now that Ash recognized Callum, it was easier to see that the other guard was his brother Edric. "Lord Alexander won't know the difference between energy manipulators killed in a public execution and manipulators killed in battle," he said. "Get rid of half. I don't care who."

Ash's heart stopped.

"What do we do with the bodies?" Callum asked.

"Bury them, burn them, leave them to rot—I don't care."

Ash struggled against the bindings, but they wouldn't budge. He desperately imagined them unweaving so that he could yank the leather mask off his face, suck in enough air to at least fight back—

He heard Callum's footsteps. He heard the click. A shot blasted, his ears ringing. In the corner of his eye he saw the flash of yellow, could see the red pooling on the concrete. More footsteps, and the alchemists all lay still, one's shoulders shaking on

Ash's other side as he tried to muffle his sobs—none wanted to pull attention to themselves. Another shot, just a few feet away. Ash's heart was beating erratically, thumping inside his chest. Callum's boots stopped in front of him. He didn't want to look up at this other Callum, didn't want his own memories of Callum's soft smiles tainted. Ash squeezed his eyes shut. A click—

36

Ash gasped and opened his eyes. He was lying on the white bed he'd left behind in House Lune. Marlowe stood against the wall, watching him like she'd never moved. Hain stood over him, watching as well, eyes deadened with exhaustion. Even tired, Ash could feel that Hain still had more strength than the average alchemist. Ash hadn't realized just how powerful his father was until now.

Ash sat up. He shook his head. "What the hell was that?"

"I needed to show you what was at stake," Hain said. "Now you see. Now you know what our world will look like if House Lune gains enough influence. You see how alchemists will be treated—hunted and killed like animals."

Ash felt sick. "You think that you're the hero, when you're only the villain."

At this, his father grew cold. He looked down at Ash for a moment, then said, "You're wrong. I do know that I'm the villain."

Ash frowned at his father as the man paced away.

"We humans have a tendency to think of evolution as something mandated to the beasts of our planet," Hain said. "We don't consider what evolution looks like for us as well. What do humans—our society—need to evolve?" Hain asked Ash.

Ash only stared, refusing to answer.

"We need people like me," he told Ash, voice soft. "We need people who will show the world conflict—what is wanted and unwanted. Peterson Lune is a fool. He doesn't even realize the role he could potentially play in our evolutionary course. He acts purely from greed. But when I find the Book of Source, I will tilt the scales in the favor of alchemy. I will destroy Lune, along with Alexander and Kendrick. I'll be the catalyst in an explosion forward on our evolutionary course."

"You'll make alchemists even more hated and feared."

"And our entire world will benefit. Our society will become polarized, and like the splitting of the atom, we will evolve into an even more powerful force. Don't you see, Ashen? If I must sacrifice myself to be the villain, to be known through history as one of the most-hated men of all time, then I will."

"You're fooling yourself," Ash said, "using that as an excuse for your own greed. You don't see that you're just like Peterson Lune—"

"You don't see how alike you are to me."

"You want me to help you spread fear? To become a mass killer? I won't do it."

Hain watched his son for only a moment. "And you don't have to."

Ash understood, then, the true reason that Hain had taken him into the parallel universes, knowing that Ash's guard would inevitably fall. He'd already rummaged through Ash's mind, and from the look in Hain's eye, Ash could tell that his father knew.

"Marlowe," Ash said, looking at her as his father came closer. "Please—we could stop him together—"

She only watched as Hain grabbed his son's arm, pulling him from the bed. Ash was tugged through the corridors. It was night. The windows were dark, halls in shadow. Ash was grateful now that Callum and Ramsay had been taken away from the village. They'd have more of a chance to survive. Ash wished he'd stayed by their side, if only to enjoy being with them for a few more hours—

Hain dragged Ash down the stairs and into the crypts. Ash cursed Lune silently. The man hadn't even bothered to station guards, he'd been so sure that Hain wouldn't dare to steal the

Book. Ash was pushed aside, forced to watch as his father began searching. Hain threw his hands into the air, and balls of light floated as he began to ransack the place. He used alchemy to fling open the stone tombs and to send valuables crashing to the floor and walls. Ash started to hope that it'd all been a trick—that the Book wasn't even in the crypt or even in House Lune—

His father stilled. He'd stopped in front of the largest tomb of all, faded gilt floral design carving through the stone. He stood over the grave. "Clever," he said.

Ash saw that the tomb was engraved to Sinclair Lune. He wondered, vaguely, if the Book had been in House Lune's possession since their founder's death, though any ability to think faded as he watched his father reach into the tomb—

"I didn't think you would dare," a voice said. Ash turned to see Peterson Lune striding forward with a hand raised. "These are the actions of a man intent on starting a war."

"Is that what you think I fear?" Hain asked, distracted, as if he'd already known Peterson was coming. "A war with Lune?"

The fight began faster than Ash could breathe. There were flashes of light, shadows that grew from the floors and grasped at necks, both men disappearing and reappearing as shots of light fired into the spaces they'd been a heartbeat before. The little scuffles Ash had found himself in with Marlowe and Randall were nothing in comparison to the battle between the alchemist masters he witnessed now. He hoped breathlessly that Peterson would win, even if it meant his own execution—Source, he hoped that his father would be killed, this nightmare over—

Ash couldn't just stand by and watch. He clenched his eyes shut and imagined a ray of light burning through the ropes around his wrists. He wasn't accurate enough in his shakiness, and felt a sharp, searing slice against his skin. He bit back a cry and pulled his hands free. There was a blinding light in the corner of his eye—he was quick enough to duck, to feel the heat against his neck—and when he looked back, stone pillars crumbled, attempting to crush his father.

Neither man noticed Ash as he crept closer to the tomb, ducking as blades flashed over his head. He got to the edge of Sinclair Lune's tomb. He looked inside. The Book was exactly like it had been in Ramsay's hands in the Akash. The faint light that glowed between the covers seemed to grow stronger—

Peterson gasped. He'd vanished and appeared again right where Hain stuck a hand into the air. His fingers were now lodged in Peterson's neck. The man gagged, hands reaching for Hain's wrist. Hain twisted, slicing through the man's throat. Ash watched as Peterson fell, already dead.

Hain whipped blood from his hand, disgusted, though his disgust seemed to be more because of the interruption and the wasted energy he'd spent.

Ash shot out a hand for the Book, but his father seemed to have noticed Ash after all. Hain flicked a finger and released a blow of energy that threw Ash into the air, smacking his back and head against stone. He crumpled to the ground, vision fading in and out. He looked up just in time to see his father holding it. The Book's plain, untitled cover and the faint light that glowed brighter and brighter from its pages looked wrong in his father's hands.

Gresham Hain paused, but only for a moment. He opened the Book of Source. There was an explosion of light.

37

Ash wasn't sure how he'd survived. Nothing else had. The remains of House Lune were like snow, ash fluttering through the air, clouding the sky so that the pale sun struggled to shine through. Above the crypt, everything was gone. The village was gone. The trees were gone. The people were gone.

He sat, frozen, back against the crypt wall. There were no traces of the Book of Source. It must have been destroyed in the explosion. Hain had disappeared with the light, too. A force that powerful, entering his body . . .

"Ash?"

He looked up, heart pounding. Marlowe limped forward, looking down at him. She was covered in white dust, save for the trickles of red that ran down her arms.

"You're alive," Ash said, voice hollow. He realized he was in shock. He tried to push himself up to his feet, but his legs were still too weak.

Marlowe slid down to the tomb and knelt beside him. Hain must've trained her for horrific moments like this. She tested his vitals quickly, checking his pulse and holding a finger up to his eyes.

"He spared you," she murmured. "I'm surprised."

Ash struggled to speak. "Is he—do you think he's—"

Marlowe dropped her hands. "He's still alive," she said. "I saw him. He came to me. But he isn't himself, not anymore—Source, I don't think he's even human. He was confused."

"What do you mean?"

"He gave me a message—not using his words, I don't think he can even speak. It was . . . a vibration," Marlowe said, struggling to describe it. "A feeling. He wanted to keep the worthy alive—to build a new world for them."

"It isn't up to him to decide who's worthy and who isn't."

Marlowe only continued. "But I saw flashes of other images, too. It's like he can't control where and when he is. He showed me other worlds, parallel realms. His body was like light. It faded in and out and in again."

"He can't control himself."

"No. I don't think he can."

"There might be enough time, then."

"Time for what?"

"Time to get to Kensington—to warn—"

"I don't think you understand," Marlowe interrupted. "I already told you, didn't I? Gresham Hain won even before he read the Book of Source. What will going to Kensington and warning the Houses do? You can't defeat him now." Ash wasn't sure why she was so angry. She glared at him. "Better to take the chance he's given you and start a new life hiding in the mountains or the woods, hoping he'll never look for you again."

"I'd rather die trying to stop him than live in his world," Ash said. "Wouldn't you?"

Marlowe didn't answer him. She only watched as Ash struggled to get to his feet.

"You're afraid," Ash said.

"Yes," Marlowe agreed. "Creator, yes, of course I'm afraid."

"But I can't tell what's scarier for you," Ash said. "Living the same life you always have, or taking control of it for once."

Marlowe stood slowly, too. They stared each other down for a long moment, neither moving nor speaking, until finally Ash said, "Help me get to Kensington. Please. It isn't too late to fight him."

Marlowe took a sharp breath, then closed her eyes. "You're a fool, Ash Woods." She looked at him again as she offered a hand.

*

Attempting to materialize to an entirely different place was dangerous, Ash knew well. There was the possibility of a backlash of energy, creating an explosion, as Ash had experienced in Hedge—but even then, Ash had to focus on multiple threads: his body's cells, keeping each bit of physical matter in mind, along with the location he wanted to enter, all while quelling the fear that he would leave an arm behind or accidentally step into a wall, instantly killing himself. No matter his curiosity, materialization was something he knew he wouldn't be able to achieve until he was a master alchemist himself.

He was surprised, then, when Marlowe, without any warning, did exactly that. He took her hand, blinked, and in a sudden shift of air, his ears popped. He felt like he was going to be sick. Ash realized he was in a new place. The room had golden walls and floors. The sofa's intricate design clashed with the portraits on the walls.

Ash staggered, and Marlowe caught his arm. "What the hell—"

Marlowe was calm. "Take a deep breath."

"You can materialize?"

"Yes," Marlowe said impatiently. "It takes a lot of energy, so I prefer not to, but this seemed a worthy exception. How else do you think I've managed to follow you so easily?"

Ash took a deep breath, just as he was told. Why was he so surprised that Marlowe could master a technique like that? Maybe he'd underestimated her, in the same way that so much of the world had underestimated him.

"Where are we?" he asked.

"House Alexander," she said. "You wanted to warn the Houses, didn't you?"

He didn't think he'd be transported to the center of the Head House Alexander itself. It took him a moment to push down his fear—to remember the importance of why he'd come. Marlowe watched as he collected himself, then said, "I've often accompanied your father here for meetings with Alexander. There's a conference room where he'd gather the Heads of the Houses for midday meetings. Come—I'll show you the way."

Ash followed her out of the golden room. The hall was just as garish. It hurt his eyes to see the sky and clouds painted on the ceiling and the wallpaper of hummingbirds and the rugs of intricate patterns beneath his feet. Ash stiffened when he saw two redguards walking down the hall toward them. Ash and Marlowe both ducked their heads and walked silently. It seemed they'd gotten away, until the sounds of the guards' footsteps paused and a voice called behind them.

"Who are you?" one demanded. "What business do you have here?"

Marlowe threw up a gust of hot energy that shot the guards back. Ash had already begun to run, Marlowe catching up and overtaking him as the stomping footsteps and shouts followed, weaving through the halls as she led the way, until finally they reached a marble floor and heavy golden doors—

She shoved the doors open. Ash rushed inside. It was a white room with a heavy stone table. People much older than Ash and Marlowe looked up with alarm. Inside, Lord Alexander himself stood at a window, peering out on his land and his state. He was a young ruler, only in his fifties in comparison to the men who were his predecessors, with pale skin and black hair, beard streaked with gray. He wore his dynastic uniform, a golden button-down with a high collar, as did the Heads of the Houses who sat at the table behind him, each in their own representative colors. The only families not represented were Lune and Thorne.

Winslow Kendrick was there as well. He half stood out of his seat when he saw Ash, fury twisting his face. "*You—*"

Lord Alexander turned to look at Ash and Marlowe with the smallest frown, as if not much managed to surprise him in his later years. "What is the meaning of this?" he asked, a glance at who appeared to be his scribe, a young man standing against the wall.

The boy opened and closed his mouth in shock for a moment, shaking his head. "I—I don't—Guards!" he yelled, walking to the doors and shoving past Ash.

Ash knew he'd only have one chance. "My name is Ash Woods," he said, striding into the room, ignoring the aghast gasps that followed as he dared to address Lord Alexander directly. "I'm the son of Gresham Hain."

There were confused murmurs. Lord Alexander tilted his head. "I didn't know that Gresham Hain had a son."

"He lies, my lord," Winslow said, staring at Ash with such intensity it seemed he was waiting for permission to kill the boy right then and there. "This is the terrorist who kidnapped my son and aided the fugitive Thorne—"

"Listen to me," Ash shouted. "Gresham Hain has read the Book of Source."

There was silence, met by a scoff, followed by nervous laughter.

"What joke is this? The Book of Source isn't real," a woman said, wearing the pale blue of Adelaide. Ash could tell, from some exchanged looks around the table, that not everyone agreed.

"He—Source, he's filled with power you can't even imagine," Ash said." He's coming here, to Kensington, to kill all of you and destroy the city."

"The boy manipulates," Winslow said.

"You need to prepare—gather your defenses, evacuate the city—"

"He should've been executed the moment he was arrested. Permission to kill him, my lord, before he causes more damage."

"Haven't you wondered why Peterson Lune isn't here?" Ash demanded.

There was an exchange of glances.

"The Elder lands are far," Lady Adelaide said.

A man wearing the green of Galahad murmured, "He should've been able to use the portal door, as he always does."

"He's dead," Ash said. "House Lune has been destroyed. The village, the people—it's all gone. And Hain is coming here next."

"But that's preposterous," Lord Galahad said. "Can we really trust a criminal and a fugitive?"

Winslow still stood, his hand on the hilt of his sword. All were quiet as they looked to Lord Alexander. He watched Ash with a narrowed gaze. Ash wasn't sure what he would do if Alexander ordered him killed.

A part of him, an ugly part he didn't want to see, whispered that maybe this was exactly what each of the Heads of Houses deserved. For whatever reason, Gresham Hain had decided Ash was worthy to let live. These people hated Ash and alchemists like him. Why should Ash work so hard to save their lives? Ash could leave them to their fate—survive the massacre and live in the new world as one of the most powerful alchemists left alive.

But Ash felt sick at the thought. He couldn't stand by and watch so many die. And besides that, there were two people in particular whose lives he wasn't willing to risk.

Lord Alexander raised his hand at Winslow Kendrick. "Imprison them both," he said. "I'd rather not get blood on the floors. We'll execute them today in the Square, alongside Thorne."

Ash bit back his frustration. Marlowe glided forward, and before Ash could scream at them to *listen*, there was a lurch.

He spun around. He was no longer in the room with the Heads of Houses. Instead, it looked like a pantry of sorts, shelves stocked with burlap sacks. Marlowe slid to the floor, Ash managing to catch her around the waist. She was breathing heavily.

"Why'd you pull us out?" Ash demanded.

"You weren't convincing anyone in that room," Marlowe said, wincing in pain.

He hesitated. "Are you all right?"

"I try not to materialize at all," Marlowe said, "much less twice within the same hour, and with another person, too."

"You need to rest."

Marlowe didn't disagree. She let Ash help her sit, leaning against a wall. She was sweating and looked like she might be sick. Ash hated the wave of nervousness he felt, knowing that she wouldn't be able to help him anymore. "Where are we?" he asked.

"I figured you'd want to find your lovers."

Source, Ash hated that word. "Are we in the dungeons?"

"The storage room of House Kendrick," she told him, grimacing as she shifted a leg.

Ash could see, then, just how easily Marlowe spent her days spying on the Houses for Hain. He laid a hand on her shoulder. "Will you be okay here?"

"Yes," she said, though Ash wasn't sure that she believed it herself. "Go. You don't have much time."

Ash left without another word, slipping through the door and pressing it shut with a click. He ran up the stone stairs and into the kitchens he now recognized, past the entryway of the Kendrick town house. He heard low voices as he raced up the stairs and to the chambers, his heart pounding as he reached Callum's door—

It was locked. He closed his eyes for a moment, hand on the knob, before it clicked. He stepped inside, shutting the door behind him.

Callum had turned, surprised. His face was bruised, a cut on his cheek and lip. Blood stained the front of his shirt, but he was on his feet. He could still speak. "Ash?"

Ash ran to him, throwing himself at Callum. Callum held him tightly, arms shaking. He bent over and kissed Ash's mouth, his cheeks. "Creator," he said, hoarse with emotion. "Creator, I thought you'd—"

Ash pulled away, hands gripping Callum's arms. "Where is Ramsay?"

Callum's voice shook. "They took her to the Square. We have to hurry—"

No more words were needed. They raced from Callum's room, down the stairs and to the same servants' halls they'd once used to escape. As they ran from the manor, through the back alleyways, Ash wanted to explain what'd happened in detail, but the story was so complicated, and both wanted to focus on saving Ramsay before it was too late. All Ash could manage to say was that Gresham Hain was coming—that he'd read the Book, and that Kensington would be destroyed. Callum took this news silently, running too hard to speak, face twisting in pain with every step. Ash wondered if the city would be like House Lune: nothing but white dust, all evidence that it'd ever existed wiped from the surface of the Earth. He wondered how many people his father would kill and how many he would allow to live. He ran faster, harder, until he and Callum came to the Square.

A crowd had already gathered. Some screamed. Some threw trash into the air. And there, in the center, were the gallows. Ramsay already stood on its platform, hands bound, the rope around his neck. He was crying. His face was pink, shoulders shaking— and it hurt even more, to see how Ramsay tried to swallow back the tears, not wanting to give the people in front of him the satisfaction. For a heartbeat, Ash wanted his father to come—to decimate all of them, to turn them to dust. Why were these the very people Ash worked so hard to save?

He shoved his way into the crowd. He clapped his hands together, gathering energy, and raised his palms to the sky. There was a burst of sparks above, loud pops crackling. People screamed, someone yelling that it was another alchemist as most started pushing against one another to escape. Callum forced his way to the gallows, shoving one guard who tried to stop him and punching the other across the face. Ash watched as Callum pulled the rope from around Ramsay's neck, helping him down the stairs. There were shouts from the guards as other reds started to push their way to the gallows, too. Ash pulled himself up, standing on the landing and looking out over the crowd. They looked back at him with hatred.

"You need to leave the city!" he yelled, but people only stared or twisted their faces with confusion. "Gresham Hain—he's read the Book of Source, and he's coming—"

Laugher echoed. Someone threw a rotten piece of fruit at him, and someone else shouted, "I knew that alchemists were evil! Didn't know they were fucking crazy, too!" The laughter grew louder.

Ash swallowed. He looked down at Callum, who held Ramsay. Ramsay stared up at Ash, brown eyes filled with fear, as if he already knew what was coming, too—could already feel the shift in energy, the storm that had been lingering on the horizon.

It was too late. Hain was already there.

38

The explosion engulfed House Alexander, aftershock blasting through the city. Ash clutched Ramsay and Callum as they huddled behind the walls of the gallows, shaking, until the winds died. Silence followed, and then the screams began. The smell of smoke and dust and burning flesh filled the air. Ash couldn't stand to look at Kensington Square, at all the people who didn't have the wall's protection.

The three got to their feet, allowing a moment to feel it, to see it—they were still alive—before they began to run, Ramsay's arms over Ash and Callum's shoulders as he limped, grimacing.

"Where do we go?" Ramsay rasped.

Ash wished he could have a moment to celebrate that Ramsay was there, that they were all reunited, but it wouldn't stay that way for long if they didn't focus on their escape. "Hedge," Ash said.

"Another major city—it'll be a target, too," Callum said, also wincing as he moved.

"Nowhere will be safe," Ash said. They had nowhere to hide. If Ash's father wanted them dead, they would be dead. "But we'll have a better chance than in Kensington."

Ramsay and Callum silently agreed, and they put effort into moving quickly.

＊

Ash looked over his shoulder. They'd left the heart of the city behind and hurried through Wynnesgrove, past the ruins of the college and over the iron bridge. People had come outside, whispering and pointing at the smoke that gushed from the center of Kensington. The houses had survived the initial blast here, but it wouldn't be long before Hain continued his destruction.

"It's too quiet," Ramsay said. "Why hasn't your father kept attacking?"

"He was confused in the Elder lands," Ash said. "He might be caught in the chaos."

Maybe he'd come to this reality for one moment, one second to annihilate House Alexander, before he fell through the seams of the universe again, fighting to control himself and return to the reality he wanted to destroy.

Ash had tried to explain what he could with gasping breaths as they ran—what had happened at House Lune, how Marlowe had helped him get to Kensington, and the reactions of the Heads of Houses. He hesitated, glancing at Callum. His father had just been in House Alexander before Hain arrived. It went unsaid, the heavy realization that Winslow Kendrick was dead.

The people of Hedge had gathered along the shore, murmuring and pointing at the fires in the distance. Some had enough sense to turn and start running, as if they could feel that they were next.

Ramsay hissed in pain. He slowed down, like he was close to falling unconscious. Callum held him close. "Ramsay?"

"I'm sorry," Ramsay gasped. "It hurts—"

"It's okay—breathe—"

There was a flash in the sky. Ash stopped to turn and saw a figure of light flickering in the clouds of smoke. Hain appeared to raise his hands, and the remains of Kensington that'd survived the initial blast were engulfed. A wave of fire reaching the sky razed across the ground. Screams erupted and the people around them fled, shoving past. This time, Gresham Hain didn't flicker out of their reality. He'd remembered himself. He lowered to the ground, disappearing into the flame and out of sight. Ash could feel it: Hedge was next.

Ash met Callum's eye. He could feel Callum's gentle thought.

There wasn't any use in running now. It was better to accept what was coming. Ash and Callum lowered Ramsay gingerly to the ground against a building's wall. Ramsay let out a cry of pain and relief as he rested, gasping for air. Ash held both of their hands tightly, as Ramsay and Callum held each other's, looking at one another, knowing that these were the last moments they had together. What could be said? They'd failed.

"I'm sorry," Ash whispered.

Ramsay and Callum watched him.

"I shouldn't have left," he said. He had a hard time meeting their eyes. "I shouldn't have lied to you and left like I did. If I'd stayed . . ."

"If you'd stayed," Callum said, "you would've been arrested and beaten with us, and Hain would've found the Book anyway." He tightened his grip on Ash's hand. "Don't punish yourself."

Ramsay seemed to agree, leaning his head back and closing his eyes. A small smile twitched onto his face. "But you're right," he managed to say. "I was pissed that you lied."

"Wish I could say I'll make it up to you sometime." Ash swallowed, nodding. "I don't think we're going to live much longer."

To this, neither Ramsay nor Callum could argue. Another explosion hit the city across the river, right on the other side of the bridge and in the heart of Wynnesgrove. There were startled screams from the people who'd remained, more now deciding to run. Ash preferred to stay with Ramsay and Callum. He wanted to feel their touch for as long as he could and pretend that they weren't moments from dying. He imagined that they'd been successful and had destroyed the Book, that they planned to escape the state and find a home together, maybe hidden away in the woods or mountains. It helped, Ash realized, to think that there was another parallel realm where this might've happened—that there was another version of him who kissed Ramsay's cheek as he sat nearby reading, joined Callum at the fire as he cooked them a meal, looking forward to spending the rest of their lives together—

Ash pulled his hands away and stood.

Ramsay reached for him again. "Ash? What're you doing?"

Callum stood also, blocking his path. "Where're you going?"

"We're not going to survive anyway," Ash said, not meeting either of their eyes. "I'm his son. It should be me who tries to stop him."

"What can you do against him—" Callum argued.

"You will *die*—" Ramsay said.

Ramsay was right. Ash had been spared once before. He couldn't see his father sparing him again. "I'd rather die trying to save you," he told them. "Please let me go."

Ramsay shook his head, already refusing—but Callum's frown faded. Ash could tell that Callum understood, even if he wished he didn't. Ash stood on his toes to kiss Callum, then leaned down to kiss Ramsay before he could argue further. He turned to leave as Callum held on to Ramsay, whispering to him as Ramsay yelled at Ash to come back.

The bridge was abandoned. The path was clear as he walked across. Smoke blew in the direction of the wind. Embers danced, stinging his skin. When the smoke cleared, Gresham Hain was there. It was like he'd been there all along—or like his father, with all his power, now knew that this meeting was inevitable, and had appeared at just the moment he knew he should.

Ash could understand what Marlowe meant now, when she said that Hain was no longer a man. His skin was translucent. Ash could see the beating organs beneath, and even those seemed to glow with energy. Ash had assumed that someone so touched by Source would be made of pure, loving energy—but something had twisted. It was as if Hain had been given the power of Source but was still tied to hatred because he was tethered to the physical world.

Hain didn't speak. He raised a hand. Ash saw images flash in his mind. Kensington, razed to the ground, only the skeletons of buildings remaining. A line of alchemists following Ash as he led them through the rubble.

"You want me to lead the alchemists you allow to live," Ash said. "The answer is no."

Ash could see the muscle and bone beneath Hain's paper-thin skin. His face warped in rage. He showed an image of Ash lying dead on the ground at his father's feet.

Ash swallowed. "Then so be it."

They both raised their hands.

Ash felt a jolt.

Time froze. Ash saw images, the threads of a canvas—him on the bridge, his body falling to the ground. He saw his father lower his hand with a flicker of regret. He saw Ramsay and Callum holding each other, both sensing that he was already gone. He saw Marlowe limping through the white dust, the wreckage, a blade stolen from the kitchens in her hand. Ash felt peace. He felt joy that he was no longer confined to his physical body, with all its wants and desires and hurts and pains. Why had he been so afraid to die? It wasn't death he'd feared, he realized, but the change— the transformation that forced him to release.

There were other energies that Ash hadn't been able to see— outlines of people who had once been in the physical realm, too, and decided to stay, to wait for their loved ones before they all returned to Source. Ash could've stayed. He could've waited for Ramsay and Callum, whose deaths were near. And there was the other energy, too, the spark between existence and nonexistence, the chaos that beckoned him and welcomed him.

Images flickered rapidly, but it didn't feel like chaos now, his body and mind overwhelmed by panic—it was only a natural state of being, shifting through the realms, witnessing the birth of planets and the death of stars, all happening as one, and beneath it all, the nothingness, the black orb that acted as the seed that grew life—

This was death, but Ash could see now that there was no such thing as death, not really. His life hadn't yet happened and was happening and had already happened, too. He watched the threads. Him as a boy, clutching his mother's hand. Him as he saw his father up close for the first time, angry and still wanting the man's love. Ash could see easily now what he hadn't seen before: His *power* had always depended on another person's agreement that he was powerful. His worthiness had always depended on another person finding him worthy. His need for validation was seeded into him before his body had even grown from his mother's cells. He'd spent eighteen years seeing himself as the victim, where life was done to him, instead of as the Creator that he was, who had built the life around him with his own desperation to be seen. He'd chosen to chase after his father, seeking the man's approval, knowing that the man wouldn't love him. Ash didn't want to take responsibility for his own life. It was easier to blame the world around him, wasn't it?

And yet he had compassion for the human boy he'd been, too. That was the life he had chosen, this boy named Ash Woods, because he was Source, telling itself a story, experiencing his life and his father's life and Marlowe's life and Ramsay's life and Callum's life and—

Ash was in a room. There was nothing but white walls and a white ceiling and a white floor. He was not in his body anymore, not really, but just as his physical body had only been a dream, so too was this experience—imagining the old body he'd once filled with his energy, which was still on the bridge leading to Hedge, eyes empty, his father now stepping over him; his body being pushed from his mother and held as he wailed, just as afraid to enter the physical realm as he had been to leave it—

Source imagined itself, too. It was the universe magnified, no limit and no end, until it shrank to a single particle of light, like a star floating in the air, hovering in front of Ash. This light held the vibration of energy that the physical body would translate as love. It was a simple reality, Ash realized. That was all existence was made of, what chaos had sparked, a simple equation that he himself had overthought and dismissed in the physical realm: Source was love. The core of every being in existence was love. Everything else was imagined. The fear, the hatred, the anger, the resentment—it'd all been a story that Ash had created.

The particle of light came closer, touching Ash's forehead. He melted away. The room melted away. Ash was light. He had no thoughts—only the vibration of love that he was made of, love that became joy and ecstasy, bubbling into the feeling of endless laughter and euphoria. He was a particle in a vibration, and he recognized the particles that were Ramsay's and Callum's and his father's and his mother's and Marlowe's and every being he had met and touched and loved. They all created the same infinite light. They were eternal.

But there was another vibration, too—an understanding that filled his fractal. There was more still. He wanted to experience more as that character he had created, the human boy—there was more to learn, more to feel and experience, even the false emotions he'd imagined. He'd had so many lives, but this was the one whose story he still wanted to complete. And wasn't returning to Source, and aligning fully with his own power, a part of his story, too?

39

Ash opened his eyes. They burned with energy. Everything inside him felt as if he'd been lit on fire, but he wasn't in pain. He stood, light glowing from him. His father had stepped over him on the bridge, and Gresham Hain now paused, turning to face Ash again.

An image filtered through Ash's mind—Ash as Gresham had seen him that day in Lancaster, looking upon the boy that he realized, for the first time, was his son—

Ash stepped forward. He touched his father's cheek. Gresham screamed.

Ash saw everything he hadn't been able to see before: the young boy his father had been in House Lune, a child told that he was worthless and taught that his alchemy was a sin—struggling to live in the streets of Hedge as he taught himself what he could, desperate for the respect that he knew he deserved. He'd told himself lies, too. Gresham Hain had convinced himself that the only value he had in this world was to be hated. He'd told himself that it was his only purpose, because without purpose, he was afraid—afraid that he really was nothing but a worthless little boy. He couldn't see that he was already worthy and loved by Source. He couldn't see how Source looked at itself, and all its fractals that manifested as lives, with unending compassion. Ash hadn't realized just how alike he and his father had been. Ash was a parallel, a sequel in his father's tale, continuing their story—but it had to end.

Gresham sank to his knees. The golden light was pulled from his skin, through Ash's fingertips. His father's skin grew thicker until it was no longer transparent. Hain was a man again, teth-ered back to this plane. His eyes became focused, less confused, as he looked up at Ash with disbelief. Ash could feel his father's understanding sweep through him: Gresham Hain had relied on the Book to align to Source and find his power. He hadn't consid-ered the possibility of someone like Ash aligning to Source with-out the Book, too.

But the energy of Source had overtaken Ash. He didn't have control of himself when he raised his hands and his face to the sky. With a jolt, the energy of the Book of Source ripped through him, exploding out of his palms and his mouth and his eyes, tear-ing through the realms and disappearing into the darkened sky as a golden stream of light—until that was gone, too.

The bridge was silent. Ash almost fell to his knees. His father's glare grew, his fury building. He staggered to his feet, his intent to kill Ash pulsing through the air. "You fucking—"

He stopped. He emitted a small gasp. Marlowe twisted the knife deeper into Gresham's side, spearing his heart. A trickle of red left his mouth as he turned, looking at Marlowe and the ven-geance that'd found him. Ash wasn't sure if he imagined it—the energy that reminded him of his mother, the energy that thick-ened the air of women and girls who had watched Gresham Hain, waiting for this moment before they allowed themselves to return to Source as well. He fell, his eyes already empty.

Marlowe was breathing hard. Her shoulders quivered as she began to cry. She met Ash's eye, and she steeled herself, as if she wouldn't let Ash witness her breaking apart. "I'm sorry," she said automatically. It seemed the appropriate thing to do, when killing another person's father—even if it was Gresham Hain.

Ash was ashamed to admit that a part of him mourned the man who was dead at his feet. A part of him still grieved that he'd never received the love he'd wanted, even after he'd aligned with Source. He was back in his physical body with all its hurts, and he couldn't easily release what he'd wanted for so long. But he also knew his father needed to die. He knew Marlowe was the one who needed to kill him.

Ash looked up and saw them. Ramsay and Callum stood at the foot of Hedge through the streams of smoke blowing on the salty breeze. Rays of white light were forcing their way through the gray haze. Ash could see survivors wandering the rubble, lost.

Ash realized that, in a way, his father had gotten what he'd wanted. There would be no returning to the life they'd once known. They would be forced to create a new world again.

40

Ash, Ramsay, and Callum stood side by side. They waited in front of what Ash could only describe as a judge and jury in Riverside's Great Hall. It was an old, rickety one-room building, made of wood that swayed in the breeze. From the sound of flapping above, it seemed some birds had made the Great Hall their home.

The new Heads of Houses sat at a table that faced them. They were a mixture of ages. After the former Heads had been killed in Kensington, a majority of the House heirs had succeeded their parents, including Charlotte Adelaide, only a few years older than Ash, and Gavin Galahad, who had been in Callum's class. Edric Kendrick was there, too. He'd inherited the position when Culver's body was discovered.

And there was the new Head of the Houses. Easton Alexander hadn't been in Kensington for the attacks. He'd been traveling abroad, learning what he could of politics from other states across the continent. He had tanned skin and brown eyes and black hair that was already turning silver, though he was only in his early twenties, as far as Ash knew. He'd taken his new task seriously, as watchful and cold as his father had been.

Ash had just finished telling his story. It was why all three had been brought before the Heads, hands bound—to explain what had happened so that, as far as Ash could tell, the Houses could decide whether they'd be allowed to live.

Edric's face was expressionless in the silence that followed. "My recommendation, my lord," he said, not looking away from Callum, "is to see the three executed as soon as possible."

Ash felt a tremor from Callum, saw his hands clench, but he said nothing as he raised his chin.

Charlotte Adelaide had pale skin and brown hair that tumbled to her shoulders. She frowned as others shifted in their seats uncomfortably. "But that's your brother, Edric."

Edric's face grew colder as his gaze slid to Charlotte. "Why does that matter? My *brother* is the reason my family was killed." He turned his glare to Callum, who was silent and unmoving. "It can be argued that Callum freeing Woods and Thorne ultimately led Hain to the Book of Source. If not for them, Kensington would be untouched."

"If not for them," Lord Alexander said, and silence filled the room now, gazes turning to him, "Hain would still be alive, and we would likely all be dead. Who's to say that Hain wouldn't have eventually discovered the Book of Source anyway?"

"But, my lord—"

Alexander stood. It seemed he knew how to command a room, just as his father had. "We must look at the bigger picture. Fear of alchemy has grown. Anyone suspected of practicing alchemy is killed, murdered—"

"Perhaps rightfully so," Gavin said.

Alexander didn't take well to being interrupted. He stared hard at Gavin until he murmured an apology. The lord continued, facing Ash, Ramsay, and Callum once again. "I've seen states where alchemy—magic, some call it; others call it science—is fully integrated into their society. We could use alchemy to rebuild."

"The followers of Lune won't be pleased," Edric cautioned.

"The followers of Lune don't even have a House," Lord Alexander said. "This could be an opportunity—a chance for a new age. And I'm assuming that if this alchemist was powerful enough to stop his father," Alexander said, meeting Ash's eye again, "then we might just need him."

Ash's gaze fell. He hadn't told the full story, choosing to follow

Marlowe's wishes. She'd asked Ash not to tell anyone that she had killed Hain, disappearing after she'd left the bridge. Ash was glad she'd escaped. He had a feeling that Marlowe wouldn't have been shown mercy if it was discovered that she'd acted as Hain's assassin and spy for so many years, even if she'd become the hero they needed all along.

The lord raised a hand, ready to give his final verdict. "I pardon you, Callum Kendrick, Ramsay Thorne, and Ashen Woods of your crimes against our state of New Anglia."

Ash felt a flood of relief. Redguards stepped forward, untying their hands, and his fingers immediately found Callum's and Ramsay's on either side of him. But there was tension, murmurs among the Heads. It seemed Edric and Gavin weren't the only ones who disagreed with the ruling.

Lord Alexander wasn't finished. "I also ask that Callum Kendrick be instated as a commander of House Kendrick."

"My lord," Edric said, finally at his limit. "I assure you, my brother will not be welcomed back to this family or House Kendrick, and not only by me—"

"He will act as an important bridge between the redguards and alchemists," Lord Alexander said, not sparing Edric a glance. "That'll be needed, in the coming days."

Ash looked up at Callum to see him raise his brows. Ash wasn't sure what bridge Alexander envisioned, when the reds had only ever been enemies of alchemy.

"Ramsay Thorne," Alexander said, looking to Ramsay, who turned to him with surprise. "Your parents left a blight on this state, but you've proven that the Thorne name can be used for good, too. While your parents killed hundreds, you've assisted in saving millions. I applaud you, Ms. Thorne."

Ramsay's voice was tight with emotion that Ash could feel coming from her in waves. "Thank you, my lord."

"I ask that you resume position as the Head of House Thorne. I'm certain that Lady Val would welcome an alchemist like you,"

Lord Alexander said, and was given a nod of agreement, "and we could use your expertise in rebuilding—perhaps innovative design to help us enter a new age."

Ramsay hesitated, but only for a moment. She nodded. "Yes, my lord. It would be my honor."

Lord Alexander's gaze finally fell on Ash. "Your father had a role as an advisor for mine," he said. "I think it'd be fitting if you joined my side as well."

There was a tense quiet. It seemed everyone thought that maybe Easton had finally taken his merciful ruling one step too far—after all, everyone knew how the relationship between the former Lord Alexander and Gresham Hain had ended. And even if Ash had stopped his father, he was still an untrained, unlicensed alchemist with no mind for politics.

Lord Alexander raised a brow at Ash's silence. "You'll be offered a place in any House as a member," he added, "though I hope you'll join House Alexander. The pay isn't the highest, but you'd have enough to live comfortably in Kensington, once we rebuild."

Ash chewed on his lip, staring hard at the floor, before he finally looked up at Lord Alexander. "Thank you, my lord," he said, "but I must decline."

This received an even larger response. There were some gasps. Not many would dare to tell Lord Alexander no to anything, much less an opportunity like this.

Lord Alexander seemed surprised into silence himself for a moment. "No?"

Ash said it again. "No."

The young lord let out a small laugh. "And may I ask why?"

Ash took a breath. "I think what you've offered would've been a dream to me, once," he said. "But I was a different person then. I'm not in a place where I'd willingly spend my days kissing the asses of House Heads." He ignored Callum's heavy, suffering sigh and glanced at Ramsay with a smirk. "No offense."

She shook her head, smile growing as she looked at him with some pride. "None taken."

"How dare you speak to Lord Alexander that way," Lady Alder said.

But Lord Alexander raised a hand. He watched Ash with even more interest now. "Fine. If that's your decision, I won't force you."

Ash narrowed his eyes. Though Lord Alexander spoke these words, his energy felt the opposite. Maybe it wasn't such a good idea, to make a personal enemy out of the new Head of the Houses just a week after he'd survived a battle with Gresham Hain—but, well, Ash had always been one to act without thinking about the consequences.

"There's only one thing that I want, really," Ash said.

Lord Alexander tilted his head. "And what's that?"

Ash smiled. "An alchemic license. I think I've proven my ability by now," he said. "Don't you?"

Lord Alexander watched him for one long moment. "Fine. A piece of paper is nothing. An alchemic license is yours."

Ash felt relief and satisfaction warm him. Just a little over a month ago, Ash had considered receiving a license impossible. It felt good, to prove himself wrong.

"I suppose there's nothing left to discuss," Lord Alexander said. "Sir Kendrick, Lady Thorne—my scribe will be in touch with further instructions soon for you to report to your respective positions within the next week. For now, you may take your leave. Rest," he added. "Grieve. You'll need clear minds."

Callum and Ramsay both bowed with respect, while Ash didn't bother, turning on his heel. He walked down the hall, opening the doors to bright blue skies and green fields. He took a deep breath. Riverside was where many in Kensington had taken refuge, overwhelming the smaller town. Ash understood not wanting to stay in Hedge or seek asylum in another city like Ironbound. Even though he knew his father was dead, he still felt coldness cover his skin at the thought of returning to a city, when images of toppled towers and streets of rubble and the smell of death filled his nightmares. He wondered if Tobin had evacuated Hedge, if Frank had made it out of Wynnesgrove—wondered if he would run into his former friends in Riverside.

Footsteps followed. Callum and Ramsay caught up to him, Ramsay smirking as if amused by his antics, while Callum looked genuinely concerned.

"Even if you didn't want to accept the position, you didn't have to insult him," Callum said. "He might not work so hard to keep you alive the next time my brother wants you executed."

"Next time?" Ash repeated, grinning as he walked along the path. "I won't be around Edric to allow a next time. No offense, Callum, but I'm sick of your family."

Callum sighed. "Me, too," the Kendrick boy said, earning a laugh from Ash and a pitying smile from Ramsay as she took his hand, continuing on their path.

There was an inn where they'd been held as prisoners while the new Heads fought and scrambled for their roles—but now that their sentencing was complete, they would be allowed to leave. They could go anywhere they wanted. They'd distracted themselves from their potential executions by imagining the life they would build together—where they would live, what kind of home they would have.

"I still think that Kensington is the best choice," Callum said, continuing the conversation as if there'd never been a pause, probably able to tell that their next home was on all their minds. "The city will rebuild quickly. We can find a town house close to the center."

Ash clenched his jaw. He couldn't imagine returning to Kensington. Cold sweat often covered his skin now, followed by a heartbeat he couldn't control. Ramsay and Callum did what they could when Ash woke up screaming at night, holding him close— just as Ash did what he could when Ramsay would freeze, losing her breath, and Callum would become stiff and silent, muttering that he needed to take a walk to clear his mind. They'd agreed, at least, that not much could be said about the horrors they'd survived. For now, sitting beside one another quietly, holding and kissing one another, was enough.

Ramsay frowned. "Do you really want to go back there—to live there?"

"We can't avoid Kensington forever," Callum said. "Especially with you as the Head of House Thorne, and me as a commander now." The pinch between Callum's brow didn't escape Ash.

"I know that my manor isn't the most comfortable," Ramsay said, "but it's spacious enough, and we can rebuild it together."

Callum sighed. "The Downs are just so *cold*."

"I'll have to go there often anyway."

"Yes, and I'll have to stay in Kensington for work, too."

Ash loved the way his shoes sank into the dirt. He loved the freshness of the air and the clearness of the sky. He could already feel the energy of seedlings beneath his feet, ready to grow roots. "What about Riverside?" he asked.

Both Ramsay and Callum stopped to look at him. "What?" Ramsay said.

"We could stay here in Riverside," Ash said, "even if it's only for a little while."

If they agreed, Ash knew the three would likely have to travel between homes if they wanted to spend any amount of time together—but he realized, at that moment, that he had no home. He had no space to call his own. He didn't want to return to Hedge, the city where his mother had lived and died. He didn't want to be in Wynnesgrove or Kensington, trying to force the respect of those around him. He only wanted peace—and here, in this small town in Riverside, Ash believed he could find it.

❋

They stayed in the inn for another few days before Callum bought a house on the edge of town, farther away from the bustle but close enough for a ten-minute walk back into its center, with a circle of shops and the market. Callum insisted when Ash tried to argue with him. "It's my house, too," he said. "We'll all be staying here from time to time, won't we?"

The cabin had bare furnishings with dusty floors and wallpaper that was torn. They began to make the house their own, scraping away the wallpaper and painting the wooden walls beneath, finding old furniture and giving the pieces a polish and shine. They managed to find a bed so large that there was barely any space in the room, but its mattress was soft and it bore all their weight, even as they began to test its durability.

Ash could feel how the others sensed it, too, the need to be careful with one another as they took off their clothes, working to find their ways back to one another again. Fragments of them had broken and shattered, and they needed the gentleness as they healed. One day, Ash was sure that they'd commiserate on losing their parents, connected on what it felt like to mourn someone who'd been so abusive. It was an interesting place to be caught, stuck between grief and gladness that they were gone.

And the garden—Source, that was Ash's favorite part. Even after the weeks passed and Ramsay and Callum both started to come and go, kissing Ash goodbye in the mornings before they left, he still had his garden. His seedlings, which he watched grow, their silent energy offering him peace. This was how he wanted to define *power*, he realized: the silent energy of the plants around him, knowing without any doubt their full connection to Source, growing in their own time without feeling the need to prove their flower's beauty or their fruit's sweetness. He decided, as he stuck his hand into the soil, that he wouldn't mind being a plant in his next life, free from the pain that still found him. It was even crueler, Ash thought, that he had felt and understood and known the peace and unending power that was Source, just to be sent back to his body again.

There was a rare night, just a month after they made their new home, that both Ramsay and Callum had returned. They cele-brated by eating a meal Callum had made them and by lying in bed together, kissing and snuggling, Ash burying his face into Ramsay's neck and sticking a leg between Callum's thighs. He could tell that both Ramsay and Callum were exhausted, even if they didn't bore Ash with the details of their new jobs. He closed his eyes, comfortable with the sounds of their slow breaths, and felt himself starting to fall asleep, too.

The orb that hung in the sky, a shadow covering the sun, its own energy wanting to pull him in, looming closer with every passing day—his mother's eyes were wide as she tried to warn him—

He woke up when he heard a scream. Ramsay and Callum had sat up, hands on Ash, eyes wide with worry, and he realized that the scream had been his own. He was breathing hard, sweating through the sheets.

"Another nightmare?" Ramsay asked.

Ash nodded, swallowing.

"Was it Kensington?" Callum asked, frowning with concern.

How could Ash begin to describe the darkness he'd seen? It was more powerful than his father had been after holding the Book. It threatened to break apart the threads of their reality. Ash couldn't stop shaking enough to speak, but he felt Callum's calming blue energy pressing through him, suggesting that he breathe. He sucked in air and let it out slowly, hands clenching Ramsay's fingers.

"It's okay," he said, forcing himself to nod. "I'm fine now. Let's go back to sleep."

ACKNOWLEDGMENTS

Thank you to everyone who helped *Infinity Alchemist* come to life:
    Beth Phelan, Marietta Zacker, Nancy Gallt, Ellen Greenberg, and the entire team of Gallt and Zacker.

    Ali Fisher and the rest of the Tor Teen team: Dianna Vega, Saraciea Fennell, Isa Caban, Anthony Parisi, Esther Kim, Heather Saunders, Dakota Griffin, William Hinton, and Devi Pillai.

    You're all rock stars! Thank you for helping my dream become a reality.

COMING SOON!

The adventure continues in 2025 . . .